'Sophie Hannah brings many gifts to crime fiction. She is a poet whose use of language is precise, and her images are evocative. As a novelist, her overriding interests lie in people on the edge and in the relationships that have driven them there.'
Times Literary Supplement

'When it comes to ingenious plots that twist and turn like a fairground rollercoaster few writers can match Sophie Hannah.'
Daily Express

'A leading writer of psychological suspense . . . Her books are so distinctive that they deserve to be placed in a separate sub-genre of their own.'
Spectator

'The queen of psychological crime . . . Fiendishly clever'
Sunday Express

'An author with an extraordinary imagination, working at the height of her powers.'
Independent

'There is an admirable, complicated cleverness about her stories . . . Think Agatha Christie at her best but updated to a time of Twitter and online dating in both its glory and ignominy.'
Financial Times

'No one writes twisted, suspenseful novels like Sophie Hannah . . . unpredictable, unputdownable and unlike anything else you've read before.'
Liane Moriarty, author of *The Husband's Secret*

'Hannah excels at dissecting human behaviour, and the way she describes little acts of cruelty can send real chills down the spine.'
Psychologies

'For those who demand emotional intelligence and literary verve from their thrillers, Sophie Hannah is the writer of choice.'
Guardian

About the author

Sophie Hannah is the internationally bestselling author of eleven psychological thrillers, as well as *The Monogram Murders*, the first Hercule Poirot mystery to be published since Agatha Christie's death and approved by her estate. Sophie is also an award-winning short story writer and poet. Her fifth collection of poetry, *Pessimism for Beginners*, was shortlisted for the 2007 TS Eliot Award and she won first prize in the Daphne du Maurier Festival Short Story Competition for 'The Octopus Nest'. Her psychological thriller *The Carrier* won the Crime Thriller of the Year award at the 2013 Specsavers National Book Awards, and *The Point of Rescue* and *The Other Half Lives* have both been adapted for television as *Case Sensitive*. Sophie lives in Cambridge with her husband and two children, where she is a Fellow Commoner at Lucy Cavendish College.

SOPHIE
HANNAH

the narrow bed

HODDER

First published in Great Britain in 2016 by Hodder & Stoughton
An Hachette UK company

First published in paperback in 2016

1

A CIP catalogue record for this title is available from the British Library

A format paperback ISBN 978 1 444 79556 1
B format paperback ISBN 978 1 444 77610 2
Sainsbury's Exclusive ISBN 978 1 473 65578 2
Ebook ISBN 978 1 444 77612 6

Typeset in Sabon MT by Palimpsest Book Production Ltd, Falkirk, Stirlingshire

Printed and bound by Clays Ltd, St Ives plc

Hodder & Stoughton policy is to use papers that are natural, renewable
and recyclable products and made from wood grown in sustainable forests.
The logging and manufacturing processes are expected to conform to the
environmental regulations of the country of origin.

Hodder & Stoughton Ltd
Carmelite House
50 Victoria Embankment
London EC4Y 0DZ

www.hodder.co.uk

For Paul Pagett, who almost guessed the right answer
to the Liv and Gibbs question

From: inessa.hughes@goochandhughes.com
Sent: 10 February 2016 11.41:24
To: Susan.Nordlein@nordleinvinter.co.uk
Subject: *Origami* by Kim Tribbeck

Dear Susan

I am thrilled to be sending you the latest (and, we hope, final) incarnation of *Origami* by our wonderful Kim. Yes, I'm afraid she's still determined to call it that! Sorry to be the bearer of bad news. I have put your case to her as eloquently as I know how, but she refuses to entertain the idea of calling it *Kim Peculiar, Kim Ha Ha*. She is of the view that it's undignified, and I must admit I can see her point. I don't know if people in France or Japan ask one another if something is funny peculiar or funny ha ha. Do you think they do? It feels very English to me. I suspect it's a title that would travel badly, and since Kim is one of the few British comedians of her generation who's starting to make a real impact internationally, I'd like her book's title to have broader appeal. And as Kim pointed out (and of course she's quite right), she's hardly a 'ha ha' kind of comedian. She's far too dark and subtle for that, and endlessly under fire from the 'Why can't you just tell funny jokes?' brigade. To put 'Ha Ha' in her title would, I fear, give rise to a few 'Ha ha? There's not a single good punchline in the book!' sort of reviews.

I also think this book will sell not because it's a comedian's memoir – a flagging genre, I suspect – but because it's essentially a true crime book: the story of Kim's involvement in the Billy Dead Mates murder investigation. For this reason, I wonder whether we might do better with a title that sounds more crime-ish? I think I can persuade Kim to relinquish her cherished *Origami* if you will, at your end, agree not to mention *Kim Peculiar, Kim Ha Ha* again. What about something referencing Billy and his books directly? *The Billy Dead Books*? Or is that too oddball?

Since the book will form the basis of Kim's tour later in the year (and I'm afraid the tour is called 'Origami', whatever the name of the book ends up being) we will need at some point to talk about a special edition of the book to be sold only at Kim's gigs, perhaps with some extra content. I've attached a full list of tour dates as requested.

I think that's all for now. I am on the very edge of my seat, and likely to bounce off it in excitement as I await your reaction to this stunning book!

Warmest regards,
Inessa

~

Kim Tribbeck in *Origami* – Autumn 2016 Tour Dates

Newcastle/Theatre Royal – 2 September
Newcastle/Metro Radio Arena – 3 September
York/Grand Opera House – 4 September
Harrogate/Royal Hall – 5 September
Scarborough/Scarborough Spa – 10 September
Durham/Gala – 11 September
Huddersfield/Town Hall – 12 September
Southend/Cliffs – 13 September
Wimborne/Tivoli – 19 September
Stoke/Regent Theatre – 20 September
Coventry/Warwick Arts Centre – 21 September
Nottingham/Playhouse – 22 September
Warrington/Parr Hall – 23 September
Ipswich/Regent – 29 September
Scunthorpe/Baths Hall – 30 September
Folkestone/Leas Cliff Hall – 1 October
Birmingham/Genting Arena – 2 October

Bournemouth/International Centre – 5 October
Stevenage/Arts and Leisure Centre – 8 October
Aylesbury/Waterside Theatre – 9 October
Hayes/Beck Theatre – 10 October
Chatham/Central Theatre – 11 October
Northampton/Derngate – 16 October
London/Southbank Centre – 17 October
Cambridge/Corn Exchange – 18 October
Aberdeen/Music Hall – 24 October
Dorking/Halls – 29 October
Swindon/Wyvern – 30 October
Carmarthen/Lyric Theatre – 31 October

from Origami *by Kim Tribbeck*

For Elaine Hopwood, the mother
I never met but always loved

I

My tip for anyone under scrutiny from the police: as soon as you try to hide something, you make it glaringly visible, like the buildings and bridges that are sometimes wrapped in white cloth by artists, making everyone stare and point at them. Pull off the cloth and you've got an unremarkable office block or a congested commuter route across water; people walk past with their heads down, oblivious.

Tell the police the truth, immediately and in detail – all your sleazy lies, all your unsavoury personal habits – and no one will pay a scrap of attention. It's kind of obvious: when you hide, people seek, whereas when you talk about something that matters to you, no one listens. Ever. This is the main way in which human beings are reliable.

Standing before detectives, I decided straight away that I mustn't appear to be a mystery. For as long as I was one, there was a danger I'd look like one, so when I first went to the police, I held up my secret and waved it around ostentatiously like an ID card in a wallet: 'Here's my secret, now let me pass.'

I wouldn't have minded, except I only had the one. A solitaire. It wasn't even current – it was the memory of a secret. Nevertheless, it was my most treasured possession and my best friend. (I've had human best friends in the past. They're overrated.) I preferred my secret to my home, my work, my remaining blood relatives. Giving it up was a significant sacrifice.

I don't regret telling the police the truth. To do anything but reveal all would have been daft. As a real person, I understand this. Only fictional characters in TV crime dramas think, 'Here come the cops, investigating a series of brutal slayings – I'd better tie myself in elaborate knots to make sure they don't find out I watched a pirated movie in 1997. Who cares if it hampers their efforts to prevent the garotting-with-piano-wire of yet another apple-cheeked schoolboy? Just nobody mention *The English Patient*. I know nothing about that. I've never seen a burnt English guy in a hospital bed in my entire life, I swear.'

The TV-crime-drama police are just as puzzling in their behaviour as the civilians they interview. Aren't they? The minute they twig something's being kept from them, they launch into their passionate 'We, the detectives, don't care about most crimes' routine. 'Look, sir, we're investigating a murder here. That's all we care about: catching *this* killer. We don't give a toss if you've parked illegally, or partaken of the contraband *English Patient* video. Just tell us what you know about this murder. If you've kerb-crawled, or lied about your age to buy booze or ciggies, we're very chilled about that. Drugs? Do me a favour! Shoplifting, carjacking – all fine with us. Have you mugged an old lady, leaving her with severe head injuries? Try not to bore us, yeah? Like we could give a shit about some irrelevant old boiler.

'Despite being employed to keep society safe from harm, we only actually want to solve *one* crime. We've decided, for some peculiar reason that is never elaborated upon, that none of the others count. We're the police equivalent of a lollipop lady who's determined to usher *one* kid safely across a road while ignoring the dozens falling under the wheels of SUVs nearby. Tell you what, I'll cut you a deal: give me something, anything, that'll take me one step closer to catching *this* killer – the only criminal on the planet I care about, even though that's utterly irrational – and I'll grant you immunity for all your other crimes, like the baby you strangled, and the fire you started in which eight nurses died.'

'I still can't risk telling the truth,' thinks the narcissistic suspect with no sense of perspective. 'I've been assured by the most eminent superintendent in the land that I could have melted my neighbour in a cauldron of boiling wax and he'd totally let me off, but there's still no way of predicting how annoyed he might be about the whole *English Patient* thing. Nope, that's a tough one to call. Better play it safe and say nothing.'

In my first real-life experience of this kind of situation, I gleaned a perverse satisfaction from giving up my shocking secret straight away. Truth is, I felt a little bit ashamed to be involved with the police in the role of boring goody-two-shoes who'd done nothing wrong, so I decided to try and annoy them. A detective's job is to ferret out what people are hiding, so how irritating must it be for them when someone's opening gambit is 'Let me tell you everything'? Imagine how furious Jamie Oliver would be if he opened his oven on Christmas Day and found a perfectly cooked turkey with all the trimmings in there that someone else had prepared earlier; it must be like that.

I shared my solitary secret with the detectives investigating the Billy Dead Mates murders as if it were a great gossipy anecdote. It *was*. I said, 'I don't know where to start. Oh, wait! Yes I do!' And laughed.

There was only one place I could start: in the middle in every sense, with the symbolic object that stood at the centre of it all, a solid barrier between one half of my life and the other – an unpainted wooden door with a silver handle . . .

~

Tuesday, 6 January 2015

Ringpull. I think the word as I swallow the object.

It happened too quickly: a hard snag in the orange-flavoured

Fruit Rush in my mouth, then gone. Nothing to be done. Unless . . .

No, I didn't imagine it sliding down. It was too small to hurt, but I felt it: a lump in liquid. And the visual evidence tells me I swallowed it: its absence from the top of the can in my hand. I must have worked it loose and dropped it in – plucking and twisting, my fingers barely aware of what they were doing. My only aim was to fill time with physical activity. Although (I realise, now that I've swallowed metal) it's a habit I have even when I don't need to distract myself: I work the ringpull loose, snap it off and drop it into my drink to get it out of the way of my mouth.

If you think about it, it makes perfect sense: only one item to dispose of if it's inside the can. And – I'd have said before today – there's no danger of it ending up in your stomach. Only a fool would swallow a ringpull.

Did I do it on purpose? Because now I have a problem, maybe, and it occurs to me that might be exactly what I wanted. Another distraction: what to do about the foreign object inside my body? Is it dangerous? If it is, I have to do something about it, which means I'll need to leave this ward and go to another one.

Did I mention how efficient I am? This will impress you: when I need, unexpectedly, to find out if swallowing a ringpull is likely to do me any harm, I'm already in a hospital – the Rawndesley General Infirmary. You can't get much more ergonomic than that.

I'd never been inside a hospital until last Saturday apart from when I was born, but I've watched my fair share of medical dramas and I've never heard anyone mention the ringpull ward. At the moment I'm in Ward 10, the cancer ward. This is where my grandmother is dying. I have to stay until she dies, unless I can come up with a really good excuse to leave.

A sharp-edged metal object that might slice my gut open

from within sounds like a brilliant excuse to me, but then I'm not an expert. And I'm not sure if the edges *were* sharp. They probably make them rounded so nobody cuts their fingers. I'd better ask someone. The nurses and doctors on Ward 10 are bound to be more interested in cancer, but anyone working on the world's top illness must first have been trained in the basics of Fruit Rush can-component ingestion, surely. I just need to catch someone's eye . . . although ideally not *hers*.

Too late. The nurse with square-cut grey hair and tortoise-shell glasses on a chain around her neck is approaching. 'You're still here?' she says.

'Yes. Marion's still dying,' I say with a shrug. 'Can't really leave halfway through.'

I don't want to discuss the ringpull situation or anything with this woman – Bridget, according to her badge. I already know she doesn't have my best interests at heart, or else she's not bright enough to work out that they might differ from her imaginary version of them. She hasn't left me alone since I decided to sit in the ward corridor. She wants me tidied away, next to the deathbed. So far this morning she's tried, 'Has the doctor sent you to wait out here?' (No) and 'You can take that chair into Gran's room if you like.' (No, thanks. Actually, I only just brought it out.)

'I know it's hard, but you'd probably feel better if you were in there with Gran,' she says now.

Stop calling her that. She's not your gran. Why not try calling her Marion like I do and always have?

Bridget extends her neck to peer sympathetically down at me. It makes me think of those sticks with pincers on the end that council workers use to pick up litter in public places.

This has been happening ever since Marion was admitted to hospital: the people who work here keep reminding me of inanimate objects, even as they move around freely, and the things on the ward remind me of living creatures. The shiny silver hand-sterilising unit on wheels makes me think of a pelican every time I walk past it.

I walk past it a lot. I leave Ward 10 as often as I can – for an extra bar of mobile phone signal for all the calls I'm not making; a drink when I'm not thirsty; painkillers from the hospital shop when I don't have a headache; a magazine I can't focus on; extra-strong mints. Any excuse. It doesn't do me much good, though; I still have to come back here, to Ward 10. A dying grandmother isn't like a crap movie at Cineworld – you can't decide to sack it and leave halfway through.

'I'm sure your brother'd appreciate the support too,' Bridget adds.

'I don't support him,' I tell her. 'He's asked the doctors to continue treatment – more transfusions, more oxygen. He wouldn't let them catheterise Marion because a nurse I've never met said she might get a bladder infection, so instead they have to keep going in and changing her, and you can see in her eyes that she *hates* it.'

My voice sounds increasingly hoarse as I say what I've said a dozen times already. I don't know why I'm bothering. No one listens. The staff here have things they've been trained to do – treat patients! Avoid infection! – and they're determined to do them.

'It's crazy,' I tell Bridget. 'My grandmother is twenty-four, forty-eight hours away from death at most. Stop rolling her around like fucking scone dough! She wouldn't want it. Put in a catheter, now. Stop listening to Drew when he talks about moving her back to her house with medical support, and maybe with daily transfusions she can regain some quality of life, and maybe she can listen to audiobooks. Who knows, maybe she can learn to play the clarinet and join a brass band!' I blink back tears. 'She can't. Just go in there and look at her eyes. She desperately wants it to be over. Drew doesn't care. All he cares about is him not losing *his* grandmother. If you had any decency you'd give her a morphine overdose. I know you can't. But you *should* be able to, because this is ridiculous!'

Bridget pulls over a chair from the nurses' area, sits down next to me and pats my hand. Who on the planet feels better after having their hand patted? Anyone who does is a pushover.

I could put an instant end to her sympathy for me by revealing that I'm knowingly making the most of my relative-of-dying-cancer-patient status to say all the outrageous things I'd want to say anyway. I'll never get a free pass to be this obnoxious again, and I'm determined to make the most of it.

'It's a painful time for your family,' says Bridget, as if this aspect of the situation might have escaped me. 'But there are ways of making it less painful. And more meaningful.'

I eye her suspiciously. 'You're going to tell me sitting in the corridor with my back to the closed doors of Marion's room isn't one of those ways, aren't you?'

'You could sit quietly by her bed instead. Hold her hand, tell her you love her.'

'I don't think I'd get a look in. Drew'll have her strapped to a treadmill by now, keeping her muscles toned in case she makes a miraculous recovery in time for this year's London Marathon. If you listen at the door, you'll hear him firing old *University Challenge* questions at her to keep her brain alert.'

After a short silence, Bridget says, 'I know you're a comedian. I don't recognise you, but Fiona told me. She says you're quite famous.'

'I can't go into a room full of death and pretend it's anything else,' I say. 'Or rather, I could, but I won't. I've spent a fair bit of time in there. I didn't like it, so now I'm staying out.'

'Well, I can't force you . . .'

'Hold her hand, tell her I love her? *No.* Do you tell everybody to do that?'

'Well . . .' Bridget looks around, as if hoping for a prompt.

'Do you have any idea how bad Marion's feeling at the moment? Not physically; emotionally. Here's what you can't know: historically, when Marion feels bad, terrible things happen to me. So forgive me if, when she's feeling worse than ever before, I don't want to get too close to her.'

'She's drifting in and out of consciousness, dear,' says Bridget. 'Whatever's passed between you, she really can't hurt you now.'

Yes she can. She can say something before she dies. She could say that me turning up after all those years made her get cancer . . .

More hand-patting from Bridget.

'I think you'd benefit from a chat with one of our counsellors,' she says.

'Do they have either a large bag of morphine and a syringe they're willing to hand over or an ability to cure terminal cancer? If not, I think I can manage without them.'

Drew would be apoplectic with rage if he could hear me. He insisted I stop making morphine jokes or else the ward staff would grow suspicious. And it's disrespectful, he said.

That's what I do, though: I joke. It's the only useful contribution I make to society. In situations where jokes don't cheer people up, I might as well not be there. Which, coincidentally, is what I want. I would love not to be here on Ward 10 today.

'How about a cup of tea?' Bridget suggests. 'And maybe after that you can go back in and see Marion?'

'Do I have to pretend I will to get the tea?'

She leaves me alone, finally; walks away with pursed lips.

Another nurse – young, with hair that's crew-cut short apart from one long, skinny plait draped over her shoulder –

approaches from the other side. 'Kim!' she says. 'Remember me? Fiona?'

'I remember your plait.'

'How are you holding up?'

'I'm okay as long as I don't have to go back in.' I indicate the doors behind me. 'Your colleague Bridget keeps trying to persuade me.'

'No.' Fiona shakes her head. 'Don't do anything you don't want to. If you want to sit here, that's what you should do. If you want to go home and sleep, do that. Whatever feels right to you.'

'I swallowed a ringpull,' I tell her.

'What?'

I hold up my Fruit Rush can. 'I feel fine and it was a few minutes ago now, so . . . no worries, I guess.'

'You swallowed the ringpull from that can? Are you sure?'

I nod.

'Then you should go to A&E.'

'Really?'

'Just to be on the safe side. I'm sure it's nothing to worry about, but you don't want to end up with a perforated—' Fiona stops. Drew has appeared beside us. I didn't hear the door open.

He's been crying again. 'They're going to give her more platelets,' he says.

'*What?* Drew, that'll only—'

'Help her live longer. Yes, that's what I want. It's what the doctors want. Strangely, the only person who seems not to want it is you.'

'And Marion. Don't forget her.'

Fiona has tactfully withdrawn, leaving us alone.

There's a burning tightness in my chest. I often get it in Drew's presence.

'She can't speak, move or make herself understood,' I say. 'She knows she's finished, and she's got a week at the absolute outer limit. Do you think she wants another week like *this*, honestly? Wouldn't you rather be dead? I would.'

'I'm not God and neither are you, Kim.'

'Neither is anyone – that's the problem! Have you persuaded them to catheterise her yet?'

'I haven't tried. I don't want her to get a bladder infection. We've been told that's a possible—'

'She *hates* being changed. How can you not see it?'

'I have to act on the doctors' advice.'

'Even if they're all dicks?'

He sighs. 'Your arrogance is . . . making this harder.'

'Drew, please. Please think properly about it. Marion has a few days left – maybe three or four, with more platelets. Imagine you're her.'

He recoils. 'Oh, well, that's a lovely thing to say, isn't it? So you want me to imagine I'm dying of cancer?'

I stare at him for a few seconds, speechless. A smiling woman in a blue and black coat is heading our way with a large Tupperware container in her hand. I can see through the plastic that the contents are beige, not dark brown. Flapjacks, then, or macaroons. That's good; a bit of variety. There's been one delivery of chocolate brownies already today. This is an aspect of life on a cancer ward that I didn't anticipate and wouldn't have predicted: at least once a day, a female relative of a former patient turns up with a bag or box of some kind of edible treat, as a thank you to the ward staff. They do so whether their loved one has survived or died. I joked to Drew yesterday about this being the equivalent of tipping a taxi driver whether he drops you at your front door or dumps you in a skip miles from home. 'What's *wrong* with you?' was his response.

The relatives of cancer patients do not, it seems, stop at flapjacks. They also sometimes send flowers and they always, without fail, bring in or send thank-you cards. There's a ward noticeboard with dozens pinned to it. Most are pastel-coloured with tasteful pictures of birds, flowers or leaves on them, though one that appeared yesterday is plain white, smaller than all the others, and actually has the word 'Death' clearly legible on the front. That made me chuckle; at some point the ward obviously treated someone with a family that was opposed to euphemism on principle. That's the kind of card I'd send, I think: 'Dear ward staff, You totally failed to defeat death, but thanks for trying. Bit harder next time, eh?'

Once the woman with the Tupperware has left her offering on the reception desk and gone, I turn on Drew. No need to say, 'Where were we?' When I'm in the middle of trying to win an argument, I never forget where I was up to.

'Is it going to be grimmer for Marion or less grim to spend her remaining time being changed by strangers? Don't you think she'd prefer to just lie there catheterised, and not be endlessly mauled?'

Drew blinks away tears. 'I can't take this,' he says. 'I need to get some air.' He moves fast. *Gone.* I don't blame him.

Fiona sticks her head out of the ward kitchen. 'Everything okay?'

'Which bit of me's in danger of perforation?' I ask her.

'Pardon?'

'From the ringpull. Gut? Bowel?'

'Oh.' She looks around with an air of guilt, checking no one's listening. 'Look, I thought about that while you were talking to your brother. My official advice has to be: go to A&E, get it checked out. But if I were you, if you asked me what I'd do in your shoes . . .' She lowers her voice to a whisper. 'Nothing. You'll be fine. It'll come out at some point, won't it? If you go to A&E, you could be waiting for hours. You might miss . . . Well, I mean, it's more important for you to be here, isn't it?'

'I might die of a perforated liver, and sue you. In that order.' I blink away tears and grin to let her know I'm joking. I'm touched that she decided to give me good advice instead of the official advice.

On the other hand, I don't want to stay here on the ward. If Drew can walk out, I can too.

'I'm just going to go and look for Drew,' I tell Fiona. 'Check he's okay.'

Without waiting for her response, I head for the exit. Once I'm out of Ward 10, I can't help thinking what I always think: 'I got out. I can't go back.'

I can, of course. Can, have to, will. I know it's physically and psychologically possible for me to sit in the corridor outside Marion's room. Inside it, with Marion: impossible. But I can do immediately outside the doors, so I won't let myself pretend I can't.

I take the lift down to the ground floor and go outside and round the corner to check on my car. This morning I found what looked like an ideal parking spot, with a huge sign next to it that said 'NO PARKING HERE', outside the Jocelyn Hodges Maternity Centre, a department of the RGI, with its own name and building.

So far, so good: no clamps. There's a woman with dark hair in a ponytail smoking outside the main entrance. Every time she moves, the sensors pick it up and the doors slide open. Then she moves again and they close. She's talking on her phone in what sounds like a French accent.

I walk round the front of my car to check no one's stuck an unpleasant note or a demand for money on the windscreen. Again, I'm in luck. I'm close enough to Ponytail Woman now to hear her side of the phone call.

'They say I can have a local, but then I can't eat or even drink water for six hours before the op, in case I need a general later, highly unlikely though that is.'

Of course you can eat and drink beforehand, I think to myself. *Just don't tell them.* What are the odds of Ponytail Woman needing a general anaesthetic? Even if she does, what then are the odds of her puking and suffocating to death? Why is the medical profession, with the honourable exception of Fiona, so intent on creating guaranteed inconvenience, and even suffering, as a means of avoiding that one-chance-in-a-million catastrophe that's bound not to happen?

I keep my wisdom to myself, in case I end up dying of excessive perforation. I don't want Ponytail Woman to spend the rest of her life saying, '. . . and it turned out that the woman whose advice I took was that idiot comedian who died after swallowing a ringpull and doing nothing about it.'

I can't think of a valid excuse for staying out here any longer, so I turn and head back towards the Death Hub. There are three people smoking outside the hospital's main entrance, all standing in front of signs that say, 'No Smoking Outside the Hospital'.

Yes smoking outside the hospital, actually. God, I wish I smoked. If only it didn't taste and smell disgusting, turn your fingers yellow and kill you.

And now here comes a fourth smoker, bursting out of the doors with a cigarette ready and waiting in her mouth. She lights it, looking up at me as I approach. Her shapeless clothes hang off her: black hoody, baggy blue jeans. 'I'm not even a smoker,' she says. 'But there are some days that just . . . you know?'

I manage a non-commital 'Mm.' She's blocking my way. 'Are you okay?' she asks.

'I'm . . . Sorry, have we met?'

'No.' She holds out her hand for me to shake. It's small and pink: no nicotine stains on the fingers. Maybe she only took up smoking today, as a way of coping with having to be here. 'But I love your work. You're Kim Tribbeck, aren't you?' Her voice is sweet and makes her sound younger than she looks.

'Yeah,' I say. 'Well, sort of. I was Kim Tribbeck and I hope to be again. At the moment I'm someone who has to be in a hospital.'

She comes to stand by my side, as if we need to keep a lookout together. 'I'm Faith Kendell – two "e"s. Most of my family pronounces it Ken-*dell*, otherwise everyone gets it wrong. I've seen you up there.'

I'm wondering if she means on stage or on TV when she says, 'Ward 10. Not much fun, is it?'

'Have you . . . Are you . . . ?'

'My mum's on the ward at the moment. Bone cancer.'

Okay, now I know how to talk to her.

'How long's she got? My gran's got a few days, tops.'

'Oh, Mum might have a year, year and a half if she's lucky. You're here with your brother, aren't you?'

I nod. 'You probably heard us yelling at each other before.'

'I won't lie: I did hear some of it, yes. Honestly, I think it can make it harder having a bigger family at a time like this. I'm an only child, so I don't have to deal with anyone else's issues. It's just me and Mum.'

I feel guilty that this woman has noticed my predicament while I haven't noticed her at all.

'Course, it'll be harder for me once she's gone. I'll be on my own then.' Faith shrugs.

I mumble something about friends and support networks. I don't know enough about friendship to be able to speak confidently on the subject. Not confidently and positively, anyway. 'Actually, it's hypocritical of me to recommend friends,' I feel obliged to add. 'Can't stand the things, myself. They're less reliable than cheap earphones and budget airlines put together.'

'I'm not much of a one for friends either,' Faith says briskly, as if I've suggested something frivolous. 'They're too much work – like houseplants.'

'I agree. Also like houseplants, they all die in the end. What's the point?' I qualify this with, 'Sorry. Ever since my grandmother's been dying, I haven't been able to stop making death-related jokes.'

'You're right, though. If only someone would say to me, "I'll be your friend, and I'll expect no more from you than a dead houseplant." That'd be good.'

'I'd say that to a prospective friend,' I tell her.

'You would?'

'Yep. Wouldn't be able to put in much more effort than a dead houseplant myself, so I'd accept being treated like one as a fair deal.'

Hooray: I've made someone laugh. More than I've managed to do on the cancer ward so far.

'Mutual dead houseplant friendship,' I say. 'It's an interesting concept. Unconditional acceptance of no effort on both sides.'

'Sounds like the way forward to me,' says Faith.

'Kim.' It's Drew, behind me. Once again I didn't see him coming.

'I'm going back up now,' I tell him.

He shakes his head. He's waiting for me to work it out without him having to tell me. From the look in his eyes, it can only be one thing that he's not telling me.

'Oh, no,' Faith whispers.

This is a bit daft. One of us ought to put it into words, to check we're not all standing here wrapped in a strange, gloomy calm for no reason. It looks as if that one will have to be me.

'Marion's dead,' I say.

Time to make a white card with nothing but the word 'Death' on the front and pin it to Ward 10's noticeboard.

My breath catches in my throat. Why do I have a sudden feeling of . . . it's not exactly déjà vu, but it's not far from it. Is it the white card on the board?

What else could it be?

Something important, says a stubborn voice in my head. *Something you glimpsed for a fraction of a second, and can't see any more.*

Lifeworld online, 2 January 2015
Same Old Story: Misogyny Kills
by Sondra Halliday

So now we know his official nickname, this killer who has claimed
four lives so far. The police didn't want us to find out, which makes
it rather strange and counterproductive that they invented such a
memorable monicker for him: Billy Dead Mates. Of course someone's going to succumb to temptation and leak a soubriquet like
that. For all the police talk of confidentiality breaches and regret-
table information spillages, they wouldn't have created the tag if
they hadn't hoped it would stick and spread.

Remember the Name The Teddy stall at your local primary
school's summer fair? This is the grown-up, serious-crime version:
Name The Evil Killer. If this monster goes down in the history books
as Billy Dead Mates, a few sad-sack cops will have made their
mark upon the world. That's what the witty alias is all about: police
egos. How much do you want to bet they're all men? The names
I've heard so far in connection with the investigation are male
without exception: DC Simon Waterhouse, DI Giles Proust, DC
James Wing, DS Neil Dunning. 'I might not have *caught* the noto-
rious killer,' these chaps will brag to their grandkids one day, 'but I
sure as hell gave him a catchy nickname.'

Just as Billy must think he's such a smartypants to have eluded
capture for so long (it's nearly four months since his first kill) so
must the detectives hunting him be patting themselves on the back
for their verbal cunning. Our Billy certainly seems, on the face of it,
to be murdering pairs of close friends. His first two victims, Linzi
Birrell from Combingham in the Culver Valley and Rhian Douglas
from Poole, Dorset, were well known 'BFFL', to use their favoured
terminology. Billy's third and fourth victims might have been older,
more affluent and less reliant on text-message acronyms to
describe their relationship, but they too were best friends for life.
Angela McCabe from Chiswick and Joshua Norbury from Spilling

were 'closer than siblings', according to Norbury's actual sibling Lisa.

It's easy to see the logic the police must have followed: 'This murderer is killing pairs of best friends! Billy Dead Mates is the perfect name for him! It's a playful reworking of Billy No Mates!'

Can't you just imagine the discussions they've been having, all these DC No-Solves who have failed to put an end to the killing spree? 'These murders must be about friendship. Perhaps he resents best friends because he never had a bestie himself,' they say to one another.

By calling him Billy Dead Mates, they're inviting us to sympathise with a murderer. 'Poor, lonely Billy,' is the subliminal message. 'If only someone had extended the hand of friendship and provided a shoulder for him to cry on, perhaps he wouldn't have grown desperate enough to kill.'

And just who might these hypothetical people be that failed to invite poor Billy to their sleepovers and summer houses? Could they be girls and women, by any chance? We're usually the ones expected to open our hearts and our legs, to provide emotional sustenance to needy men incapable of taking responsibility for their own actions. Make no mistake: although no male detective has said so explicitly, if Billy has been lonely all his life, then the underlying assumption is that somewhere, somehow, a woman is to blame. Perhaps his mother didn't let him play out with the other children on their street, or an ex-girlfriend humiliated him by mocking the size of his todger. Does he maybe have a shrewish wife who never lets him go to the pub with the lads after work?

I'm beyond certain that if I were to put all this to DI Giles Proust or DC Simon Waterhouse, they would vehemently deny they're thinking along these lines. They'd insist that they blame Billy and no one but Billy for the four murders he's committed so far. They would claim that the name Billy Dead Mates, with its implicit reference to Billy No Mates, was in no way intended to elicit sympathy for a killer. To which I would say, 'Oh, really? Then why aren't you calling him Billy Dead *Women*?'

That's right, folks. He might have killed two pairs of best friends, but it's telling that the police are pushing that angle so hard, isn't it? We know that nearly all of the violence in our patriarchal woman-hating society is male. This isn't a controversial feminist assertion; it's a simple fact. Toxic masculinity is responsible for more than 90 per cent of fatal assaults in the UK. The overwhelming majority of murders of women are committed by men. Yet, again and again, the police and the media conspire to conceal what's going on, which is nearly always the same thing: lethal male violence against women and girls.

Here we have a killer who has killed *three women.* Please note: there is no need for the helpful among you to submit comments along the lines of 'But one victim was a man! Don't forget Joshua Norbury!' That doesn't change my fundamental point: it's an outrage that a male killer can murder three women, and be reported as having done so all over the national media, and yet the words 'misogyny' and 'male violence' are not even mentioned. It was the same when Godfrey Cornish murdered his daughter Holly. Why are we so reluctant to name this plague that's claiming more and more lives all the time: pernicious male brutality and the deeply entrenched belief among men that female lives don't matter? Why do those with the power to control the story reach instead for a nickname like Billy Dead Mates that directs us, however subliminally, to side with the perpetrator rather than with his victims?

I'm aware that we don't yet know for sure that this killer is a man. The police haven't found him! He might be a woman! O come all ye mansplainers and men's rights activists to tell me that women can be killers too. I don't deny that, but the fact is that the over-whelming majority of murderers in our society are male. I don't believe the police would have coined the nickname Billy Dead Mates if they believed there was an equal chance of the culprit being a woman.

This monster – Billy Dead Women – might or might not be taking lives because he harbours some deep-seated resentment around the issue of friendship. We don't know that he does, and neither, presumably, do the police. Yet this is the feature of the situation that everyone is keenest to talk about. 'How intriguing!' we say to one another in wine bars as if it's the latest episode of *CSI*. 'Pairs of best friends – how novel! How distinctive! Whatever might his motive be?'

Well, let's think about it, shall we? We know that Billy has murdered three women, and that the majority of his victims are female. We know this beyond doubt, but it's something no one wants to discuss. That's not the story that's got the media excited. That's just boring old misogyny, the most familiar motive in the world – so old hat that our society regards it as barely worth remarking upon, let alone eradicating.

2

6/1/2015

Simon Waterhouse feared that DC James Wing from Bournemouth and Poole Police was under the impression that the two of them were becoming friends, or might do so in the future.

It would never happen. It couldn't happen if Simon didn't let it, and he wouldn't. He'd stand firm against the threat. Thankfully, Dorset was nowhere near the Culver Valley. Soon as they'd caught Billy, Wing would be out of Simon's life, which was as it should be. Agreeing about a couple of things didn't mean anything; it wasn't a sign that you were on the same wavelength. More likely to be coincidence.

It was nothing personal against long-legged, curly-haired James Wing, who was more intelligent than many even if he did have the irritating habit of rolling his eyes when he spoke, like a thwarted teenager. Simon simply wasn't the sort who allowed people to latch onto him.

The couple of things that he and James Wing had agreed on so far had first been mooted by Wing. On both occasions, Simon was put out to find himself in the position of seconder. If they were good ideas, he ought to have had them first.

Not that anyone apart from him and Wing thought they were valid points. Of the six officers in the sterile, green-walled room at Paddington Green police station in London, representing three Major Crime teams from different parts of the UK, only Simon had supported Wing when he'd opened today's meeting by saying it was stupid that they were calling the killer Billy Dead Mates.

'Because it might be a woman, you mean?' DS Sam Kombothekra, Simon's sergeant and line manager, had asked.

'No.' Major eye-rolling from Wing. 'Some women are Billies, usually with "ie" at the end.'

'Billie Piper, Billie Jean King, Billie Holiday,' DS Neil Dunning, their host for the day, chipped in quickly. Of course – it would matter to a man as petty as Dunning that he should list all the female Billies before anyone else did. Simon had worked with him before, hampered by a marked lack of cooperation and good faith on both sides. He'd wondered, before his first encounter with Dunning on the Billy case, if there might be some scope for burying hatchets. Seconds after walking into the room – in Bournemouth on that occasion, with pockmarked white walls and a faint smell of cauliflower cheese – Simon had known there was no chance. How had Dunning managed to get all his hard feelings to that initial briefing without the help of a suitcase on wheels?

'I was going to say Billie Holiday,' said Dr Kerensa Moore, the psychological profiler who was their guest for the morning. The low turnout was due to her presence, Simon suspected. No one wanted her or believed they needed her; she was an unwelcome gift inflicted on them by the London higher-ups. There would have been between twelve and twenty detectives here if she hadn't got involved. As it was, there were three from the Culver Valley, two representing the Met on home turf – Dunning and DC Grace Woolston, a woman with chipped green nail polish and two cats that she talked about as if they were people – and a lone James Wing from Bournemouth and Poole.

'Billy Dead Mates doesn't work for two reasons,' Wing said. 'One: it's too Little England. No one in America knows what a Billy No Mates is.'

'They do now, thanks to us,' said Dunning. 'The few who are interested, that is.'

'It makes us look like parochial hicks in the eyes of the rest of the world,' Wing insisted.

'Is your new friend serious?' DI Giles Proust asked Simon, who flinched. The F-word; the very one he didn't want to hear. In front of Wing, too. Proust – the third and most senior member of the Culver Valley delegation – was a cunning bastard. He seemed always to know the worst thing to say to Simon, and he always said it. Billy's might be flawed but Proust's nickname was perfect: the Snowman, inspired by the icy wasteland he had in place of a heart.

'Are you serious, DC Wing?' A new friend for Simon, as Proust saw it, was a shiny new victimisation opportunity for him. 'Are you this murderer's public relations manager? You're worried he might not *catch on* internationally?'

'I'm worried about how it looks, yes. If we can't name our serial killers, thinks the *New York Times* and *USA Today*, then maybe we can't catch them.'

'The *New York Times*?' Proust snorted. 'You're aiming high. So far one talk show host with a haircut like a bad wig has given Billy a token mention, and one blogger from Dayton, Ohio, has written a ponderous screed – which, in any case, contains an explanation of the nickname: "In Great Britain, a friendless individual is colloquially described as a Billy No Mates." And all is clear. I see no problem.'

'My bigger issue is that the name Billy Dead Mates is misleading,' said Wing.

At the word 'misleading', before the explanation, Simon had got it. He'd understood. Everyone else's blank expressions told him that he was alone. Just him and Wing, who'd thought of it first.

'Why isn't it accurate?' Sam Kombothekra asked.

'He's killing pairs of best friends,' Proust said loudly and slowly. 'They're *friends*, which is synonymous with "mates". They're murdered, which is synonymous with "dead".'

'He's killing pairs of best friends, yes, but they're friends with *each other*,' said Wing, eye-rolling again, 'not with him. To call him Billy Dead Mates implies he's killing *his own friends*. And we've no reason to think he is. The opposite. There's been no connection found between the two pairs. Linzi Birrell and Rhian Douglas existed in a very different world to the one Angela McCabe and Joshua Norbury inhabited. We've found nothing to suggest any overlap—'

'They were all murdered by the same person,' Proust interrupted flatly. 'I call that overlap.'

'I was going to say "nothing to suggest any overlap in their friendship circles. We're as sure as we can be that Linzi and Rhian had no friends or acquaintances in common with Angela and Joshua. So it's not *Billy*'s mates who are dead, is it?' Wing sat back and folded his arms.

'Aren't you being too . . . ?' Sam Kombothekra began hesitantly. 'I mean, if you think of it as "Billy *of the* Dead Mates". . .'

'Like Tess of the D'Urbervilles.' Kerensa Moore smiled.

'Why does this matter?' Proust had adjusted his voice to its coldest setting. When alone with his team – Simon, Sam, Colin Sellers and Chris Gibbs – this tone would guarantee silent compliance for the foreseeable future, unless Simon was feeling particularly bloody-minded.

Kerensa Moore stared down at her feet and frowned, no doubt deciding not to do anything as rash as make a harmless remark ever again.

James Wing, by contrast, appeared impervious. 'No.' He directed his reply to Sam, bypassing Proust who sat between them. 'Billy Of The Dead Mates That Aren't His doesn't work. Everyone who knows the saying behind the name knows it's Billy No Mates as in Billy *has* no mates. When you change the phrase slightly, the silent reference remains: leading people to assume . . . rather, *mis*leading them into assuming that it's *Billy*'s mates that are dead – that he's killed his own friends. Billy *has* dead mates. Can't you see the problem?'

'I'm looking at him right now.' Proust stared at Wing.

'I think DC Wing's got a point,' Simon forced himself to say.

'I'm not sure most people are that literal-minded,' Kerensa Moore said with a nervous glance at Proust. 'Hardly anyone would get as far in their thought process as "Billy of the", "Billy has", etcetera.'

'Maybe so, but it's not ideal that we're calling him by a name that misrepresents him,' said Wing.

'I take your point, but I just don't see that it does,' said Sam.

'Then you don't take his point, Sergeant,' offered the Snowman. 'You reject his point.'

'No, I can see what he's saying, completely, but the name works for me. At the most basic level . . .' Sam shrugged. 'He's killing pairs of best friends and we're calling him Billy Dead Mates.'

'Also, you don't know for certain that the two pairs had no one in common,' said Kerensa Moore.

'We pretty much do,' Simon told her. 'Unless all four murder victims were keeping their friendship with Billy secret from everyone they knew. These weren't secretive people, though.'

'Well . . .' Moore swallowed visibly. 'I haven't been invited to start, officially, but . . .'

Proust waved his hand at her in a batting-away gesture – one that would say quite unambiguously to an untrained observer, 'Get out of my sight.'

'He means start,' Simon told Moore.

'All right, then. Given that we've reached this point in the discussion naturally . . . I think we have to consider the possibility that Billy was, secretly, a friend of each of the four victims. Extensive interviews with all four families have turned up no one who knew them all, yet we believe that each of them – Joshua, Angela, Rhian and Linzi – invited Billy into their home, and that three of the four made him at least one cup of tea . . . Who would you welcome into your home and make tea for, when you've not mentioned to your nearest and dearest that you're expecting a visitor?'

'A canvasser, a charity worker, a market researcher doing a survey,' Simon reeled off the first three possibilities that occurred to him.

'Maybe, yes.' Kerensa Moore rewarded him with a smile. 'Or maybe a secret friend who persuades normally open people to enter into a conspiracy of silence with him. Either way, this killer is skilled at manipulation. Four murders, unsolved, and no leads apart from a sighting of a blonde woman at one crime scene who is as yet unidentified.'

'Our blonde woman's gone up in smoke, I'm afraid,' said James Wing. 'But I can think of one possible lead no one's mentioned. You're all going to hate it.'

'Let Dr Moore say her piece.' Proust glared at Wing. 'I'm not ready to hear another of your opinions. It hasn't been long enough since the last one.'

What possible lead did Wing have in mind? Why couldn't Simon think of it?

'I don't think it'll surprise any of you to hear that I think Billy has issues around friendship,' Kerensa Moore went on. 'The obvious conclusion, I suppose, would be that he or she never had a best friend and always yearned for one. But somehow . . . I don't know. I think I'd expect someone with that motivation to kill, for example, several of their former classmates, or a group of friends on a fun night out together. Not one pair, then another – and more pairs in the future for all we know.'

'Are you making this up as you go along, Dr Moore?' asked the Snowman. 'I swapped a sizeable chunk of budget *for all you know*, and so far it seems to be not a lot.'

'It's not much,' Kerensa Moore agreed. 'I'll come to that later. There's a very specific reason why I'm able to glean so little in this case – these cases, I should say – but I want to stay with the friendship thing for a while. Pairs of two being killed makes me wonder if Billy was the third and least powerful of a trio of friends. You're going to ask me for supporting evidence.' She smiled at Proust. 'I have none. It's no more than informed guesswork, but that's what struck me: the rejected member of the three-that-was-a-crowd taking symbolic revenge on the other two by killing pairs of best friends.'

'What an entertaining story,' said Proust. 'I have one too: Billy was deserted by his wife who ran off with her best friend after deciding she was a lesbian. Symbolic revenge. Who's to say my theory's any less likely than yours?'

'Which is why I said: no evidence.'

'You said, "informed guesswork". Informed by what?'

'It's a theory based on observations I've made in the past, in other cases, that were later proved to be sound. One thing I *am* sure of: Billy is a serial killer in name only. You're a great deal more likely to catch him if you forget everything you think you know about serial killers in your search for him.'

'What—?' James Wing began.

Moore raised a hand to shut him up. 'Billy has the victim tally of a serial killer, but he lacks the correct mindset. Serial killers might have three victims, twenty-three, thirty-three or a hundred and three, but those victims are always either individuals—'

'Everyone's an individual,' Dunning and Grace Woolston said in unison.

'Apparently not,' James Wing muttered in Simon's ear, as Simon was thinking the exact same thing. So that was Wing's point doubly proven.

'The victims of serial killers, 99 per cent of the time, are individuals, killed individually,' said Moore. 'Serial killers rarely target groups, even groups as small as two, and in the rare cases that they do – Zodiac, for example – they kill the whole unit, be it two or three or however many, at the same time. But I can't stress enough how exceptional that is. Normally, serial killers collect *individual* victims that fit a certain type.'

'So Billy's abnormal even within his abnormal category?' Sam asked.

'A freak among freaks,' Proust summed up.

'He's methodologically freakish, yes,' said Moore. 'If he was waiting until each set of best friends was together and shooting them in pairs, I'd have a clearer basis to work from. But what Billy's doing is nothing like anything I've seen before from a serial murderer. He's *choosing* pairs – I mean, we have to assume he is – but he's *killing* as if each victim were an individual.'

'I suppose people with close best friends are also individuals,' Sam Kombothekra said.

'That statement contributes precisely nothing to the discussion,' said the Snowman. 'Less than nothing. When are you next planning to hand in your resignation, sergeant? We're due one soon, aren't we?'

Simon watched Kerensa Moore's eyes widen, and was relieved to see that she was getting the picture. He found it impossible to relax when he and his team were thrown together with strangers; he waited nervously for Proust's first attack and Sam's first capitulation, jumpy until everyone had the measure of everyone else.

'There's no precedent for paired victims or a victim group *not* killed together,' said Moore. 'Which means we can't assume about Billy what we'd assume if he were a more conventional serial killer – if he'd killed, say, four red-headed women, or four bald men.' She looked at Proust's shiny head for a second, then quickly away. 'We can't assume he experiences a build-up of stress for a period, then kills to achieve release, then kills again when the stress starts to mount. It makes it very difficult to know anything about him, really. I just don't . . . again, it's a gut instinct, but I don't think the drivers here are the same as for most serial killers. This is a unique situation.'

Grace Woolston held up a creased copy of *Lifeworld* magazine. 'What about Sondra Halliday's theory?' she asked.

Proust growled like a prodded bear. 'I've heard that name

too often already. Not that it *is* one. The name is Sandra. Do we need to waste time on every fool with an opinion?'

'This one only briefly, I think,' Moore said. Her tone was upbeat but firm. Simon wondered if she had small children. 'There's nothing whatever to substantiate Halliday's theory that hatred of women is behind these killings. I read up on her and I'm afraid she's got form. Everything, according to her, is caused by a global epidemic of woman-hating. I'm not exaggerating: sunburn, indigestion, flat tyres on cars. Oh, all right, I *am* exaggerating.' Moore smiled. 'But not by much, I promise. I've looked at her Twitter output. It's not only men she accuses of misogyny. Any woman who disagrees with her analysis of anything gets found guilty of it sooner or later. You might be an overt misogynist or someone with what she calls "internalised misogyny", but "not a woman hater" doesn't seem to be an option in her book. Yesterday on Twitter, another female journalist tried to inject a bit of balance by saying feminists should ideally want equality between the sexes, not to vilify and shame men. Halliday described her as "patriarchy's bitch" and told her to eff off.'

'Halliday's a fanatic,' said Simon.

'Yes,' Moore agreed. 'She's manifestly wrong, I think. She's made no attempt to explain why Josh Norbury ended up dead if Billy's project is to kill women.'

James Wing sat forward in his chair. 'What if it's the other way round?' he said.

'The other way round . . .' Proust pretended to ponder. 'So that would be: what if the project of all women is to kill Billy Dead Mates? Which is nonsensical. DC Woolston, is it your *project* to murder our murderer? I hope this isn't your so-called new lead, Wing. For your sake.'

'Lead was the wrong word. And not *all* women – just Halliday. And not to kill Billy, no – because in my hypothesis Sondra Halliday *is* Billy. And her project would be – if the hypothesis were correct – to kill men. Or at least, one man: Joshua Norbury.'

Proust looked around the room. 'Would someone who shares a first language with DC Wing care to translate? Waterhouse?'

Wing turned to Simon. 'I don't know about you, but I'd quite like to be told that Halliday couldn't possibly have killed Norbury – or any of the four.'

'Hang on,' said Grace Woolston. 'She didn't know Norbury, did she?'

'Do you know that for sure?' Wing fired back.

'Well, no, but . . . I mean, is she of interest? Seriously? Or are you plucking this out of thin air?'

'I said it was a hypothesis, that's all.'

'No harm in trying to alibi her out.' Simon pulled his phone out of his jacket pocket. 'I'll ring Charlie, tell her to ask.'

'Your wife Charlie?' Grace Woolston asked. 'Won't Sondra Halliday speak to men?'

'Sandra,' Proust amended.

'What?' Simon frowned. 'Yeah, I'm sure she would, but Charlie might as well ask her.'

'I don't see why,' said Neil Dunning. 'I didn't think Sergeant Zailer was anything to do with Billy.'

'She isn't.'

Proust drummed his fingers on the table beside him. 'Come on, Waterhouse – you have the attention you crave. The floor is yours. Spit it out. Why?'

'Because Charlie's with Sondra Halliday now,' said Simon.

~

Sergeant Charlie Zailer was not where she was supposed to be. She was in London, in a café near King's Cross called Drink, Shop & Do, with her sister Olivia, having successfully delegated her Sondra Halliday duties. *Drink, Shop, Get Someone Else To Do*. What sort of name was that, anyway? The 'Do' part was alarming. Brightly coloured plastic crates full of buttons, bobbins, piles of cloth and every kind of craft material lined the walls of the room Charlie and Liv were in, as if it were the most natural thing in the world to leap up and stitch an impromptu patchwork quilt in between sips of coffee. Charlie found it hard to empathise with anyone who wanted to do any more than they absolutely had to while out at a café. Since everyone knew it was possible to drink tea and eat cake without resorting to embroidery . . .

The tea, to be fair, was delicious. As was the chocolate and beetroot cake. Still, Charlie was sceptical about Drink, Shop & Do. A comma *and* an ampersand in the name of a café? It was too fussy. Anyone who chose that name had to have something not quite right about them.

Charlie was more cynical and suspicious about everything these days. It was Liv's fault. Charlie had come to the conclusion that there were two kinds of lies: the really bad, corrosive ones in which her sister specialised, and the harmless ones that Charlie preferred.

Like this meeting with Sondra Halliday. Strictly speaking, Charlie hadn't lied to Simon; she'd told him she'd set up a meeting with Halliday, and that part was true. If Simon had chosen to assume that Charlie herself would be present at the meeting then that was his silly fault, and he ought to listen more precisely to what people said. In fact, the meeting Charlie had arranged – the one she assumed was currently in progress – was between Sondra Halliday and the Culver Valley Police officer that, as a strident radical feminist, Halliday simply *had* to meet as soon as possible, if only because the prospect was so hilarious each time Charlie thought about it: DC Colin Sellers, a man who regularly announced his intention to go out and pick up a woman – any woman – with the words 'I need a new ride', and who then did so without a morsel of shame, or consideration for Stacey, his wife of more than twenty years.

Sellers, despite being the least trustworthy of husbands, was too trusting of his friends and colleagues. When Charlie had told him Simon wanted him to try and make Sondra Halliday see reason, he'd accepted it without question. He hadn't wondered why Charlie was the one asking when Simon saw him every day and could easily have made the request directly. Having prepared an answer, Charlie volunteered it anyway: 'Look, Simon can't ask you because he's not supposed to be doing the tasking, is he? Sam is, which is a fat lot of good to anyone. Sam's convinced himself that tiptoeing around Halliday's bullshit is the only way to avoid being a vicious male brute. So . . . keep this to yourself, okay?'

Sellers wasn't very good at keeping things to himself. Nobody was supposed to know, for example, that he'd recently joined a Weight Watchers group in order to meet potential new rides with ample cleavages, after a disappointing run of 'double fried eggs', as he charmingly called them, but somehow everyone at the nick did know. The consensus, with which Charlie concurred entirely, was that Sellers was jealous of his closest friend at work, Chris Gibbs, who'd been having an affair with Charlie's sister Liv for several years, and, more recently, had been pretending to have split up with her.

Charlie couldn't help looking at her sister's cleavage, which was on display today as always. It was an all-outfits, all-weather cleavage.

'What are you grinning about?'

'Your tits.'

'Oh.' Liv looked resigned. 'In case you're wondering: yes, I regret asking.'

'You know Sellers has joined Weight Watchers?'

'Yes! Hysterical!'

'I reckon he was jealous and that's why he signed up. His best mate had a busty girlfriend – you – and he thought, "I want one of those". Weight Watchers is the perfect trawling zone for him: women with big boobs and negative body images, so he can easily talk them into bed with a few calculated compliments.'

'That's so *gross*.' Liv wrinkled her nose. 'He's so . . . ugh. How can he prey on people like that?'

'You, of course, would never stoop so low.' Charlie smiled and felt powerful. She was enjoying her meeting with Liv and, although she wasn't there, she was enjoying Sellers' with Sondra Halliday simultaneously. What might be happening, right now this very second? Was Halliday taking notes for her next *Lifeworld* article? Was Sellers telling her his double-rejection-at-the-women's-refuge story? That was a classic.

If Charlie had met Sondra Halliday as per Simon's instructions, it wouldn't have been nearly as jolly. Harsh words would undoubtedly have passed between them, and perhaps even a cup of coffee in the face if Charlie hadn't been able to restrain herself. She'd had a grudge against Halliday ever since the journalist had written a string of vicious and unfair think-pieces about a Spilling man called Godfrey Cornish: an arterial surgeon at the Rawndesley General Infirmary who'd killed his thirteen-year-old daughter Holly in 2006, when Charlie was still working as a detective.

It was a tragic case. Godfrey and his wife had been devoted parents, adored their daughter, did everything they could for her. Then Holly had started to get ill. Doctors examined her and could find nothing wrong. Meanwhile, Holly continued to deteriorate. Her parents, desperate to comfort her, kept telling her not to worry, they'd find out what was wrong and cure it. After a few agonising months spent visiting specialists, the diagnosis came: Holly had a rare terminal illness, a non-hereditary genetic condition that afflicted 1 in four million people. She would be dead within six months, her parents were told; nothing could be done. Godfrey Cornish decided he couldn't bear for Holly – a girl who loved life so much – to know she was dying. So he killed her: gave her an anaesthetic that ensured she wouldn't wake up.

He then went straight to the police and told them what he'd done and why. He was convicted of murder. Charlie and her team had been shocked. They hadn't wanted the CPS to prosecute and, when things had gone the other way, they'd been sure Godfrey would be acquitted. His wife had stood by him throughout, and he'd finally been released from prison last year.

Sondra Halliday, in a series of columns in various national publications, lumped Godfrey Cornish together with every thug who'd ever beaten his girlfriend to death and every cheating husband who'd arranged a hit on his wife so that he could marry his younger, prettier lover. Typical pernicious male violence was her verdict and all she had to say on the matter. She railed against the journalists who reported the incident as 'Tragic case of devoted father's desperate attempt to spare his daughter pain.' Halliday poured scorn on anyone who tried to tell the true story, and suggested that a more accurate headline would be 'Yet Another Male Person Murders Yet Another Female Person.'

Charlie, who knew from first-hand experience of the man that Godfrey Cornish didn't have a misogynist bone in his body, had hated Halliday ever since. Sellers, on the other hand, claimed to love all women; that was what made the delegating to him of this particular task so perfect.

'Are you leaving the rest of that cake?' Liv asked.

'Yes,' Charlie said before picking up the chunk that was left and putting it in her mouth.

'But . . . you just ate it.'

'Yep. I lied.'

Liv's mouth flattened into a line.

'Do you miss Gibbs?' Charlie asked her.

'Miss him? I still see him. I don't know why you're so obsessed with us ever since we split up.'

You didn't split up. You lied about that. I just don't know why.

'We told you and Simon at the time that we'd always be close friends, and we still are.'

Yeah. Close friends who fuck each other's brains out. What you told us at the time was as big a lie then as it is now.

'How are things with Dom?' Charlie couldn't let it go. 'Is your relationship with him better or worse now than it was when you were seeing Gibbs on the sly?'

'I think it's probably better,' Liv said vaguely, looking away.

'And Gibbs' marriage?'

'I . . . yes, I think it's fine.' Never had anyone wanted to get to the end of an answer so quickly.

'Well, that's good.' Charlie smiled. 'It's bound to be easier all round if you're not keeping secrets.'

She wasn't expecting enthusiastic agreement from Liv on this point, so she wasn't surprised when none materialised.

How can you not suspect that I'm asking you all these questions and sitting here with this knowing smile on my face because I know? Don't you care if I know?

Maybe you don't mind me knowing you're lying as long as I don't know why.

Charlie's relationship with her sister had changed beyond all recognition. Though on the surface it appeared the same as it had always been, Charlie now had to produce convincing conversation – things she might have said to Liv before – while in her mind, always present behind her spoken words, flowed a soundtrack no one but she could hear: *You big fucking massive shameless liar. Why do you think you can do this? How can you imagine I might believe you, knowing I have a brain in my head? And Simon? Do you really think he'd fall for it?*

Suspecting that Liv and Gibbs had pretended to split up rather than actually split up, Simon and Charlie had subtly spied on them for a while. They'd followed them to Cambridge and discovered that their accommodation there was a double room at the DoubleTree by Hilton Garden House hotel. They'd followed them, unobserved, and seen them holding hands and kissing in the street – all of this while, according to what

Charlie had been told, Liv was in Dublin reporting on a literature festival for the *Observer*.

The most surprising thing about those days in Cambridge was that Liv and Gibbs had been out for lunch once and dinner once with another couple that Simon and Charlie hadn't recognised: an Asian man and a white woman. Both had looked friendly and respectable, but couldn't be, Charlie had decided. Whatever peculiar, underhand thing was going on, chances were it involved them too. Liv and Gibbs didn't have friends that she and Simon didn't know about. If they'd kept these people secret, there had to be a reason for it.

In any case, they certainly hadn't broken up as advertised. Instead, after several years of having a relatively open affair that they freely discussed with Simon and Charlie, they'd suddenly announced that they were no longer an item, and they'd stuck to their lie ever since. Simon had recently decided to wash his hands of the whole thing; it was Liv and Gibbs' business and no one else's, he'd told Charlie one day. She'd barely been able to believe it. Her feelings on the matter hadn't changed at all, and could be summed up as follows: if she didn't find out the truth in the next five seconds, she'd swell up like a big black boil and burst.

The temptation, with Liv sitting across the table from her, was to ask outright. Charlie had pictured herself doing it countless times: *Liv. I know it's a lie. I saw you and Gibbs canoodling on the streets of Cambridge. Tell me what's going on.*

Over and over again, Charlie had rejected the direct approach. It was a strategy that could work quite well with a normal liar, someone who'd be embarrassed to have been caught out; it wouldn't work with the kind of person who'd stand in front of you on her two legs and say, 'Oh, didn't I tell you? I had both my legs amputated yesterday.' Charlie had no doubt that Liv, if put on the spot, would insist that she and Gibbs had never been to Cambridge together and that therefore Charlie and Simon must have seen people who looked very like them: a simple case of mistaken identity.

If Liv said that in response to an open and honest appeal, Charlie would loathe her forever after. She wouldn't be able to help it. And she didn't want to feel that way about her only sibling. She preferring goading and snooping and behaving nearly as sneakily as Liv; that made things feel more equal.

'So what made you pick this place?' she asked. 'Have you got something else to do near King's Cross?'

'No.' Liv's eyes were wide and innocent. 'I thought it'd be easier for you, that's all – King's Cross is your station.'

Funny how you've never thought that before in all the years I've lived in Spilling.

'What are you in London for, anyway?' Liv asked.

'I was supposed to be meeting a journalist.'

'Ooh, which one? I probably know them.'

'Sondra Halliday.'

'Oh – nasty piece of work. She once savaged me on Twitter for daring to praise a man. I'd addressed precisely no remarks at all to her, ever, and she tweeted at me something like "Why don't you just suck his cock and have done with it?"'

'Maybe she knew about Gibbs and decided you were a loose woman.'

'Char, why do you keep bringing up Gibbs?'

'No reason.'

'Look, I'd better go.' Liv did the looking-at-watch gesture, though she wasn't wearing one.

'It's five to eleven. Do you have somewhere you need to be?'

'No. No, I'll just . . . I don't know, I might do a bit of shopping. Are you going straight from here to meet Sondra Halliday? I'll walk you to the tube.'

So Charlie was getting the tube, was she? That was news to her. She couldn't be bothered to tell Liv she wasn't, in fact, meeting Halliday. Clearly Liv hadn't picked up on the rather obvious clue provided by the words, 'I was supposed to be'.

Because she doesn't care. She only cares about getting you out of the way.

Charlie forced herself not to mention Gibbs' name again as they paid the bill, and again as they walked along the busy road, raising their voices to be heard above the traffic.

When they arrived at the entrance to the underground, she managed to produce a last-minute display of warmth and affection: all fake. She needed Liv to be convinced, so that she'd go off and do whatever it was she needed to do – so she wouldn't be on her guard.

After the hugs and the see-you-soons, Charlie walked slowly down the steps to the underground. When she got to the bottom, she counted to ten. Then she turned round and hurried back up to ground level. Her phone was buzzing in her bag. She decided to ignore it.

She looked around. No immediate sign of Liv. And hundreds of people who weren't Liv, obstructing her view.

Charlie ran towards the station. If Liv was catching a train to Rawndesley, on her way to see Gibbs, why was she in such a hurry? With Simon, Sam and the Snowman all in London today for the big briefing, and Sellers busy with Sondra Halliday, Gibbs would be holding the fort at the nick. He wouldn't be free to see Liv until early evening.

Charlie's heart pitched forward inside her chest as she caught a glimpse of the furry collar of her sister's coat. Was it her? The walk said yes – hips swaying from side to side more than they needed to. Then the glossy blonde head came into view. Yes, that was her.

Gotcha.

Liv was in the queue to go through the barrier. She had a ticket in her hand. She must have bought it before meeting Charlie so that she'd be all prepared for her day. That was interesting.

Charlie pulled her own return ticket out of her pocket and picked up her pace, determined not to lose sight of her quarry. It wasn't every day that an opportunity like this presented itself. She was going to enjoy playing Follow That Liar.

3

from Origami *by Kim Tribbeck*

Who remembers the unpainted wooden door with the silver handle, the one I mentioned a while ago and then never explained?

The police remember it, I'm sure – but then they know the whole story, and it's not one you'd forget in a hurry.

The door is in my house. It divides the main part of the house from the cellar. (I never know whether to call it a cellar or a basement. There's no wine in it, so cellar feels wrong. And basement sounds creepy. Let's call it the lower-ground-floor flat beneath my house.)

You're right: I'm putting off telling you my secret. What if you hate me once you know? Actually, I've just remembered: I only care about your opinion because I know you all like me. You're my select few. You've paid to come and see me, or to buy my book. That's something I wish I could make people in my personal life do, to prove they're really keen. Let them put their money where their mouths are.

I'd make an excellent hooker, appreciating payment as I do. All the men who've had sex with me over the years and *not* paid – not a moment went by when I didn't doubt their level of commitment.

Right, here goes. And if you stop liking me once you've heard my secret, I'll stop giving a shit what you think, so that'll be easy.

My new detective friends liked me *more* once I told them, but that's because they can only hold in their minds two categories of person: Not A Murderer and A Murderer. As soon as I explained, they thought, 'Ah, yes – an unscrupulous bitch but Not A Murderer'. I was flattered. It was like getting into the top stream for English all over again.

Okay, so before I start, you need to understand the layout of the building where I live. It's four storeys tall, two rooms wide – one on either side of the front door or the stairs – and only one room deep. They're big rooms, but still, as houses go, it's an oddity. Gabe and I nicknamed it Flat Stanley when we first bought it.

The part I inhabit, the main house, is three floors: ground, first and second. Then there's the lower-ground-floor flat, which in the past has been part of the house, but it can also be self-contained. At the moment it's rented out to a doctor from Copenhagen, Nils Danius. He and I hardly speak, though whenever we do I wind him up by insisting his name means 'Do not resuscitate' in Danish.

The lower-ground-floor flat has separate access from the street. It has its own front door, reached by descending ten or so steps from pavement level, so it can easily work as a separate residence, but only if the wooden door between the house and the cellar remains closed and locked.

You can lock it from either side. Since Nils Danius took up residence, there has been no key in the lock. He doesn't have access to a key. I do. If I wanted to, I could open the door and invade his territory, but I don't. I keep the key tactfully far away from the door, to remind myself that, for the time being, I mustn't even think about going in there. Not that I want to.

I used to want to. Every night, towards the end of my relationship with Gabe. I suppose I should introduce him properly: Gabriel Kearns. On paper he's still my husband, but we no longer live together. We'd been married for about nine years when we realised each of us was regularly disturbed in the night by the snoring or fidgeting of the other. Our guest room – the only other room in the house with a comfortable bed in it – was in the converted basement. Nils Danius now sleeps in that bed, but he didn't then, and one day Gabe and I realised our marriage wouldn't fall apart if we didn't share a bed all night every night. (It would fall apart later for other reasons.) We could still have sex – on the sofa, usually, with *Gogglebox* on in the background – and then we could both get a decent night's sleep in different rooms, two floors apart. This discovery thrilled us both.

(Enjoy your smug laughter while you can, youngsters. Sleep matters. You'll realise that once you turn forty. This kind of thing will happen to you too.)

The one who commuted to the lower ground floor was always me, since I'm capable of moving my brain cells and limbs after 10 p.m. and Gabe isn't. Our relationship improved once we were no longer exhausted all the time, but it still wasn't perfect. It had never been perfect. That's why I needed a lover, whose name was Liam.

Hands up all those who expected me to accept an imperfect husband and not defend myself with a lover? Nope. Sorry. I've always believed fidelity should be earned with good behaviour, not taken as read. Demonstrate to me that you can load a dishwasher in a way that doesn't make me want to start my next sentence with the words, 'Only a lunatic . . .' and then we'll talk sexual exclusivity.

Liam was a fan, or so he said. He emailed me via my website to tell me that I was his favourite comedian. If this sounds as if I'm summarising, I'm not. His message read, 'You are my favourite comedian.' No 'Dear Kim', no 'Warm Best Wishes' at the end. Still, this gave him the edge over Gabe, whose favourite comedian is Larry David.

I wrote back one of my standard 'Thank you so much' emails and Liam replied straight away: 'You're not brilliant, but all the other stand-ups I've seen are dire.' I replied, 'Actually, I am brilliant.' 'Meet me for a drink and I'll explain why you're not,' he fired back. 'Be brilliant rather than dire at making me want to have a drink with you and maybe I will,' was my response.

We met for a drink and it very soon turned into more. I found Liam incredibly attractive, partly because he was nothing like Gabe – he was blonder, bigger, stronger-looking – and partly because he hardly ever smiled or spoke. He was a mystery to me. He lived with his sister and refused to explain why, or admit that an explanation was required beyond, 'Some people live with their siblings, just as others live with their spouses. What more is there to say?'

Sex with Liam always made me think, 'Yes, he's worth bothering with and this is why – I must remember this, how I feel now.' The nothingness around the sex, on the other hand, was perplexing. One evening the word 'bored' came into my mind. I knew something more was needed or else I wouldn't be able to make it last. That's when I had a brilliant idea: a way to make an advantage out of Liam's silence.

I invited him to my lower-ground-floor lair at midnight. It couldn't have been more straightforward. I knew Gabe never fell asleep later than eleven. Barring an emergency, he'd be dead to the world until his alarm went off at seven the next morning.

On the agreed night, I did something I'd never done before when I reached the lower ground floor. I moved the key from the house side of the door to the cellar side, and I turned it in the lock. Now Gabe couldn't get in even if he wanted to. Now my underground lair was mine alone, to do with as I liked. Then I unlocked the door to outside, and waited for Liam to arrive.

He turned up at midnight as arranged and we spent our first whole night together. It was amazing in a way that defies description, partly – no, mainly – because of that locked door, Gabe's proximity, the whole secret cellar thing. Do with that gory psychological detail what you will.

I caught up on sleep between 7.30 a.m. and 2 p.m., while Gabe was out at work. Thank God for the schedule of a stand-up comedian, I thought to myself; it's lucky I'm not an accountant or a chiropodist, or almost anything else. (Also lucky for people with money and feet, not only for me.)

It turned into a regular thing. Not every night, but two or three times a week. Sometimes four. Liam would arrive at midnight, spend the night with me in the basement, and leave at 6 a.m., a safe hour before Gabe's alarm was due to go off. Liam's sister worked nights, so she never knew what was going on. 'She wouldn't like it,' was the most Liam would say on the subject. 'She's a worrier.'

I never worried. I loved living two lives, one on either side of the wooden door. For those of you hoping for drama and retribution, I'm going to disappoint you. Nothing went wrong. No nosy insomniac neighbour stuck his oar in to ruin everything; Gabe never heard any suspicious noises. If someone had walked into our house at night through the main front door, he might have heard them and thought, even in his sleep, 'Wrong sound to be hearing now', but from the master bedroom it's impossible to hear a person entering the building on the lower ground floor.

I had a plan in case of emergencies. In the incredibly unlikely event of Gabe waking up at 2 a.m. and coming to seek me out – which I figured would only happen if he was ill, otherwise even if he were awake he wouldn't want to disturb me – he'd find the wooden door at the top of the stairs to the basement locked. He'd be puzzled, and probably start knocking and calling my name. 'What? I'm asleep!' I'd yell in a fake sleep-fogged voice, while Liam quickly dressed. 'Hang on a minute, Gabe, for Christ's sake! Give me a chance!'

Would Gabe, at that point, think, 'Hm, this is suspicious. I can't get into my cellar the usual way, so I'll run outside, down the steps, and get in through the other door'? I didn't think he'd ever do that. He'd wait there, wondering what the hell was happening, until I came to let him in.

While he waited, Liam and I would proceed on tiptoes to the other door, the one to the street. I'd unlock it, Liam would slip out into the darkness, and I'd call out, 'Gabe? Gabe?' Then I'd say, loudly, 'Fuck! I'm an idiot!' I'd then lock that door and hurry to unlock the other one. 'I went to the wrong door,' I'd tell Gabe. 'I was half asleep and thought you were outside, knocking to get in – silly me!' There's no way Gabe would have suspected me of secretly letting my lover out of the house. He'd probably have asked why I'd locked the door and I would have said, 'I don't know – I always lock both doors before I go to sleep as a matter of course, for security.'

None of this ever happened. I successfully deceived my husband. Past tense. My two-year cellar adventure with Liam is over, as is my marriage to Gabe.

When I told the police, the part they found hardest to believe was that I got away with such a close-quarters deception for so long. I assured them that I did, that Gabe, Liam and I had all survived unscathed – because in real life, contrary to every book and movie and Netflix drama you can think of, the loved ones of depraved adulteresses sometimes don't die in tragic accidents or come down with fatal illnesses. I know! Pretty surprising, isn't it, after what we've been led to believe? You really can have sex with a man who isn't your husband without prompting a victim-blaming deity to have him clipped purely to spite you.

Still, maybe the reason Gabe's still alive is because I mainly only cheated on him while he was asleep. When he was awake, I was faithful to him. That ought to count for something. That's a reasonable compromise. I said all this to the police, who couldn't tell if I was joking.

~

Tuesday, 6 January 2015

I return from the hospital to an empty house; hardly surprising since I live alone. It feels strange and predictable at the same time. Normally I love turning my key in the front door and knowing that everything will be exactly as I left it. I used to dread coming home when I lived with Gabe, and not only because of Gabe himself. There were all the tiny irritations to contend with: the bin liner attached only to one side of the kitchen bin, drooping down low on the other; the jar of Nescafé with the gold foil seal only half torn away, because why waste time tearing off the whole thing when you can shake the coffee powder out of one side of the jar forever?

Today, because I am now officially someone with No-Grandmother-Not-Even-A-Shit-Grandmother, the emptiness feels too much. I would quite like, I think, to walk into the kitchen and see two discarded pairs of shoes under the table and a pair of balled-up socks on the dresser shelf, stuffed between the cereal bowls and the dinner plates.

There are other men. Perhaps I could get the strewn shoes and the balled-up socks without the accompaniment of a drug addict – that would be good.

I make myself a coffee, trying not to notice the Nescafé jar's clean circumference, absent of all foil, and take it through to the lounge. I turn on the TV to break the silence and sit down on the sofa, aware of myself doing both. This is what a pretentious art-house film about a lonely woman would look like.

Aimlessly, I flick through the channels. Everything looks unappealing, but anything's better than thinking. As of today, my brother Drew is the only family I have. I'd be better off with no one at all.

Eventually I settle for one of those endless news channels, the kind with a ticker moving along the bottom of the frame: 'Aston Villa signs Sir Andrew Lloyd Webber to be its new chairman', 'Bus crash in Eastbourne kills nineteen people, seven of them trombone players'. The headlines are so dull, you're forced to alter them to keep yourself awake.

Dull is good, though. Hypnotically tedious. Maybe if I fix my eyes on the screen, I'll drift into a catatonic state and re-emerge a month or two from now, when hopefully I'll know what to do again, and how to get on with the rest of my life.

I wish I liked alcohol more, or cigarettes. Instead, my favourite things are weak instant coffee and cheese and crackers. If only my tastes were different, I could be well on course for an early death by now – not in a depressing suicidal way, but in a way that would be indistinguishable from having too much fun. I'd like to die of Too Much Fun, if only to spite Drew. I don't want to give the bastard any chance to feel sorry for me.

On the world's dullest news channel, there's a policeman talking about the Billy Dead Mates murders. He looks a bit like that newsreader Matthew Am-something-something. Coincidentally, this man also has an unpronounceable surname that has appeared in a box beneath his face: DS Sam Kombothekra of Culver Valley Police.

As someone who lives in Rawndesley, I probably ought to be more worried than I am about this serial killer on the loose. He's killed twice so far in the Culver Valley. Selfishly, I allowed my concern to dissolve when I read an online news report saying that Billy Dead Mates was targeting pairs of best friends.

That rules me out as one of his victims, I thought, and lost interest immediately. The three best friends I've had in my life so far were all chronically disappointing. The first was loyal but so dull she made me want to scream. The second was unreliable – a shape-shifter; less a person in her own right than a series of complex calculations. She told me what I wanted to hear, then walked over to someone else and told them the opposite.

My third best friend was Sarah Durdy. Sarah was a high-status girl at our school: a Tier One. I was a middling Tier Two: I was clever, wore good clothes and had a healthy and fearless disrespect for authority; on the other hand I was unpredictable and, because I didn't care about anyone else's status, I often mixed with the lowest-ranking people.

Sarah Durdy decided I was worth befriending at the beginning of sixth form because she wanted to go out with the boy whose best mate was my boyfriend at the time. She thought I could help her to achieve this, and I did. We remained friends after we'd dumped them. Sarah decided we needed to look further afield; the boys at our school were immature creeps, she said. We needed real men. Her solution was for us to join a tennis club.

I'd never been remotely interested in tennis or any sport, but it didn't occur to me to say no. I looked up to Sarah. She got what she wanted in all things; it never crossed her mind that there might be any other outcome. I admired that. And one of the things she wanted was full ownership of me. It occasionally felt stifling, but mainly I liked it. Sarah acted as if I belonged to her; meanwhile, *chez* Tribbeck, I continued to feel more like a visiting foreign exchange student who had overstayed her welcome than a member of the family.

Within a couple of weeks of us joining the tennis club, I'd met someone I fancied in a frenzied, out-of-proportion way. He wasn't a grown man but he wasn't a boy from our school either. He went to a boarding school in Oxfordshire, and was only around in the school holidays, he told me. His name was Dorian, and he was so gorgeous that it didn't matter. He could have been called Toenail and I'd have felt the same.

Sarah said she thought he was aloof and superior, but was encouraging nonetheless. She told me to go for it, ask him out, he might be less full of himself than he seemed; she'd never ask him out in a million years, but I definitely ought to.

So I did. And to my astonishment he said yes.

Sarah turned away when I told her the amazing news, as if I'd slapped her across the face. I was scared. I'd seen her freeze others out before, but she'd never been like that with me. 'What's wrong?' I asked her.

'Nothing,' she said angrily. 'It's just, I would have thought you'd have *noticed*, that's all. Seeing as how you're supposed to be my *best friend*.'

'Noticed what?' I asked, utterly bewildered.

'That *I* fancy Dorian too!' she spat at me. Then she started to cry and said, 'I've *tried* to keep it to myself because I could *see* how much you liked him. I did what a good friend does: I stood back, I supported you . . . And you didn't even *care* that I liked him too! All you cared about was your ugly selfish self.'

This was a lie. I have never been ugly and, although I am now arguably one of the most selfish people on the planet, I wasn't as a teenager. Sarah produced, through her tears, some kind of psycho-verbal formula that I didn't understand, involving sin debt and friendship severance packages. I was too upset to follow the detail, but the gist was clear: I had to end my relationship with Dorian. Fast. And hand him on to Sarah.

All this I did without complaint. Sarah and Dorian went out together for two weeks before she dumped him for a friend of her older brother's. I decided, after that experience, that the words 'best friend' were meaningless; I had no interest in securing myself another one. Ever.

Now, listening to DS Sam Kombothekra tell the woman interviewing him that there are still no leads and police have decided it's time to appeal to the public for help, I find myself thinking it's a shame Billy didn't start his killing spree while I was still at school. He could have identified Sarah Durdy – the worst best friend since records began – and done the world a favour by removing her. I like to think he'd have spared me, once I'd told him the Dorian story.

Better to have no relationships than bad ones: that's what I tell myself. Which makes it annoying that I'm stuck with Drew. I don't think I can bring myself to say to my own brother, 'I never want to see you again.'

I hear the words 'little white book' and my memory swings away from Sarah Durdy and towards the more recent past: a large hall, a bar near the door, a stage; the audience sitting at round tables – my least favourite formation. I much prefer rows. Tables make the performer – or at least this performer – feel excluded before she starts. On either side of the stage, glittery silver stars painted on black walls . . .

A man coming towards me, his hand outstretched . . .

My breath hardens and sticks in my throat as I listen to DS Sam Kombothekra.

'In all four instances so far, the victim has been given one of these little white books. This isn't one of them – it's a mock-up, but it's very similar to the real thing. Billy's four victims each found a small book like this in his or her home, or among his or her possessions, several weeks before the murder occurred in each case.'

A close-up shot of the book in Kombothekra's hands fills the screen. A blank, white cover. The size is exactly the same.

'But no words inside,' I whisper to myself, suddenly light-headed. If there were no words inside the books given to Billy's victims then this has nothing to do with me.

Kombothekra's next comment demolishes that idea. 'In each book – in some cases on one of the inside pages and in others on the front or back cover – there were some handwritten words. One line, usually – from a poem. The lines chosen were macabre ones, some directly referencing death.'

Death in a little white book. Or maybe not in it, but *on* it, on the front . . .

It's gone.

Something was in my mind then that seemed to matter. It escaped before I could grab hold of it.

Wherever that stage was with the silver stars painted on black and the bar by the door and the audience at round tables, he was there: Billy. The same night I was.

I threw away the book he gave me. Was that him?

It can't have been.

It must have been.

I was scared of him – wanted to get away. There was some-thing about his manner that made me feel threatened. But . . . no, he definitely looked kind. You have to look kind and harm-less if you're approaching a stranger.

But Sam Kombothekra said the four victims were dead within

several weeks of being given a little white book. The silver stars gig was . . . when was it?

Gabe was with me. And . . .

Christ, it was painful, dragging Gabe around with me everywhere. But he was there, so it must have been last year. My 2014 winter tour; February or March.

A little white book with four words handwritten at the bottom of the inside back page in black ink: 'Every bed is narrow.'

Do those words directly reference death? It never occurred to me. I thought it had to be either pretentious whimsy or an unusual pick-up line, though I wasn't sure how he imagined it might work as the latter. I remember trying to work it out, thinking, 'If a man hands a woman a book containing one line that refers to a bed, it has to be a come-on.' My next thought was, 'But if every bed is narrow, surely that means you're better off not inviting anyone to share yours – then you'd have more space.'

I suppose it could mean a grave, if you really wanted to stretch it: we're all alone in the grave.

Lovely thought. Thanks for that, mystery man. Looks like I was right to want to run away from you.

'The lines appear to be paired,' DS Kombothekra tells his interviewer. I don't want to hear any more. This has nothing to do with me. Just because I too was once given a tiny white book. Just because . . .

Liam. You have to ring Liam.

'So, the first and second victims, who were best friends – they each got lines from the same poem,' says Kombothekra. 'The same is true of the third and fourth victims: two lines from the same source – again, a literary source.'

Literary? That never occurred to me.

'We'd like to appeal to anyone who has seen a book similar to this one here, or been given one – anyone for whom this is ringing any bells at all – to contact us as a matter of urgency.'

This is crazy. I'm being roped in by a TV policeman. How absurd. Don't they know my grandmother's just died?

I tossed the little white book in the nearest bin and hardly thought of it again.

Literary. A quote, then? Perhaps a well-known one. I feel as if I'm trapped in a surreal dream. All the details are clear but impossible.

I force myself to get up, walk to the kitchen, pull my phone out of my bag and tap the Google icon. I type the words 'Every bed is narrow' into the search box.

Shit. Oh, shit.

The line 'Every bed is narrow' comes from a poem. It's the last line of the first verse. I start to read the poem from the top and get no further than the first line.

No, no, no. Oh, God. You have got to be kidding me.

A loud, undignified noise startles me. A fraction of a second later, I realise that I made it.

Death. A little white book. That has to mean . . .

Leaving the TV on, I stuff my phone back in my bag and run to the front door. On the other side of it, I fumble with the keys. Can't leave the place unlocked, not if a killer might be after me. I need to talk to the police, but first I must go back to my least favourite place in the world: Ward 10 of the Rawndesley General Infirmary.

4
6/1/2015

They were all staring. Anyone'd think they'd never seen a man walk back into a room after making a phone call before. Proust's jibe rang in Simon's ears: *You have the attention you crave. The floor is yours.*

The words would stick in Simon's mind for too long. Speaking in public, never easy for him, had just got harder.

'Any joy?' James Wing asked.

'She didn't pick up. I'll try again later.' Simon stuffed his phone back in his pocket.

'Why is Sergeant Zailer with Sandra Halliday, Waterhouse? Has marriage to you driven her to seek out the nation's foremost misandrist?' The Snowman chuckled.

'I asked Charlie to have a word. Didn't trust myself to do it without losing my rag.'

'Because you hate women?' Neil Dunning asked neutrally.

Twat.

'You might as well ask Waterhouse if he hates stilt-legged llamas, DS Dunning.'

And another one.

'No, I hate people who prefer their stupid biased beliefs to the truth,' Simon answered Dunning's question. 'Halliday might be talking shit but she's making herself heard, and it's not helpful.'

'No one with a flicker of brain activity would listen to her,' said Proust.

'You'd be surprised,' said Kerensa Moore.

'I wouldn't,' Simon told her. 'Anything you don't have to be clear-sighted and intelligent in order to agree with is going to attract a lot of agreement. As a general principle.'

'Spot on,' said James Wing. Simon flinched. He could do without Wing's endorsements.

'Halliday's writing about Billy all over the place and she's winning people over,' Wing went on. 'I've also checked out her Twitter feed. Yesterday and the day before, the hashtag #FuckYouBillyDeadWomen was trending. She started that. People are lapping up her bullshit. Dunderheads, yes, but there are plenty of them. What I'm wondering is: is Halliday as obtuse as she seems, or does she have a particular reason for wanting to shove Josh Norbury's murder to one side and direct us all to disregard it?'

Keen to expand on his clever-clogs theory, Wing turned to Kerensa Moore. 'You said it yourself: in her various outpourings on the subject, Halliday's made no attempt to explain why Josh Norbury was killed if Billy's motivated by hatred of women.'

'He was a gay man,' said Neil Dunning.

Everyone stared at him.

'Gay men aren't women,' Simon told him.

'I know that. I just meant—'

'He wasn't camp, he wasn't effeminate.'

'I meant I can imagine a woman-hater who might also hate gay men,' said Dunning.

'You can imagine him, or you are him?' Simon enjoyed asking. He noticed a small smile from Grace Woolston and his mood improved still further.

'So now we're playing Pin The Prejudice On The Serial Killer,' Proust snapped. 'Sandra Halliday's made him a misogynist, and now Dunning's made him a homophobe. Is it my turn? I'm going to say that he's a terrible racist. All of his victims so far are white, aren't they?'

'Sondra Halliday might be deliberately creating a smoke-screen,' said Wing. 'The desired victim – the only victim that matters – might be Josh Norbury, and the three women could have been murdered first to send us up the garden path. A false flag operation, if you like. Then along comes Halliday to interpret things in a way that casts Norbury aside as irrelevant. If we believe her take, we barely give him a thought. We consider only, or mainly, the three female victims.'

'That sounds unlikely in the extreme,' said Kerensa Moore. 'Sorry, DC Wing. The first-three-victims-as-cover-for-the-fourth is ingeniously baroque, but sadly this is real life. And Halliday might see the world through a warped lens, but I don't think she's dumb. She knows the police won't neglect to investigate Joshua Norbury's murder on grounds of gender, or because of anything she wrote in *Lifeworld*.'

'Have you read her blog?' Wing asked.

Moore nodded. 'I think I've read every word she's published, for my sins.'

'I think we all have by now,' said Sam Kombothekra.

'That's three words, then,' said Neil Dunning. '"I", "hate" and "men".'

Proust smiled. Sam looked stricken. Simon could read his mind: he was wondering if it was okay to laugh at Sondra Halliday or if that would make him guilty, as all men must be of all crimes. Of everyone in the room, only Sam was fretting, thanks to Halliday, about what kind of reprehensible misogynist he was and what he ought to do about it.

That was why Simon had sent Charlie to tackle Halliday, because of doormats like Sam who were too easily persuaded. Tell men every day, endlessly, that they hate women whether they realise it or not, and some will believe you. Some will start to hate, at the very least, the women accusing them unfairly; others might lump all females together and decide to act on their newly discovered contempt for half the population. Every time Halliday put fingers to keyboard, she rammed home the message that there was violent hatred in the air all around us, and that was dangerous. Simon didn't think it was possible to release that much boiling resentment without putting lives at risk.

Not that Charlie would succeed in talking her round. Zealots like Halliday listened only to acolytes who echoed their own fantasies and prejudices.

James Wing stood up. He said, 'On Halliday's blog, though she doesn't go into detail, she refers to two sexual assaults in her past. What if one of the men involved was Joshua Norbury?'

'He's *gay*. Was, I mean.' Neil Dunning looked surprised to be having to make the point again.

'Gay men don't rape women,' said Kerensa Moore.

'All right, forget that theory.' Wing was starting to sound desperate. 'Halliday could have hated him for any number of reasons. She wants revenge, so she kills him – after killing three women first, as a decoy. Then she pops up as a commentator on the Billy murders, saying, "Notice the dead women, not the dead man!" Come on, we're all familiar with criminals who can't keep away from the scene of the crime – Halliday's failing to keep away by setting herself up as primary media voice on the issue. Think what a buzz that'd give her.'

'I agree we need to rule her out, but I don't believe she's Billy,' said Simon. 'Her schtick's convincing. She means every word of it, from the heart. Wing, what did you mean about the blonde woman lead going up in smoke? I know we were going to go over the four in date order, but maybe we can do Rhian Douglas first if there's been a development?'

'Yes, let's hear it,' Proust decreed.

'I'd like to suggest something,' said Kerensa Moore. 'Apart from this new breakthrough, whatever it is—'

'It's the opposite of a breakthrough.' Wing rolled his eyes. He hadn't done it at all while accusing Sondra Halliday of murder, Simon realised. Did that mean something?

'Well, we'll hear about the negative breakthrough in a minute,' Moore said, 'but otherwise, you're all up to speed on all four, aren't you?'

'We are,' said Sam.

'Then instead of each team, or a team representative,

presenting their own, why not do each other's? I promise you, when you listen to someone else talking about *your* investigation, however well informed they are, you'll find yourself thinking, "They forgot X or Y". Or sometimes they'll pick up on things you mentioned in passing but didn't spot as significant.' Moore circulated an encouraging smile around the room – the facial expression equivalent of handing out copies of a useful pamphlet. 'Shall we try it?'

'I think it's a very sensible approach,' said Sam.

No one protested. Simon thought it might throw up some interesting results, though there was a parlour game aspect to the idea that made him want to reject it out of hand.

'DC Woolston, do you want to start with Rhian, since she's not yours?' Kerensa Moore asked. 'That way DC Wing can get us all up to speed sooner.'

'Please, call me Grace.' Woolston rose to her feet. 'Rhian Douglas,' she said. 'Billy's second victim. Twenty-three-year-old nursery worker. She'd worked at Little Chimps day creche in Poole, Dorset, for six years. Address 17 Nettle Edge, Poole. Rhian was shot in the back of the head on 21 October 2014, between 1 and 3 p.m., while her boyfriend Dolan Todd, a twenty-one-year-old car mechanic, was out at work at Green Fleet Cars, where he's worked for two years. One neighbour, Samantha Granger of 19 Nettle Edge, might have heard the gunshot. Chances are she did, but she wasn't sure because she was taking delivery of some shopping at the time, and she thought the loud noise she heard might have been the back of the supermarket's van slamming shut, or another neighbour's too-loud TV, a neighbour she's currently involved in a legal noise dispute with.

'The driver of the delivery van was subsequently found and interviewed, and he also remembers hearing a noise that sounded like a gunshot. He assumed it was a gun, but not a real one – he thought it was on the loud TV next door. I'll come back to the deaf neighbour later.'

'Oh, so will I,' said James Wing ominously.

Grace Woolston said, 'The evidence tells us nobody broke into Rhian's house, so our working assumption is that Rhian invited her killer – Billy – into her home. She made him a cup of tea. Her body was found by her boyfriend on his return from work at 6.30 p.m. – she was on the floor close to the sink. The kettle was on the floor beside her. We're thinking Billy might have said yes to a second cup of tea, then shot Rhian while she was standing at the sink filling the kettle.

'There were two mugs on the kitchen counter near where the kettle usually sat, both containing tea dregs, and two used teabags in an otherwise empty kitchen bin – all this goes towards consolidating our theory that Billy takes the welcome guest route in.'

'When are you going to mention the little book?' Dunning asked.

'Now. A few weeks before she was murdered – boyfriend Dolan doesn't remember exactly when, but he says between two and three weeks before – Rhian found something in a cloth tote bag that she'd taken into work with her. She swore that when she took the bag in, all that was in it was a scarf and a copy of the *Daily Mail*. When she took it home at the end of the day and unpacked it, she found a little hand-made book: white folded paper with staples in the middle, about five inches by five inches – stiff card, really, more than paper. Only eight pages in total if you didn't count the cover; twelve if you did. There was nothing to suggest who'd put the book there, or what it meant. Most of the pages were blank, but on one towards the back, someone had handwritten the words, 'I wonder if it hurts to live' in black ink, cursive writing. Rhian had no idea what this meant, and described the experience of finding it in her bag as "creepy". More later on these little books, since each of Billy's victims received one in similar circumstances.'

'Yes, let's come to the books later,' Kerensa Moore agreed.

'The investigation into Rhian's death soon established that, unless she was keeping something well hidden, there was no obvious reason for her to get herself killed,' Grace Woolston went on. 'No trouble at all at home, in the extended family, friendship circle, at work, with any of the families whose kids she babysat for – nothing. Boyfriend didn't do it – he was at work surrounded by people all afternoon. He's got no criminal record, there's nothing amiss about him as far as we can tell, and he's obviously devastated – DC Wing and his team said that wasn't an act?'

James Wing nodded his confirmation.

'Billy left his DNA on the mug he drank his tea from. We know it's his because he did the same at two of the other three crime scenes – Linzi and Angela. Josh Norbury was shot before he got as far as making Billy his first cuppa, so there was nothing there. The DNA profile we're assuming is Billy's from three of the four scenes matched none on record, so we're none the wiser. We've taken samples from anyone and everyone connected to all four victims, and there was no match for our Billy DNA. Things were looking bleak. But then, once all obvious avenues of investigation had been covered and had turned up nothing, a stroke of luck occurred.'

James Wing muttered something inaudible, then said, 'Only to un-occur a few weeks later. Sorry. Go on, Grace. It's painful, but I'll sit it out.'

'Right,' said Woolston. 'Well, another of Rhian and Dolan's neighbours, seventy-one-year-old Muriel Pearson – the deaf lady I mentioned earlier, with the too-loud TV in the noise dispute – she lives at number 20 Nettle Edge, and she remembered suddenly, long after she'd told us she hadn't seen anything suspicious on the afternoon of Rhian's murder, and long after we'd said, "Are you absolutely sure?" and she'd said, "Oh, yes, quite sure!" – she remembered that she had, lo and behold, seen a blonde woman behaving suspiciously outside her house.'

'And we got all excited,' said Wing bitterly. 'We imagined

that if we could only scrape Blondie's cheek with a wooden stick, we'd get our DNA match with the Billy mugs.'

'Further probing based on what Muriel Pearson was watching on telly revealed that she might well have seen this woman at around the time Rhian was killed,' Woolston went on. 'What she described was this: she was watching TV, with the volume turned up *very* loud because she's completely deaf—'

'Yeah, and even though she can't hear any better with the volume up as high as it'll go, because she can't hear sod all, she still puts it up to max, because she's hard of hearing – so if she's ever going to hear anything, it's only going to be with the volume on full, isn't it?' Wing shook his head. 'As if the fu— As if the telly's going to restore her hearing by yelling at her at the top of its voice.'

'DC Wing, I understand that this is your case and you want to—' Kerensa Moore began.

'Sorry, Doc.' Wing held up his hands. 'All right, I'll shut up until it's time for my star turn.'

Grace Woolston went on in the weary tone of one who expects to be interrupted. 'Muriel Pearson was sitting in her living room watching TV, volume way way up, and she had a sense there was, as she put it, "someone else there when there should have been no one else there" – because she was alone in the house as far as she knew. Then she saw something out of the corner of her eye, so she turned to her left and got the fright of her life when she saw a woman with blonde hair – straight, shoulder-length, heavy fringe down to just above her eyebrows – standing right outside her house and staring in through her window. Muriel's eyesight's pretty good – much better than her hearing. It was assumed she was as reliable a witness as any.'

'That's right, rub it in,' James Wing muttered.

'The blonde woman wasn't looking at Muriel,' said Woolston. 'Instead, she was looking straight ahead, but she was smiling, as if she'd just spotted a friend, when in fact she was staring at the far wall of Muriel's lounge. Understandably, Muriel was unsettled by this – even more unsettled when, instead of stepping back from the window, the woman moved to the side in a way that looked – and I quote – "funny and just not right". She was heading for the front door, Muriel assumed, but when Muriel went to look there was no one there. The blonde woman is – or I suppose I should say "was", from DC Wing's hints – a person of interest.'

'Was,' Wing agreed. He sat forward and rested his head in his hands briefly. 'I'll start with the geography, because it matters. Rhian Douglas and her boyfriend Dolan lived in the first of a row of four tiny terraced cottages, numbers 17 to 20 Nettle Edge, which isn't a proper street. It's unmade: a mess of bumpy potholes and about as narrow as it's possible for a road to be – only a few centimetres wider than one car or van. No pavements. When I stand in Rhian and Dolan's living room with my car parked outside, I can't see the wheels.'

'Why would you want to see the wheels of your own car while interviewing a witness?' Proust asked.

'I didn't say I would or did, did I?' Turning pointedly away from the Snowman, Wing said, 'As you all know, we assigned our mysterious blonde at the window to a sketch artist. Before we had a chance to do anything with his handiwork, we got a call: Muriel Pearson's son. Asked if I'd go round and see his mother again. She had something she needed to discuss, he said. She was worried about it, and scared . . . As you can imagine, that was enough to get me haring round there. At first the old lady was all het up, apologetic, she never meant to tell a lie, all that. Since we all know people who say that usually *did* mean to lie, I thought, "Oh, here we go", made the right noises and sat back, waiting for the confession.' Wing laughed and shook his head.

'And?' said Simon.

'Muriel Pearson didn't lie. But she did make a mistake. A fu— An important mistake, the correcting of which leaves us with no more mysterious blonde woman to search for. She was never there.'

'The blonde woman was never there?' said Sam.

'Nope.' Wing smiled enigmatically. 'No grinning blonde lady outside the window who moved to the side in a peculiar way. It didn't happen.'

'So how did a woman with decent eyesight, who didn't mean to lie . . . ? I don't get it,' Grace Woolston said.

'Muriel Pearson's house is next door to number 19, where Samantha Granger lives,' said Wing. 'That's Samantha Granger who was *having her shopping delivered* at the time a shot was heard, remember? Delivered by a man in a van?'

'So . . . the driver, he was who Muriel Pearson saw?' asked Sam. 'She saw a man and mistook him for a woman?'

'Nope.' James Wing was enjoying this too much. Simon wanted to press his face against a wall, sideways on, so that his mouth looked squished and stupid. He shook his head to banish the violent image. At one time, long ago in his police career, he'd have jumped out of his chair and made his fantasy a reality.

'The woman Muriel saw wasn't a real woman, or a man,' said Wing.

'A eunuch?' said the Snowman with a heavy sigh.

'It was a picture – a life-size picture – of a woman. Blonde, yes, grinning, yes, and seemingly staring at Muriel Pearson's living room wall because, being an image, her eyes could only stare straight ahead. Anyone here ever seen an Asda delivery van?'

Grace Woolston gasped, covered her mouth with her hands, then spluttered with laughter. 'Oh, my God!'

'I have.' Sam was nodding. 'Yes, a blonde woman with a fringe, smiling. She's on most of the Asda vans, isn't she?'

'I've seen her too,' said Neil Dunning. 'But wait a second, you're not seriously telling me—'

'That anyone could mistake a picture of a woman for an

actual woman?' Wing cut him off. 'I thought that too. So next time Samantha Granger had an Asda delivery due, I made sure to be in Muriel Pearson's front room. It was uncanny. If I hadn't known it was the Asda van lady, yeah, I reckon I might have thought she was real. Muriel Pearson lives in a tiny, light-deprived cottage. Her window's pretty small and the van would have been right up against it. From where she was sitting on the sofa watching telly, she wouldn't have been able to see its top, sides or wheels – only a woman's face and upper body. She assumed, as I think at least a few others might have, that it was a real woman.'

'Who slid to the side,' said Grace Woolston, trying not to laugh.

'Yeah, as the van drove off, obviously,' said Wing. He shrugged. 'I don't think I need to spell it out, do I? Our one promising lead's down the pan.'

'Muriel Pearson had never seen her neighbour's shopping being delivered before that day?' Simon asked. 'Most people who shop online have a regular supermarket they use. How come Pearson wasn't already familiar with the blonde woman on the side of the Asda van?'

'She sits in her chair all day long watching telly she can't hear, barely taking her eyes off the screen,' said James Wing. 'Maybe the day Rhian was murdered was the first time the van driver parked in that particular spot, right outside Muriel's window. In any case it was the first time Muriel saw or noticed her.'

'You asked her that?' said Simon.

'Yes.'

'I never thought the blonde woman was Billy,' said Proust. 'If you've just shot someone, you don't wander along the street and smile in at the neighbours before disappearing – you scarper.'

'Simon, what are you thinking?' Sam asked.

'He's wondering when to launch his brilliant new theory,'

said the Snowman. 'The Asda lady – the real woman in the photo – secretly follows the vans that bear her image, and murders the people they deliver shopping to – except in this case she miscalculated and got an innocent neighbour by mistake.'

'There's nothing implausible about a real person being there that day as well as the picture on the van,' said Simon. 'We know someone else was in the vicinity: Rhian Douglas's killer. Who might, for all we know, be blonde and smiley, with a fringe – and for all Muriel Pearson knows, if she'd never seen that van before and sits in her chair all day, never looking out of the window. How does she know?'

'She positively IDd the Asda van picture as the woman she saw at the window,' Wing said. 'When I showed her the photo, she turned pale and started to cry. "That's definitely her," she said.'

'Your ignorance of the female anatomy is, as ever, your Achilles heel, Waterhouse. Real women don't slide to the side as if on wheels. They walk. On these things they have called legs.'

Unbelievable. They'd all missed it.

Simon smiled and stared at the wall, like a picture of a man on the side of a van.

~

'Do you really believe all this?' DC Colin Sellers held up page 27 of *Lifeworld* magazine so that the woman opposite him could see her own words. Would she turn away in embarrassment when confronted by her own stupidity?

The two of them were sitting at a window table in the Artesian bar of The Langham hotel in London; her choice of venue, not his. While he waited for an answer to his question, Sellers silently listed all Sondra Halliday's worst physical features – too-small eyes, too-small forehead, bitten nails – in a futile attempt to persuade himself he didn't fancy her.

He did.

She had as many good attributes as bad: long legs that tapered to exactly the sort of bony ankles he liked best, shiny brown waist-length hair, a trace of a northern accent, a gurgly laugh that was achingly sexy, and a way of looking at the world that should have angered Sellers but instead fascinated him. That a person who shared the same planet and probably watched some of the same TV shows as him could have such alien ideas in her head . . .

That's if Halliday was serious. For as long as they'd been talking, Sellers had wondered if she was about to admit that her whole personality was a wind-up.

'*Shit*,' she said loudly, startling him. A waitress nearby adjusted her smile setting from 'warm and effusive' to 'brave face', and moved so that she was standing directly in front of the elderly couple to whom she was serving mint tea, blocking their view of the sweary lady.

Sellers could guess how Sondra Halliday would feel about being called a lady. She'd said something incomprehensible about her 'biological sex' within twenty seconds of arriving, but, although the words were all ones Sellers knew, their order resembled nothing he was used to.

'Pardon?' he asked now.

'There was a silent "shit" at the end of your question.' Halliday speared one of her dim sum with a chopstick and stuffed it into her mouth, then used the same chopstick to tap the page in *Lifeworld* where her article was printed. 'Am I serious about all this *shit* that I write and have the gall to publish? Yes, I am. Would you ask a male columnist if he meant what he wrote?'

'Yes, if—'

'Or would you assume he did, because men have natural authority and are therefore deserving of your trust?'

'No. If a man, woman, cat or dog wrote what you've written about these murders, here, on Twitter, on your blog . . . I'd have to ask them if they were doing it for a dare. You can't honestly believe hatred of women is the motive for these killings. One of the victims is a man.'

Sondra Halliday sighed. 'Have you actually read what I wrote? All the way through, like a good little boy?'

'Several times.'

'Then you'll remember the part where I said, that, yes, one of the victims, Joshua Norbury, was male, but 75 per cent of Billy's victims were female. Want one of these?' Sondra skewered another dim sum, a bright green one this time, and waved it under Sellers' nose. 'I've ordered too much as usual.'

'No. Thanks.' He took refuge behind his cup of tea. 'It looks like a frog's bollock.'

'Ha! Yes, it does. Actually, it *doesn't*.' Halliday ate it, as if to make sure. 'Yum. Tastes great, however it looks.'

Sellers tried not to wonder how Sondra Halliday tasted.

'It might look like we *imagine* a frog's bollock would look, but I for one have never seen a frog's bollock in the flesh. Have you? I bet they look nothing like spinach and cashew nut dumplings. Yet we could probably get every single person in this bar to agree these dim sum look *just like* frog's testicles, rather as you and your cop mates have persuaded the world that Billy Dead Women's killing spree is all about pairs of best friends – and everyone nods along because most people have never thought to wonder what murder looks like in a society that hates women. You know what it looks like to a radical feminist? Lots of men killing lots of women, all the time, while every official mouthpiece falls over itself not to call these murders what they are: misogyny.'

'I dispute that,' Sellers cut in when Halliday paused for breath. 'We have no reason to think the motive—'

'Motive! You know what? *Fuck* your motive. Motive's nothing but what the killer says his reason is – his smokescreen, which he then gets you to parrot all over the place. In doing so, you aid and abet his concealment of what's really going on: misogyny.'

She liked to end her statements with that word, Sellers had noticed. 'Statistically, your argument's crap,' he told her. Not something he'd normally say to a woman with hair he wanted to stroke and ankles he wanted to lick, but he'd certainly say it to any man talking bullshit.

'How so?' Halliday sounded interested.

'100 per cent of Billy's victims had one best friend they were much closer to than to any of their other friends. 100 per cent of his victims were murdered either shortly before or shortly after those best friends were also murdered. Not 75 per cent, but 100. That means there's a higher chance these killings are about best friends, friendship, something along those lines, than about woman-hating. I mean, Billy might just as easily have killed two all-male pairs of best friends.'

'Except he didn't.'

'No, but I'd say that's not relevant.'

Halliday laughed. 'You're so stupid, it's almost endearing. That's the whole point of my article. People like you – no offence intended – always think it's irrelevant when men murder women. I don't. I *don't* believe the man-murders-three-women feature of your exciting little murder mystery is neither here nor there. And I never will, no matter how many times well-intentioned mansplainers tell me it is. It's *disgusting* the way it's presented on the news – "Ooh, what could possibly be going on in this killer's mind? Why pairs of best friends? Aren't we all so mystified and on the edge of our seats?" No, we're fucking not! I know what's going on. It's the same thing that's always going on. Men are hurting, maiming, raping, killing women and girls. Same old, same old.'

'Misogyny?' said Sellers. She'd forgotten to add it.

She eyed him suspiciously, as if she suspected him of stealing something that belonged to her. Sellers was disappointed. He'd been hoping for a 'Yeah' or a smile.

'I've spent my working life locking up a good few of the men you're thinking of, the ones who murder women,' he said.

'Some of them, yes, without a doubt, had a problem with women as a . . . a group, but—'

'The word you're looking for is "class".' Halliday swallowed a yawn. 'Women are the inferior class in an exploitative hierarchy. As a man, you ought to be more than a little bit ashamed of the way *your* class oppresses mine, unless you're actively working to change it, and somehow I *really* doubt . . .' She looked Sellers up and down, then gurgle-laughed. 'Oh, it's not your fault. I just get bored of having to educate clueless people to make them see what's right in front of their eyes.'

'I think Billy's different from most men who kill women,' said Sellers. 'We all do – all the detectives involved, from three regional forces. We all agree it's likely to be about the pairs, the friends thing—'

'Oh, wait – you all agree, all you men?' Halliday interrupted him again. She dropped her chopstick and planted her elbows on the table. 'How about this, then: I and other feminists *all agree* that your expertise – ha! – amounts to nothing more than wilful blindness.'

'Charming,' Sellers muttered.

'Oh, wait, that's right: I'm female, so you expect me to charm you. If I don't do that, I've failed.'

'I don't expect anything. Actually, I do now. I expect you to carry on being rude. Any chance you might want to surprise me?'

Sondra narrowed her eyes at him. 'Wow. You really are sleazy as all fuck, aren't you? You're actually flirting with me.'

'No, I wasn't. I was asking you if you'd consider dropping the rudeness – interrupting me, telling me I'm an idiot who knows nothing. Not flirting. I decided about thirty seconds ago not to bother flirting with you. No offence.'

This seemed to please Halliday. She smiled. 'And before that?'

Sellers decided to give it to her straight. 'When I first saw you, I thought, "Yeah, wouldn't mind getting conker-deep in that."'

'"That"?' Halliday raised her eyebrows. 'Wow. Meeting you has made all the work I do feel *so* much more worthwhile.'

Sellers shrugged. 'I never claimed to be refined,' he said. 'I'm a working-class Yorkshire lad and always will be. I'm from Donnie – or Doncaster, as southern jessies say. How about you? I can detect a bit of . . . Hull, is it?'

'Sorry. I don't share my personal details with woman-haters.'

'Then you can tell me. I love women. What, just because I said something crude? If I batted for the other side, I'd be equally keen to get conker-deep in . . . I don't know, Brad Pitt or Johnny Depp.'

Sondra Halliday laughed. 'Poor DC Sellers and his hurt manfeelz.'

'My what?'

'I see I've struck a chord. I'm flattered that you think Brad Pitt and Johnny Depp are my male equivalents in terms of attractiveness. To return to the business at hand – your unsolved murders . . .' She cleared her throat. 'Much as I shouldn't have to spend my spare time teaching Women Are Human Too as a foreign language, I can't resist. You're so ignorant, you've ignited my missionary zeal. Let's do a little thought experiment. Did Hitler hate Jews?'

'Course he did. He killed millions of them.'

'He killed disabled people too, though. Maybe that means he wasn't an anti-semite. He didn't kill *only* Jews. So maybe when he killed those six million Jews, it wasn't about anti-semitism at all.'

'Come on, that's just daft.'

'Uh-huh. As daft as trying to pretend a man who kills three women might not hate women.'

Sellers shook his head, still half wondering what Halliday had said before about his 'man field'. What the hell was that? He'd have to Google it. 'The comparison doesn't work,' he said. 'Hitler *admitted* he hated Jews. He was all about anti-semitism – that was his . . . his thing, his vocation. Billy

Dead Mates has never said anything to indicate he hates women.'

'He's killed three of them, for fuck's sake,' Sondra Halliday snapped. 'Admittedly he's taking the show-don't-tell approach, but I'd say his message is clear.'

'And I say it isn't, and you're living proof.' Sellers pulled off his tie and undid the top button of his shirt. 'The only message I'm getting from Billy is about best friends, nothing to do with gender.'

'You mean biological sex, not gender.' Halliday sounded tired.

'Same thing, aren't they?'

'No. One is real, the other's a socially constructed instrument of oppression and subordination. If you want to think Billy doesn't hate women, fine, you go ahead and think it. I know that he does. I'm happy to disagree if you are, since we're never going to see one another again *please God*. And I'm not sure why this godawful meeting was necessary. Do the police really find it so threatening to have a mere woman disagree with them?'

'Why'd you agree to meet, then?' Sellers asked. 'No, we don't find it threatening, we find it irritating and unhelpful. My colleagues and I have devoted a lot of time and attention to putting out the right message in the media. It's not ad hoc, it's carefully thought out. The name Billy Dead Mates wasn't leaked, it was released deliberately.'

'But I heard a DCI—'

'Claim on *ITV News at Ten* that it was leaked? Yeah, me too. Like I said: there's a strategy.'

'Please don't interrupt me when I'm speaking,' Halliday said coldly.

'You've interrupted me more than once.'

'Yes, and that's fine. You know why?'

'Because you're rude and selfish?' Sellers guessed.

'If I'm rude and selfish, it's for a good reason. Men have

been silencing women for millennia, DC Sellers. If a member of the oppressed class interrupts an oppressor, that's fightback. That's necessary resistance.'

'You're joking.' Sellers laughed, but not for long. 'You're *not* joking? Fucking hell.'

'"Sexist Pig Detective In Woman-Has-Non-Compliant-Thoughts Shocker",' Halliday muttered.

'Like you said: we don't need to agree. I came here today to ask you – politely – to *please* stop writing, publishing, blogging about Billy and these murders. You're muddying the waters, and making it harder for us to control what's out there. That could lead to us taking longer to catch him, which in turn could lead to more deaths. Of women, perhaps,' Sellers added.

Halliday was nodding. She couldn't be about to announce her intention to cooperate, could she? It seemed impossible. 'How very familiar all this sounds, even though we've never had this conversation before,' she said.

'What do you mean?'

'How ultra-reasonable *you* sound! Who could say no to such a request, when lives are at stake?'

'You?'

'Damn fucking right, me. I'll concede it's not *all* your fault – you've just come with your individual request and you can't understand why I wouldn't submit, shut my feminist mouth, help the good old police who, after all, only want to catch a killer, and, as you point out, that would benefit women – his future victims.'

'Right. So what's the problem?'

'Oh, only that men who believe they're well meaning, reasonable, enlightened, have been trying to derail every conversation started by women about how to demolish misogyny since time began. They don't realise that's what they're doing – of course not. They always have a great excuse. "Shut up about misogyny because you'll only make it worse, you'll make women targets for even more male violence." "Shut up about misogyny because we're trying to catch a murderer and you're interfering with our media message." Obviously I want Billy Dead Women rotting in a jail cell as soon as possible, but, no, I'm sorry, I won't be silenced about what's patently going on here. The misogynistic element won't disappear from this case if I stop mentioning it. Unless we notice and name the problem, we can't solve it, and that's my priority. Just as yours is catching Billy.'

'It *isn't* what's going on, though.' Sellers sighed. 'What if Billy killed two more pairs of best friends and all four victims were men? Would you concede then that you were wrong?'

Halliday tilted her head to the left. She seemed to be considering it. 'Maybe. Though I predict that won't happen. He's started out killing many more women than men for a reason. Mi—'

'Misogyny.'

Halliday clapped. 'I suppose you deserve some credit for getting the right answer, even if you don't really believe it. Look, you asked why I agreed to meet you—'

'Is misogyny the answer to this question too?'

'I'm not going to stop writing about Billy, but I might help you catch him.' Halliday reached inside the bag that was sitting by her feet. Much rummaging and under-breath swearing followed as she failed to find what she was looking for. Sellers hadn't spotted the slogan on the bag when she'd first arrived; it must have been on the side facing her body. It read: 'Women who seek to be equal to men lack ambition'.

'Aha. Here it is.' Halliday slammed a book down on the table. *Beloved*, by someone called Toni Morrison. Sellers had never heard of it. 'Someone sent me this anonymously. If it was just the book, I'd be clueless, but it was accompanied by a *very* bizarre letter-cum-passive-aggressive-death threat that makes me wonder if I might know who sent it. I could be wrong, but I think it was him. Billy.'

'Him or her,' said Sellers. 'Billy might be a woman. Don't let the name mislead you.'

'Oh, yes, how silly of me!' Halliday sneered. 'I forgot how keen men always are to cast a woman in the leading role when that role is "villain who needs punishing". Do you have *any idea* how few serial killers are women?'

'Doesn't matter,' said Sellers. 'Billy might be one of the few. If *she* is and we only allow ourselves to suspect men, we'll never catch her, will we?'

'How convenient. When the statistics turn against you, suddenly statistics no longer matter.' Halliday sighed. 'Ugh, look – saving you from your festering bigotry isn't my job or responsibility. I'm here to do my bit to save women's lives, so here it is – take it. I think it's from the *man* . . . sorry, the *male animal* you're calling Billy. Which would make it a significant clue.' She pushed the book across the table at Sellers. 'Letter's inside the front cover. And if you catch him thanks to me, I want proper credit. Men have been taking credit for women's achievements since the dawn of time. You might have thought we were planning to put up with that forever. Well, here's a heads-up: we're not.'

'It's not something I've thought about at all,' Sellers said truthfully.

'Of course it isn't,' said Halliday. 'Because you don't see women as fully human.'

~

Neil Dunning stood up and moved to the front of the room to talk about Linzi Birrell's murder. He did it in a 'This is how it's done' way, awarding himself points as he went, no doubt. Simon's loathing for him intensified.

'Linzi Birrell, twenty-three, address 1c, 143 Klessen Road, Combingham,' said Dunning. 'Billy's first victim. I'll cover the background first, then the murder. Linzi lived with her fiancé, twenty-eight-year-old Ahmed Shoaib, in a rented flat above a toyshop. They chose it because Linzi was a Harry Potter fanatic. Ahmed wanted to live somewhere quieter, off the main drag, but Linzi liked seeing the kids going in and out of the toyshop with their magic wands or whatever, so they stayed where they were, in one of Combingham's main shopping areas. Linzi desperately wanted to have kids – she and Ahmed had been trying for a year or so, and she was worried about her fertility because she'd been on the pill for years and thought it might have had a lasting effect. No worries about Ahmed's fertility: he had two kids with his previous girlfriend Dawn Tooke.'

'Dawn Tooke the kids,' James Wing quipped, to half-hearted laughter.

'Linzi and Rhian Douglas went to primary school together in Poole,' Dunning went on with a more severe expression to deter further heckling. 'They became best friends there, and then when Linzi's family moved to Combingham they kept in touch. Almost constantly. They were the kind of female best friends who said they loved each other all the time and sent texts with a dozen kisses at the end of them. Rhian also loved Harry Potter – though that wasn't mentioned before, when we were discussing her.'

'Sorry,' said Grace Woolston.

'Don't apologise,' Kerensa Moore told her. 'That's why we're doing this. To see what strikes us as important and worth mentioning when we hear the same facts from different people.'

'Linzi worked nights for an agency, cleaning – most recently at Combingham airport,' Neil Dunning resumed his exposition. 'She was killed on 19 September 2014 between three and six in the afternoon. When she was murdered, she'd presumably recently got up and dressed after being asleep for a few hours after her night shift. She was found dead fully dressed in blue jeans and a black and white New Look top.

'It's a pity there's no one here from Combingham,' said Kerensa Moore. 'I know the Spilling team took over Linzi's investigation once Joshua Norbury entered the picture, but it'd be nice to have Combingham's input.'

'The only reason they aren't here is their own resentment,' Simon told her. 'Once we were given overall control, they wanted nothing to do with it. Two of their DCs were meant to be coming today. Guess what? One phoned in sick and the other had something more urgent come up.'

'We don't need them, today or ever,' said Proust. 'If a murder's not gang-, drug- or race-hate-related, they don't know where to start.'

'I assume most of the crime they see is one of those three things?' James Wing asked.

'It is,' said Sam. 'Which is why, at first, they pursued the race angle. Linzi's fiancé is Pakistani, and her ex-boyfriend, the one she left for Ahmed, was the worst kind of white: a member of the English Defence League. He lost his job a while back and took it out on Linzi, so she sensibly dumped him for the more promising Ahmed, who's an accountant.'

'Why the race angle and not the straightforward jealousy angle?' Wing asked.

'Combingham are race-hate-crime obsessed,' said Simon. 'Their hypothesis was white thug or thugs who weren't about to take it lying down when one of their own – as they'd see Linzi – shacked up with a Pakistani man. Only problem was they had nothing to back that up, and no theories as to why Linzi found a small white hand-made book in her coat pocket two weeks before she died, containing nothing but one line of poetry distributed over the double-page spread at the centre of the book: 'I measure every grief I meet.'

'A line from an Emily Dickinson poem,' said Sam. 'The same poem Rhian Douglas had a line from in her little white book.'

'Combingham Police had high hopes a witness might turn up,' Dunning raised his voice a fraction to remind them all of who was supposed to be speaking. 'Someone who saw Billy being let in through the door next to the toyshop that leads up to the flats. But no one saw anything, or if they did, they didn't come forward. Despite Linzi's flat being opposite a chip shop, a café and a betting shop, there were no witnesses to speak of. Probably a case of too much going on in a busy shopping area, so that no one saw anything.

'Linzi, like Rhian, was shot in the back of the head – in the lounge, though, not the kitchen. She was found in front of the cabinet where she kept all her Harry Potter paraphernalia. Nothing had been taken, Ahmed told police later, but the doors were open and there was a model of Dumbledore on the floor next to Linzi's body. We're thinking maybe Billy asked Linzi to show him the Harry Potter stuff, and when she was facing the cabinet, with Dumbledore in her hand, he came up behind her and shot her. All the people who lived in the other flats above the toyshop were out at work, so no one heard a shot – but that's not surprising. That road, there's buses roaring by constantly.

'On the coffee table in the lounge were two mugs, one containing the dregs of a cup of tea, the other of coffee. We know from Ahmed – who alibied out early and satisfactorily – that Linzi drank coffee always, never tea. Angela McCabe, victim number three, was the same, and at her place too there was one tea, one coffee mug found near her body. At the Rhian Douglas crime scene there were two teas; Rhian was a tea-drinker. I think it's safe to assume Billy's a tea-drinker too, therefore.'

'If I were a serial killer with a strong preference for coffee, it'd probably occur to me to ask for tea at my crime scenes,' said James Wing.

Simon disagreed and said so. 'You're about to do something as momentous as commit murder; you'd want your regular go-to comfort drink. It's not as if "Suspect drinks tea" or "Suspect drinks coffee" is going to bring a police team to your door – millions drink both.'

'True if your pool of potential suspects is everybody out there,' said Kerensa Moore. 'Less true if we narrow it down to a few possibles. In that scenario—'

'In that scenario, we fall to our knees and praise the Lord,' said the Snowman. 'Can we press on? Who's doing Angela McCabe?'

'I haven't finished Linzi Birrell.' Dunning looked shocked that anyone would try to cut him short. 'Linzi and Ahmed had been subjected to a fair amount of racist abuse from local unsavouries, but nothing that stood out, no one who seemed passionate about it – just the predictable comments shouted in the street, things overheard in pubs. Low-level everyday stuff – nothing to suggest anyone'd take it as far as murder.'

'Another thing Combingham flat-out refused to acknowledge,' Simon said. 'As well as my question they'd never answer: wouldn't racists kill Ahmed instead of Linzi, or as well as?'

'Combingham detectives interviewed most of the town's population – everyone who'd ever had a racist thought – and they got nowhere,' said Dunning. 'Same when they interviewed Linzi's and Ahmed's families, colleagues, friends. Nothing. As per Billy's other three victims: no red flags in the finances, no affairs – just nothing. Little white home-made books with lines from poems in them, and apart from that? Diddly squat. There was a brief moment when suspicion fell on the owner of the caff opposite Linzi's flat, Hot-n-Tasty. That's the caff's name, not the owner's. She's called Miff Sheeran. And she didn't once leave Hot-n-Tasty on the day Linzi was killed – it's been confirmed by about twenty people who were also there – so she was quickly ruled out, and no one had pinned their hopes on her anyway. Ahmed insisted Miff wouldn't hurt a fly, and her DNA wasn't a match for Billy's at the scene, so . . . that was a never-very-promising lead down the drain.'

'Though it's worth remembering that Miff Sheeran denied Linzi ever made a complaint about a lasagne,' said Simon, sensing that Dunning was about to move on without mentioning this.

Proust groaned. 'Please not the lasagne again.'

'I just think it's odd she lied, that's all,' said Simon. 'Linzi can't have been the first customer who'd complained.'

'I honestly think she might have been,' Sam said. 'Hot-n-Tasty isn't the kind of place where customers have especially high expectations of the food.'

'Three people in the caff on the day in question, two months before Linzi was murdered, confirmed they'd overheard the row between Linzi and Miff about the lasagne,' said Dunning. 'Though to be fair, two called it a discussion. Third says it was definitely heated – claims Linzi ended up picking up her phone and the Harry Potter book she'd taken in there with her to read over lunch and walking out, leaving the lasagne on the table after only one mouthful.

'Once she'd left, Miff sat down at the table and ate the lasagne herself, loudly announcing it to be delicious. All three witnesses separately reported the same altercation, which I'm sure no one wants to hear in detail again: Linzi claimed it wasn't the same, it was worse, but couldn't say how. Miff said if she was accusing it of being worse she must surely be able to explain in what way today's lasagne was different and worse than usual . . .' Dunning raced through the substance of the five-month-old argument in a bored voice. 'Miff then, er, tried to blame Linzi for having the same thing twice – on the grounds, presumably, that if she never repeat-ordered the same dish, she'd be more likely to avoid dashed hopes and dissatisfaction.'

There was a ripple of laughter around the room – as there had been, traditionally, whenever this particular detail had come up.

'Linzi said, "But it's not the same,"' Dunning went on. 'Miff said, "Darling, if you don't want it, I'll happily take it off your hands." That's when Linzi walked out and Miff sat down and gave a public performance of really enjoying the lasagne, for the sake of PR. Though you'd have thought not fighting with the customers might have been a more sensible approach.'

'Ahmed said Linzi never mentioned this altercation to him,' Simon cut in again with another detail at risk of being omitted, one that had bothered him a bit. 'She'd been attacked unreasonably by the owner of the café across the road – why wouldn't she tell her fiancé?'

'Because it's a boring-as-shite story?' Grace Woolston suggested.

Probably. Simon made the concession silently.

'After Linzi's death, fingerprints were found in her flat, as they were at all the murder scenes,' said Dunning. 'But *different* unidentifiable fingerprints in each case, suggesting Billy either wore gloves or wiped away all traces of his or her presence at the crime scenes. I don't think the latter option's practical, personally . . .'

'Me neither,' said James Wing. 'We'd have found a few of Billy's prints at all four scenes, enough to tell us it was the same person. We know that anyway from the little books, but that's circumstantial.'

'Which means we don't know it,' said Simon. 'We mustn't ever forget that we're *assuming* the same person killed all four, because of the books and the other similarities. Doesn't make it true.'

'Of course it's the same killer,' said Proust impatiently. 'Can we please not waste time?'

'The gloves thing bothers me,' said Grace Woolston. 'You're in someone's house chatting away, and you haven't taken off your gloves? Wouldn't they be suspicious?'

'They might if they had reason to fear you,' said Sam, 'but the victims invited Billy into their homes, which suggests trust, not fear. In which case, you'd simply think, "Funny he – or *she* – hasn't taken the gloves off."'

'Happens all the time,' said Dunning. 'Visitors come round and sit there in their coats, even when you've got the heating up, saying, "I'll take it off in a sec, just let me warm up first."'

Simon imagined that anyone visiting Dunning might keep their coat on to effect a quick getaway when things became unbearable.

'Gloves are slightly different,' said Proust. 'I think DC Woolston has a point. No one walks into a heated building and leaves their gloves on.'

'You're *all* right, I think,' said Kerensa Moore, playing the role of diplomatic parent. 'No one does that, true – or very few people – but *if* someone you trusted enough to invite into your home and make tea for happened to do it, what would you do? Sergeant Kombothekra: what would *you* do?'

'Oh!' Sam looked pleased to be chosen. 'Well, if it was someone I knew well, I might say, "Aren't you going to take off your gloves?" in a light-hearted way. I wouldn't want to upset them or make them feel awkward.'

'Sergeant Kombothekra would find his own woolliest gloves and put them on, lest his guest should feel alone and misunderstood,' Proust told Moore.

'But if it was someone I wasn't close to – and there are plenty I trust in that category – I wouldn't say anything. I'd just think, "That's unusual" – but people are, aren't they?'

'Right.' Kerensa Moore nodded. 'The very answer I wanted. I think we can assume, in the absence of evidence to the contrary, that Billy figured he could keep his gloves on and no one was likely to query it because of basic politeness.' No one disagreed with this.

'He wore gloves, but left DNA from his mouth on the crockery,' said Proust. 'Is he a moron?'

'I'd say not,' said Moore. 'I think the gloves might have been as much about avoiding skin contact with the gun as anything else. Symbolic distance from the act.'

'I'm done with Linzi Birrell,' said Dunning. 'Who wants to take Angela McCabe?'

'I will,' said Simon. 'Angela McCabe, forty-seven years old, address 7 Bradby Avenue, Chiswick. Happily married, two children, ten and eight. Killed 11 November 2014. And with his third murder, Billy moves to a different socio-economic bracket. Angela McCabe was upper middle class and so was Joshua Norbury, whereas Linzi Birrell and Rhian Douglas both came from working-class backgrounds and led working-class lives. Angela and Josh had been best friends – like particularly close siblings, we're told – for nearly fifteen years, since they met on a . . .' – Simon cleared his throat – '. . . holistic holiday in Crete, where they were on the same creative writing course.'

'Yet I keep hearing that they weren't hippies,' Proust said. 'When in fact only a hippie or someone of that persuasion could hear the word "holistic" without gagging.'

'I can promise you they weren't hippies or anything like that – really,' said Grace Woolston. 'Angela McCabe was trying to write a screenplay and went on many creative writing courses – this one was in the sun, by a beach, so she thought, "Why not?" She had reservations about the holistic stuff, but she thought she could just ignore it.'

'And what was Joshua Norbury's excuse?' Proust asked.

'The crime we're here to investigate is murder,' Simon told him. 'Not going on the kind of holiday you disapprove of. Norbury was young, gay and single and wanted to meet someone in the same situation – hopefully the love of his life. He'd been told by a mate that those holistic holidays were the place to go. Josh didn't meet a romantic partner, but he did make a best friend for life: Angela McCabe.'

Simon stood up, walked over to the window and looked out at the blocks of flats opposite. He found it easier to speak in a group situation when he wasn't looking at the people he was talking to. 'Angela and her husband Russell owned a four-storey townhouse in Chiswick with a large outbuilding in their back garden, from which they ran their business: a small kung fu school. That's a martial art. They didn't make a fortune from it, but they didn't need to. Both

Angela and Russell had inherited an eye-watering amount of family money, so the school was more of a hobby than a necessity.'

'Not fair, that,' said Grace Woolston. 'It was a proper business: professionally run and the classes were popular. Just because the McCabes had money doesn't make them dilettantes.'

'All right, fine,' said Simon. 'Crime scene: kitchen of the McCabe home. Same as the previous two victims: cups with remains of drinks found – one tea for Billy, coffee for Angela. Angela, like Rhian Douglas, was shot in her kitchen, but – key difference – Angela was the only one of the four not to be shot in the back of the head. She was shot here.' Simon pointed to the spot between his eyebrows. 'By her body, on the floor, was a biscuit tin and biscuits scattered everywhere. Theory: Billy was preparing to shoot her in the back of the head while she was facing the kitchen worktop, mugs, kettle, etcetera, but then she turned round, biscuit tin in hand, to offer him a biscuit – so he shot her face to face.'

'I think Billy's conflict-averse,' said Kerensa Moore. 'He likes – maybe even needs – everything to be friendly.'

'Then he ought to consider not murdering people,' said Proust.

'I'm not saying he's a great guy who should be let off,' Moore clarified. 'Only that his preferred M.O. – cups of tea first, then shot to the back of the head while unobserved – suggests he might be uncomfortable with overt hostility. He wants people to like him – right up until the moment he shoots them dead.'

'That's . . . not a given,' Simon changed course to end his sentence more tactfully than he'd first intended. 'He might just be efficient, or risk-averse. Why allow your target to see you produce a gun and aim it at them when you can wait till their back's turned and surprise them? If they've got even a split second's advance warning, they might duck out of the way and then you've lost control of your kill.'

'Wow. Spoken like a true scary murderer!' Kerensa Moore laughed.

'How do you think I catch these people year after year?'

'Fair point, DC Waterhouse. You're right: your analysis of Billy's character is as likely as mine to be correct. It's good to air as many as we can come up with. There might be other equally plausible possibilities. Let's hear as many as we can.'

'Yeah, let's – later,' said Simon, whose tolerance for Moore's isn't-it-all-jolly tone was fast evaporating. 'I'm in the middle of recapping Angela McCabe. Like Linzi and Rhian before her, Angela also found a small white home-made-looking book, stapled in the middle, with no more than one word on each page. Together, the words added up to a line from a poem by Ella Wheeler Wilcox, an American poet: "Somebody's baby was buried to-day". Angela found the book in her handbag. Her husband said it was her favourite bag; she always had it with her. Anyone could have followed her and slipped it in at some point. After dropping her kids off at school, Angela was in the habit of going for a coffee at the Whole Foods Centre on Magnier Road in—'

'Whole Foods Centre!' Proust pounced on it. 'And we're expected to believe she's not a hippy.'

'The point is, it would have been easy for Billy to learn that Angela could be found there most mornings,' said Simon. 'At the Whole Foods Centre. Easy for him to be there too one day and slip the booklet into her bag.'

'Also worth mentioning that Angela got a line from the same poem that Josh Norbury did, in his little white book,' said Grace Woolston.

'Norbury's line was "And a shadow seemed drawn o'er the sun's golden track",' said Sam.

'Yes, this is crucial,' said Kerensa Moore. 'Sorry, DC Waterhouse – I know you're keen to go on, but we need to state at every opportunity: this is Billy's way of telling us that it's about pairs of best friends, in case we were too slow to work it out. Rhian and Linzi got lines from the same poem. So did Angela and Joshua.'

'The pairs thing was frustrating in the case of Angela,' Simon went on. 'The unmissable link to Linzi and Rhian via the little white book, I mean – because if that hadn't been there, telling us it had to be the same killer, there'd have been an obvious suspect for Angela's murder: thirty-six-year-old Gisela Bloor, receptionist at a car showroom in Ealing. Bloor has been semi-stalking Angela's husband Russell for years, making a nuisance of herself in the guise of being a dedicated kung fu student. Russell McCabe wasn't interested in her and nothing ever happened between them, but Gisela told everybody, including Angela and Russell, that *she* and Russell were destined to be together. It's what the universe wants, apparently, she told anyone who would listen – and it would happen eventually whether Russell accepted his predetermined fate or not.'

'Another unhinged hippy,' said Proust.

'She's the most selfish individual I've ever met,' said Neil Dunning. 'She left her husband and son to pursue Russell, to be available for when he finally saw the light, which he insists he never will. Now that Angela's dead, he seems even more determined. Can't say I blame him. Gisela'd make anyone's skin crawl, but she's not a murderer. She was stroking shiny hatchbacks in the showroom the day Angela was murdered. No payments to hitmen, either – not that we can find any trace of. Also, if you'd met her, you'd know she'd never put herself out to find a gun and learn how to use it – the universe is expected to do all the work and bring her what she wants without her having to make an effort.'

'Gisela could be Billy,' Simon insisted. 'Somehow, some way – even if it looks, for the moment, like she couldn't.'

'Then so could Sondra Halliday,' said James Wing. 'Just as likely, given her obsession with the Billy killings – and we don't know she has alibis.'

'What's Gisela's motive for killing Rhian and Linzi?' asked Neil Dunning. 'Big fat nothing.'

Simon ignored him. 'Another suspect for Angela, initially, was the obvious: husband Russell McCabe. Her death meant the debt on their house being paid off *in full* by Zurich Insurance – they had a £485,000 interest-only mortgage on it. At the same time, they had nearly two million quid in various savings accounts and investment portfolios, and owned outright a six-bedroom holiday home in Burnham Market in Norfolk. So, did Russell McCabe murder his wife to get his mortgage paid off? We think not, because he was teaching kung fu classes all afternoon. Also, one of the kung fu pupils claims she looked out of the window at one point and saw Angela with someone else in the kitchen of the house. We think that someone else must have been Billy. As far as Russell McCabe knew, or as far as he's told us, his wife wasn't expecting any visitors that afternoon. And that's our one and only sighting of Billy, folks – by a witness who happened to glance out of a window and see someone about 80 feet away, for a few seconds. We got nothing more from that sighting than "a person", and even that was qualified by "not sure, might have imagined it".'

'If you're done, I'll do Josh Norbury,' said James Wing.

Simon nodded and returned to his chair. He wanted it to be Gisela Bloor but he didn't believe it was, not deep down.

'Joshua Norbury, forty-five, single,' said Wing. 'Gay. Had a flat in the old Corn Exchange building in Spilling. He worked as a manager at a chemical waste plant between Rawndesley and Combingham. Murdered – shot to the back of the head – on 17 December 2014. Like Rhian and Angela, killed in his kitchen. Josh was found by his cleaner, Andras Nagy, two days after his death. There were mugs on the kitchen counter, but they were clean. Empty. Billy was getting impatient, perhaps, on his fourth killing expedition – couldn't be bothered to do the cup-of-tea-and-friendly-chat part of his routine, so shot Norbury before the first drink was made.' Wing rolled his eyes.

'I mean, you can see his point. Why waste time socialising with someone who'll be dead within the next half-hour?'

In this instance, thought Simon, the eye-roll was at odds with the sense of what Wing was saying. Why hadn't someone close to him had a word, tried to make him quit the habit? Wing had mentioned a 'partner'.

'Josh Norbury was well liked, lots of friends, nothing dodgy or dangerous in his personal or professional life. No one saw or heard anything – no leads, nothing to go on apart from a little white book with a line from a poem: "And a shadow seemed drawn o'er the sun's golden track". Ella Wheeler-Wilcox.'

'Norbury shouldn't have died,' said Simon with feeling. 'Soon as Angela McCabe was murdered, Norbury, as her best friend, should have had round-the-clock protection. It's bullshit to say no one was sure it was pairs of best friends Billy was going for when Linzi and Rhian—'

'Don't harp on, Waterhouse,' Proust snapped. 'What's done is done. What wasn't done – well, there's not much that can be done about it now. Billy was not, at that point, known as Billy. The friends pattern only revealed itself after Norbury was killed.'

'No, it didn't. To anyone who had their eyes open—'

'Let it go, mate.' Wing patted Simon's knee. Simon swung his leg away.

'So where does all this get us?' Proust asked. 'Anywhere at all? We had two decent motives for Angela McCabe, none for anyone else, unless you count vague suggestions of racism for Linzi Birrell, which I don't. But since all the Culver Valley racists, in any case, have alibis, as does Russell McCabe, as does Gisela Bloor, we have . . . nothing. We're up a well-known creek, it seems to me.'

'The Culver Valley has to be significant,' said Simon.

Everyone looked at him.

'Pairs of best friends – fine, maybe Billy's motive is friendship-related, but there are pairs of best friends all over the country. Two, one in each pair, from our patch – that can't be a coincidence.'

'With only two pairs, it can, I think,' said Neil Dunning. 'Course, if there were to be a fifth and sixth victim—'

'Let's hope and pray that doesn't happen,' said Sam. 'Even if we never catch Billy, that's a price worth paying to avoid more murders.'

'No.' Simon said. 'We don't make deals like that, even in our minds. We hold out for both – no more murders, and Billy behind bars.' *Or Billy dead*, he added silently.

5

from Origami *by Kim Tribbeck*

Shall I tell you the least disappointing thing Liam ever did? He bought me a brilliant birthday present, the best thing anyone's ever given me.

Big deal, you're probably thinking. Isn't that what lovers do – give gifts that you treasure forever, or at least until you decide you'd rather wrap your thighs around somebody else?

Well, no. If those lovers are Liam, then that is categorically not what they do. That's why I said 'least disappointing'. Liam, I'm sorry to say, is a disappointing man. Let's put it this way: he would never be asked to stand in for Cyrano de Bergerac. If there was ever a conversation along the lines of: 'Cyrano's gone AWOL – can anyone think of a man who's equally able to convey romantic passion with eloquent brilliance?', I guarantee no one would pipe up with, 'Yes, of course! There's Liam Sturridge from Rawndesley!'

Romance wasn't Liam's thing. Compliments weren't either, though he did once whisper, 'That's amazing,' while I was giving him a blow job. That was the only time in two years that he used a top-tier enthusiastic adjective. (I don't include 'favourite', from that first email he sent me, in which he told me I was his favourite comedian.)

On our first date, at the Hourglass in Rawndesley, we each bought our own drinks: a red wine for him and a brandy for me. There were royal blue upholstered booths along two walls. Liam pointed to a free one and said, 'Let's sit there,' when he saw me heading for one of the round tables near the window. From this, I gathered that he wanted privacy.

He sat next to me in the booth instead of opposite as I'd expected him to. I opened my mouth to start chatting at the exact moment that I felt his hand on my thigh. I ran through all the obvious checks in my mind: is it definitely his hand? Could it be there by accident? How do I feel about this?

It was, without doubt, the least annoying thing he'd done since writing to introduce himself. His fingers on my skin were an interesting proposition, until he pressed them in harder, like someone testing an avocado for ripeness. Without lowering his voice, he asked, 'Is this okay?'

'Is *what* okay?' I fired back in my best superior voice.

'This,' he said as he reached up and pulled my underwear to one side. 'I can stop if you don't like it.' I'd worn my best lingerie, telling myself this was only because it was closest to the top of the drawer.

'Let me see,' I said, running a quick check on my feelings to see if I hated him. The results were unclear. I suspected my reaction was a false negative, as I believe they say in scientific circles. 'It's better than your crap opinions about comedy,' I concluded aloud.

'I can stop talking altogether if you like?' he suggested as he pushed his fingers inside me.

'Yes. I . . .' I gasped. 'I'd like it if you could stop talking shit, yes. And emailing me your ill-informed opinions.'

'You turned up tonight in spite of the shit I've been talking,' Liam pointed out.

'Yes, but not for any reason that reflects well on you.' I raised my left hand and waved my wedding ring in front of his face. 'I'm finding my husband annoying at the moment. I'd probably have come out to meet a Morris dancer. Or one of those people whose hobby is researching their family history.'

'Why's your husband annoying?' Liam asked, stroking away quite expertly.

I couldn't really speak at that point. Silently, I opened my book of Disappointing Husband anecdotes. Page 45: Gabe once emptied out my nutmeg jar, throwing its legitimate contents in the kitchen bin so that he could use it to store his skunk-weed. He needed an airtight container so I wouldn't smell it. Skunk has a horribly strong stench and I'm unfashionably zero-tolerance about any kind of drugs.

The next day, when I needed the nutmeg to put in a sauce, I couldn't find it. I asked Gabe to help me search the kitchen, swearing I'd bought a new jar only the other day. Gabe hunted with me quite happily, emptying out the pantry and the dresser drawers – all the time knowing the jar was in the glove compartment of his car, which I opened a week or so later when we were driving to his mother's, to see if he had any extra-strong mints. The nutmeg jar full of weed fell into my hands.

Gabe was sorry, sorry, sorry – for taking drugs, for lying again. His sorry phase lasted for the first ten or so years of our marriage. It was followed by the rational-defiant era. Now that Gabe and I are no longer together, I sometimes ask myself which was better. Did I prefer constantly playing hide and seek with pieces of silver foil dotted with tiny burned holes, searching my home for proof of the weed habit he denied, or was it better, all things considered, to have to listen to rapturous descriptions of £320 vaporisers that were so much better for you than bongs and that would enable Gabe to get wasted while protecting his lungs?

'I'm not going to discuss my husband, tonight or ever,' I said as Liam's fingers continued with their due diligence. 'I'd . . . aah . . . feel too disloyal. My husband is fine.'

I loved Gabe. I probably still do. He's the funniest, cleverest, most interesting man I've ever known. He always had some new fad on the go that he raved about until I was so sick of it, I could scream – yoyos, fencing, a particular brand of Greek olive oil, old issues of *Punch* magazine . . .

I wanted to be as loyal to him as I could, which meant not discussing him with Liam. I'd had a little bit of a vent and I wanted to leave it there. And for all of you who are thinking there's no point fretting about loyalty to your husband while a stranger's got his fingers inside you, I would respectfully say this: what crap.

Have you ever been on a diet, one of those calorie-counting ones? First week or two, you're as strict as anything. Half a potato: 37 calories. 100 grams of etiolated Quorn: minus 7 calories. You lose half a stone, then a whole one. But then disaster strikes! You've already used up your 39-calorie-a-day allowance, and someone offers you a four-cheese pizza with extra Gorgonzola, and you can't resist! You guzzle it down and exceed your calorie quota to the tune of 17,000.

We've all been there. Question is, what do you do *then*? Most of us give up. We've failed. No more diet for us, only failure and shame and Gorgonzola pizzas every night from now on. Whereas if we could think to ourselves instead, 'Oh, well, it's only one slip-up – back on the thin broth tomorrow,' we could continue to starve ourselves quite successfully, until we're no more than bags of bones covered in fine downy hair.

I digress. The point is: that's how I feel about loyalty. So a stranger's fingers are exploring my private parts – I'm the first to admit it – but does that mean I have to give up altogether on being loyal to my husband? I believe that if we all practised as much loyalty as we could, the world would be a better place. To this day, I'm glad I never bitched to Liam about Gabe.

Liam didn't care either way. He said so. 'Don't tell me if you don't want to. I was only asking to be polite. I don't care.'

'I just need to get out of the house sometimes,' I explained. 'Well, often. Actually . . . whenever I'm in the house.' It was true and it wasn't. No one understands about the true-and-not-true thing that you have if you're a real person with an on-stage persona that's a different version of you.

'Are you going to put that line in your next comedy show?' Liam asked.

'Maybe,' I said. (Update: yes, Liam, I am. I'm going to put it in a book too.)

'Are you married?' I asked him. 'I'd need an X-ray to see if . . . ah . . . if you're wearing a wedding ring.'

'No, I'm not married. And I don't care that you are,' he said solemnly, as if nothing had ever mattered more to him than not caring.

I laughed and admitted to myself that I found him interesting. What kind of creature is this? I wondered. He was nothing like me – nothing at all, mentally or physically. I'm medium height with dark brown hair, brown eyes, olive skin, a long-ish face. Liam is a tall, well-built strawberry blond, with ivory skin and eyebrows that look, under the light, as if they've been added with gold highlighter pen.

He seemed not to care about my words, ideas or feelings. All he wanted – that evening and whenever we met subsequently – was to touch me. It was the one constant, from that first evening in the Hourglass to the last time I saw him, when I ended our affair: his physical urgency. He behaved like a starved animal that had found a raw steak and was determined to get the most out of it in case he never saw its like again. After a session in bed with him, I'd feel raided and devoured. I loved this aspect of our relationship, and told myself – because, like many women, I'm a dumb-arse who uses sex to try and get love – that Liam enacted his feelings instead of verbalising them.

Meanwhile, his emails were a joke.

'It was good to see you yesterday. When next? L'

'Can't come tomorrow. Weds maybe. L'

'Sorry, been busy all day. Yes, tonight okay. L'

I felt lucky beyond belief if I ever got an email from him that was unrelated to the arrangement-making process. Once he sent me a message saying, 'Have you read *The Sportswriter* by Richard Ford?' I hadn't, but after hearing that Liam thought it was 'good', I bought and read it immediately.

He loved books; that was one thing I knew about him. He never used the word 'love' about them, but he carried a printed list in his trouser pocket of the books he wanted to read, divided into categories, each with its own distinct box in a formal-looking table: History, Politics, Fiction, Sociology.

One night, after we'd been seeing each other for more than a year, he mentioned his office in Rawndesley. I reminded him that he worked in Spilling. 'That was my old job,' he said. 'My new one's in Rawndesley.' He'd switched companies three months previously, it turned out. 'Why the hell didn't you tell me?' I asked him. All I'd ever known about Liam's work was that it was something to do with applying for patents for technical products.

He looked surprised. 'I didn't realise I was supposed to,' he said. There was no 'supposed' about it, I explained; it was simply that I'd have thought he might want to tell me, because it was news – good news. 'I don't regard myself as interesting, so I'm not interested in talking about myself,' Liam replied, before reaching inside my top to grab a breast.

Our sex sessions were long – longer than Gabe and I had ever managed, even in the early days. After a night with Liam, I was usually left stuck in a Y shape, wondering if anyone had invented a physiotherapy routine for coaxing legs back together again after they'd been wide apart for too long. I pictured a strict, shouty, secretly-devoted-to-me nurse in a white hat and tunic yelling, 'Come on, Kim, don't you dare give up, d'you hear me? When we started this morning, your legs were a full 180 degrees apart and look how far you've come – now they're only at 90 degrees! Are you really going to quit now, like a loser, or are you going to keep working to get the gap down to 45?'

I had two birthdays during the time Liam and I were sleeping together. For the first, he didn't buy me anything. I wasn't surprised. He wasn't the kind of person who bought presents and I didn't expect one. As far as I was aware, he didn't know when my birthday was. I'd mentioned it once or twice in the weeks before, moaning about how difficult special occasions are to navigate when you don't like any members of your family, but Liam hadn't picked up on it.

On my second birthday that fell during the time we were together, Liam arrived at our basement rendezvous carrying a brown paper bag, which he thrust at me as I opened the door to let him in. 'What's this?' I asked.

'Have a look,' he said.

I opened the bag and pulled out a book that looked fifty years old: a small hardback with a maroon cover that had nothing on it apart from the title, *Delirium of the Brave*, and the author's name, Terence Nithercott, in gold letters on the spine. There was no dust jacket, and nothing to indicate what sort of book it was. Two of the cover's corners were sort of swollen: thick and bumpy, like callouses. This is beside the point but: how does the corner of a hardback book end up swelling into a massive bump? I mean, what is that? Joint inflammation?

Turning the stiff, yellowed pages, I smelled a dusty old house that belonged to a smoker. Rightly or wrongly, I pictured a quiet death in an armchair, a grey cardigan missing most of its buttons, a house clearance.

'It's your birthday,' Liam told me.

'I know,' I said, distracted, obsessing about the tragically deceased former owner of *Delirium of the Brave*. Then, realising what I'd just heard, I said, 'Oh! Do you mean . . . is this a birthday present for me? From *you*?' It seemed so unlikely, I had to check.

'Yes,' said Liam.

'Ha!' I couldn't help blurting out. 'How . . . astonishing.'

I moved swiftly on to the next mystery: if Liam had wanted to buy me a gift, why this book? I glanced at the first page, which introduced an archaeologist from Dublin with an Irish mother and a Scottish father. His name was William

Balbirnie, and his determination to begin his story at the moment of his birth led me to suspect that his narrating adult self wasn't presently involved in any kind of urgent predicament.

Oh dear, I thought. There was no way on earth I would ever read this novel. I'd told Liam more than once that I loved science fiction, fantasy, horror. What was he thinking, for Christ's sake? *Delirium of the Brave* by Terence Nithercott, published in 1952?

'You haven't spotted it, have you?' he said. 'Look at the printed dedication and then at the handwritten one.'

It sounded like a clue. I wondered if it would turn out that Liam had chosen this book for a good reason, rather than simply because he was crap.

I should say, I was already a cynic about presents by that point. I had no hope left. For my fortieth birthday, Gabe had bought me – as a little extra, to be fair, but still – a mug with a really bad drawing of Lionel Richie on it, and the words 'Hello, is it tea you're looking for?' Later that day Marion had given me a Kobo e-reader, even though I must have said at least three times in her presence that I'd never want one. I knew she'd heard me say it, too; she'd replied, 'You and me both. You can't tell me those are real books they put in there!' Drew, meanwhile, bought me a bottle of aftershave he'd mistaken for perfume for my fortieth. I decided, after that poor performance, to cancel all future landmark birthdays.

Delirium of the Brave by Terence Nithercott was a real book. Just not an overwhelmingly appealing one. All the same, Liam's clue intrigued me, so I went in search of dedications.

The printed one was fairly unremarkable. 'For Penelope, in appreciation of many wonderful summers at Lillieoak. May there be many more.' I pictured a sandy-haired, bespectacled Nithercott trogging up the grand driveway of a country house, battered brown suitcase in hand, preparing to recount his entire life story, starting in the womb, to anyone brave enough to open the front door.

'This copy of the book's unique,' said Liam.

I searched for handwriting and found some barely legible scrawl.

'"Dearest . . . Pineapple"?'

'Penelope,' Liam corrected me.

'Oh, right. "Dearest Penelope, As I have always been, so too is this book, by printing press and now by hand – dedicated to you. Fondest regards, Terence". Hang on! This is the same Penelope, yes? It must be.'

'*Yes*.' Liam emphasised the word. This sudden foray into speech with expression startled me so much, I looked up at him. My sex robot was smiling. I'd never seen excitement from him outside of a sexual cause-and-effect situation. I'd never heard eagerness in his voice before. His enthusiasm was always exclusively physical. Until now.

'See? It's unique,' he said, breathing fast beside my ear. 'The only copy of the book that's signed from the author to the dedicatee.'

'Unless Penelope lost this one and asked him for a replacement,' I said. 'Maybe somewhere there's another copy: "Dear Penelope – this is the last one you're getting, you ungrateful cow".'

Speaking of ungrateful cows, I hadn't said thank you yet. Did I forget to mention that I'm disappointing too? I'm pretty much incapable of taking anything nice at face value. Does this go some way to explaining my choice of husband and my choice of lover? When I speak scathingly of disappointing people, please don't think I'm glowering down on Gabe and Liam from any great moral height. They are my tribe, my kith and kin. Disappointing people are my people.

'I doubt Penelope would have lost the book. No one would lose something like this.' Liam responded to my flippancy as if I'd been deadly serious.

I was almost ready to thank him effusively for the present. First, though, I had to make absolutely sure that it was as good as I thought it was. 'Liam, did you buy this book for me for *any other reason*?' I asked.

'No. What other reason could there be?'

'I don't know. Maybe you thought I'd enjoy reading about an Irish archaeologist?'

'Who cares what the story's about?' Liam shrugged. 'I didn't even look.'

'So you bought it for me, even though it might be the worst book in the world, because it's dedicated and signed to the same person?'

'Yes. That makes it unique. I bet I'll never see that in a book again. I never have before.'

'Well . . . thanks.' I wanted to say much more. I wanted to ask him if he understood that he'd done something almost magical, that he'd bought me the perfect present. If the book had looked gripping, or like a lost classic, that wouldn't have been as good. A popular book would have ruined it altogether. It was *better* that it was *Delirium of the Brave* by Terence Nithercott, a novel the world had forgotten, one that looked impossible to enjoy. This way there was nothing to overshadow the two matching dedications, nothing to make us think there was anything about Terence Nithercott that mattered more than his relationship with Penelope.

'They must have been in love,' I said to Liam. Did he only see her in the summer? I wondered. It didn't sound as if they lived together. Was one of them married?

'Who?' Liam asked.

I sighed. 'Terence and Penelope.'

'There's no reason to think that,' he said robotically. 'Anyway, who cares?' Then he took the book from my hand and put it down on the desk by the bed so that he could get started on the main business of the night.

I felt as if he'd hit me with a brick.

He still bought me the book, he still did that, I recited silently to myself.

As he pulled off my clothes, I wondered what it was about the dedications that had so appealed to him if he didn't care about the relationship between writer and recipient. Simply that the book was a rare object? If Terence and Penelope didn't matter, and if you *also* didn't care about the story in the novel Terence Nithercott had written, then what did it mean to call the book unique? Why even bother calling it a book? It's only folded paper, right? If you're someone like Liam, what's the difference between that and literature?

Why not just call it origami?

~

Tuesday, 6 January 2015

'Come on,' I breathe. 'Come on, for Christ's sake.'

Finally the lift doors slide open. I burst out onto the fourth floor of the Rawndesley General Infirmary like someone who's been trapped for hours, and march along the corridor so fast it makes my calves ache. This is a new experience for me: hurrying to get to the cancer ward. I'm not here to visit a sick person, so there's no need to stand still for ten seconds adjusting my scarf, no need to wonder if it might be sensible to nip to the loo or make a phone call first – anything to put off the awful moment of reaching those blue-grey doors.

Today, belatedly, I can do it the way we're all supposed to: rush to get there, *quick, quick, I have to get to the hospital, it's urgent, look how dutiful I am.*

I press the buzzer outside Ward 10, wondering how long I'll have to wait. There's an instant click followed by a different buzzing sound, a higher note. I push the door on the right and it opens.

That's strange. If any of the nurses had seen me, they'd have assumed I was here for a Marion-related reason and let me in, but none of them could have. I was standing to the right of the glass part of the door. Which means someone chose the minimum-effort route, too tired or depressed by her job to check.

I could be anybody.

I doubt the hospital has a huge problem with people sneaking into the cancer ward who have no business being there. The smell alone would be enough to put off anyone but a fanatic. If I believed in God, I'd be profoundly grateful to him for the human inability to remember odours. It's comforting to think that once I've left here my mind won't be able to recreate the sugary, soapy stink of Ward 10.

If the nurses have been lax about the buzzer once, they must have done it dozens of times. Anyone could have got in. Anyone could have walked, as I am now, along the white-walled corridor, past the hand-sterilising unit on wheels, the kitchen, the always-dark, always-empty TV lounge to the noticeboard opposite the ward's reception.

Anyone, or someone in particular: the man police are calling Billy Dead Mates. He could easily have got as far as the noticeboard with the help of a reassuring I-belong-here smile. He could have pinned up a card, or something that, to a novice eye, would look like a card . . .

Checking is a necessary formality, that's all. I have to check before I go to the police with this, but I know I'm right. I can't believe I didn't make the connection straight away. When you don't expect to see something in a particular place, you miss it even when it's right in front of you.

The white card is still pinned up on the noticeboard, with the word 'Death' in large handwritten letters – except now I know it's not a card. It's a little book, stapled in the middle, containing a line from a poem. Like the one I was given by a stranger at my gig, wherever it was, and the ones Detective Sergeant Sam Kombothekra was describing on the news – the ones Billy Dead Mates gives to his victims before killing them.

There are no nurses or doctors behind the desk. At the far end of the corridor, two men wearing normal clothes are shuffling from foot to foot as if no one's told them the right way to stand. Patients' relatives. They won't get in my way. The conditions are perfect.

I'm about to pull out the drawing pin and take the white book down from the board when I hear an exclamation followed by the sound of a door swinging shut.

'Kim! You're back.'

It's Fiona, the only Ward 10 nurse I like, though I'd love to cut off her plait. It's as annoying as watching a dog running around with its lead still attached and trailing behind it. Fiona must have been in room 6, the one closest to the noticeboard. And now she's come out of it, reminding me that there are other rooms along the ward corridor besides the kitchen and the always-dark TV lounge – the numbered rooms with lives ending inside them, struggling to hang on or praying for release.

I know some patients get better and leave. While I was waiting for Marion to die, I saw two people pack up their things – slowly, helped by loved ones – and swing through the blue-grey doors in the optimal direction. Still, I didn't quite fall for it. Once you've been in here even briefly, how can you shake off those numbered rooms? They've got you, just by letting you see that they're there and waiting.

I can't think about any of this now: the horror of Ward 10, or the shame of having only just discovered, at the age of forty-two, that death is unavoidable and so entirely not ideal.

I have to push all that out of my mind and think instead about the lives I can save: mine, hopefully. And maybe someone else's too – though every time that idea presents itself, I dismiss it as too crazy. I'm looking forward to dumping my suspicions in the lap of the police. Will they laugh and tell me I'm mad?

I'm not part of any kind of pair. I haven't had a best friend in living memory. How can I be on Billy Dead Mates' radar? Why would he choose me? It makes no sense. DS Sam Kombothekra said these murders were about pairs of best friends. He sounded sure.

And I'm still alive – that has to mean something. None of the facts can be discounted. Maybe Billy has two lists: pairs of best friends, whom he kills, and people with no friends who get his sinister little books but whom he doesn't otherwise bother or harm.

'Billy', for God's sake. Why am I thinking about him as if he's a mate and we're on first-name terms?

'Kim?' Fiona peers into my face, twisting her plait around her index finger. 'Who let you in?' She looks around.

I wrestle down a burning desire to tear the little white 'Death' book off the noticeboard and make a run for it.

'I've no idea. Someone who couldn't see me and didn't know who I was. You should probably . . . I mean, not *you*, but someone should . . . ' *Shut up, idiot.* I don't want Fiona to think I'm criticising her. My exchange with her, brief and ludicrous as it was, is the only good memory I have of this ward. I don't want to ruin it. Still, it should be much harder to get into a hospital cancer ward. No one wants to be in here. The entrance procedure should reflect that, I feel. Symbolically it's important; we all want to see death banged up in a high-security facility.

'Are you all right, Kim?' Fiona asks. 'You don't look it.'

Good point. I must look odd: sweaty, tongue-tied. Bereaved and traumatised. I perk up a bit when it occurs to me that that's not a convenient lie. I *am* bereaved and traumatised. Officially. If I described myself in those terms, no one would say, 'Oh, come on, don't exaggerate.'

Excellent. So how can I use this to get what I want?

I need the card that isn't a card. I need to get it quickly and painlessly. Then I'm out of here.

Wait. Taking the card wasn't part of the original plan. Checking you were right and then, if you were, ringing the police – wasn't that the idea?

I know that's what I ought to do, but I lack the will power. Standing around, waiting . . . the passivity would drive me crazy.

Where's the harm in grabbing the white book and taking it straight to the police? I'd have to touch it, but the prints of whoever pinned it to the board would still be there, wouldn't they?

I should think about saying something to Fiona round about now, or I'll cross the line from grieving into plain rude. 'Sorry,' I say. 'It's just weird being back here, that's all.'

'Yes, a lot of people say that. I'm surprised to see you back so soon.'

'Well, I couldn't be bothered to wait till I got cancer myself.'

'What?'

'Joke.'

'I thought you'd be at home, catching up on sleep.'

And then, around a week to two later, you thought I'd reappear with a Tupperware box full of chocolate brownies or macaroons to say thank you for everything you did for my dying relative, like everyone else does. Like all the well-balanced bereavement-to-baking people.

'I came back to visit my favourite medical expert,' I tell Fiona with a smile. Getting out of here with the little book in my bag will be easier if I'm casual about it. 'I think your assessment was correct. You know – the ringpull situation? Nothing bad's happened to me yet. If I was internally perforated, I'm sure I'd know by now.'

Fiona manages an anxious half-smile. 'Honestly, Kim, are you okay? Are you sure you wouldn't like—'

'A leaflet about the hospital's counselling service? Positive, thanks. And they'd like it even less.'

'Who?' Fiona looks confused.

'Your counselling people.' I mean, Christ, who'd want to meet me?

'I don't get what you mean.'

'Nothing. Another bad joke. I've got an idea: why don't I stop making them?' A strange, high-pitched laugh leaks out of me. You'd never guess I was a professional performer; my acting couldn't be worse if I tried. 'I was passing, so I popped

in to . . . I don't know, to check this place was real, I suppose.'
I sound as pathetic to myself as I must to Fiona. 'Nothing
about the hospital or the ward felt real when I was here before.'

'Lots of people say that.'

I should wait till she moves away, but she's showing no sign
of going anywhere. I'm too impatient to think up a decent lie.
My arm's twitching with the need to grab the white book.

Do it fast. Over and out.

Trying to appear open and confident rather than furtive, I
reach up, pull the drawing pin out of the noticeboard and take
down the booklet.

'What are you doing?' Fiona says.

'Have you seen this?' I ask her, but I don't hand it over.
Flicking through it, I find its insides empty. There's just 'Death'
on the front cover and the other four words on the back cover.

Death devours all lovely things.

Thanks to Google, I know it's the first line of a poem by
Edna St. Vincent Millay, an American poet.

> *Death devours all lovely things;*
> *Lesbia with her sparrow*
> *Shares the darkness,—presently*
> *Every bed is narrow.*

It's the same poem that contains the words in the little white
book I was given at a gig in 2014.

The narrow bed is the waiting grave, evidently: the symbol
of our ultimate, inevitable isolation. What a cheery thought.
No wonder so many of us try to stuff our earthly beds full of
as many people as possible while we still can.

This book I'm holding and the one I was given are a pair.

I pass it to Fiona. She looks at it. 'People are funny,' she says
with a shrug. 'Funny peculiar, I mean, not funny ha-ha. Apart
from you. You're funny ha-ha, being a comedian.' She adds
this quickly, as if afraid I might be offended otherwise.

'Do you know who it's from? Or to?'

'Oh, it's for us – the nurses and doctors here.'

'How do you know?'

'All the cards on the board are for us,' says Fiona. 'They're thank-you cards.'

'It doesn't say thank you anywhere on it.'

'No, well . . . not everyone's very good at expressing themselves.'

'But this is a book, not a card. Look. It has several pages.'

Fiona nods. 'I'm sure it's full of meaning for the person who sent it, or brought it in.'

'Do you know who that was? Or which it was – sent or brought?'

'No. I hadn't noticed it till you showed it to me. Why do you ask?'

Because I think it's the handiwork of a serial killer. Isn't that jolly? More exciting than cancer.

'No reason.' I hold out my hand to take the book back.

'Do you want it?' Fiona looks confused. 'But . . . it belongs to the ward. It was on our noticeboard.'

'It's not addressed to you and you don't know how it got there. Whereas I . . . Look, I can't explain, but I think I might know something about this . . . thing, and I need to take it with me. I'll bring it back, I promise, but can I take it?'

'I don't think so, Kim. I'm sorry. It's just that often people who've been in here come back –'

'I know. With caramel slices.'

'– and if they've brought in a card for us and they see it's not on the board—'

'This isn't a card, it's a book. Trust me: it might be on your noticeboard, but it's not meant for you. It's meant for—' I stop myself, remembering I have no proof of anything. It's a theory, and an outlandish one at that.

'I'm really sorry, but I'm going to need to stick it back up on the board,' Fiona says firmly. 'I wouldn't be allowed to let you take it.'

I could tell her the truth and admit I need to take the book to show the police. Somehow, I doubt she'd hand it over even then. Who in their right mind would hand over possible evidence in a serial murder investigation to a sarcastic comedian who swallows parts of Fruit Rush cans? Fiona would do the right and sensible thing: she'd promise to look after the white book until the police were able to come and collect it.

That's not good enough. Once it's out of my sight, I don't know it's safe. I need to take it with me, whatever I have to do.

'Will you do me a favour and let me have a quick last look at it?' I hold out my hand again.

She falls for it. Once the book's back in my hands and I'm flicking through it again, I say, 'I'm sure you're right, but can you check?'

'Check?'

'Yeah, with whoever's in charge – the ward sister or whoever. You never know, she might say it's fine to let me take it.' I smile hopefully.

Fiona looks uncertain. 'She's not here at the moment.'

'Yeah, where is everybody? Buried under piles of flapjacks?'

'I suppose I could try and . . .' Fiona glances at the phone on the desk.

'Please ring her. I know it sounds weird, but this matters to me. I can't explain why.'

'All right.'

'Thank you! You're a star. Really, I'm hugely grateful, whatever the result.'

Fiona walks round to the other side of the ward's reception desk. I wait till she picks up the phone, then make a dash for it, clutching the book. Surprised I can move so fast, I crash through the blue-grey doors, turn left and run. I was planning to take the stairs, but the lift's doors are open. It's full of people, one of them horizontal and on a trolley. If this were an action movie, I'd climb under the white sheet covering Trolley Man and hide next to him.

As it turns out, I don't need to do anything so drastic. I hold my breath, but Fiona doesn't appear, and I hear no running footsteps before the lift doors slide shut.

Less than twenty seconds later, I'm outside and making my escape.

~

If there's anybody reading this who doesn't already dislike me, prepare to move over to the other side when I describe the rigmarole associated with me going to the police station to tell them what I knew, or thought I knew, or feared, about their quarry Billy Dead Mates.

It's the same when I need to go anywhere: the rigmarole goes before me, to see how the land lies. I only follow if I'm given suitable assurances. Yes, even when there's a murderer to catch and my life might be at risk.

You're confused. Until now, I haven't sounded like a prima donna. Let's face it, anyone who lets a stranger stick his fingers into her after only a cursory introduction – that has to be a down-to-earth person, you'd think.

You'd be right. Deep down, I'm approachable, with no airs or graces. There's a problem, though: if you let it be known that you're reasonable, with a normal-sized ego, enemies and idiots will try to do terrible things to you, and they'll succeed more often than they would if you were a monstrous neurotic protected by a six-foot-high blockade of restrictions and requirements.

That's why I armed myself with a list of rules people have to obey if they want to come anywhere near me. Writing it – knowing I meant every word, however preposterous – was one of the most satisfying things I've ever done. I kept thinking, 'This can't be me, laying out all these conditions' – not the same me who once waived her fee to do a charity gig hundreds of miles from home, only to discover on arrival that there was a raffle involved and that one of the prizes was dinner with me at a dismal local restaurant in several weeks' time – which meant travelling back to the Isle of Wight at my own expense to spend an awkward evening with a pensioner called Shirley.

It would be remiss of me to abandon this anecdote without mentioning the photographer, who was supposed to turn up during our dinner and take photographs for the local paper, but who was caught in traffic, and so arrived only when the prize-winner and I were leaving. We had our coats on and were standing outside on the pavement, about to step into our respective taxis, but the poor photographer! He'd had such a hellish drive, and he was here – late, but hopefully not too late – with all his kit. Of course, since it had snowed that day, the chance of getting some Winter Wonderland shots – me and Shirley trying to keep our fake grins fixed in place while our teeth chattered and further snow fell on our hood-less heads – was too good to miss, the photographer was sure we'd agree. I don't know what made him so sure; he knew nothing about either of us. Perhaps that was why he was so determined to interview me as he snapped away.

What is it you do again? They never tell me much about who I'm photographing. Oh, a comedienne. You as funny as Morecambe and Wise, are you? I love Morecambe and Wise. They say women aren't as funny as men, but I can't see why that should be the case, personally. Are you funny? What sort of funny are you? Go on, try and make me laugh. I'll give you an objective assessment, I promise – a mark out of ten. Ten for hilarious, zero for didn't crack a smile. I don't flatter people, me – I tell it straight.

That incident should have been my last straw. Bizarrely, it wasn't. Clearly there's a huge part of me that has no self-respect whatsoever. That's why I need the protection of a multi-clause terms and conditions document.

My breaking point came when a PR firm for a comedy festival sent a car to collect me from home one day at 4.30 a.m. The driver rang the doorbell, waking me and Gabe. Luckily, it wasn't a Liam night, but it easily could have been. 'What . . . ?' I demanded, bleary-eyed. 'Who are you? What do you want?'

'I'm here to collect Kim Tribbeck and take her to an interview,' the driver told me.

I was confused. I had interviews scheduled for later that day in London, to help promote an up-and-coming comedy festival, but the first one wasn't until 2 p.m. I'd been planning to get the 10.30 train from Rawndesley. When I sought clarification, I was told by a sleep-fugged PR person (to whom I greatly enjoyed giving a taste of her own rest-wrecking medicine) that she was sorry it was such short notice but an amazing opportunity had come up: a TV interview! On some obscure Sky channel that nobody watched! Had no one told me?

No. No one had asked me either.

I dismissed the driver as politely as I could and went back to bed, after a brief conversation with Gabe. He said, 'Why are you so polite? Why don't you tell all these people to fuck off? Not just the ones who send cabs at four thirty in the morning – *all* of them. You're great at telling *me* to fuck off, and you enjoy it so much. Why not branch out to other people?'

My God, he's right, I thought. I *love* telling people to fuck off, and when I don't dare, I love thinking it secretly, in my head.

'What would X do if this happened to her?' Gabe said, naming a famous high-maintenance female comedian. 'Can you imagine? That PR firm'd be closed down within the week. Shortly thereafter, all its former employees would die of radiation-like symptoms.'

'This would never happen to X,' I said. 'Everyone knows X takes no shit, so no one risks – oh!' I stopped as the obvious way forward struck me.

That was the night my life changed. First thing the next morning – the proper morning – I pulled out of the comedy festival associated with the unwanted wake-up call and sat down to write my commandments.

From now on, I vowed, I would be the highest-maintenance comedian of them all. I'd make X look like a pushover. Anyone who wanted to see me, book me, interview me, catch a glimpse of me as I sailed by, would have to jump through so many hoops, they would hopefully decide it wasn't worth the hassle.

Composing my list was a challenge. I needed hoops and had none. Hoopless all my life so far, I had no idea how to go about constructing or acquiring them. The drafting process took several weeks and many hours of revision, but I finally came up with something I was happy with and that, as an added benefit, made me laugh whenever I read it through. People would think I was an out-and-out lunatic. Fantastic. Maybe they'd all leave me alone.

My list was – and is, since I haven't changed it in the intervening years – as follows:

KIM TRIBBECK – EVERYTHING YOU NEED TO KNOW IF SHE'S HEADING YOUR WAY

1) Earl Grey tea must be available, with proper semi-skimmed milk – no milk substitute or powder. The tea should be accompanied by a mug, not a cup and saucer. The mug should not be chipped or stained, and should be a standard cylindrical shape: not wider at the top or the bottom.
2) Sparkling water must also be available, in a full bottle that's not yet had its seal broken, with a glass that's made of glass, not plastic. The glass should be a standard cylindrical shape – as wide at the top as at the bottom.
3) A packet of pickled-onion-flavoured Monster Munch crisps must be provided for Kim. Other than this, food should not be provided unless specifically requested. It should not be assumed that Kim will eat with anyone associated with the event or interview, either beforehand or afterwards.

4) FOR INTERVIEWS AND GIGS – the proposed venue must always be inside a proper building with a roof and walls, not in a tent or outside.

5) FOR INTERVIEWS – the proposed interview room must have an armchair with a straight back and arms, and a footstool for use with the armchair.

6) FOR INTERVIEWS – the interviewer must arrive at precisely the agreed time. To make sure to avoid being late, the interviewer should aim to arrive twenty minutes early and wait near the agreed venue in order to appear punctually. However early the interviewer arrives, he or she must not approach Kim or demand her attention until the agreed time. If the interviewer presents him- or herself to Kim even as little as a minute early or a minute late, the interview will be cancelled.

7) If overnight accommodation is involved in the arrangement, nothing smaller than a king-sized bed is acceptable. It must also be possible to open a window in the room to outside. Kim must have a room with the best view available from any of the rooms in the hotel. If she arrives at a hotel with (for example) sea views and is allocated a room without a sea view, she will leave immediately and whatever event she has been scheduled to do will be cancelled.

8) No autographs or photographs are permitted unless pre-arranged.

9) All autographs will take the form 'To [insert relevant name], Best wishes, Kim Tribbeck'. For example, Kim will not sign anything 'To Mum' for someone else's mother. She will not write 'Happy Christmas' or 'Happy Birthday' to people she doesn't know, and she will not write a message that is compromising, cryptic, undignified, that she doesn't understand, or that's none of her business, for example: 'To Gary, Rebecca will never

forgive you for betraying her' or 'From one hilarious comedian to another!' Kim will never agree to put her name to someone else's words in that way, and, if asked to, she will refuse an autograph altogether.

10) If permission to take photos has been granted, the photos must be action shots – mid-interview or mid-gig. Kim is too busy to devote separate time to being photographed.

11) If permission to take photos has been granted, the photographer mustn't ask questions or try to engage Kim in conversation.

12) You may not ask Kim for help of any kind with your comedy career, or that of a loved one, however talented you believe yourself or that loved one to be.

13) Kim will not listen to jokes or anecdotes and tell you if they're funny or not.

14) Kim will not do an impromptu routine or tell you a joke if you are not a paying audience member at one of her gigs.

15) Kim will not discuss other comedians, or the nature of comedy and what makes funny things funny. She will not explain to you why she is funny, or how.

16) If something happens between you and Kim when you meet that she later wants to use in her act, she reserves the right to do so. In having any dealings with her, you risk being used as material.

17) Get Kim's name wrong – either her first name or her surname – and she will walk away, even if it happens halfway through a live TV interview. Her first name is Kim, which is not short for Kimberley, and her last name is Tribbeck, with the emphasis on the second syllable.

18) If you want to put Kim's name on the cover of another comedian's book, attached to some praise from Kim for that comedian, Kim's name and quote must be positioned on the front cover of the book. The moment you

decide to move her quote to the back cover because Ricky Gervais has also given you a puff, consider Kim's consent for you to use her name and words withdrawn. Similarly, if you've booked Kim to appear at a comedy festival and then subsequently print a brochure in which other comedians' names appear on the front cover and Kim's does not, consider Kim's event cancelled.

A police interview is obviously different from a comedy festival appearance or a press interview, but since I didn't have time to draft a new list specially for Culver Valley CID, I emailed the all-purpose list to the detective I spoke to on the phone and told him to do his best.

~

Tuesday, 6 January 2015

I'm met in the police reception area by the same man I spoke to on the phone: DC Christopher Gibbs. With barely a word spoken, we're off to a not-ideal start. His first question is: 'Was that list a joke?'

'No.'

'You're a comedian, though,' he says suspiciously. We established on the phone that he's heard of me but never heard me. He doesn't like stand-ups; he prefers sketch shows and sitcoms because they're 'a team effort – not all about someone's ego'.

If my team contained DC Gibbs, I'd root for my opponents. He's a small, muscly man in his forties with eyes like black pebbles, a bunched-up forehead and thick, dark brown hair in a once-short style that needs a trim.

'I'm a comedian,' I confirm. 'That doesn't mean I'm always joking. It's like you and police work. When you go to the dentist, you genuinely want your teeth checked. You're not there to make the dentist confess to murder.' *You fucking idiot.*

'And you think you can help us with Billy?'

'I know I can.'

'This had better not be a wind-up, Ms Tribbeck.'

'I came here with serious intentions,' I tell him. 'Although I'm finding you quite amusing. Don't forget number sixteen on my list: "If something happens between you and Kim when you meet that she later wants to use in her act, she reserves the right to do so. In having any dealings with her, you risk being used as material."'

'There's nothing funny about me,' says Gibbs. 'No one so much as smiles at anything I say, apart from . . . ' He stops.

'Do tell.'

'I give my mate a hard time sometimes, about the way he carries on with women. That makes people laugh,' Gibbs says in a monotone.

'Right.' I try not to imagine those people, or how desperately bored they must be if this scowling drone is their idea of a fun night out. 'Well, I wish we could chat all day long, but I need to get this done and get on with my life, so . . . '

My life. Is it possible that Billy Dead Mates wants it to end? It seems so unlikely. It's not me I'm worried about, in any case.

'Follow me,' says Gibbs. 'We've got the only interview room that has a window you can open. It's locked at the moment, but it does open.'

'Interesting,' I mutter as I trail after him along a high-ceilinged, echoey corridor with bare brick walls. 'Are you going to unlock it when we get to the room?'

'No. I don't think anyone's seen the key for months, if not years.'

'Then that's not really meeting my requirement, is it?'

'The open-window thing only applies to overnight accommodation, as I read it,' says Gibbs.

Annoyingly, he's right.

'Then why mention a window that might – though, in fact, doesn't – open?' I ask.

He stops and turns to face me. 'Look, I don't know what other people are willing to put up with from you, but I'm on a multiple murder investigation. I've got better things to do than run around pandering to a diva before I've heard if she's got anything useful to say.'

'I promise you, you won't be disappointed.'

Gibbs looks as if he already is. 'I've got your pickled onion Monster Munch and I've got you a bottle of mineral water. That'll have to do.'

If he were running a comedy festival, I'd walk away. This is a unique situation, so I'll make an exception.

It strikes me as odd that Gibbs should be so unaware of the little white book in my bag, while I can't forget its presence for a second. I've had to put up with it shouting its message at me all the way to Spilling police station: *Death devours all lovely things.*

'No one could meet all the conditions on your list. You must know that, and want everyone to fail.'

'Not true,' I say with relish. I often say in interviews that stand-up comedy is my vocation, but that's a lie. Deep down, I know that defending myself is what I was born to do. I think this probably means I've been attacked too often; I'm a bit sick of it by now.

Gibbs is waiting for further clarification.

'I want to increase my odds of encountering bare minimum civilised conditions, that's all. If I didn't send my list as a calling card ahead of time, I might not even get water.'

The interview room we end up in is about as bad as I expected it to be. It's one of those rooms that's trying too hard to be nice, to shake off the taint of the building that contains it. The bristly blue carpet looks brand new and there's a smell of recent fitting lingering in the air. There are three white walls and one that's custard yellow, beige curtains with tie-backs, a cheap wooden table, round, with four almost-matching chairs. My crisps and water are on the table next to a green glass vase with some daffodils in it – two bunches, each one with its stalks still bound together by a red elastic band.

In the centre of the room there's a strange installation that might be a stolen exhibit from a contemporary art gallery: a straight-backed chair with tears in its maroon fabric and lumpy yellow foam spilling out of it. There's a large suitcase in front of the chair, with wheels and a pattern of pink and white circles on a purple background. The case is lying on its side, touching the seat of the chair.

'What the hell is that?' I ask Gibbs. It's such an unexpected sight that I don't connect its presence in the room with mine.

'We don't have footstools here,' he says. 'I found an old suitcase in a cupboard – it should do the job. It's the right height and you can put your feet on it.'

'Which means this is the armchair I asked for? Next to the, er, footstool substitute?'

'Yes. I'd have thought that was obvious.'

'It has no arms. Its guts are falling out.'

'It'll do.'

I smile at him, provoked by his unwillingness to do anything but glare coldly. 'You accused me of wanting everyone to fail. I reckon that entitles me to a reciprocal accusation. You get a kick out of depriving people of things you know they want. Don't you? I must be your dream come true – someone with a long wish list! So many things you can enjoy denying me. Why do I get the sense that forcing me to sit in a chair that's leaking its stuffing in a room with no tea and a locked window is the most fun you've had in years?'

He looks bored by my analysis of him. 'The thing is, everyone wants in on Billy,' he says.

'Pardon?'

'No one knows who he is, but that doesn't make him any less famous. Everyone wants a piece of the action, including has-been comedians trying to revive their flagging careers. You're here trawling for material, not to help us. You've as good as said so already.'

'No, that's not what I—'

'If you had anything real to offer, I'd have heard it by now.'

I perch on the edge of the suitcase, open my bag and pull out the white book I stole from Ward 10's noticeboard. 'I offer you this real thing,' I say, handing it to Gibbs.

He inspects it, then stares at me with barely concealed fury. 'Where did you find this?'

I tell him.

'You knew its significance, yet you touched it? You moved it? Why didn't you call us straight away?' He pulls a clear plastic bag out of his pocket, drops the book inside it and puts it down on the table, at the outer edge. I almost make a joke about Monster Munch contamination, but I manage to restrain myself.

'Don't split hairs,' I tell him. 'I saw it and realised it was important, so I brought it straight in.'

'Is there anyone who can verify you're telling the truth about finding this book pinned to the noticeboard of the RGI's cancer ward?'

'Yes. A nurse called Fiona. I asked her if I could take it. She said no, so I distracted her and ran off with it.'

'Maybe you pinned it up on the board yourself first,' says Gibbs.

'Why would I . . . oh, you mean maybe *I'm* Billy Dead Mates? No, I'm not. But I'd love to know how it came to be pinned up on that noticeboard, which is partly why I'm here. I haven't got the authority to ask and make people tell me, but you have.'

Gibbs walks over to the table again. He glances down at the book but doesn't touch it. Instead, he takes one of the bunches of daffodils out of the vase, pulls the red elastic band off the stalks and winds it around his fingers. 'How did you know Billy sends books like this to his victims before killing them?'

'I got in from watching my grandmother die, switched on the telly and saw a detective talking about it on the news. I realised – belatedly, like an idiot – that the card I'd seen on the ward noticeboard probably wasn't a card. How did I know? Because I'd seen one exactly like it before. Not just seen; been given. Which is why I'm kicking myself for not having spotted it straight away, but I was focused on hideous death at the time – that's my excuse.'

'You were given a small white book like this one?'

'Yes.'

Gibbs does his daffodil thing again, this time with the second bunch. He removes the elastic band and stuffs it into his pocket. The other one's still wound round the index and middle fingers of his right hand. I wonder if he has a red elastic band fetish. There's more wrong with DC Christopher Gibbs than is observable by the human eye; I'd bet good money on it.

'Chronological order might help us,' I say, and launch into the story of my involvement with the little white books of Billy Dead Mates, starting with the stranger who handed one to me at a gig I did almost a year ago. As I speak, DC Gibbs' pebbly eyes seem to stare harder and grow blacker and more intense with each new development. I can see how someone might rather confess to a murder they hadn't committed than be on the receiving end of those eyes for a moment longer.

I tell him about Ward 10, Marion's death.

He's ready with a question when I finish, before I've had time to take a breath. 'Where was this gig you did, where the man gave you the book?'

'I told you: I don't remember.'

'You don't *remember*? How can you not remember?'

'I thought you might ask that, so I brought you this.' I fish around in my bag and hand him a crumpled sheet of A4 paper.

He starts to read it aloud. 'Shrewsbury, Theatre Seven,

2 February. Lowestoft, Marina, 3 February. King's Lynn, Corn Exchange, 4 February—'

'Can we fast forward through Skegness, Salford and Sheffield? At the risk of spoiling the reading experience for you, I end up, twenty-seven gigs later, at the Motorpoint Arena in Cardiff and that's the end of my first 2014 tour.'

'And at one of these gigs, this guy gave you a small white book very similar to that one' – he points down at the table – 'but you can't tell me which?'

'I can't. I'm sorry. I normally do a longish tour – twenty-five to thirty gigs – twice a year. I have lists of where I've been, like that one, but going to so many places and performing the same routine in all of them has a weird effect on my memory. I can describe to you in detail the room we were in, the man's appearance, our interactions, all of that—'

'Good, because that's what I'll need you to do,' says Gibbs.

'Fine. I can picture the theatre in my mind very clearly, I just can't tell you which it was. I tried Googling a few of the venues while I was waiting for you just now, but hardly any of them have pictures on their websites that show a big enough area of the auditorium, or the general layout – it's pretty much useless trying to identify the place that way. A couple of things I *can* tell you: my husband came with me to that particular gig. Our marriage wasn't in great shape at the time – we've since split up.'

'Congratulations.' If Gibbs is joking, there's no sign of it on his face or in his voice.

'Thank you,' I say. 'Early in 2014, we were both still kidding ourselves that it could work, and one of the ways we thought we might salvage our relationship was for my husband to trail around after me like someone with nothing better to do, even though he has a full-time job. We called it spending more time together. It was totally impractical – why would he want to listen to me doing the same routine twenty times in one month, all over the country?'

Why would I want him there after each performance, killing my post-show buzz by saying darkly, 'The same jokes in the same order, *every fucking night*. I stopped laughing after the fourth time. If I have to listen to it again, I'll maim anyone within reach who laughs. I'm starting to hate laughter.'

It was supposed to be funny, I think. That's what Gabe always said the next morning, when he'd swear he hadn't meant any of it. *Yes, of course I want to come to tonight's gig. Why wouldn't I? I'm looking forward to it. We agreed I'd be there for as much of the tour as possible, and that's what I want to do.*

'So why did he go to all your gigs if that's how he felt?' Gibbs asks. 'Why not watch the show once and leave it at that?'

'Good question.' I have a matching good answer, but it's not one I'd better share with a policeman. It involves an illegal drug habit. 'Look, my marriage isn't the point here. I only mentioned Gabe was there that night because it might be useful. He might remember where the theatre was if you describe it to him – which town, I mean. He also moaned about how far away it was – he had to drive home afterwards and be up early for work the next morning. That narrows it down in terms of possible venues. Gabe regards anything more than an hour and a half as a long drive, so the theatre can't have been one too close to Rawndesley.'

'The two of you live in Rawndesley?'

'Yes. Though not together any more.'

Gibbs nods. 'I need to get all these details – your address, husband's address, his work and contact details . . . You're right: he might remember where the theatre was, so we need to talk to him. This white book you were given – I'm assuming you haven't brought it with you. Do you still have it?'

I stand up, walk over to the table and open the bottle of sparkling water. No glass. I'll have to drink from the bottle, which I suppose is no more undignified than using a suitcase as a footstool. Some spoilt prima donna I turned out to be. I decide to leave the pickled onion Monster Munch alone; I don't fancy having to suck sticky crisp particles off my fingers in front of DC Gibbs. 'Does it matter where the theatre was?' I ask him.

'The . . .' He doesn't want to talk about the theatre any more for the time being. He thinks he made that clear. 'Does it matter? Yes. Obviously.'

'It's not obvious to me. Let's say Gabe remembers and it turns out it was the Everyman in Cheltenham. That doesn't tell us Billy lives in Cheltenham.'

'It tells us he might. Or he might have strong links to the place,' says Gibbs.

'Purely because he's at a gig there? I disagree. This is a man who goes round giving small white books containing lines of poetry to people he subsequently murders. His victims live in a range of different places, right? He's presumably chosen each pair of friends in advance – and then, from what I've heard in various news reports, he goes to where they live to kill them. Has gun, will travel. So he could be from anywhere, and he came to my gig at wherever-it-was because *I* was there – not because it was where he lived, or near where he lived.'

'And he gave you a little white book, *but then didn't kill you*,' says Gibbs pointedly, as if by still being alive I'm messing with the neat pattern. 'Maybe because it was too near his home, and/or because you saw him.'

'Didn't kill me *yet*,' I say. 'He still might. Part of the reason I'm here is to try and make sure that doesn't happen.'

'His four victims were all dead within a few weeks of being given a book. Also, if the man you met was Billy himself – if he handed you the book in person – that's another big difference.' Gibbs drags a chair away from the table and sits down. 'You didn't answer my question: where's the book he gave you?'

'I threw it away. Don't look at me like that. Now, with the benefit of hindsight, I wish I'd kept it, but I thought he was just a weird guy. I had no idea he was a serial-killer-in-waiting.

I chucked the book in the nearest bin, just as I would have if he'd given me a leaflet advertising conservatories or double-glazing. Or maybe I just left it on the table in the venue – I don't remember. Either way, I don't have it any more.'

'How sure are you of the precise wording inside the book you were given?'

'A hundred per cent. "Every bed is narrow". I never forgot the words, because . . .' I stop, having stupidly said too much. I'd rather not tell Gibbs this part of the story, and now I'm going to have to. 'Something weird happened later that night – one of those funny coincidences, although at the time I was a bit freaked out and wondered if there was a connection. Though there was no way the two things could have been connected.'

'Go on,' says Gibbs.

'I stayed in a hotel that night. The hotel was very near the theatre – no more than a two minute walk. I remember the route: leave the theatre, cross the road, head right, first left, walk along a bit, the hotel's on your left. I can describe the hotel reasonably well, I think – one of those fusty three-star places where a really depressing wedding might happen – navy carpet with a fleur-de-lis pattern, that type of place.'

Gibbs stares blankly at me.

'Sunday lunch carvery?' I try harder. 'Plastic rack on the reception desk stuffed full of leaflets advertising pantomimes, water parks, country houses?'

Still no facial expression from Gibbs. 'But you can't tell me which town or city the hotel's in, or its name.' He sounds unimpressed.

'No. Sorry.'

'Carry on.'

'Do you remember on my list of terms and conditions, I specify bed size if overnight accommodation's involved?'

'How could I forget?'

'No smaller than a king, I say. Well, this hotel decided to

try and pretend that a bed *smaller than a double* was a king. I dragged the receptionist up to the room and made her look with her own eyes. The bed was about the size of the average sofa-bed, but she wouldn't accept that because somewhere on her computer system, it said that the bed in room 21 was a king. That wasn't my actual room number, I was just . . . you know.'

It's hard to imagine a tougher crowd than DC Gibbs. I don't know why I'm bothering to dramatise any of this for his benefit; he's as receptive as a slab of stone.

'It didn't matter that the bed was on the small side, because there was only going to be me sleeping in it, but still . . .' Why am I saying this? I'm fairly sure there's absolutely no need, and it's nowhere near true. The narrow bed mattered a lot. And even when I sleep alone, I like a big bed. If I have to travel halfway across the country and entertain hundreds of people, it's reasonable to try to create conditions that make the experience bearable.

'And this incident with the small bed in the hotel alarmed you because of the words in the book you'd been given that night?'

'Yes, a bit. Not seriously. I just thought, "How odd. On the same night, a man hands me a little book containing the words 'Every bed is narrow' and I go to my hotel to find my bed there is way too narrow." It was a funny coincidence. Peculiar, not ha-ha.'

'Not really,' says Gibbs.

'Here's something else that's weird: I'm not Billy's type. I don't have a best friend, or any friends. All the evidence suggests they're more trouble than they're worth. Point is, I'm not part of a pair – yet the line of poetry in the book I was given is one of a pair with the one from the hospital noticeboard. They're from the same poem, by Edna St. Vincent Millay. Verse one contains both lines: "Death devours all lovely things;/Lesbia with her sparrow/Shares the darkness,—presently/Every bed is narrow." I wanted to ask you . . . did the two pairs of best friends Billy killed get lines from the same poem? As me and the cancer ward noticeboard, or as each other?'

'As each other,' says Gibbs. 'First two, the lines came from a poem by a woman called Emily Dickinson. Second pair, the writer was an Ella Wheeler Wilcox. Both poems, like yours, were about death.'

'And all three by female American poets whose first names begin with E.'

'Do you think that means something?' He's not looking at me, and sounds as if he's asking himself.

'I've no idea. I mean, if you want American women poets who write about death, why not pick Sylvia Plath? She's the obvious one.'

'You're the anomaly,' Gibbs neatly summarises how I feel about myself most of the time. 'The lines come in pairs. All Billy's victims so far are pairs of best friends, but you don't have a best friend. Yet you get a book containing a line that's one of a pair. A man – maybe Billy, maybe not – hands it to you instead of leaving it in your bag or among your possessions, and then you're *not* murdered weeks or even months later.'

'No need to sound so miffed about it.' I smile at him. 'There's still time.'

'But you don't consider yourself to be in danger, do you?' This sounds like an accusation.

'I believe I might be, yes.'

'You don't seem scared.'

'I'm not.' *Not for myself.* 'Logically, it seems I might be on this guy's list. Emotionally, I can't really get far enough past the unpleasantness of witnessing a cancer death at close range to believe in these murders that seem so . . . well, sensational. Improbable. I know they're real – I've heard about them on the news – but they don't *feel* real.'

'They do to the loved ones left behind.'

'Yes, I'm sure they do. But I'm someone else's loved one left behind – well, barely tolerated one, anyway – so my fears are elsewhere. You know what?' I laugh. 'This Billy stuff, for me . . . it's a welcome distraction. Not that I want him to shoot me dead, but if I get to avoid what my grandmother went through, if I get to avoid spending any more time on a cancer ward, that's quite a big consolation.'

'Let's go back to your no-best-friend claim. You're sure there's no one?'

I take a deep breath. If he doesn't already think I'm crazy . . .

'There's no one. But . . .'

But the little white book on Ward 10's noticeboard didn't come from nowhere, for no reason. It wasn't intended for nobody.

'Billy might think there's someone,' I say.

~

As embarrassing experiences go, trying to explain to a police detective about your imaginary friend is up there with the best of them. Briefly, I'd entertained an idle fantasy about befriending the woman I'd met outside the hospital while Marion was dying: Faith Kendell. Her misanthropic world view had impressed me. I felt obliged to divulge to DC Gibbs that words on the subject of friendship had passed between us.

Friends are too much work – like houseplants.

I agree. Also like houseplants, they all die in the end. What's the point?

If only someone would say to me, 'I'll be your friend, and I'll expect no more from you than a dead houseplant.'

I'd say that to a prospective friend.

You would?

Yep. Wouldn't be able to put in much more effort than a dead houseplant myself, so I'd accept being treated like one as a fair deal.

Mutual dead houseplant friendship – it's an interesting concept. Unconditional acceptance of no effort on both sides.

Sounds like the way forward to me.

Could Billy have been listening? Even if he had been, it made no sense. He'd given me my white book nearly a year earlier, when he'd had no way of knowing that on 6 January 2015, I'd be at the RGI visiting my dying grandmother. So what was he doing there that day, with a white book containing a line from the same poem? He had no reason to believe I'd meet a woman outside the hospital whom I'd briefly consider befriending, before rejecting the idea. In any case, the 'Death devours' white book was pinned to the ward's noticeboard before Faith and I had exchanged a single word. Try to put it together and it makes no sense. So why can't I shake it from my mind?

Gibbs agreed it was ludicrous to imagine what I was imagining. The best way to prove how unlikely it was, I suggested, was to check Faith was all right, maybe offer her some protection. What harm would that do? Because, let's face it, if that white book wasn't intended for her, who was it meant for? There were no other candidates for the role of best friend to me on Ward 10 of the RGI that day. It *had* to have been meant for Faith – who, by the way, I'm sure would start to irritate the hell out of me if I ever got to know her better. I was already getting a bit sick of her by the time I'd finished giving DC Gibbs as complete a description of her as I could remember – small frame, black hoody, baggy jeans, very short brown hair, brown eyes.

Could Billy have pinned up that little white book on the board and then sent someone in that he'd lined up to befriend me artificially? This, I decided, was the single most ludicrous suspicion I'd ever had.

Still, I tried as hard as I could to persuade Gibbs that Faith Kendell might be in danger, not because I thought it was likely but because I believed there were no other possibilities.

Don't ever think that, boys and girls. Don't be as naïve as I was. There are always other possibilities and plenty of them

– ones you couldn't come up with in your most demented dreams. Or at least I couldn't, and neither could Chris Gibbs.

Detective Constable Simon Waterhouse on the other hand – he was a different story.

Typed copy of handwritten letter received by
Sondra Halliday on 4 January 2015

2 January 2015

Dear Mrs Halliday

I hope you don't mind me addressing you as such. Your
Wikipedia entry tells me you're married to the chef
Oliver Halliday, so it seems the obvious thing to call
you.

I hope you enjoy the enclosed novel, *Beloved* by
Toni Morrison. It is a work of genius in my opinion.
You might wonder why I, a complete stranger, am
sending you a book. It's because I want to teach you.
I don't know if you're capable of learning, but I
have to try.

("Why?" I imagine you asking.)

I have to teach you because the only other thing I
want to do to you is kill you. Nearly every day, you
are doing severe harm to the thing that matters to me
most in the world. You have your cause and I have mine;
they are not the same thing. They are, rather,
stratospheres apart - and you've been lying about my
agenda in order to further your own. I have an itch
inside me, telling me that the only thing I can do to
stop this is put an end to you. Then this thing I care
about won't be ruined.

At the same time, I would do almost anything to stop
myself from killing you because it would be morally
wrong. Unjustifiable. It would make me into something I
could not bear to be: a person driven by hate and anger
and desperation to become a murderer. That, too, would
ruin everything for me, in a different way.

There are some dilemmas that one cannot resolve
alone, so I sought help. I don't expect you know what
an Ishaya is, do you? Neither did I, but I was lucky
enough to find one and she's changed my life. Lane.
She is the wisest, kindest human being I've ever
known. She is, in every way, a truly good person.
Instead of condemning me for wanting to kill you,
which would have made me angrier and more bitter
than I was when I first sought her help, she told me
she admired my passion, my commitment to the things
I held dear. She persuaded me that killing you would
be quite wrong not by making me feel ashamed, but by
telling me it was completely understandable that I
might have murderous impulses.

I don't want to let down either Lane or myself.
That's why you're still alive and will hopefully
remain so. Thanks to Lane, also, I now have all the
theory at my fingertips. I know the rules for living
a pain- and anger-free life. I could preach all day
long if I wanted to, and if I'm still unable to
practise because the pain and anger remain lodged
inside me and seemingly won't be shifted, at least
I'm in a better position than I was before. It's a
bit like having the perfect recipe, but being unable
to bring oneself to set off to the supermarket to buy
the ingredients.

Lane, in my position, wouldn't want to kill you. I
still do. In that sense, my sessions with her have
failed, but in another more important way, they've
succeeded. Because here I am, not killing you.
Instead, I'm writing you a good old-fashioned letter
explaining that I've decided to opt for teaching and
preaching instead. Read the book I've sent you.
That's the lesson for now. What does that story tell
you? What does it make you think? I will send you

another story in due course - one of Lane's next
time, I think. The thing I love most about her is
that she teaches through stories.

Yours,
A Secret Detractor (I suppose, since I'm
certainly no admirer)

6

7/1/2015

'I don't remember hardly anything about it apart from America and slavery,' Charlie told Simon. They were on their way into work. For the first time since they'd moved in together, he'd handed his car keys to her as they left the house, without a word of explanation. To ward off any questions Charlie might have asked, Simon had got in first with one of his own – about *Beloved*, the book that had been sent anonymously to Sondra Halliday.

'It was powerful and unsettling, but not much fun,' Charlie went on, not sure he was listening. What was bothering him so much that he couldn't drive? It couldn't still be the old lady from Poole, could it? Muriel Pearson, who'd mistaken a picture of a woman on the side of an Asda van for a flesh-and-blood person? Did Simon suspect her of being Billy Dead Mates? Or her son, the one who'd rung DC James Wing to explain that his mother had made an embarrassing mistake? It wouldn't be the stupidest plan Charlie had ever heard: make a complete tit of yourself in front of the police and they're less likely to see you in the role of killer; you move seamlessly from the suspect category to Official Joke of the Investigation.

Charlie knew better than to ask Simon if he was thinking along the same lines. He always took longer to tell her when she seemed desperate to know.

She steered the car to the left to miss a dark lump on the road: brown with patches of red. She looked away quickly to avoid seeing spikes if there were any there to see, and told herself it probably wasn't a hedgehog. The thought of hedgehogs or elephants being killed bothered her in a way that animal deaths in general didn't.

Simon didn't know this about her. She wanted to tell him, but now wasn't the time. If he wasn't paying attention to her description of *Beloved*, which he'd asked about, then the topic of disproportionate sympathy for hedgehogs was unlikely to engage him.

'I was into Sue Grafton's *A is for Alibi* series at the time,' Charlie reminisced aloud. 'I really resented having to read anything I hadn't chosen myself – bit inconvenient when you're studying English Lit! – and I raced through *Beloved* without paying too much attention because I couldn't wait to start *D is for Deadbeat* or whichever one was next. I remember that the heroine was a woman called Sethe. She killed her baby daughter to save her from a life of being a slave. She loved her so much, she couldn't bear the thought of her going through the suffering and horrors that she – the mother – had been through. Oh – the dedication was memorably chilling. It wasn't "To" or "For" anyone, like normal dedications, it just said, "Sixty million and more", meaning all the black Americans murdered by slavery.'

'It has to mean something that Billy – or someone – sent that book to Halliday, that particular novel. Why *Beloved*?'

'The answer to that question's only relevant if Billy sent it.'

'Which we're officially 80 per cent certain he did, and probably more like 99 per cent certain unofficially,' Simon reminded her. He dug his thumbnail into the pad of his index finger, turning it from pink to white. 'It makes no sense. He's already killed four times. If he wants to kill Sondra Halliday, why not do it? Why's that morally wrong when killing the others isn't?'

'If I had to guess? Sondra Halliday hasn't got a best friend, so in his eyes she doesn't deserve it.'

'Having a best friend isn't a capital offence.'

'Simon, he's a serial killer, not the Archbishop of Canterbury. Maybe he's morally confused, to put it politely.'

'Letter doesn't sound confused,' Simon muttered.

'I followed Liv yesterday.' Charlie half hoped he wouldn't be listening.

'Followed her where?'

Damn. 'To Cambridge.'

'You mean . . . followed her without her knowing?'

'Yup. A proper undercover surveillance operation.' Charlie was tempted to take her voice to a falsely upbeat pitch: a defence against the frown lines she knew were etching themselves more deeply into Simon's brow with each word she uttered. She resisted the temptation, and spoke normally. 'We met for coffee in London. Liv suggested the venue: a place called Drink, Shop & Do – about fourteen footsteps from King's Cross station. That's not her neck of the woods and the café was everything she'd normally hate, so I had a feeling she'd be catching a train from King's Cross after she'd said goodbye to me. I asked her if she was, and she denied it – said she'd chosen somewhere near King's Cross because she knew that was where *I'd* be coming in to. Seemingly she'd forgotten she'd never done that ever before, even though I've been catching trains from Spilling to King's Cross for many years—'

'This isn't doing you any good, Char,' Simon cut in. 'It's become an obsession.'

'Says the man who's never been obsessed with uncovering the truth.'

'That's different. When it's work—'

'Liv's my sister, Simon. I have to know, whatever it is. You used to feel the same way, remember? Last time I followed Liv to Cambridge, you were with me.'

'Yeah. I also want to know, but . . . there's a limit to how much prying you can and should do when it's someone else's private business. Let yourself be driven to extremes and the result can be catastrophic.'

'Wow.' Charlie giggled. 'You're a really . . . abstract, non-specific harbinger of doom, aren't you? "Do a thing, and a thing might happen – scary scary!" Why the change of tune? This wasn't your attitude at first. You know what I think? I reckon you assumed it'd be easier than it has been to find out the truth. We stalked Liv and Gibbs all the way to Cambridge – I thought that'd be enough, we'd definitely come back with the answer. But it wasn't enough, and rather than risk more failure, you decided to pretend to respect their privacy.'

'I felt like a prurient creep.' Simon's voice sounded thinned out. 'Whatever they're up to, it's not our business.'

'Right. So I shouldn't tell you what happened when I followed Liv yesterday?'

Simon swore under his breath. 'Tell me. Following her's wrong, though. You can't do that to someone you know. It's not about her – I know she's not being straight with us, but . . . it's about how you want to behave, or it should be. The kind of person you want to be.'

'Well, that's easy.' Charlie smiled to herself. 'I want to be the kind of person who uses her cunning and ingenuity to find out the truth about her lying toe-rag of a sister. And – would you believe it? – that's who I am!'

'Tell me what happened.'

'I like your extra-strict voice. Very sexy.'

Simon no longer flinched when Charlie said 'sexy' or 'sex'. He didn't seem to be afraid of the act itself these days either. He was mellowing in many ways – all ways, really, that didn't relate to his work. He now ate food in pubs and occasionally restaurants in front of other people, not just Charlie, without being in a bad mood about it and trying to find a way to avoid it happening. For the first time in years, Charlie had a sex life that made her happy. The only downside was that the unmistakeable change for the better could never be mentioned or, God forbid, discussed. Simon was still Simon; an attempt to drag it into the light might drive him away again. Charlie wasn't prepared to risk it. Unable to talk about the improvement and the possible reasons behind it, she felt as if she couldn't rely on it lasting.

'Well?' Simon was still waiting for her amateur sleuthing report.

'I pretended to get the tube – went down into the underground so that I was out of sight, counted to ten, then went back up again to street level. There was no sign of Liv. I thought, "Well, I've lost her, haven't I?" As you do if you say goodbye to someone in central London and then walk away. Chances of finding them again are close to zero, but I headed towards the main station, feeling stupid about my hunch that was probably going to amount to nothing, and there she was. I followed her into the station. She went to stand in front of the high-up screens with the train times on. I hovered at a safe distance, closer to Kiosk than to her—'

'To where?'

'Kiosk. You know,' Charlie said impatiently. 'The place sort of under the arch that does the amazing hot sandwiches – pork and apple sauce, salt beef . . . I usually get the pork one. It's so good. They always give you a free bit of crackling with it too, which is the best bit.'

'Never heard of it,' said Simon.

'It doesn't matter. Point is, I kept out of the way and Liv didn't see me. She was in a world of her own anyway, not looking out for me.'

'She'd said goodbye to you. Most people don't expect to be tailed.'

'Especially not by their sisters!' Charlie tried to sound as proud as she could of her achievement, to counter Simon's disapproving tone. 'I assumed she was heading to Spilling to meet Gibbs after work, though it was a bit early still. Why would she go so early? I hovered in the doorway of WHSmith and made sure to stay well behind her. Every time she looked as if she might be turning in my direction, I ducked into the shop and hid. I could still see her clearly – I had a good vantage point, peering out from behind a big square "Deal of the Week" board.'

'She could easily have seen you.'

'Yeah, I know. Luckily, she didn't. If she had, I'd have said, "Just suddenly had a craving for a can of Dr Pepper, so I came back up from the tube" – a barefaced lie I'd have been quite happy telling. I find it hard to persuade myself I owe her any honesty at all these days.'

'So what happened?' Simon asked. 'She caught a train?'

'Yes, about ten minutes later, to Cambridge.'

'Hardly surprising. We know Liv's got friends in Cambridge – we've followed her and Gibbs there before.'

'Oh, come on, for God's sake!' Charlie's forehead felt hot. So did her palms on the steering wheel. 'Suddenly you're all "Yawn, yawn, nothing to see here." This isn't personal for you like it is for me, Simon. Imagine if it was your mother behaving like Liv. You'd have to know, wouldn't you? That's how I feel. I have to find out.'

'Yeah,' Simon breathed. To Charlie it sounded like someone giving up.

She was too embarrassed to describe her elation that was as strong now as yesterday: she'd followed Liv, and she'd completed her mission successfully. As a result, she had new information. Ever since, she'd felt as if there were a helium balloon inside her, giving her a floating-above-everything sensation. Why was it so frowned upon to be noticeably excited once you were a grown-up?

The strange thing about it was her being police. Before she'd transferred out of CID, Charlie had worked on many serious crime investigations, closed plenty of cases, found out useful information that had helped to identify and put away criminals, so why did illicitly following her sister to Cambridge feel like the most exciting thing she'd ever done?

Illicit. It was all there, in that word. As a detective, it had been her job, and therefore less fun, to poke around in other people's business. There was also the novelty factor. Charlie could barely believe it but it was true: in all her years as a DC and then a DS, she'd never straightforwardly tailed somebody one-to-one. Doing so – even better, to her own sister – had given her a rush of joyful adrenaline that was hard to describe. She'd found herself hoping it would take many more months to get to the bottom of Liv's deception.

'Has Gibbs ever mentioned a Nikhil Gulati to you?' she asked Simon. 'Liv hasn't to me.'

He didn't take the bait.

'That's his name – the male half of the couple we saw Liv and Gibbs with in Cambridge that time. Shall I tell you how I know? When Liv got on the Cambridge train, I did too. I watched her make a beeline for the first coach – first class; only the best for Liv! – and made sure to get on a few coaches along, in standard. It was a train for King's Lynn, but it stopped at Cambridge and I had a strong suspicion that was Liv's destination, so that's where I got off, concealing myself in a swarm of business suits. Liv was just ahead of me, at the ticket barrier. Again, I was lucky. She didn't see me.'

'Very lucky,' said Simon.

They'd arrived at the police station car park. Charlie drove past two narrow spaces and pulled into one with no car on either side of it. She turned off the engine.

'I followed her out of the station. There's a turning circle immediately in front of it, and a taxi queue to the right. I expected Liv to go for a cab, but instead she headed left and went to stand at the edge of the circle. I thought, "She's waiting for someone to come and pick her up," and sure enough, a few minutes later a Skoda pulls up, the window comes down and there he is – Nikhil Gulati. I didn't know that was his name then, obviously. I'm jumping ahead.'

'Can the rest wait?' asked Simon, opening the passenger door. 'I've got work to do.'

'You know what I think? You're secretly pissed off that I'm

the one who's found all this out and not you. No, it can't wait! The rest won't take long. I'd have told you sooner if you hadn't been obsessing about that old woman and her Asda van.'

'I want to interview her myself,' Simon murmured, his eyes glazing over.

Charlie raised her voice. 'I bribed my way to the front of the taxi queue – literally, I shoved a twenty-quid note in the hand of the first woman in the queue, leapt in a cab and yelled, 'Quick, follow that Skoda!'

'Wouldn't have been any consolation for all the others waiting,' said Simon.

'God, you're right! Let's worry about them forever.' Charlie opened her door, pulled her cigarettes out of her bag and lit one with the lighter inside the packet. 'I was sure the car-chase ruse wouldn't work, but, amazingly, it did. My cabbie was able to stay close enough to the Skoda to see each turn it took. Round the ring road we went, past the Backs, and we ended up on a side street next to the Punter pub. Nikhil parked, he and Liv got out; into the pub they went . . . Once the coast was clear, I got out of my taxi, gave the driver a large tip—'

'Expensive day,' Simon observed.

'. . . and set about peering discreetly in through the windows. The woman was there: Nikhil's girlfriend, partner, whatever – she wasn't wearing a wedding ring. I still don't know her name. For the next two hours, she, Nikhil and Liv had lunch. I'm guessing you don't want to know what each of them ate? Because I could tell you.' Charlie grinned to herself. 'My surveillance detail was *that* successful.'

'Skip it.'

'Eventually they finished lunch and asked for the bill. Liv paid. They all got back into the Skoda and headed off. I'd had time to hide, meanwhile, behind a parked van. When I was certain they'd driven off, I went in and threw a bit of my police weight around, in the nicest way possible. I found out the table had been booked by a Nikhil Gulati. I've Googled him – he works for a wine company.'

'How is it helpful to know that?'

Charlie held her breath for a few seconds. Then she said, 'You'd have thought three people having lunch together might chat, wouldn't you? They didn't.'

This snagged Simon's interest. *Finally*. 'They sat in silence?'

'Oh, no, they talked. Non-stop, but it was . . . I don't know, a business meeting or a planning session for a bank heist or something. There was nothing casual or relaxed about the conversation – and believe me, you didn't have to be an expert on facial expressions and body language to work that out. I tried to lip-read and failed.'

'It's easy to misinterpret something you see through a window,' said Simon.

'You're thinking about Muriel Pearson and the Asda van again, aren't you?'

'I'm thinking I need to go and speak to her. But James Wing'd find out, and it's his patch. He'd want in.'

'As you would if Wing wanted to ask questions unilaterally on your patch,' said Charlie.

'True. But I don't want him around for this.'

'For a particular reason, or just your usual megalomania?' Charlie took a long, deep drag of her cigarette. Knowing there would be no reply, she didn't wait. '*Why* are you so fixated on this old lady?' She always vowed not to ask and she always ended up begging.

'Isn't it obvious?' said Simon.

'No. Like everything else you think is obvious – no, it isn't.'

'I've told you what was said at the London briefing yesterday. Word for word.'

'And still I fail to intuit your conclusions, spoilsport that I am. So what's the real reason you're not tearing down to Poole to grill this old biddy? Don't pretend you give a toss about offending James Wing.'

'I'm not ready yet.'

'What would have to happen for you to be ready?' Charlie threw her cigarette end out of the car, squashed it with her shoe, then climbed out and stretched her legs.

Simon followed her lead. He slammed the passenger door shut. 'I want to be surer of the answer I'll get before I ask the question,' he said.

'Follow that logic and—'

'Yes. That's what I'd like. To know, without asking. Just listen in silence to all the shit everyone spouts all day long, and work it out in my head, and *know*. Only speak when I'm certain. I'm sick as fuck of asking this, that, the other. It's demeaning.'

And a crucial part of your job.

No point in saying it.

'I like the sound of this new regime,' Charlie said instead. She pulled a red lipstick out of her bag and ran it over her lips as they walked up the steps to the front door of the nick. 'When you've given up asking questions, can you start answering them instead? That would be amazing! Let's practise now. I'll ask, you answer. What is it about an old woman stupidly thinking a picture on a van is a real person that's obsessing you so much?'

'Her son.' Simon's eyes were cloudy and distant. '*He* was the one who rang up James Wing and said his mother had made an embarrassing mistake – and we weren't even told his name! Wing didn't think it worth mentioning.'

'You think the son could be Billy?'

'What? No.' Simon looked confused, then annoyed, like someone who'd had his concentration broken by the blare of a car alarm. 'I mean, he might be, but I doubt it. I'd better go.'

He pushed through the double doors into the building. Charlie did the same a few seconds later. He hadn't bothered to hold them open for her. He never did.

~

'Books are important!' Sam Kombothekra raised his voice to be heard over the lunchtime din in the Brown Cow.

'As part of a healthy lifestyle, Sergeant?' asked Proust. Simon stopped himself from smiling just in time. He'd never laughed at one of the Snowman's witticisms and wanted to keep it that way.

'I'm waiting till the food arrives,' said Gibbs. 'I'm fucking starving.'

'Waiting to do what, detective? Burst into song?'

'Talk,' Gibbs clarified.

Sellers was pushing his way through the crowd towards their table. He had a pint in one hand and was unbuttoning his coat with the other. 'Congratulate me,' he said.

'Another blind woman pregnant?' Gibbs muttered.

'Shut it, gobbo. I hope you ordered for me.'

'Yeah. Weight Watchers bar, wasn't it?'

Sellers made a face. 'I think I've found Lane the Ishaya. If I'm right, her full name's Marjolein Baillie. Lives in Rawndesley. She's an Ishaya of something called the Bright Path, whatever that means. Known to family and friends as Lane. I spoke to her husband – she's away till next Tuesday on a meditation retreat, but we can speak to her the next day, the Wednesday.'

'Another reason to think Billy's local,' said Simon. 'His therapist, mentor, whatever is Culver Valley-based, as were two of his victims, as is Kim Tribbeck who he might have lined up as a future victim.'

'I was just saying I think books are important, whatever else is,' Sam filled Sellers in. 'Billy gives his victims books before killing them, he sends Sondra Halliday a book, he admires someone called Lane who teaches through story. But why those lines of poetry, and why *Beloved* by Toni Morrison? We ought to be able to get something from that. We've got not only his choice of victims to go on now, but also his choice of literature.'

'You're assuming Billy wrote the letter to Sondra Halliday,' said Simon.

'He did.' Sellers looked around for somewhere to dump his coat. Not finding anywhere convenient, he folded it up, put it on his chair and sat on it. 'Report just came in from the prof. In court, he'd have to say there was an 80 per cent chance the writing was Billy's, same as in the little white books—'

'80 per cent? Is that all?' said Proust. 'Can't he do better? As he's not a real professor, I'm not sure his opinion has any worth.'

'Malcolm Coulthard's a world expert in forensic linguistics and author identification,' said Simon. '"Emeritus" doesn't mean "not real". He was the Foundation President of the International Association of Forensic Linguists, an expert witness in more than two hundred criminal and civil cases. Experts don't come much better. Plus, if you're going to hold a grudge against him for being technically retired, didn't he say he'd consult with the professor who now runs his old department?'

'He did and he has,' said Sellers. 'They want a bit more time to put their formal report together, but when I pushed, what I got was an official 80 per cent and an informal "Yep, that letter's from Billy". I just got off the phone with Coulthard – there's no doubt in his mind.'

Simon made an impatient noise. 'There might be no doubt in his mind that the letter to Sondra Halliday and the lines from poems in the little white books were written by the same person, but *we* need to remember we don't know for certain that person's Billy. It's just about possible that someone's giving out white books, and someone else is doing the killing. I know we're assuming they're one and the same, but we shouldn't forget that's all it is: an assumption. We especially shouldn't forget it now that this comedian's turned up alive and well, saying she was given a book early last year. That's a big blow to our presumed pattern, isn't it?'

'I think James Wing's right,' said Gibbs. 'We need to alibi out Sondra Halliday. She's ended up centre stage. First she's writing about Billy, now he's writing to her . . . We need to focus on her.'

'Want me to talk to her again?' Sellers offered.

'I didn't want you to talk to her yesterday,' Simon reminded him. 'I wanted Charlie to do it. I wonder . . .'

'Lonely as a cloud, but not as pretty,' Proust contributed.

'If Billy was the man who gave Kim Tribbeck the white book, he wasn't to know she can't match a memory of a place to that place's name because of the number of shows she does in one tour. Did he want her to say to us, "He was at my gig in, say, Falmouth" because he lives nowhere near there? That could explain why on that one occasion he let himself be seen, if he wanted to mislead us.'

Sam frowned. 'It'd be a risk for him. He's surely safer if no one's seen his face.'

'Kim got her book first, and could well have been Billy's first intended victim,' said Simon. 'We should remember that. It might mean he hadn't settled on an optimal M.O. yet. I'm sure Kerensa Moore'd tell us that sometimes, with serials, the first kill's different – more spontaneous, less thought through – before the scrote sorts out his ideal routine.'

'I don't need Moore to tell me that,' said Gibbs. 'We all know it's true.'

A waitress appeared at their table with a plate of steaming hot food in each hand. Everyone was having the house shepherd's pie with extra Tabasco sauce. Gibbs pointed to the table in front of him to ensure he was served first.

He stuffed two forkfuls into his mouth in quick succession, then said, 'Why's Kim Tribbeck still alive? Little white book means rapidly approaching death for all the others, so what makes Kim different? Unless it's important to her to look like a potential victim. Because otherwise you might think Billy'd make sure to kill her pronto, if she saw his face.'

Simon passed the plate the waitress had put down in front of him to Sam. Sam always volunteered to be last; it got on everyone's nerves. 'Take it and shut it,' Simon told him. To Gibbs, he said, 'You think Kim Tribbeck, famous comedian, might be a serial killer?'

'No. But only because I've met her and . . . it's not her, I don't think, but there's no reason in theory why a famous person shouldn't be a murderer. Maybe some of the impulses that make these people seek out fame could also make them more likely to kill. Egotism, the idea that everyone should do their bidding.'

'Monster Munch,' Sellers murmured without moving his lips.

'Fuck off, Dong-caster.' Gibbs picked up the empty peanut packet on the table and dropped it into Sellers' pint.

'Kim Tribbeck's a well-known TV face,' said Sam. 'She's always popping up on some panel show or other. If your doorbell rang unexpectedly and you found her outside . . .'

Sam broke off while two waitresses put the remaining plates down on the table.

'I wouldn't let her in,' Simon said once they'd gone. 'I'd look around for hidden cameras. Whether I could see them or not, I'd slam the door.'

'That's you, mate,' said Gibbs. 'Most people'd be excited a celeb was asking to come in and talk to them in their homes. They'd assume their life was about to take a turn for the more glamorous, probably – maybe that they were about to be offered some sort of TV opportunity.'

'Which is what happened,' said Proust briskly. 'They ended up on the news. They're all big names in the media now. For crying out loud!' Sometimes there were warning rumbles before one of his rage avalanches; on other occasions, they came from nowhere, startling everyone.

'We need to rein ourselves in before we lose our bearings.' The Snowman slammed his pint glass down on the table. We've got *nothing*, so we're inventing things that ought to embarrass us. Sandra Halliday, Kim Tribbeck — we don't seriously believe either of these women is a killer of four people, do we?' The wrong answer, his manner made clear, would disgust him forever.

Simon decided to brave it. 'We don't know. It's more likely to be the man at the gig who gave Tribbeck the white book, but anything's possible.'

'In one sense, our confusion's a good thing,' said Sam. 'We have new names and new faces, as yet unnamed, to consider: Kim Tribbeck, Sondra Halliday, this man at the comedy gig. Each new person we add to our list is someone we can take a DNA sample from, potentially — and maybe get a match with three of our four crime scenes.'

'I want uniforms taking any samples from here on in,' Simon told him. 'Separate from any interviews we do — separate occasions altogether, I mean. The two don't mix well if we want to establish trust.'

'I didn't realise your interviews were about establishing trust, Waterhouse.' Proust chuckled. 'I thought they were about making people want to jump out of the window.'

'What if Kim Tribbeck's not Billy, but this is still all about Kim?' Gibbs said. 'She gets a white book but she also gets to live. She gets hand delivery while the others don't. She hasn't got a best friend, but all the others have. She's the special one, isn't she?'

'Different doesn't mean special, Detective, whatever your primary school teachers told you.'

'Has anyone read the book?' asked Sam. '*Beloved*, Toni Morrison?'

No one had.

'I'll read it tonight,' said Simon.

'Good idea, Waterhouse. Run yourself a bubble bath and read a novel. That'll help us.'

'You know it will. That book was chosen out of all the ones that might have been sent. We need to know why.' Turning to

Gibbs, Simon asked, 'What do we know about Kim Tribbeck's life and anyone in it who might not be favourably disposed towards her?'

'Or, turning it on its head, who might be,' Sam said. 'Kim's alive and unhurt. That could mean Billy *is* favourably disposed towards her. She's scared, I suppose.'

'Not noticeably,' Gibbs told him. 'Her gran's just died and somehow that's left her scared of cancer and hospitals and illness, but not of being shot by a maniac. It sounded a bit too convenient when she said it, but I still can't persuade myself she's killed anyone. In terms of people in her life who might be of interest: estranged husband, estranged lover – she dumped them both. Sister of estranged lover's worth looking at too. Her brother hid the affair from her because he thought she wouldn't like it – saw Kim during the night when his sister was at work. Kim also has a brother she can't stand, with whom she's clashed big time over various family issues . . .'

'Four excellent suspects full of juicy DNA, right off the bat,' said Proust. 'Good. Better.'

And not dismissed as far-fetched because not in any way famous, Simon noticed. How could you describe anyone as an excellent suspect with no idea of why a series of murders was happening?

'Kim's definitely got issues with her family,' said Gibbs. 'Dead grandmother included. She gave me a long list of bad presents they've all given her over the years.'

'Bad presents?' The words made Simon's skin prickle. He couldn't have said why. 'Like a little white book with hardly any words in it?'

'No. Keep up, Waterhouse! Someone *else* gave her that: a man she didn't recognise, not a relative. We'll call him excellent suspect number five.'

'Is the list of bad presents in your notes?' Simon asked Gibbs. 'I'd like to see it.'

Gibbs nodded. 'Something else: Kim didn't like thinking or talking about the man who gave her the book. She seemed to have an aversion to the memory.'

'Did you ask her why?' Sellers was barely intelligible through a mouthful of shepherd's pie.

'No. It felt like an important question – perhaps one to come at from a more sideways angle, a bit later on. I had a feeling she'd deny and clam up if I asked outright. Plus I was busy asking her other things – mainly about this Faith woman who might or might not be in danger.'

'We need to get her details from the RGI, check she's okay,' said Sam.

'Do we, Sergeant?' Proust pounced on the suggestion. 'Frankly, Kim Tribbeck's story about Billy secretly watching at the hospital and taking it upon himself to nominate Kendell as Tribbeck's best-friend-in-waiting—'

'Kim didn't present that as fact,' Gibbs cut in. 'It was a theory, to explain the "Death devours" book on the cancer ward noticeboard. She admitted it was far-fetched.'

'We need a police artist sketch of this guy from Tribbeck's gig,' said Sellers.

'I had another idea,' said Gibbs. 'I didn't think Kim'd go for it and we can't force her, but when I suggested it, she didn't say no. I asked her if she'd revisit all the stops on her tour from early last year. I offered her a police driver. Me, if that's what it takes. Though I was wondering if maybe . . .' Gibbs looked at Simon.

'Charlie?' he said.

'And she said yes?' asked Sam. 'Kim agreed?'

Gibbs nodded. 'Eventually she agreed.'

7

from Origami *by Kim Tribbeck*

He put on a specially reasonable tone to ask me. It sounded unnatural, as if he was straining to achieve it. And I was terrified.

It's funny, the things that scare you.

I wanted to cry, or hide. I wanted to say, 'No, no, impossible! I can't go back to those places.' Except it wasn't impossible. It was practically and scientifically feasible. I had no good reason to refuse. No bad one either.

I couldn't understand why the prospect of revisiting my old tour venues was so frightening to me. It was only – to put it casually, though I felt anything but casual about it – going back to some places, harmless theatres and auditoriums. It would be time-consuming, yes, but I wasn't touring at the moment. Also, I knew it was the right thing to do. I could see the same glaringly obvious truth Gibbs saw: I was uniquely placed to help the police. How could I refuse? I fought hard with myself inside my head.

Don't you want to catch Billy Dead Mates?

Of course.

And stop him murdering more people?

Yes.

Then what's the problem?

I don't know. Can't put it into words. I just quite desperately don't want to do it. I—

'Kim?' Gibbs was waiting for my response.

'I'm sorry. It's a big ask, that's all.'

'I know.'

'Are you sure it's necessary? I mean, you don't know this guy at my gig was Billy. Even if we find the right venue, how's that going to help you find him?'

'We've been through this. It could be a pointer to him living in the area or having family connections there. We'd be able to make enquiries with some of the other people there that night. Maybe someone saw him who can help us ID him. You'll need to give a description to a police artist. The sooner we get a sketch of this man to circulate—'

'I'm happy to do that. Can't we just do the sketch and forget the historical comedy tour reenactment?' I wiped beads of sweat from my upper lip.

'What are you so afraid of?'

It was the same question I'd been asking myself. 'I don't fancy another encounter with Scary White Book Man.'

'Interesting. You're not scared of Billy Dead Mates the killer, though we have reason to believe you might be on his target list, but you *are* scared of a man who gave you a white book at a gig last year.'

Yes. 'I don't believe they're the same man.'

'That was my point,' said Gibbs. 'If they aren't, how come the one you're more scared of isn't the one who kills?'

It struck me later that it was the retracing-of-steps aspect of Gibbs' proposal that terrified me. I am someone who never stays in the same hotel twice; it's a firm policy of mine. I didn't want to see where I'd been. I could only cope with dragging My Life So Far around with me everywhere I went on the strict condition that I never had to look in its direction, let alone re-enter it.

There would be no way to explain it to DC Gibbs, and no point trying, but I was relieved as well as alarmed to have worked out the truth about myself. In the two or three nights after Gibbs asked me to reconstruct my old tour minus all the laughs, I had some horrible nightmares in which some of the theatres I'd gigged in and the hotels I'd stayed in had become entangled with other scenes I'd been happy to leave behind: a screaming row Drew and I once had that I never thought about because I couldn't bear to, except that in my dream it took place in the lift I once found myself in on tour, with the manufacturer's name, 'Schindler', emblazoned across its interior wall. This prompted many comments about how you shouldn't really joke, should you, but it was rather an unfortunate name for a lift, wasn't it? Another of my nightmares featured Sarah Durdy, my best enemy, after the Dorian-from-the-tennis-club incident. In the dream, Sarah patiently tried to convince me that, yes, you *could* do something wrong over and over again for as long as possible, then turn round and say, 'Sorry!' to the person you'd hurt and would still be hurting if opportunity allowed, and yes, really, you were truly sorry and would never do it again – unless of course you got the chance to. Dream Kim found both Sarah's explanation and her contrition unconvincing, and told her so. Our showdown took place in the foyer of an old music-hall-style theatre I once played (God knows where), with elaborately patterned floor tiles, in front of the audience that had paid to see my gig.

Worst of all was the nightmare in which my grandmother climbed on stage halfway through my set at St George's Hall in Bradford (this time I remembered the venue) and shouted to the audience, 'Will one of you take her? We don't want her!'

Going back wasn't safe for someone like me. I could only cope if I looked determinedly ahead. And then I realised I had the answer to another of Gibbs' questions: why don't I fear the future, especially when it might contain my murder at the hands of Billy Dead Mates?

It's because the future's always been the best bit, the bit that's not the past – it's not losing your family, or finding them when you're eighteen and being hurt by them over and over again; it's not finding your husband's hidden stash of drugs for the twenty-seventh time, and having to believe his lame promises that he'll give up, he swears, he means it this time;

it's not realising that your lover, who's supposed to have hidden depths, is nothing more than a blank hard surface; it's not being handed a small white book by a man who looks at you in a way that stops your breath and makes you want to run . . .

The future is none of those things. It's where the good things are finally going to start happening. That's why it's not scary.

I thought everyone knew this.

From: inessa.hughes@goochandhughes.com
Sent: 11 April 2016 09.21:34
To: Susan.Nordlein@nordleinvinter.co.uk
Subject: *Origami* by Kim Tribbeck

Dear Susan

Thanks for your email. I'm so glad you love the book as much as I do! And I'm delighted to hear that your jaw hit the floor at the Liv and Gibbs revelation. Mine did too. I agree it's a legal minefield, but it's such an intriguing part of the story and I suspect Kim might dig in her heels and refuse to publish without it. Surely Nordlein and Vinter are covered on the legal front by the simple fact of the Liv and Gibbs element being verifiably true?

I'm afraid I haven't been able to talk Kim out of her favourite hobby of defending Billy Dead Mates on Twitter and Facebook. She jokily refers to it as 'my pro bono work'. 'Who would you rather I defend?' she said when I first broached the subject. 'Joanna Lumley? Prince George the royal toddler? All the people who've done nothing wrong and are being vilified by nobody?' I didn't give up *quite* straight away, but I'm afraid I lost the battle. Kim's argument is 1) she's not for a moment claiming murder is acceptable, and 2) blanket condemnation and writing people off as evil only adds to the sum total of pain in the world.

Do you think her portrayal is too sympathetic? I felt for poor old Billy when I read Kim's book, in a way that I didn't at all when I heard the news reports. I'm afraid that at that point my only thought was, 'What a monster!' We should be prepared for some negative feedback along those lines, I think: that Billy's depicted as being almost a regular, flawed human like the rest of us, albeit one who took a senseless obsession too far. Though I've read and reread the manuscript and there's absolutely nothing in there than condones or justifies the murders.

I'm sorry to report that I didn't get very far when I tried to raise the thorny subject of how Kim portrays herself in the book. I told her we didn't recognise *Origami*'s spiky, slightly hard-hearted protagonist as the kind, warm, compassionate Kim we all know and love. To no avail: she claims that since she did, thought and felt all the things she attributes to herself in the book, it is accurate and not in need of amendment. (She also told me quite firmly that she is funny, but not a nice or good person, and that I shouldn't imagine she was just because she makes me laugh.)

This is certainly the most surprising and dramatic project I've ever worked on! I passionately believe it will be worth it and I do so hope you agree.

Warmest best wishes as ever,

Inessa

PS I LOVE *The Narrow Bed* as a title, but Kim is not keen. She has suggested *Every Bed Is Narrow*, which she thinks is more interesting – but also, I fear, less commercial a prospect! She also said that even if we end up calling it something else, its 'real' name will always be *Origami*.

8

from Origami *by Kim Tribbeck*

I blame my unsuccessful marriage on the phrase 'opposites attract'. I met Gabe on a train, having tried not to. I did the polite quick-smile-eyes-down manoeuvre to signal that I wanted to read my book in peace, but he was determined to talk to me, and full of energy, confidence and ideas he wanted to share with a random stranger. He didn't recognise me from *The Village Parallel*, a TV show I had a minor part in at the time, so I didn't suspect him of talking to me only to be able to tell his friends later.

By the time we'd arrived at our destination (we were both going to London – me to see my agent and Gabe to pitch for new business), we'd disagreed about at least ten things, starting with people who claimed they could only sit facing the direction of travel on trains. Gabe thought they were bullshitters who'd been getting away with it for too long.

I disagreed. I was happy to sit facing either way myself, but I'd met a handful of people over the years who soon felt dizzy on a train if they weren't looking forward. Why would they lie about it? 'Status,' Gabe replied without hesitation. 'If you're whiny and sensitive, you're seen as special. If you muck in like a trouper, no one notices or cares.'

'That's too cynical,' I told him. 'If you're right and it's bullshit, they're not doing it in a calculating way. It's a psychological defence reflex. Probably means they weren't fed often enough as hungry babies or something. Now they're adults, they've worked out a few strategies for getting their needs met, but they have to make sure those needs keep coming, as the cue for endless reassurance. When the needs stop, the meeting of them stops too. Then they're catapulted right back to their childhood misery.'

'Oh, I'm sure that's what they've all agreed to *say* if challenged.' Gabe nodded emphatically, as if no conspiracy could get past him. 'It's up to you if you want to take the word of the backwards-facing cabal over mine.'

I couldn't help laughing. In our early days, Gabe did this all the time: veered towards the surreal when he was losing an argument – not in order to win; purely for entertainment's sake. It made me realise how dull and rule-bound most people's conversation was. As I told Marion when she asked about the new boyfriend I hadn't yet let her meet: 'He's as much fun to chat to as a gay man, but straight.' Marion frowned and said she didn't think she'd ever spoken to a homosexual.

Gabe was as infuriating as he was amusing. I soon learned that his moral code bore no resemblance to mine. He was happy to wander around with disused marjoram jars full of sprigs of skunkweed nestling in his every pocket, but he thought cheating on your partner was scummy. He was sweetly naïve about sexual exclusivity being an integral part of romantic love. On that first train journey, he proudly declared himself to be the if-you-kiss-anyone-else-it's-over type, and I showered him with good-natured ridicule for it. (That's right: he read the small print before he opted in, in case any of you are worried about him.)

As Gabe said in his speech at our wedding, the woman in seat D14 and the man in seat D16 had nothing in common but powerful sexual attraction. This was what convinced me, before our train had pulled into King's Cross station, that I'd met my future husband. Opposites attract, don't they? Every romantic book and film ever made tells us that thinking someone's an utter twat is a crucial pre-love stage that can't be bypassed or else your relationship is lacking something.

If I were a romantic novelist, I'd want to send out a different message: imagine the same words and behaviour minus the attractive physical shell – would you still be interested? Or would you want to tell the person to fuck off? If the latter, do not marry.

To be fair, it wasn't only Gabe's physical beauty that drew me to him. His verbal and intellectual dexterity were partly responsible. But still, in retrospect: do not marry. Divorcing a clever, witty man is no fun at all.

~

Monday, 12 January 2015

Gabe's already there when I arrive at Dempster's Café. He's holding his iPhone in one hand and typing on his MacBook Air with the other. I don't need to take a closer look to know that he's got at least four tabs open on his laptop. Why doesn't he—

I stop myself mid-thought. Gabe is not my responsibility any more. If he wants to try to do too much at once, that's his problem. That and his drug addiction.

'Oh, you're here,' he says, looking up. 'Get a drink – I'll be with you in five.'

Minutes. You have to add minutes.

'Is your meeting with yourself running late?' I say mock-sweetly.

'Are you comparing a work conversation by email to masturbation?'

'I was thinking more of self-absorption than anything sexual, but now you mention it . . .'

'Ha! You're doing it!'

'What?'

'I feel like a school teacher suspected of pushing illicit chocolate doughnuts onto already overweight schoolchildren.'

'*What?*'

'You're assessing the size of my pupils.' Gabe grins. 'And drawing bad conclusions.'

'That's the worst joke I've ever heard,' I tell him. On the substantive issue, he's right. 'It's a hard habit to break. I'm afraid it'll carry forward into any relationship I have from now on. I'll stare into the eyes of future beloveds, searching for pupil dilation of the drug-induced variety.'

'No one would put up with that apart from me.'

'Is that because you're an extra-special saint?' I relent and finally respond to his smile with one of my own. 'I need a coffee – do you want another?'

Gabe shakes his head. 'Already had two.'

Dempster's was his choice, not mine. I don't like the way they use every inch of wall space to try and flog appalling 'computer art' and I don't like their customers. It's almost against the rules to come in here without at least one Apple device – Gabe and I have argued about this before, and I still maintain it's not just a modern life thing. There's a café three doors down where you can walk in at any time and not see a single MacBook or iPad mini. Dempster's is the kind of place that might at any moment decide it's not a café but a 'connectivity hub' or some such nonsense; if you order a slice of cake here, you get it on a plank of wood or a shard of black slate.

I buy a double espresso, carry it over to Gabe's table and sit down. 'So, are there really people out there who look at their romantic partners and don't zoom straight in on the eyes in search of evidence of recent bonging?'

'I'll be able to give you a definitive answer once my *Guardian* Soulmates profile goes live,' says Gabe. 'That's what I've said I'm looking for: an intelligent, sexy, funny, loyal woman with no narcotics-policing tendencies.'

Unfortunately, he's joking. I wish he would look for someone else and stop lobbying to get me back.

'I'm sure you and she will be idyllically happy together,' I say. 'Most people are on your side – they see nothing wrong with using marijuana to stupefy yourself day in, day out. Soon it'll be fully legal everywhere. What a depressing thought.'

'And yet, all these years later, I'm not stupefied, am I? All the things you said would happen to me – slower reactions, duller brain . . . See any evidence?'

'No, but you're relatively young. And I don't want to live with a drug addict any more than I'd want to live with a man who was plotting to blow up St Paul's Cathedral.'

'What's the connection?'

'Vandalism – of yourself, of a beautiful building. It's the same thing.'

'Well, either that or it's a totally different thing and you're a fanatic.' Gabe shrugs.

'Yup. One or the other. The great thing is, we don't have to have this argument any more. Now we're apart, you can smoke as much weed as you want. I don't care.'

Gabe runs his hands through his hair. 'I hate us being apart. I want you back, Kim. I'm not going to give up.'

'Oh – you left off the word "drugs" there. You're not going to give up *drugs*. That's why you're not getting me back. Might as well face it, Gabe.'

'What if I *did* give up the weed?'

I laugh. 'What a brilliant idea! Why didn't I think of that?'

'You think I never will because I never did, but you're wrong. I didn't before because I didn't believe you meant it when you threatened to leave me. Now I see you did. That changes everything.'

'Gabe.'

'Mm?'

'I left you *ages* ago. Since then, have you smoked skunkweed every day?'

'No.'

'Oh, fuck off. Gone back to lying about it, have you?'

'I'm not lying! I bought a vaporiser – treated myself, to cheer me up after getting dumped.'

'Right. A machine that allows you to ingest the same amount of weed while also indulging your passion for new gadgets.'

Gabe grins and nods. 'Also, it's much easier on the lungs. Not at all carcinogenic – which was one of your issues, wasn't it, body-vandalism-wise?'

'Yet the destruction of your mental faculties proceeds apace. I'm not impressed. But I will rephrase my question: since I booted you out of the house, has a day passed without you smoking or vaporising skunkweed?'

'Nope,' Gabe says proudly.

I sip my tea to hide the sting of pain. I shouldn't feel it any more, but I do.

'So your question – what if you did give up weed? – is a pointless one, isn't it? You never will, because you very much don't want to.'

'I'd give up like a shot if you'd have me back. Why not try me? Accept the challenge: if you're right about me and I screw up on day one, leave me again. There's no way I could fool you, not with your state-of-the-art pupil-measuring techniques. But if I'm as good as my word, we stay together.'

'As good as your *word*?' I raise an eyebrow. 'Gabe, in a contest between you, Pinocchio, The Boy Who Cried Wolf and Bernie Madoff, your word would come stone cold last. You've lied to me about drugs hundreds of times. For all I know, you've found some cunning anti-pupil-dilation device that'll help you outwit me. Sorry, but I'm not falling for it.'

'No such device exists.' Gabe looks annoyed about this. 'You're a coward.'

'I'm a realist,' I correct him. 'If you were capable of giving up, you'd have done so the second I said we were finished. That's what I'd have done if I were you and wanted me back. I'd have said, "Okay, I didn't think you meant it, but you clearly do, so I'm clean as of now. I'll take regular drug tests—"'

'Well, I will.' Gabe smiles. He looks so reasonable. Reasonable and sexy. I want to hit him. 'Come on, who else are you ever going to meet who'll let you test their urine whenever the mood takes you? We're a match made in heaven. We could even turn it into an exciting sexual role play: you could be a Thai airport official, and I'll be the hapless passenger who's had his luggage tampered with, and—'

'Gabe, stop it.' I don't want to chat to him like we used to. It's dangerous. He knows it, the bastard.

'Kim, listen. No, I didn't respond to being dumped by immediately getting "clean", as you call it – though, you know, I continue to shower and wash my hair every day, and brush my teeth. Why didn't I ditch the weed on the spot? Because there was no incentive. You'd left me! I felt like shit. I still do. Whether you like it or not, I *enjoy* smoking weed. For all I knew, you were done with me for good and wouldn't have me back even if I *did* make a colossal sacrifice for your sake—'

'Yes. That is the situation, perfectly summarised.'

'I can give up skunk, no problem.'

'No, you can't.'

'Yes, I can. But only if you guarantee you'll make it worth my while.'

'Fuck off, Gabe.'

'Promise me that if I'm drug-free for a year, you'll take me back and stay with me until such time as I reoffend.'

'No.'

'I'll take a drug test every day if you want me to.'

'No! I don't want to live with a man I have to test for illegal substances every day, or, actually, ever. Most people don't do that – you do know that, don't you? The way normal people live?'

'Your anti-weed prejudice is a relic from a bygone era, Kim.' Gabe looks sad for me. 'Most people—'

'I don't care about most people. I hate most people. If I ever have another relationship – which is by no means guaranteed – I need it to be one in which drugs aren't an issue, any more than arson or gambling is an issue. If no man exists who can give me that, I'll stay celibate. Look, can we talk about what we came here to talk about?'

'That's what I'm doing,' Gabe says. 'I care more about our marriage than about Billy Dead Mates.'

Two women at a nearby table look up from their iPad minis. I scare their eyes away with my best scowl.

'Then you ought to want to help make sure the police catch him before he kills me,' I say to Gabe. As I say this, I can't help thinking how unlikely it sounds. I feel as if I'm reciting lines I've learned for a play.

'From what you told me on the phone, he's not going to do that. If he wanted to, why wait so long after giving you the book?'

'I don't know. What if there is no "why"?' For some reason, I want Gabe to take the threat to my life seriously, even if I can't.

'Isn't there always a "why"? It might be a crazy one, but it'll make sense to him if to no one else.'

'Who cares? Look, the guy needs to be locked up, that's all. Have the police contacted you?'

'Yeah. They're coming to talk to me this afternoon. I've told them they're wasting their time. I don't remember where it was that he gave you the book. I didn't see him do it.'

'Let me describe the room to you, just in case it jogs your memory – though God knows it hasn't worked on mine. I don't trust the police not to miss out details. If you even think you might know . . . You don't have to be sure.'

'All right, let's give it a go.' Gabe squeezes his eyes shut. 'It might be a conveniently heroic way to win you back if I help catch a serial killer.'

I smile, knowing he can't see me, and wonder if the reason I'll never take him back is that I prefer him when he's like this: trying hard to impress me. If I gave him another chance, he might give up drugs but he would also – inevitably – give up trying to win me over.

'Kim, seriously. Will you let me move back in until the police have caught this guy?' He's opened his eyes and I haven't even started on my description. No will power whatsoever. 'Just for my peace of mind, and yours? Purely for platonic protection?'

'The police have said they'll provide protection if and when they think I need it. At the moment, they believe I'm safe enough.'

'Safe enough for them's not safe enough for me. Look, I mean it. I'll not even mention our relationship for the whole time I'm there. I'll be your bodyguard, not your husband. *And* . . . I'll do loads of skunk.'

'*What?*'

'Yeah, to prove that this isn't me trying to move back in as a husband. If I were doing that, I'd be a drug-free zone, wouldn't I?'

I squeeze his arm. 'It's a kind offer, but I'd rather be protected by someone who's not stoned to oblivion.'

Gabe closes his eyes again. 'Describe this room then, if this is the only way you'll let me help.'

I go through the details one by one: long black stage, about two feet high, with steps down on both sides, also black. Very scuffed wooden floor, pale wood with a herringbone pattern. A huge room that was a perfect square shape with an additional bit added on that was sort of funnel-shaped. All the audience sitting at round tables, about ten people at each one. There was a bar area to the left of the stage, in the funnel part of the room. To leave the hall you had to walk past the bar. Once you'd passed it, the room narrowed. This was the neck of the funnel, and it led to a single door: navy blue with a square glass panel at the top. On the wall furthest from the blue door there was a purple velvet curtain, half pulled, with a black net curtain behind it, partially covering a white wall. The purple wasn't lilac or mauve or pink; it was livid purple.

'Kim.'

'What? Have you remembered?'

'No. I'm not going to. Sorry. I don't know what livid purple is, and I don't remember the colour of any curtain I've ever seen, I'm afraid. Couldn't tell you what the curtains look like in our house, for example.'

My house. I'll have to buy Gabe's share so that I can think that legitimately. He's not quite as out of my life as I need him to be.

My phone is buzzing. 'Pray for me,' I tell Gabe as I reach into my pocket to pull it out. 'With any luck, this'll be a detective, phoning to say they've arrested Billy and I can have my life back.'

That's what I want, isn't it?

Please don't leave me alone with my life, Billy.

'Hello?'

'Kim, is that you?'

'Yes. Who's this?'

'Fiona.'

The name is familiar, and the voice, but I can't place her.

'From the hospital.'

'Oh. Right.' The nurse with the tiny Rapunzel plait. 'Look, I'm sorry about the other day. I just needed to get that little book to the police as soon as—'

'I'm not calling about that.'

'Then what?'

'You need to come down here now.'

'Where? To . . . to the hospital?'

'Yes. Ward 10.'

'Ward 10's a cancer ward,' I say sharply. 'Far as I know, I don't have cancer. Unless you tested me on the sly while I was visiting.' This is crazy. I shouldn't panic like this at a phone call.

'Just come,' says Fiona. I hear a click and then nothing.

～

I brace myself as I turn the corner, eyes down, watching my feet on the mottled blue hospital lino as if it's the only way to keep track of where they're going. They might as well belong to a puppet whose movements I can't control. The self-consciousness I feel inside the RGI turns me numb every time.

This is the last time, I say to myself. *I'm not coming back here again, no matter what.*

I look up when I can no longer avoid it, expecting to see the double doors to Ward 10. Instead, I see Fiona leaning against the wall outside the ward, looking anything but relaxed. Her eyes are red from crying.

Then I see movement through the glass panel – a dark-haired man with his back to me. He turns slightly and surprise jolts through me before I've worked out why. *Wait, is that . . . ?*

It is. It's DC Gibbs.

'Yeah,' breathes Fiona. 'The police are here.'

That's to be expected, right? I asked them to check Faith Kendell was safe. This is nothing to panic about.

'I overheard them talking about whether to ring you, when to ring you, how to handle it . . .' Fiona shrugs. 'Thought I'd take the decision out of their hands. I knew you'd want to know sooner than they'd want you to. I'm so sorry, Kim.' She starts to cry. 'I just can't believe it.'

'Believe what? What's going on?' Hearing my own question, I realise there's only one thing it can be. *Oh, no.* My throat tightens. 'Is it Faith Kendell? Is she dead?'

'What?' Fiona sounds surprised. 'No.'

'No?' I need to check. It would be my fault if Faith were dead; I'm not sure how, but it would be.

'No. Kim, that's not it.'

I touch the wall with the palm of my left hand: a solid surface. 'Thank God,' I mutter.

The double doors swing open and a hulk of a man in an ill-fitting suit appears on the corridor. 'Kim Tribbeck? I'm DC Simon Waterhouse. What are you doing here?'

'I . . . um . . .' I don't want to land Fiona in any trouble.

'Never mind. Now you're here, we should talk.' He turns to Fiona. 'Where can we go for privacy?'

'I'll show you.' Her voice is efficient, despite the tears streaming down her face.

I'm third in line as we walk along the main ward corridor. Chris Gibbs is sitting with his head in his hands beyond the reception area. Like someone who's lost someone, or losing them. He looks up when he sees us coming and lurches to his feet.

Fiona ushers us into the always-dark TV room. She turns on the lights to reveal a ribbed maroon carpet, pale yellow walls and turquoise curtains, pulled closed. There are two yellow-upholstered armchairs and a long, thin walnut-veneer table covered in magazines. All the bright colours in the room are screaming, 'Don't look at death! Look at me!'

I sit down.

Gibbs turned away when I looked at him and tried to say hello a minute ago, but now, when he thinks I'm looking at Waterhouse, he's watching me. I can feel his stare.

'Can I bring anybody a drink?' Fiona asks.

'No, thanks.' I need to know what the hell's going on here. No milky drink is going to delay that by even a second.

There's no protest from Waterhouse or Gibbs. Fiona withdraws, closing the door behind her.

'What the fuck's going on?' I blurt out. 'Fiona said Faith Kendell's not dead – is that true?'

'Faith Kendell's not the person we need to worry about,' says Waterhouse.

'Then who? Tell me.'

'When we came here today, it was Faith we were primarily concerned with – on your tip, because you speculated about Billy maybe thinking the two of you were friends and giving Faith one of his white books for that reason.'

'We asked the ward staff about the book – how it ended up on the board,' Gibbs says.

I'm nodding so hard, it's making my head throb. 'And?'

'It was found in Marion's room. In her bed.'

'In her . . . her bed?' The connection between my brain and my words has stretched too thin. *Every bed is narrow*, I think to myself. *Narrow, narrow, narrow.*

'One of the nurses found it a couple of days before Marion died, tucked underneath the mattress with one corner sticking out,' says Waterhouse.

'And no one thought to tell me or Drew? They find a weird thing like that in a patient's bed and say nothing, just stick it up on the noticeboard?'

'From what I can gather, they were busy, confused . . . they didn't want to add to your or Drew's distress, so they put it up on the board because it looked vaguely as if it might belong there. They had no reason to think it was connected to anything untoward.'

'So the book wasn't meant for Faith,' I say, trying to make my brain work faster. It was . . .' I stand up and try to walk, but there's a wall everywhere I look. 'But that's not right, is it? I mean, Marion's not my best friend. I didn't even like her! And Billy didn't shoot her. She died of cancer.'

'You'll feel better if you sit down and try to stay calm,' Waterhouse tells me.

'No.'

'Yes. Do it.'

I sit.

'Kim. Listen. Marion had terminal cancer. She would have died of it very soon. A day or two later, the doctors think.'

'Would have? She *did* die of it.'

'No, she didn't,' says Waterhouse. 'Kim, I'm sorry to have to tell you this, but it's looking very much as if Marion was murdered.'

Sophie Hannah

11 January 2015

Dear Mrs Halliday

Last time I wrote, I promised I would send you one of
the stories from Lane's collection. Here it is: 'The
Two Sisters'. I've also sent you another novel: Thomas
Hardy's *Jude the Obscure*. Apart from non-natural
death, these latest two offerings do not have a lot in
common. They are, in some ways, diametrical opposites.
You might want to think about that.

Your Secret Detractor

~

The Two Sisters
from *Stories of Enlightenment*

An elderly couple was found murdered at home. They'd been shot
while asleep in bed in the middle of the night. When the police set
about investigating this heinous crime, they found that no one had
entered the house by force, so they spoke to the couple's two daughters, both of whom had keys to the family home.

The elder daughter was a frivolous, party-loving hedonist who spent
all her spare time having fun. She spent her money on luxuries like
fine wine, perfume and beautiful jewelry. The idea of saving for a
rainy day was alien to her.

The younger daughter, by contrast, lived frugally. How, she wondered,
could anyone care about jewelry in a world full of poverty and injustice?
The younger daughter spent all her time fighting for causes she believed
in, she told the police. She battled against those who sought to deprive
the needy; she wrote letters condemning politicians who neglected the
disabled, or demonized immigrants in pursuit of election success. She
lived within her means and never ran up debts of any kind.

'My older sister must have done this,' she told the police. 'She and I are the only ones with keys to the house. She's been spending money on designer handbags recently, and she took out a loan to buy a yacht she couldn't afford. She might be my sister, but she's a totally reprehensible person.'

The police questioned the older daughter, who protested her innocence. Like her sister, she was aware that only the two of them had house keys, and so she said, 'If I didn't do it, she must have, or there must be some other explanation.'

'Like what?' asked the police.

'I don't know!' The older daughter looked bewildered. She was clearly not enjoying being interviewed. 'I don't want to think about it. Can I go now? I'm going to a movie premiere that's bound to be huge fun.'

Neither sister had an alibi for the time of the murders. Their parents' house was searched for fingerprints, and none belonging to any strangers were found. The elderly couple had become very reclusive in their old age and had made a will that divided their estate equally between their two daughters, who both earned good salaries. Despite this, the elder daughter, who loved shopping and partying, was in considerable debt, while the younger sister had accumulated significant savings.

A week after the murders, the police reviewed their notes on the case. They had no leads and could prove nothing. Reluctant to give up, one of the detectives had an idea. 'It's got to be one of the daughters,' he said. 'No one else benefited from these deaths.'

His colleagues agreed the killer was likely to be one of the two daughters.

'I've got an idea, then,' said the detective. 'Let's tell each sister that we have incontrovertible proof that she's the killer. Continue to claim innocence, we'll say, and that will count against you when it comes to sentencing. But admit to your crime and you'll be treated more leniently. We say this to both of them, and see if either one breaks down and tells us the truth.'

One detective objected. 'We should only say all that to the one who killed her parents,' she said. 'Only one of those two sisters could conceivably be guilty of murder.'

Everyone agreed she had a point. 'All the same,' said one officer, 'I'd be happier if we dangled the bait before both sisters. I mean, I agree it's super unlikely that the younger sister suddenly decided to become a murderer—'

The detective who'd intervened held up her hand. 'Did you think I was referring to the older sister when I mentioned the only one who could conceivably be guilty?'

All the detectives in the room nodded.

'Hell, no,' she said. 'The opposite. The elder sister is selfish and hedonistic, but she can't bear to spend a second of her life not having fun. She's almost allergic to the absence of pleasure. Now, you're going to say that she was in debt and needed her inheritance, whereas the younger sister didn't, but the older sister didn't care about debt. I doubt she ever gave a thought to how much she owed. She'll have buried her head in the sand and pretended everything was fine, because she could only bear to exist in a world that contained happy, fun things and no depressing realities.'

'Whereas the younger sister—' one detective began, as light started to dawn.

'Yes. The younger sister worries about money even though she's comfortably off. That's why she saves: too much. A single woman, earning what she earns, with disproportionately large savings – *that's* someone who worries about money.'

'If the older sister went to the chair for murder, wouldn't the younger sister inherit her share of the estate too?' one detective asked.

'Wait,' another officer said. 'Everything about the younger sister's life tells us she's a good person.'

'Stop thinking about good and bad,' said the female detective who strongly suspected the younger sister. 'Take the judgment out of it. Think in terms of happy and unhappy. The older sister likes to surround herself with happy experiences. Now think what we know of the younger sister. She *fights* injustice, *condemns* inequality, *disapproves* of spending money on fun, wants to *destroy* capitalism.

All those things she's putting her energy into are negative actions.'

'But she does it all for noble reasons,' somebody said. 'To make the world a better place.'

'I think she might genuinely believe that but, again, look at the words she chose to describe her activities. She could have said she *helped* the poor and *supported* the disabled. She didn't, because she's full of anger, and therefore much more likely to be the killer.

'The simple truth is this: if we put our energies into anger, fighting, disapproval and condemnation, we're unlikely to end up making the world a better place. The only way we can do that is by contributing our positive energy – our love, kindness and compassion. Many who are full of anger and hate, many who feel the need to be forever at war, attach themselves to undeniably good causes as a sort of disguise. "Look," we say to ourselves. "That person must be doing it right, she's spending all her free time attacking . . . whatever the particular appalling thing might be." But no; if the impulse is an attack impulse, it can only do harm.'

It was decided that only the younger sister should be confronted in the first instance. Within five minutes of being told about the nonexistent proof that she'd murdered her parents, she admitted to the murders. Despite having more than enough money, she was terrified that some worst-case scenario would befall her for which her savings would prove inadequate. She killed her parents for her inheritance, hoping that would lessen her anxiety, and had no qualms about trying to frame her sister, whom she regarded as a decadent waste of space.

The group of detectives who solved the crime worked differently afterwards. As well as thinking about evidence, they tried to be attuned to positive and negative energies in those they interviewed. The result? Unsurprisingly, their solve rate hit a record high and stayed high thereafter.

9

12/1/2015

Natalie. Charlie had a name at last – only a first name, but still, it felt like a big step forward. She celebrated with a sip of ginger beer from the can on her desk. It was warm and flat, leftover from yesterday, but she was in too good a mood to care. Ginger was a taste that nothing could destroy, especially when you'd just found a short, grainy film on the web of Nikhil Gulati giving a best man's speech and, in it, referring to his girlfriend as Natalie.

The film was on the YouTube channel of Philip Sier, the groom. Nikhil's speech had made Charlie laugh twice. It was witty without being attention-seeking; it kept the spotlight firmly on Philip and Emily, whose special day it was. Best of all, it referred to 'my better half, Natalie', who was also present and whose embarrassed face helpfully filled the screen at the exact moment her name was mentioned.

Charlie opened the Liv and Gibbs file on her computer and added the new information – 'Nikhil Gulati's girlfriend's name: Natalie' – to what she already had. She'd found out quite a bit about Nikhil. No criminal convictions, no history with the police – that was the first thing she'd checked. He wasn't on Facebook, but she'd found him on Twitter and LinkedIn. He was Associate Marketing Manager for the R & T McElwee Winery in Linton, Cambridgeshire. Before taking that job in 2011, he'd had a similar role at Gallo wines in Uxbridge. His Twitter feed revealed him to be the doting owner of two pugs – Doug the Pug and Peppa Pug – as well as a member of the Liberal Democrat party and addicted to spicy foods, the hotter the better.

Nikhil had joined Twitter in 2012. There were several references among his tweets to 'Her Outdoors', which had led Charlie to speculate that the girlfriend had a non-office-based career. Her Outdoors wasn't addicted to Twitter as he was, Nikhil told one of his followers on 11 April 2013; she thought he was crazy to waste so much of his time on it. Charlie, by contrast, was glad he had, because it was his Twitter activity that had led her to Philip Sier, Nikhil's best friend since university.

And now, thanks to Sier's YouTube channel, she'd been able to add the name Natalie to her notes. Everything was shaping up nicely.

Charlie felt like doing something to celebrate. She had a sudden urge to be on the move. One minute it presented itself as excitement, the next as anxiety. Everyone was capable of doing something life-ruiningly stupid, but Charlie believed her sister to be more capable of it than most, and they were too close, their lives too intertwined, for Charlie to maintain a safe emotional distance. Not caring – taking no further action – wasn't an option.

The only way to kill the fear was to find out the truth.

Charlie considered watching Nikhil's best man speech again in case she'd missed something: a subtle but vital clue. Unlikely. She'd watched it more than ten times already.

Don't be crazy, Zailer. She had to be at a multi-agency Spotlight on Domestic Violence forum in Combingham in . . . Charlie looked at her watch. *Shit.* Ten minutes ago.

By the time she got to the meeting they'd be forty minutes into it. That was unacceptable. It was better to fake a migraine, better to go somewhere else altogether, where she couldn't be late because she had no appointment and no one was expecting her.

Somewhere like the McElwee winery in Linton, Cambridgeshire, where Nikhil Gulati worked.

~

'I don't know why you're looking so aghast. Hmm. It's interesting.' Sondra Halliday tilted her head to look at Sellers from another angle. Either that or she thought he'd hidden the explanation for his behaviour up his nose. 'Are you really *so* disappointed to find I have an alibi? Four alibis, to be precise.'

The news of Marion Hopwood's murder hadn't yet been made public, so Sellers had only asked to know Halliday's whereabouts on the other four relevant days.

'I wonder which of my attributes has you itching to lock me away forever. I'm sure it can't be because I'm a woman with a strong opinion that differs from yours, so I'd love to hear what it is.'

They were at the Langham Hotel again, sharing a pot of English Breakfast tea this time; no frog-bollock dim sum in sight. On the phone, Halliday had said something about needing a long spoon before she could eat in Sellers' presence again. He'd had to look it up.

'I'm not disappointed, but I think I must have misheard you,' he said. 'Would you mind repeating what you've told me?'

'My alibis? Which one?'

'All of them.' If he narrowed it down for her, she'd be better able to second-guess him. She had to be lying . . . but then, why offer a false alibi that was so improbable? And for Josh Norbury's murder, too: the one man, the one victim of Billy Dead Mates that she preferred to ignore.

It probably meant nothing.

'You seriously want me to repeat where I was on four separate occasions?'

'Sorry. I wouldn't ask if it wasn't important.'

'Oh, to be able to say "important" as if there's no subjectivity involved!' Halliday sighed. 'Okay: Linzi Birrell: I was in the *Lifeworld* office all day. Rhian Douglas: I was on a train in the morning, to Gobowen – nearest station to Oswestry, where I spent the afternoon interviewing a woman who'd exited the sex trade after many years being prostituted and exploited. Angela McCabe: I was in Oxford at a Focus On Femicide conference all day. Joshua Norbury: I was at home in the morning writing a piece for *Lifeworld*, then in the afternoon I went to Hertford to collect a painting: my mother-in-law's Christmas present. Satisfied?'

'First time round, you said more about the Christmas present.'

'No, I didn't. I said, "my mother-in-law's Christmas present" and I moaned about having to sacrifice an afternoon to pick it up. It was a painting of a boy and a cat and it was shit. Joan had seen it in an exhibition at a place called Gravelly Barn—' Halliday broke off. 'Do you want to know any of this?'

'Not really. I'd like to know why you sacrificed your after-noon, though. Since it was a present for your husband's mother, why didn't he go and get it?'

Halliday snorted. 'Who buys your mother's Christmas presents? And birthday, and Mother's Day – you or your wife?'

'My wife. But she's not a radical feminist.'

'Really, Conkers? I'm astonished to hear that.'

'You *are* a feminist. An obsessive one. Which is why, for Josh Norbury, I don't believe your alibi. No way you'd do that: go and collect a picture for a man's mother when he could do it himself. You wouldn't be married to the kind of bloke who'd ask you to.'

'Oh, God, you're serious, aren't you?' Halliday groaned softly into her tea. 'I'm a feminist, yes. That doesn't mean every single action I perform is a feminist action.'

'Do as I say, not as I do? Doesn't that make you a hypocrite?'

'Wow! I think you might be right! Am I doing feminism all wrong, do you think? Please, advise me and let me learn from you, a misogynist shitbag.'

'That one struck home, didn't it?' Sellers chuckled. 'What's the point in calling homicide "femicide" when you run errands for your husband like a skivvy? Shouldn't you try to practise what you preach? Especially when it's so easy. If you'd told him to sort out his mum's present himself, he'd have done it, wouldn't he?'

Halliday stared at him as if she wanted him dead.

'Maybe you're too scared to rock the boat at home, and all

that fighting talk in *Lifeworld*'s just a way to vent your frustration. It must be easier to assert yourself in print than in real life.'

'You think my fear that I'll disappoint my husband if I don't serve him like a good wife invalidates my feminism? Where do you think that fear comes from? How do you think it worms its way inside all women, even the ones like me who know it's poison?'

Too many words fired at him too quickly; it took Sellers a while to untangle them. Once he had, he said, 'Yeah, but a principled feminist would . . . you know, feel the fear and do it anyway, wouldn't she?'

Halliday stood up. 'I'm going. You're an ignorant twat who thinks "femicide" means "feminist-language-for-homicide". It means *the murder of women by men,* you prick. It means Linzi Birrell, Rhian Douglas, Angela McCabe. Guess how many more names we've added to the list since those three? Go on, guess.'

'Hang on: you've put Linzi, Rhian and Angela on which list?' Sellers asked.

'UK victims of femicide.'

'But if that means killed by a man—'

'If you're about to tell me Billy might be a woman, don't bother. He *isn't*. Every woman in the country with a best friend, scared to set foot outside in case she's next, knows Billy's a man. You only don't know because *you're* a man – you have the luxury of being not afraid.'

'So you were scared to come here today, were you? Because here you are – in the five-star surroundings of the Langham Hotel. And you look as if you're about to head out onto those mean streets again, so . . .'

Halliday was gone: marching away at speed, her bag flying out behind her. Today's slogan was, 'If I had a hammer, I'd smash the patriarchy.'

Sellers left a twenty-pound note on a saucer, grabbed his jacket and ran to catch her up.

'Are you *following* me?'

'Yeah. What about Josh Norbury?'

'What about him?'

'Did you add his name to your list of femicide victims?'

'No. He was a man. Once again: femicide is the murder of women by men.'

'If you can include three women who might not have been murdered by a man, surely you can stretch the definition even further to include a male victim.' Sellers didn't know why he was provoking her. He knew she wasn't Billy; she couldn't be. The mother-in-law's present thing hadn't been a lie; Halliday's anger when he'd called her a hypocrite had been too real.

'Fuck off, Conkers. Leave me alone, or I'll cancel my appointment with your lackey who's been chasing me for a DNA sample.'

'You didn't give me what I came for: Billy's latest letter and book, the story about the two sisters . . .'

'Oh, yeah.' Halliday unzipped her bag and pulled out another plain black one. She handed it to Sellers. 'The Two fucking Sisters. Of course, the one who fights for good causes and isn't totally frivolous turns out to be the killer. Men have to demonise women who attempt any kind of serious work. And you honestly think Billy might not be a man?' She walked away, laughing.

Silently, Sellers made a vow: he would solve the murder of Joshua Norbury if it was the last thing he did on this earth. He knew it was wrong of him to care more about Norbury than about Billy's other victims simply because of his sex, but, thanks to Sondra Halliday, he did.

He pulled his phone out of his pocket and scrolled down the contacts list until he got to Lisa Norbury, Josh's sister. No, he wasn't going to check in with Waterhouse or anyone else first. For once, he was going to follow his own instincts.

~

Arriving at the McElwee Winery's large, half-empty car park on a sprawling, grey industrial estate, Charlie was disproportionately delighted to spot Nikhil Gulati's car straight away. *There it is!* she thought. *Everything's coming together!*

The comedown was fast. Of course his car was here. He worked here and it was a weekday. This couldn't be notched up as a new gain. Still, Gulati might easily have been abroad on a business trip or at a meeting out of the office, so Charlie allowed herself to count the presence of his Skoda as a good omen. It made speaking to him a possibility, assuming that was what she decided to do.

She'd spent most of the drive from Spilling to Linton trying to manufacture a reason for needing to interview Nikhil Gulati that had nothing to do with her sister. She'd considered asking him about his relationship with Philip Sier, and a few questions about Sier and his wife Emily.

Charlie had her police ID with her, though she'd nipped home to change out of her uniform, so she could compel Nikhil to talk if she chose to. He was unlikely to refuse on account of her not being with Cambridgeshire Police, though he might want to ring Spilling nick before agreeing to be questioned.

Even if he didn't, it was a risky approach to take: if word got back to Culver Valley Police that Charlie had used her police status in the service of a personal obsession, she'd lose her job. Also, it would be massively unfair to Nikhil Gulati and Philip Sier, who might both suffer unnecessary anxiety as a result.

No, she couldn't do it. Out of the question. Pity, though; it would have been the easiest thing in the world to say, at some point in the conversation, 'I'll spell my surname for you, since you'll never have come across it before: Z-A-I-L-E-R.' Surely Nikhil would then mention Liv, giving Charlie the opportunity to say, 'But that's extraordinary! She's my sister.'

To which Nikhil would say . . . what? 'Oh, really? My girlfriend Natalie and I have regular kinky orgies with Liv and her boyfriend Chris. Isn't it a small world?'

It wasn't sexual, Charlie was certain of that. She and her

sister were different in many ways, but one thing they shared absolutely was a conviction that sex ought to mean two people in a room together and no more. They'd discussed it often over the years.

Whatever was going on between Liv and Gibbs and Nikhil and Natalie, it was something more . . . administrative than passionate. What Charlie had seen through the pub window the day she'd followed Liv to Cambridge was something being arranged, or an important issue under discussion. It was driving Charlie crazy that she couldn't burst into the McElwee Winery and demand to know which, and what.

She opened her car door and smoked two cigarettes in quick succession reconsidering and rejecting the official police visit option three or four more times. It was infuriating that she could never risk her job because Simon was forever risking his – though he wouldn't be fired now unless he burned down the nick or strangled a suspect. Proust, Superintendent Barrow, all the higher-ups – they knew they couldn't afford to lose him. All of them would die rather than use the word genius, but they knew he was. Apart from in the pages of fiction, there was no detective in the country – perhaps in the world – as inspired or talented as Simon, no one else who could provide the kind of answers he came up with against the odds.

Charlie had to keep reminding herself that she, on the other hand, wasn't special. It was a mistake to think that being Simon's wife afforded her a certain amount of protection. She should have been doing the job she was paid to do today, not skiving off to solve her own pet mystery.

If only she could bring herself to confront Liv. That would be much easier to do now she had names to use. 'I know about Nikhil and Natalie,' she could say coldly. Or angrily, impatiently, with tears in her eyes – that might work better. 'I know what's going on, Liv. You should have told me the truth.'

Except Charlie didn't want to find out that way. Her sister

had chosen to deceive and manipulate her, and now she wanted to find out in spite of Liv, not with her help – not even by tricking a confession out of her.

Charlie tensed as she saw a door open: a McElwee Winery door. Two men in suits walked out of the building. One of them was Nikhil Gulati. Without stopping to think, Charlie got out of her car. 'Hey!' she shouted, walking briskly towards him. 'Wait!'

The two men heard her and stopped.

Running over to them with the wind blowing her hair across her face, she said, 'Am I in the right place for Missingham's, the printers?' It was the only name-business combination she remembered from the twelve or so signs at the entrance to the industrial estate.

She nodded and made grateful noises as Nikhil Gulati's balding, bearded colleague directed her back the way she'd come. Then she turned to Nikhil and said, 'This is going to sound weird, but . . . I swear I've seen you before. Recently, too.' She pretended to make an effort to summon the memory. 'Oh, I know! You weren't by any chance in the Punter pub in Cambridge last week, were you? During the day?'

'The pub, during the day?' Nikhil's colleague tutted and laughed. 'Naughty, naughty.'

Nikhil looked surprised. 'Yes. Yes, I was.'

'I was too!' Charlie smiled. 'Wow – what a coincidence.'

'You must have an exceptional memory,' said Nikhil.

'I do. Everyone's always saying that. See something once, I remember it forever. Actually, I remembered you especially because you were with two women, weren't you?'

'Two women!' Beardy pounced on the cue Charlie had offered him. 'Have you been up to no good, Nik?'

'Oh, no, it was nothing like that,' Charlie said. 'They were having what looked like a very complicated discussion, but all above board, I'd say.' She followed up with a giggle.

Nikhil smiled politely but unenthusiastically. 'We need to

make a move, so – you know where you're going now, for Missingham's?'

'Yes. Yes, thanks, both of you. Sorry for accosting you.'

Charlie returned to her car feeling riled and embarrassed. Had she made it too obvious that she was up to something?

All the way home, she replayed the scene in her mind to try and work out if Nikhil had reacted like a man with something to hide, or like a person who, quite understandably, saw no reason to account for his behaviour to a complete stranger.

By the time she arrived in Spilling two hours later, she still wasn't sure.

IO

from Origami *by Kim Tribbeck*

Monday, 12 January 2015

'Murdered? My grandmother?' I laugh and can't stop. In my head, my giggles look like barbed wire. 'Don't be silly. People don't murder terminal cancer patients. I mean, what the fuck's the point of that? Murdered how?'

'We believe something, perhaps a poison, was injected,' says Gibbs. 'We'll know more soon.'

Thank God Drew's not here. Thank God.

'Why? Why would a shooter of best friends kill a dying old woman with no friends? Why? There's no reason. It wouldn't happen. I don't believe you.'

Fiona believes it. That's why she was crying.

Waterhouse pulls a notebook and pen out of his jacket pocket. 'I need to ask you some questions.'

'I suppose, on the upside, it's one in the eye for cancer,' I say. 'Right? Poisonous substance one, cancer nil on this occasion. Ha!'

'Before you arrived, we spoke to Marion's oncologist,' Gibbs says. 'He explained how Marion would have died, if her disease had taken its natural course. She'd have slept more and more, with her breathing becoming increasingly shallow until she stopped waking up, stopped breathing altogether. But the nurses report her having a substantial wakeful interval shortly before she died.'

'That's true.'

'They were all surprised she went so fast, but they didn't question it because . . . well, she was dying. They expected her to die, and she did. Until we asked if there was any chance she could have been killed by something or someone other than her illness, no one thought of it.'

'They weren't suspicious when they found a creepy book in her deathbed, with the words "Death devours all lovely things" inside it?'

'No.' The way Waterhouse says it makes me suspect he asked somebody the same question in the same incredulous tone. 'People behave strangely when their loved ones are dying. The nurse who found it assumed that either you or your brother left the book there, or else it was a sort of . . . present, tribute, whatever, from someone else. A token. Normally she'd have passed it on to the relatives but she was afraid you'd find it upsetting so she pinned it on the noticeboard instead. Kim, I want you to think hard: while you and your brother were here, in the last few days before Marion died, did you see anyone go into her room who wasn't a member of hospital staff, or who might not have been?'

'No. That doesn't mean they didn't. They could have, easily.'

'The nurses told us that either you or Drew was with Marion the whole time.'

'Drew was with her, sitting next to her bed, nearly the whole time – apart from when he nipped to the loo or down to the food court to get food and coffee. And once or twice he fell asleep in the chair next to Marion's bed, he told me. I've no idea how long for. And obviously at night he slept on the camp bed the nurses put in the room for him. I suppose someone could have gone in while he was asleep.'

'What about you?' Waterhouse asks. 'While Drew was taking a bathroom break or eating, weren't you here?'

'I was here in the ward, but not in the room with Marion. The day she died and the day before – Monday and Tuesday – I didn't go into her room at all.'

'Why not?'

'I didn't want to. I spent Saturday and Sunday in there, after which I decided I didn't enjoy being in a room with a dying person. It's a more unpleasant experience than you'd think, believe me.'

'So where were you Monday and Tuesday?'

'Sitting in the corridor.'

'Where exactly, in relation to Marion's room?' asks Waterhouse.

'About three feet to the right of the door.'

'That's easily close enough to see who goes in and out.'

'It is if I'm looking. Mainly, I wasn't. I was fiddling with my phone a lot of the time – Googling what happens if you swallow a ringpull.'

'A ringpull?' Waterhouse glances at Gibbs. 'From a can?'

'Yeah. I'd accidentally washed one down with Fruit Rush and I was trying to find out if I could risk doing nothing about it. I was also answering emails, reading Twitter – anything I could to distract me from Marion dying. I was aware of nurses going in and out of her room all the time; after a while I stopped paying attention. It annoyed me too much. They'd refused to catheterise her in case it gave her a bladder infection – obviously those are hugely annoying to dead people – and they refused to put an end to her misery, so I tuned out and focused on my little screen.'

'Could someone who wasn't wearing hospital clothing have gone in without you noticing?'

'Seventeen people wearing "I'm a serial murderer" leotards could have gone in and I'd have been none the wiser. This is what I'm trying to tell you.'

Waterhouse sighs.

'What about the ward itself?' asks Gibbs. 'Surely those seventeen people wouldn't have been buzzed in.'

'Don't count on it,' I tell him. 'When I went back to the ward to get Billy's white book, they buzzed me in without seeing my face or hearing my voice.'

'Great.' Waterhouse sounds despondent. 'Well, you're now one of a clear third pair. Not a pair of best friends, but a pair. Relatives this time.'

'I didn't even like Marion,' I tell him. 'And she went one better: she formally expelled me from her family – bullied my mother into giving me up for adoption. It's almost as if we knew a serial killer would one day decide to kill pairs of people who had a close bond, and set about trying to get ourselves off the hook!' I giggle. 'Sorry. Making jokes is what I do – whatever the occasion.'

'A pair of relatives, not best friends, with no close bond,' Waterhouse murmurs, looking down at his feet. 'And the M.O.'s not Billy's usual, either: poison instead of a gun. But the white books and the poem quotes in Marion's and yours being from the same poem make it undeniable. This is Billy's handiwork.'

'Well, unless there are two of them,' I suggest.

Waterhouse's head jerks up as if someone's yanked it with a rope. 'Why d'you say that?'

'I don't know.' I shrug. 'Kind of neat, I suppose: a pair killing pairs. Maybe one's targeting best friends and the other's going for grandmothers and granddaughters.' I mustn't laugh at this. Really, really mustn't. I'll treat myself to a new car if I can hold out.

Thankfully, my hysteria subsides.

'What put that into your head?' Waterhouse demands. He's almost shouting.

I sigh. There is no levity in this man. 'Nothing,' I say. 'Ignore me. I was being silly. I've watched too many TV shows.'

He turns to Gibbs and says, 'The interval between the planting of the book and the kill is shorter than it's ever been: less than a week. That makes Kim, among the six recipients of white books, a real anomaly. Why's she still alive?'

Charming.

'We need to talk to her brother,' says Gibbs.

I'm sure he doesn't mean to imply that my ongoing existence is Drew's fault. It only sounds that way.

~

I hated you then, Billy. The power of my loathing for you shocked me. I felt as if you were deliberately trying to take the story of me and my family – a story that mattered to me, perhaps too much – and turn it into a small, insignificant part of your bigger, more newsworthy drama. Marion and I had nothing to do with Linzi Birrell, Rhian Douglas, Angela McCabe and Josh Norbury. Yet suddenly we were all thrown together and defined solely by our relationship to you – your victims and prospective victims. Our fate seemed to have nothing to do with who we were or what we'd done.

How could someone plan to kill Marion *and* me? How could you, Billy, fail to see that I'd defined myself all my life as 'Not Marion; against everything she stands for' – so that if you wanted to murder her, I ought to have been the very last person on your list? How dare anyone kill Marion for any reason apart from as revenge for what she'd done to me?

Illogical and incoherent, I know; I'm simply trying to describe the chaos that was raging in my mind as I sat and listened to DCs Waterhouse and Gibbs talk about how they needed to speak to Drew, because I was such a disappointing, unreliable witness.

No, I'm not, I protested silently. I know so much more than my brother does about death. I'm the one who can be objective about it. Drew was thinking of his own loss while Marion was dying. I didn't feel I stood to lose in the same way, so I thought about her deprivation, and how everything she had – her breath, her thoughts, her memories – was about to be wiped out forever.

If I could have saved her life, I'd have done it in a heartbeat. I viewed her death as the most horrifying tragedy: not because it was Marion, but because it was *death*. Drew was too busy crying over his grandmother to notice the encroaching epidemic that was – is – coming for all of us. That's why he could stay in the room and I had to get the hell out.

What I didn't realise was that Death had a human representative on Ward 10 that day: you, Billy.

I don't hate you any more, not now that I understand why you did what you did. The five murders you committed were horrifying and unjustifiable, but once I knew your reason – the bizarre, meticulous logic of it – the personal antipathy I felt fell away. Yours was a mindset that only intense suffering could have produced. That's why I can't condemn you as evil through and through. I think you honestly believed you could redeem your own suffering by creating its equal and opposite. And while you planned and carried out your crimes, you were temporarily anaesthetised: focusing on creating pain for others prevented you from experiencing your own agony.

I understand all that because I, too, go to great lengths to avoid feeling the pain that's lying in wait for me.

Would I ever commit murder? I doubt it. But I understand why you did. In order to make sense of your thought process and how you must have felt, I've had to build a model of your mind inside my own. I've forced myself to inhabit that model and, when I do, everything you've done makes perfect sense.

I'm writing this book because I want it to make sense to other people, too; not only to you, me and Simon Waterhouse. Also because it seemed the obvious thing to do. There has to be a book about you, Billy. How can there not be?

11

13/1/2015

Sam Kombothekra was finding it hard to concentrate on the questions he wanted to ask Kim Tribbeck's husband. Gabriel Kearns's rented one-bedroom flat in the Kornbluth Tower in Rawndesley was unlike any living space Sam had seen before. Every object his eye landed on looked either rare and beautiful or intimidatingly expensive – a glossy orange curve-edged coffee machine; a leather jacket with a phoenix emblem on the back; original oil paintings, mostly fruit-in-bowl still lifes – but everything was in the wrong place. The leather jacket was slung across the kitchen sink; the twelve or so paintings were laid out like floor tiles on one side of the living room; the coffee machine was in the corner of the bathroom, balanced on a blue-painted wooden crate that was playing the role of a table. Also on the crate was a yellow pottery mug with a pair of Calvin Klein boxer shorts stuffed into it.

On a black-and-white-striped rug in the living room was something Sam at first mistook for an ornate oriental teapot: a brown glass thing with two waists, three curved bobbly bits, and a silver spout-type thing protruding from its side. It looked like the kind of contraption from which a genie might emerge to grant you three wishes. Seconds later, Sam recognised it for what it was: a more elaborate than usual drug-taking device. A bong, he supposed you'd have to call it, though no other bong he'd seen looked so much like a work of irreplaceable art. The glass was subtly patterned; you had to look closely to see the tiny leaves, birds and flowers. It was a beautiful object. Shame about its function. As the father of two boys,

Sam sometimes felt as if he spent all his spare time telling his sons how important it was that they never touch drugs. Would they listen? Probably not.

Gabriel Kearns's flat, unlike the homes of most bong owners, did not reek of cannabis. It smelled faintly of spices – nutmeg and cinnamon. The scent had to be artificial, but Sam could see no oil burner or air freshener.

Kearns reappeared in a new outfit: red jogging bottoms and a white zip-up sports top with a logo on it that Sam didn't recognise. Eye-wateringly expensive, no doubt. Sam tried not to disapprove of the bare feet. When he'd let Sam into his flat, Kearns had been wearing brown jeans, a striped shirt and brown suede shoes. He'd vanished into his bedroom almost immediately, calling out, 'Won't be long!' Evidently he thought sportswear was more suitable for a police interview.

'Right, then.' Kearns arranged himself in a cross-legged position on his lounge floor. 'I hope you got yourself a drink while I was in the shower. You and I have serious business to do today.'

'What do you mean?' Could he be talking about providing details of his whereabouts on the dates of Billy's murders? That, as Sam had explained on the phone, was the purpose of this meeting.

'What do you think I mean?' Kearns laughed. 'I'm not letting this fucker Billy Dead Mates make a dog's breakfast of my love life. The intel I've had so far suggests he might want to kill my wife. If she's dead she can't take me back, whereas if she lives I'm going to make sure she does, you see. So how are we going to stop him from killing her and instead usher him into a claustrophobic jail cell? Note: I say "we", not "you". I'm at your disposal, Sergeant.'

'Um . . .'

Sam was still formulating his reply to the surprising onslaught when Kearns launched a new verbal assault. 'Of course, Kim's in danger twice over, as I see it. Not only from Billy, but also from you guys.'

'I'm not sure what you mean,' Sam said truthfully.

'One of the murder victims was Malevolent Marion. I know it's not public knowledge yet. Kim told me. See, I'm still the one she turns to in times of trouble. She won't be willing to pretend she didn't have a low opinion of the old bag, so you're bound to suspect her.'

'Suspect Kim? Of killing Marion?' Sam wanted to be sure.

'Yes.'

'Why would she want to kill the others, though – Billy's first four victims?'

'She wouldn't. Kim would never kill anyone. I would, without hesitation. Don't worry, I'm not Billy. I have alibis for every one of the five: full house.' Kearns beamed at Sam. 'I was at work while Billy was doing his stuff – my colleagues at De Bonis will vouch.'

Sam believed him, and half wished he didn't. There was something of the pantomime villain about Gabriel Kearns; he was a man one might enjoy hating.

'I've never bought into any of that self-serving sanctity-of-human-life claptrap that people like to put about,' Kearns said. 'Have you?'

'I have, yes.'

'Oh. Well, I suppose you'd have to, to do your job. Back to Kim . . . I hope you heard my point: killing's not in her repertoire and never could be. She's too contrary.'

'What do you mean?'

'She's a warrior and a contrarian. Her need to quibble and find fault is so strong, she'll do it with herself if there's no one else around. If she were seriously considering killing Marion, she'd immediately start arguing with herself: "Who are you to decide if someone lives or dies?", "What if you're the troublemaker and Marion's lovely and harmless?" Kim's said that to me more than once. It's what her repulsive brother thinks, what Marion herself thought, and her husband Trevor before he carked it. That's the Hopwood family folklore: Kim's the stain on their otherwise perfect family. She's never done them any harm apart from try to talk about the whole them-abandoning-her thing in an honest way, but they didn't appreciate her being around to remind them of their own shoddy behaviour.

'Anyway . . .' Kearns uncrossed his legs and recrossed them with the left one on top this time. 'Kim knows the score, but it's hard to shake off the fear that the official family lie might be true. Ultimately, she wouldn't feel confident enough in her membership of the Hopwood family to kill a Hopwood.'

Sam wasn't sure he followed the logic of this. Kearns had presented it as if it were a self-evident truth and beyond question.

'I like you, Sergeant. I trust you. You want Billy behind bars, I want my wife back. Let's work together on it. I've already been to the police station to provide a DNA sample as requested, and I know you're working hard at your end too. Give me a call when you're ready to set up another meet. In the meantime, I'm counting on you to keep Kim alive and out of prison.'

A meet, without the 'ing' on the end? Was this what the cool young people were saying these days? The cool slightly older people too, by the sound of it. Gabriel Kearns looked around Sam's age.

'It's good to hear you have confidence in the . . . um . . . investigation, Mr Kearns. I'll be in touch if there's anything else I need.'

Asserting himself was Sam's least favourite activity, but being addressed as if he were Kearns's right-hand man, receiving his patronising if favourable appraisal, made Sam wonder if there were any circumstances in which he might lose his temper. He was forty-seven years old and so far in his life he never had, not fully. When he saw it happen to people around him, he felt sorry for them and thought a version of 'How awful to suffer from a condition like that', as if he'd witnessed an epileptic fit.

On the threshold of his flat, Kearns's parting words were, 'You keep Kim in one piece, man. I need her.' Unbelievable.

As if anyone he didn't require for wife duty could be killed all over the place and it wouldn't matter at all.

Kearns slapped Sam hard on the back before slamming the door in his face.

What an absolute, premier league, gold-plated . . .

What a selfish man. That, Sam decided, was a reasonable conclusion.

~

The ticket machine at Silsford Marketplace car park was broken. Sellers went back to his car and fumbled in the glove compartment for the crumpled half-sheet of A4 on which, years ago, he'd written 'Ticket machine broken – couldn't pay and display, sorry!' for occasions such as this one. Each time it proved necessary to communicate this message, he congratulated himself on taking good – well, good-ish – care of his home-made notice.

He'd identified within himself two prejudices against Liam and Isobel Sturridge, whom he'd not yet met but was on his way to interview. One, funnily enough, was parking-related. Their house was on Castle Terrace, the narrow and so-steep-it-was-almost-vertical approach to Silsford's ancient castle that loomed over the town. Sellers was more favourably disposed towards those who lived in houses that enabled him to park in their driveways or immediately outside their front doors. Failing that, he was willing to undertake a short, level stroll from his car to his destination, but the Sturridges' house was a worst-case scenario: an upward slog that would have him sweating rivers within seconds. He'd said as much to Gibbs before setting off from the nick, only to be told that it was his own fault for being a fat bastard. Sellers had wanted to point out that he'd lost nearly a stone already, but, frustratingly, that line of defence was no longer open to him at work; Charlie Zailer had told everyone that Sellers had joined Weight Watchers for the deep cleavages and nothing else, and now he couldn't mention his new eating regime or his weight loss at the nick without everyone shouting 'Cleavage!' and laughing.

Even if he'd lost the full four stone his group leader, Maeve, said he needed to lose, he'd still be in trouble here; you'd have to be a trained athlete to take this ascent in your stride. There were damp patches on his shirt already and he was only a third of the way up. He crossed the bridge over the River Culver, wondering how much of this stretch of it was made up of the sweat and tears of bastards fat and thin, and perhaps the occasional non-bastard too. Liam and Isobel Sturridge must have strong leg muscles, he thought.

His other prejudice against them, sight unseen, was the brother and sister sharing a house thing: too weird. Sellers didn't care how well they got on – it wasn't right, grown-up siblings living together. It suggested they'd failed to build any new relationships away from the family nest. The desire to strike out on your own was natural, wasn't it? Sellers had once stayed a week with his brother and sister-in-law after Stacey had kicked him out for pissing into her wardrobe while drunk, when he'd risen from bed in the middle of the night and walked purposefully towards it, firmly believing it to be the loo. If only he'd aimed into his own wardrobe instead of hers, he might have avoided banishment. As it was, he'd ended up at Jeanette and Ed's house and spent a crazy-making seven days observing their schizophrenic approach to child-rearing at close range. Sellers' nephew Finn was a fledgling tyrant, endlessly appeased by his mother and periodically terrorised by his father. In the hushed, quaking voice of a supplicant, Jeanette would offer eight-year-old Finn every conceivable bribe – ice cream; extra pocket money; extra gems in Clash of Clans, his favourite game – if he'd only be good enough to consider stopping wailing and kicking, please? After several hours of this, when he'd decided the wailing had gone on for too long, Ed, having so far ignored the unfolding drama as if it wasn't happening, would leap to his feet with a snarled 'Right, that's it!' and Take Finn Into The Utility Room.

Sellers had never managed to work out what happened in

the utility room. Whatever it was, no sound could be overheard by someone listening at the door. Sellers had enjoyed trying to guess: mouthed threats of limb amputation and disinheritance followed by the bloody murder of the pet rabbits in the garden? Whatever Ed did, it worked. Finn would emerge from the utility room ten minutes later with a mechanical happy-and-good-child grin on his face, and for at least two hours he would sit quietly in a chair asking for nothing. The whole performance was exhausting to watch, and Sellers had resolved never to stay with his brother again.

At last, he'd reached the Sturridges' house, a large four-storey townhouse that could have been stunning but was letting itself down badly with stone windowsills that had almost crumbled away and hardly any black paint left on the railings.

There was no doorbell, only a heavy iron knocker that made Sellers wonder if, in addition to learning new eating habits, he ought to work on his upper-body strength.

A man – presumably Liam Sturridge – opened the door and said tonelessly, 'You're late.' He stood back to let Sellers in. He was tall, with coppery blond hair cut very short, and had the build of an athlete – thanks to the steep approach to his home, no doubt. He was wearing a white shirt with jeans, black socks on his feet.

Sellers apologised for his lateness, then blamed it on the hill and the broken ticket machine in the car park. Sturridge gave him a look that said, 'You should have taken potential late-making obstacles into account and allowed enough time.' It was one of Sellers' wife Stacey's favourite looks, but she was an amateur compared to this guy. Sturridge's large, slightly bulging eyes were ideal for staring disapprovingly. Even their colour worked: unusually dark blue; as if they'd started out ordinary blue, then been discoloured by the murkiness of the person in front of them.

Sellers introduced himself, producing his ID, which Sturridge made a point of not looking at.

'I know who you are,' was the response. The face had yet to crack a smile.

'And I'm assuming you're Liam Sturridge, joint owner of this house?'

'Why else would I be here?'

'I need to check. Sorry. This'll be easier if you drop the hostility, mate, okay? I've just got a few questions and then I'll be off. You're not under suspicion of anything.' Cheery banter had always been Sellers' preferred manner for interviews, as it was for most things in life.

A surprised expression appeared on Sturridge's face. It was . . . extreme was the only way Sellers could think to describe it. As if nothing at all made sense any more. 'I'm not being hostile,' he said. 'Why do you say that? I've said nothing out of the ordinary.'

Sellers thought back over their conversation so far and decided Sturridge was right. He'd said very little, so there wasn't much to go on. He had an unusual manner but perhaps he wasn't antagonistic. Maybe he was just a bit weird. Lots of people were.

Sturridge didn't look like someone about to offer refreshments, so Sellers asked if he could use the bathroom, and drank from the cold tap until he was no longer thirsty. He raised each arm in turn to examine the sweat stains on his shirt in the mirror. Could be worse, he decided; it shouldn't be noticeable if he kept his arms at his sides.

Sturridge led him through the kitchen to a long, rectangular conservatory – or maybe garden room was a better name for it, because this wasn't the usual white plastic crap that most people on Sellers' street had stuck onto the backs of their houses. There were two disintegrating wicker chairs in the furthest two corners, and apart from that nothing but size-matched piles of books, stacked neatly in rows. Something about their orderly presentation suggested they were waiting to be taken somewhere for an official purpose, rather than a random scattering of personal possessions.

'Ran out of room in the house?' Sellers asked.

'What? Oh, the books. Isobel refuses to throw anything away.'

'Is she around? I'd like to speak to her too if I can.'

'I don't know. I suppose she's somewhere.'

Sellers revised his diagnosis from just a bit weird to quite a lot weird. It was like talking to a machine that had been programmed to look and speak like a human. For the first time since Billy had started killing, Sellers found himself thinking, 'Yes, this is a man I can see murdering again and again.' Which, he knew from past experience, didn't mean Liam Sturridge was a murderer.

'That is one dramatic view.' It wasn't something Sellers could remember having said before, but he couldn't help being impressed by the edge-of-the-world visual plunge through sharply descending woodland to the river and the fields and hills beyond.

'I never look at it.' Sturridge sat on the edge of a wicker chair. Either he liked being uncomfortable or he didn't expect to be there long. 'So: what do you want to ask me? I've checked at work: four of the dates you asked about – September, November, December and January – I was there all those days. If you need confirmation from them, I can give you a name and number. I wasn't working on the October date. I was off sick, so I'd have been here.'

'Where's work?'

'Harbinson Mortlock Ltd. I work on the patenting side.'

'Thanks.' Sellers made a note.

'Do you have any other questions?'

Was he serious? They'd only just got started.

'Yes. Quite a few. You were involved in a relationship with Kim Tribbeck until recently, correct?'

'Yes. I wouldn't have bothered if I'd known she was going to bring the police to my door.'

'Mr Sturridge, we need you to think hard about whether you might know something that can help us. Kim believes, as do we, that she might be in danger from Billy Dead Mates. We—'

'Why do you call him that? It sounds infantile.'

'We thought he was targeting pairs of best friends. At first. Until Kim's grandmother, Marion, was murdered.'

Sturridge shrugged. He said, 'I don't want Kim to be harmed, but whatever happens to her, it's nothing to do with me. I'd rather not be involved.'

Charming. What had a talented, successful woman like Kim Tribbeck seen in this man?

'Kim's told us she ended the affair between the two of you. Is that true?'

'Yes. It was hardly an affair.'

'What was it, then?'

'I don't know.'

'Was it a sexual relationship?'

'Yes.'

'And it lasted two years?'

'I suppose so. I didn't keep track of its duration.'

This man was unbelievable. Sellers was sorry to be interviewing him alone. He'd never be able to convey the full oddness of the demeanour that at one moment seemed blatantly disdainful and the next merely robotic.

'Were you upset when Kim ended it? Angry?'

'Neither. It was a relief.'

'Why?'

'It made life easier, I suppose.'

'Were you also thinking of calling it a day?'

'No.'

Give me strength.

'How did your sister feel about your relationship with Kim?'

'I don't know. Ask her.'

'She knew about it, then?' Many men conducting affairs with married women would make an effort to keep it to themselves. The rule was well known: if you don't want to get caught, don't confide in anyone. Sellers pushed the thought away; his own discretion record was pitiful. All his colleagues and friends knew he regularly cheated on his wife. The situation was far from ideal.

'Isobel didn't know for a long time,' said Sturridge. 'I didn't tell her.'

'So how did she find out?'

'Why don't you ask her that question?'

'I'd like to. Do you know where she is? Do you know if she's at home?'

Sturridge shook his head.

'Do you think she worried you and Kim might want to make a go of it full time and she'd be left on her own?'

'No. Isobel's already on her own, in the relationship sense. I'm her brother, not her husband or boyfriend.'

'Yes, but the two of you live together.'

'We share a house. That's it.'

'So Isobel might have feared you leaving the house to move in with Kim.'

'Why would she?'

'Because then she'd be left living alone.' *Isn't it obvious, you stupid twat?*

'I don't know,' Sturridge said after some consideration. 'Seems stupid to me. What's wrong with living alone?' He might more aptly have asked, 'But is living with me any different from living alone, when a fridge magnet would probably be capable of providing more entertainment and companionship?'

'Did Kim ever mention to you that she'd been given a small white book by a man she didn't know?'

'No.'

'Oh, hello!' A female voice injected a welcome burst of energy into the room. Sellers turned in his chair and saw a small, thin woman with unusually short brown hair in a strange, tendrils-blown-forward-onto-her-face kind of style, as if she'd stood with her back to a strong wind. She was wearing a knee-length navy-and-pink-striped cotton dress with a pale pink wool cardigan over it, and white sandals with gold buckles. 'Are you

DC Sellers? I'm Isobel Sturridge. Liam, why didn't you tell me he was here?'

'You didn't ask me to.' To Sellers, Sturridge said, 'Are you finished with me?' He stood up.

'I think so, but if you could wait and not go out? Just in case I think of anything else.'

'I'm not going out, so I don't need to wait. I can get on with my day, as I would if you'd left or never arrived.'

'You're not going to work?'

'No. Day off.' With that, Sturridge left the room.

'Your brother's . . . a character.' Sellers smiled at Isobel.

Instantly her smile vanished. She bit her lower lip. 'Do you think?'

No. I think he's a noticeable absence of character, but that's trickier to broach.

'I worry he doesn't have enough in his life. Especially now he and Kim have split up.'

'Did you know Kim?'

'No. Liam never introduced us. He's very private.'

'So you weren't jealous that he had a girlfriend, or worried he'd desert you if things got more serious between them?'

'No.' She seemed to be telling the truth. 'Liam won't ever live with anyone apart from me.' This was said in a reassuring tone. Sellers found it chilling.

'Has he said that?'

'No, but he wouldn't last five minutes on his own.'

'But . . . if he were to move in with a woman, he wouldn't be on his own, would he?'

'He couldn't live with a woman for five minutes.' Isobel laughed. 'Apart from me – but that's different. I'm his sister.'

'Let's say he did move out, though, and get married or something. Would you mind? How would you feel about living alone?'

Sellers waited for Isobel to tell him that Liam would be back within five minutes. He was surprised when she said, 'Me? I'd be fine! We lead pretty separate lives.'

'Right.'

She leaned forward. 'You can't honestly think Liam would kill anyone and needs an alibi?' She looked as if she was waiting for Sellers to start laughing so that she could join in.

'We have to rule him out – because of his connection to Kim Tribbeck, and the fact that she's been threatened, probably by the person we're looking for. It's nothing personal against Liam. It's a formality.'

'I see. Well, what about me? Shouldn't you ask me for my alibis for all the dates of the murders? And – oh – do you want some DNA from me? Liam said someone rang up about DNA.' Isobel stuck out her tongue, then put it away again, as if realising she must look odd, sitting there with it sticking out.

'I don't do that part,' said Sellers. 'I don't have a kit on me. But if you and your brother could follow up on the phone call you received, I'd appreciate it. We need to rule you out on the DNA front. And yes, I'd like to ask you about your whereabouts on the dates in question, if that's okay? Again – only a formality.'

Sellers didn't fancy Isobel Sturridge at all. If she made a pass at him, he'd give her the knockback. Wasn't often he felt that way. He did a quick analysis of his aberrant response to her and decided it was her teeth that were the problem. There was a noticeable vertical groove at the centre of each of her front teeth, creating a disconcerting two-halves effect.

'I was at work for all five,' Isobel said once Sellers had told her the dates. 'I work nine thirty to five thirty, Monday to Friday.'

'Where's work, then?' he asked her.

'The famous Rudolphy's.' Isobel was unable to keep the pride out of her voice.

Whatever Rudolphy's was, its fame hadn't spread as far as Sellers. Typical Silsford resident, he thought, imagining that everything that happens in Silsford is of inherent interest to the world. Two elderly Silsfordians had turned up at the nick last week – Spilling nick – to complain that the police in Silsford weren't concerned enough about the dreadful wind-tunnel effect created by the new Waitrose on Bicknacre Road. What did Spilling Police intend to do about their negligent colleagues in the neighbouring town? they demanded to know. Answer: nothing.

'It's a labour of love more than a job,' said Isobel. She couldn't have sounded more self-satisfied. 'I mean, the money's negligible. People are always saying how much they envy me, when they're earning three times my salary!'

Sellers heard the silent addition loud and clear: *And yet, we all know I'm in the better situation.*

'So – aren't you lucky?' She laughed.

'What do you mean?'

'My alibi is Rudolphy's! Which means you've got an excuse to go there now, to check it – and emerge several hours later and several hundred pounds poorer!'

'I'll be the one in need of an alibi if I spend several hundred pounds without my wife's permission.'

'Unless you spend it on her,' said Isobel forcefully. This was the hard sell, all right. She looked sad, as if Sellers had spoiled all her fun. He resolved not to spend a single penny in bloody Rudolphy's, whatever it turned out to be.

His phone buzzed in his pocket, providing him with the perfect excuse to leave. 'I've got to take this call,' he told Isobel, though he knew it was only a text landing. He was keen to get out of the Sturridge house and away from the Freak Siblings, and was relishing the prospect of a slow walk down the hill with dazzling views and fresh air to accompany him: compensation for what he'd suffered on the way up.

The text was from Lisa Norbury, Joshua's sister. Sellers probably wouldn't have followed up on his original message. They'd already been over Josh Norbury's house with a fine-tooth comb; he knew he'd find nothing useful. After his last encounter with Sondra Halliday, it had felt important to Sellers to show he cared about the dead man she barely bothered to mention, but he'd be showing no one but himself, effectively. It was a vanity exercise.

Still, this was the one thing he'd set in motion without consulting any of his team. If he cancelled it, he'd feel lame. He had to see it through. Sighing, Sellers started to compose a text to send to Lisa in reply, sounding more grateful and enthusiastic than he felt.

~

Gibbs wanted to talk about alibis for Billy's first four kill dates, but Drew Hopwood wanted to talk only about money. Mostly, what he wanted to say was that money mattered not a jot to him. It mattered so little that, at every opportunity, he brought the conversation back to it.

'If I could trade what I'm going to inherit from Gran for her still being alive, it'd be a no-brainer. I'll be getting something in the region of three hundred grand, but I'd swap that for having her back any day of the week. She was like a second mother to me.'

Gibbs decided Hopwood was a no-brainer. You didn't have to be Einstein to do a passable impression of a non-materialistic person: just don't insert the words 'roughly three hundred grand' or 'around three hundred k' into your every sentence.

Hopwood had arrived at Spilling nick like an applicant for a prestigious job, clean-shaven and eager for his interview in a smart grey suit, navy tie and shiny black shoes.

'When Angela McCabe died, her husband was the financial beneficiary,' Gibbs told him. 'With Joshua Norbury, it was his sister, Lisa. In the absence of other suspects, motives, leads, we looked at Russell McCabe and Lisa Norbury very carefully. We eliminated them both – neither could have committed the murders. I hope you can appreciate that we need to go through the same formalities with you.'

'What do you mean?'

'Eliminate you, as the sole beneficiary of Marion's estate,' said Gibbs.

'What about the other two? Billy's killed five people.'

'Linzi Birrell and Rhian Douglas had nothing to leave, so no motive there. Is there a reason why you're unwilling to tell me where you were on those days, Mr Hopwood?'

'Not at all. I just find it unbelievable that you'd suspect me. I loved Gran like a second mum.'

'Yes, you've said.'

'When I heard she'd been . . . I can't even say it!' He covered his mouth with a clenched fist. 'I wouldn't have killed her for three *million*, let alone for three hundred thousand. This is all . . . I'm sorry, but it's absurd for you to think it.'

'If you'd worked for the police for nearly twenty years and seen as much profit-motivated crime as I have, you wouldn't find it absurd. So, where were you on the dates I keep asking about? I know you were at the RGI the day Marion was murdered.'

'Working, I guess.'

'You guess? I was hoping you'd be able to offer me something more solid than a guess, Mr Hopwood. You knew you'd be asked to account for your whereabouts, didn't you? I told you when we spoke on the phone.'

Hopwood's sigh suggested a good man whose generous nature was being shamelessly exploited. 'Look, what am I supposed to do? I work alone a lot of the time. The first four murders all took place on weekdays and I wasn't on holiday, so I was definitely working. But . . . I'd only be able to prove where I was if I'd had meetings on those days, and I'm afraid I didn't.'

Gibbs was looking at his notes on Hopwood, which told a different story. 'It says here you work for a company called Struthers Breary. Just you, is it? No colleagues? Don't bother answering. I happen to know that firm's owned by a husband and wife team, Gaby and Tim Breary. I know them personally, and I'm a hundred per cent certain they don't only employ you.'

Another long-suffering sigh from Hopwood. 'They employ hundreds of people, and most are based at head office. Some aren't. I'm not. I make a very specific kind of wire for them – I have a lab in my garden where I've worked since I set up as a sole trader, and they're fine with that. I don't like busy, noisy environments. One of my conditions when I started working for them was still being able to work in my own lab. If you know Gaby and Tim so well, why don't you check all this with them?'

Gibbs nearly laughed. Gaby Struthers – as he still thought of her – was the kind of person who'd dish out fake alibis to loyal members of staff without the slightest qualm. She'd done much, much worse. Gibbs tried not to think about her role in the Francine Breary murder case; every time he did, he wanted to punch a hole in a wall.

'So what you're telling me is that on the dates of Billy's first four murders, you were in your own personal laboratory making special wires, and no one will be able to verify that?'

'Basically, frustratingly, yes.' Hopwood offered an apologetic smile.

'On Tuesday 6 January, when Marion was murdered, you were at the hospital with her, in her room nearly all the time.' Gibbs stared at him. 'You say you saw no one else in or near her room who shouldn't have been there.'

'I didn't, but I fell asleep for small spells. I was exhausted. And . . .'

'What, Mr Hopwood?'

'I assume you've considered Kim? My sister?'

'As a suspect, d'you mean?'

'Well, just . . . in the same way you're considering me.' Pink spots had appeared on Hopwood's cheeks. 'If you think three hundred grand give-or-take is a viable motive, how about *no* three hundred grand? How about *lack* of inheritance?'

'Marion left everything to you and cut Kim out.' Gibbs made a note. Hopwood was right: brother and sister both had a motive. Opposite motives, equally strong. 'Well, it's kind of you to be willing to divide it equally between you.'

'What? I never said . . . I'm *not* willing. I mean—'

'You seem upset, Mr Hopwood.'

'Did Kim tell you I'd promised her half the money?'

'No, she didn't. You misunderstood me. I wasn't talking about your three hundred grand, give or take. Well, take, anyway,' Gibbs amended. 'When I said it was kind of you to divide it equally I didn't mean Marion's money. I meant suspicion of murder. That, you're willing to share with your sister. Aren't you?'

'I don't deserve this!' Drew Hopwood looked around the small interview room as if hoping to spot someone in a corner who might defend him. 'I've done everything you've asked of me – paid for my own travel to and from your police station so that I could give a DNA sample, answered all your questions politely, and this is how you treat me? Carry on like this and I'm going to be speaking to your boss, I'm sorry to say.'

Gibbs grinned at him. 'I recommend you do that. I think you'd enjoy it.'

'Do you address all recently bereaved people in such a heartless way?'

'I don't know. You'd have to ask them.'

'I have some experience of bullies,' said Hopwood. 'They try to intimidate until they see it won't work, then they slink off underneath the nearest stone. You can't scare me, DC Gibbs. We're in Britain, one of the most civilised countries in the world, in the twenty-first century. I've murdered no one, therefore I have nothing to worry about. I won't be going to prison. Kim, as my next of kin, won't be getting her hands on Gran's money by framing me for five murders so that I can't legally inherit – much as you and she and all your cronies would no doubt love for that to happen!'

Not another one. You could divide people into two groups, Gibbs had always thought: those who had a realistic idea of how little they mattered to you, and those, like Drew Hopwood, who imagined a detective he'd known less than an hour gave a single shit about any aspect of his life. The suggestion that Gibbs and his colleagues were conspiring with Kim Tribbeck to cheat Hopwood out of his precious three hundred grand, that any of them would *love* for that to happen, was laughable. *You're just a name in a file, mate, until I can find more evidence.*

'Have a think, look at any records you've got, and see if you can do better for those four dates,' Gibbs told Hopwood. He rose to his feet to signal that the interview was over. 'Imagine you've got three hundred grand riding on it – that might help you to focus.'

12

from Origami *by Kim Tribbeck*

Tuesday, 13 January 2015

'Battery acid?'

Remember how you felt when a detective told you someone had murdered your grandmother by injecting battery acid into her? That there was no doubt from the post mortem, and also a syringe had been found, but there were no fingerprints on it?

Of course you don't. It doesn't happen to most people, only a select few.

'As I understand it, it's not quite the same chemical—' Waterhouse breaks off. Decides to change course. 'Essentially, yes. In layperson's terms: battery acid.'

When I don't respond, he asks me what I'm thinking.

We're in my kitchen, sitting across the table from one another, mugs of coffee in our hands. At one time, I'd have associated a scene like this with 'A friend pops round for a chat'; now it's more 'An enemy whips out a gun and shoots you in the head while you're putting on the kettle'. I was pleasantly surprised when Simon Waterhouse didn't, which shows how far my definition of good news has stretched lately.

'Is Billy a psychological sadist?'

'Why do you ask that?' says Waterhouse.

'Only explanation I can think of.'

'Meaning?'

'The four victims before Marion – none of them had terminal cancer, did they? From what I've read, they were all relatively young and healthy.'

'Correct.' Waterhouse's way of speaking reminds me of an

automated till in a Tesco Express. *Please insert payment. Unexpected item in bagging area.*

'My guess is that's why Billy gave me the first book but still hasn't killed me. He was planning to – I was first on his list – and then he found out Marion, who was meant to be second for the chop, had terminal cancer. He made a new plan: kill the other four first because there's no point waiting, and only kill Marion once she's had a chance to suffer the full extent of her illness.'

'That's an interesting theory.' Waterhouse addresses this unexpected praise to my kitchen window.

'If you want someone dead, chances are you hate them, right? It might irritate you to think that by murdering them, you could spare them some pain that was coming their way naturally. So you wait as long as possible and kill them just before they're about to die. You're a sadist.'

'And you're saying originally Billy planned to kill you before Marion, but changed his mind because there was a clock ticking on her and not on you?'

'My theory's way sicker than that. He didn't want me *or* Marion to miss out on a cancer death. It was gruesome for both of us – more for her, but it's no fun being a spectator, believe me. And Billy might have assumed I loved Marion deeply, which of course would have made it more painful for me.'

Waterhouse takes a long slurp of his coffee. I wish I hadn't given him the hideous 'Hello, is it tea you're looking for?' mug.

'Didn't you?'

'Didn't I what? Oh – love Marion? I don't know. I expect I did in a way, but . . . of the feelings I've always been aware of having for her, love didn't figure prominently.'

'Is that a tactful way of saying you hated her?'

'There were moments when I hated her. I was always scared of her.'

'Why?'

'Long story.'

Most people would have said, 'It's okay, we have plenty of time,' or words to that effect. Waterhouse says, 'I have to hear it, so . . . maybe condense it down a bit if it's really long.'

Thanks for your sensitivity, mate.

'Bullet points?' I smile. If I could summarise it all in list form, it would be less likely to upset me. 'I'm not sure there's a short version, to be honest. My mother fell pregnant with me at fifteen and my father ran for the hills when he found out. My mum begged to keep me – I found this out later from her best friend at the time – but her parents, Marion and Trevor, were worried about the shame she'd bring on the family. This was 1971, so I don't know how bad it would have been for them – it was hardly the 1840s or anything, but I suppose if you're the respectable façade type . . . and my grandparents definitely were. So I was given up for adoption.

'Mr and Mrs Tribbeck adopted me. That's how I think of them in my head: Mr and Mrs Tribbeck. They were good people, they did their best, but I'm not in touch with them any more. Not a day went by when they didn't demonstrate that, while they adored their three flesh-and-blood children, I was their good deed. They approved of themselves for having taken me on. For my whole childhood I was the perfect, well-mannered, parent-pleasing suck-up – top grades at school, Duke of Edinburgh Award star, tidying my room every night even when it didn't need tidying—'

'That doesn't sound like you,' Waterhouse cuts in.

I laugh. 'You don't know me.'

'You're a big part of a big case – means I need to find out about you. I've watched some of your stuff online. You portray yourself as a rebel, always doing what you want no matter what the world thinks. Going your own way.'

'Yeah, that's me now. I'm bright enough to realise when a tactic's not working. Being the perfect child didn't make me or anyone else feel I was a proper member of the Tribbeck family. I was a lonely, unhappy kid and now I'm a lonely, unhappy adult, but at least I get to be myself and make other people unhappy too – you'd be surprised how much that takes the edge off.'

Waterhouse scowls into the dregs of his coffee. I'm sensing that of all the people he's ever met, I'm the one he disapproves of most. At the same time, he strikes me as the sort of man who might make everyone feel that way.

'That was a joke,' I explain. 'Well, partly. Don't worry, I'm not expecting sympathy. I was trying to make you laugh, but . . . I can see that was overly ambitious.'

'Carry on with what you were saying. The Tribbecks adopted you . . . ?'

'Yes, and did their best, which was probably more than adequate, and better than I could do myself in a similar situation, but I didn't have a fantastic time growing up in that house. To put it mildly. I had the chance to trace my biological mother when I was eighteen – should have left well alone, but I'm not the sort of person who can ever do that – so I leapt at it. Found out very quickly that she'd died the year before. Choked to death after getting a piece of chicken lodged in her throat. Her best friend was with her at the time but couldn't help her. Horrendous. Last time I saw Cheryl, she still wasn't over it.

'They were close, her and my mum. Cheryl was able to tell me stuff I might have been better off not knowing: Elaine desperately wanted to keep me—'

'Elaine? Your mother's name was Elaine?'

'Yes. Why's that important?'

'Was it ever shortened to Lane?'

'Not as far as I know. Why? Cheryl calls her El – I think most of her friends did, and Marion and Trevor insisted on the full Elaine and didn't care what she wanted to be known as.'

'Never mind. Go on.'

'My mother hadn't planned to get pregnant so young, but

once she found out she was, she desperately wanted to have the baby: me. She'd already figured out that her parents were twats, and she had no siblings, so having a baby seemed to her to be the only way of securing a halfway decent relative for herself.'

'This is coming from Cheryl, all this information?' Waterhouse asks.

I nod. 'And she's convincing. I don't think she's just saying it to make me feel I was wanted. Some of the details I've heard are too specific, and Cheryl's not imaginative enough to invent them. Elaine wanted to keep me. She talked about me every single time Cheryl saw her – being forced to give me up haunted her. It became an obsession. She never forgave Marion and Trevor. And there was an added twist that made it all so much worse for her.'

I need extra supplies of oxygen to talk about this bit. My lungs feel squeezed of air before I've even started. 'Elaine got pregnant again while still a minor. Almost exactly a year after she'd given me up for adoption, she had my brother Drew. Different dad, also made himself scarce very quickly.' *Time for a joke, to cheer us all up.* 'I mean, no one likes to speak ill of the dead but clearly contraception wasn't my mother's strong point. Marion and Trevor went into full doom mode once again – family shame panic – and insisted on another adoption. Elaine was distraught *again* – and then a miracle happened. Drew was born, Marion took one look at him in the hospital and her heart melted. She couldn't bear for him to be given away, so she talked Trevor round, and suddenly the family shame didn't matter any more because everyone loved Drew so much.'

I smile brightly. 'If you're wondering whether I was a hideous baby and Drew a cute one, I don't think so. I've seen photos of us both – we look remarkably alike.'

'Probably a generational thing,' Simon says. 'I know my parents wanted a boy. Not me, probably – a different boy.'

I lean forward. 'Did you just make a *joke*?'

'No, I was being serious.' He looks embarrassed, and seems keen to move briskly on. 'So your mother kept your brother? He wasn't adopted?'

'Nope. Marion did all the childcare, Elaine was free to go about being a teenager, but Cheryl says she wasn't happy. She adored Drew, but her relief at being able to keep him, and her love for him, only increased the pain of having given me up. And Cheryl says—'

I break off. This is the hardest part to say, as I know from telling Gabe ('Jesus Christ! What a pair of unmitigated cunts! Isn't this the perfect opportunity never to see Marion and Trevor again, since they're also mind-numbingly dull?') and Liam ('Families are strange. Are you wearing anything under that?').

'Cheryl says Elaine would have ended up hating her parents *less* if they'd made her give Drew up for adoption too. She'd have been bereft again, and she'd much rather have had Drew than a better opinion of her parents, of course, but . . . it was the hypocrisy she couldn't stand: the double standard, and the brick-wall refusal to acknowledge it. Marion wouldn't accept that it was cruel or wrong in any way to force Elaine to give away one baby then allow her to keep the next purely because she felt instant love for one and not the other. It *wasn't* a generational thing or a boy/girl thing. Marion apparently said that she looked down at newborn Drew and he looked up at her with so much love in his eyes that she simply couldn't go through with the adoption plan.'

I breathe out long and hard, trying to exhale the tension that's accumulated from telling my least favourite story. It doesn't work. 'So there we have it: Drew got to stay chez Hopwood, and got to have a mother who loved him, because he was able to provide evidence of love for Marion early enough to save himself. I didn't.'

Simon shrugs. 'I still think it's more likely to be the boy thing. The rubbish about eyes was a less offensive-sounding excuse.'

'Less offensive?' I laugh. 'How d'you figure that? I'd *rather* it was because I was a girl, but I don't think it was. I think Marion just didn't warm to me. I'd prefer "Marion's a sexist idiot" to "I'm inherently unloveable" as an explanation.'

Could he be right? Even if he is, I'll never convince myself.

'If you're about to ask me why I sought out the Hopwood family after the only member of it who gave a shit about me had died . . . I wanted to meet my brother. I thought I might have hit the nuclear family jackpot: at last, a blood relative who was neither dead nor a conspirator in a plot to banish me. Unfortunately . . .' I stop. This bit's going to be harder to convey.

I used to think Drew was simply uninterested in anyone but himself. Then Gabe and I got together and I noticed Drew related to Gabe differently. He asked him proper questions. That's when I realised how uninterested in me he is. The questions he asks me are always what car I'm driving at the moment, how much I think my house is worth, which airline I think is the most reliable. That's because he's interested in cars, houses, travel. He hides his refusal to ask me anything about myself amid an extensive and varied assortment of questions about all the things I know about but care nothing for, bombarding me with trivial enquiries as a way of blocking me – of demonstrating that I'm not someone with a heart and soul that matters, as far as he's concerned.

Questions Drew never asks when I see him include: how are you? What have you been up to? How's work going? Are you writing new material at the moment? Have you decided what your next tour's theme will be yet? Any love life developments?

Gabe, on the other hand . . . I watched time after time as my brother chose the exact right words that would enable my husband to expand on all the things that mattered most to him: the films of Michael Haneke, the legalisation of marijuana, Gabe's work for a verbal branding company.

Since Gabe and I split up, Drew's first question to me is

always, 'How's Gabe? Have you heard from him? What's he been up to?'

Another of my brother's strange and discouraging habits is suggesting I'm probably guilty of everything I criticise others for. If I get an uncooked chicken breast in a restaurant and complain, he points out that I once served him an inedible meal; if I say a politician's a hypocrite for dodging inheritance tax and then condemning tax avoidance, he reminds me of the time I said everyone should give blood and then chickened out because I'm scared of needles.

If I'm murdered, Drew will appear on the TV news and tell the nation that, however unfortunate Billy's actions might have been, mine also, frankly, had always left a lot to be desired.

According to my brother's rules, nothing bad can be allowed to have happened to me, nor may I notice wrongs done. It's a form of protection from harm that's anything but reassuring.

'On the surface, Drew was keen to welcome me to the Hopwood family,' I tell Waterhouse. 'He'd just lost his mum. As a bloke who doesn't like to be short-changed, he knew he was down to the tune of one close relative and he was happy to be able to fill that gap. Marion and Trevor went along with the "Of course you're one of us" routine – probably to please Drew – but there was a silent, non-negotiable condition attached to all of this: nobody was allowed to mention the backstory.'

'You mean—'

'Everything I've just told you: my adoption, Drew's planned adoption, Marion not being able to go through with it, Elaine hating her and Trevor as a result, my miserable childhood with the Tribbecks. We all had to pretend nothing out of the ordinary had happened, that Drew and I were equal members of the family who'd never been treated at all differently . . . I went along with it at first, but it soon started to rankle. I didn't have the guts to walk away, so I rebelled covertly, hinting whenever I could at the traumatic experience I'd had that my brother hadn't. That's what really set them against me: I was a troublemaker, determined to rake up horrible things from the past. I didn't want to be like that but the enforced silence got too much for me. Marion never apologised, or acknowledged any aspect of what happened to me. Instead, she behaved as if I'd chosen to go on a very long holiday, then reappeared with the sole intention of putting a dampener on everyone else's happiness.'

'I have to ask, because I know you could have; you had plenty of opportunity . . . Did you kill Marion?'

'No. Cancer and Billy Dead Mates did, between them.'

'Did you know, or know of, any of the four other victims: Linzi Birrell, Rhian Douglas, Angela—'

'I know the names. No. Never heard of any of them until they were in the paper after they were killed.'

Waterhouse pulls a small lined piece of paper out of his shirt pocket and hands it to me. 'These are the dates they were killed. I'll need to know what you were doing on the afternoons of those days.'

'For most of them I was probably being driven from one gig to another. Look up Kim Tribbeck autumn tour 2014 – you can also talk to my driver, Dmitri Pescov. I'll give you his number.'

I reach for one of the pens on the shelf above my head, write Dmitri's number on the back of the lined paper and pass it back to Waterhouse.

'Thanks. For what it's worth, I don't believe you killed anyone.'

'I'm more worried about being killed, to be honest,' I say. Worried. Still not scared. It seems too unreal, all of it. And confusing. An hour before Waterhouse arrived, a uniformed police officer was sitting where he's sitting now, scraping the inside of my mouth with a wooden stick to get a DNA sample.

Apparently no one can decide if I'm a danger or in danger.

'Your worry's understandable,' says Waterhouse. 'I'm hoping

that once you've had your session with our sketch artist and we've spread the image of the man who gave you the book far and wide, we'll be well on our way to catching Billy. In the meantime, I'm glad you're going away with Charlie tomorrow. That'll give you some protection while we make progress.'

My tour-in-reverse, in search of the mysterious gig venue that I can't identify. I'm dreading it.

'Let me ask you something. Who might want to harm you?'

'Apart from members of the public who tweet me death threats because I'm not funny?'

'Are there many of them?'

'No, and please don't waste your time tracking them down. They're saddos letting off steam. I feel sorry for them. Who might want to harm me seriously? Gabe, Liam, Drew. I can't think of anyone else.'

'Your husband, your ex-boyfriend and your brother.' Waterhouse makes a note. I imagine it says something like 'Only knows three people in entire world. All probably want her dead.'

'To turn that question around and look at it another way: who, if they'd planned to kill six people and you were one of the six, might not be able to bring themselves to harm you, even if, theoretically, they wanted to?'

This one I have to think about. I'm surprised by my conclusion. 'Strange as it sounds . . . the same three people. Gabe. Liam. My brother Drew,' I say. 'No one else would care enough to spare me.'

~

I was surprised when I met Charlie and she was a woman. Waterhouse hadn't mentioned it.

My first thought: if a Charlie can be a woman, maybe a Billy can too.

When she introduced herself to me – the police officer who was to be my chauffeur for however long it took – I knew it was too late to call off the gigless tour. I considered feigning an illness: sharp pain in my stomach. Maybe that ringpull I swallowed could be brought into play, I thought.

I didn't want to let anyone down, but I feared I would, whatever I did. If I helped them find the man who gave me the little white book, I'd be leading them to the wrong person. I didn't know why I was so certain that man wasn't Billy, but suddenly I was.

So why had I felt so uncomfortable when he approached me? My instincts had told me there was danger . . .

Not danger of murder, though.

I shook my head to banish the incoherent swirl of thoughts. It would be easier, I knew, if I stopped thinking, got into the car and let Sergeant Charlie Zailer drive me around the country as planned. It wasn't as if there was anything else I wanted or needed to do at that moment.

She was tall and thin, with wavy dark brown hair cut to just above shoulder-length, pale skin and no make-up apart from bright red lipstick. 'You're not wearing uniform,' I said.

She looked down at herself. 'Actually, I am. This is it.'

'No, I mean . . . when we go on our blast-from-my-past tour, I'd rather you wore regular clothes. Otherwise I might feel like I'm an escaped loony who needs a uniformed attendant.'

'I'm glad you raised this.' Charlie perched on the edge of the table in the corner. 'I'd rather not play driver to a spoilt star with an over-inflated ego.'

Star? Was she deluded? 'Is that your way of saying it's important to you to wear uniform?'

'I've seen your list of requirements: a gold-plated dressing room, a Filipino butler with a six-pack to polish your toenails between interviews, etcetera.'

'Wow. Seems there really are a million different ways you can interpret the words "pickled onion Monster Munch".'

We were going to be getting into a car together soon whether we wanted to or not. Since Charlie Zailer was unlikely to stop being an arsehole – people rarely did – I decided I'd have to be the one to make the effort. 'I only made that list because I'd been treated badly by an event organiser one time too many,' I said. 'Feel free to ignore my list, and wear whatever you want. You're right, it's none of my business.'

'I probably don't need to wear the uniform,' she said. 'Leave it with me. First things first: we need to draw up a schedule. Where we go and in what order. Also hotels – I want to get on and book them.'

'Hotels?'

Every bed is narrow.

When I'd first read those words in a little white book, I'd thought they meant that any bed you share with another person feels too small. Even in the early days of our relationship when I couldn't get enough of his body or his conversation, I'd wished Gabe would sleep somewhere else at night and not next to me. I'd have suggested it, but you're not supposed to. People who are in love are meant to want to sleep side by side, so I tried to want to. It took me more than a year to work out that Gabe's intermittent snoring was the perfect excuse to make a case for separate rooms.

'B and Bs more than hotels, probably,' said Charlie. 'I have to try and keep costs down. If we're travelling all over the country, we're going to need to sleep somewhere – unless you want to start from the Culver Valley every morning.'

'No. Sorry. Hadn't thought it through.'

'Are you okay?' She peered at me.

Totally, and not at all would have been an honest answer. For as long as I could remember, I'd been absolutely fine and a complete mess.

'If it's okay, I don't want to stay in any of the hotels I stayed in before, when I gigged in those towns. I don't like going back to old haunts if I can avoid it.'

'Fine. I've got the list from your agent of where you stayed while on tour. I'll avoid places you've been before. Chances are they're beyond our budget anyway.'

'And we'll have our own rooms? I mean, separate? No twin rooms to save money?'

'Of course not.'

Thank God for that.

'Once we've identified the event venue we're looking for, we're also going to need to go to whichever hotel you stayed in – the narrow bed hotel – to check it's the right one.'

That was the main one I didn't want to revisit. *Damn.*

'Simon wants to know for sure. He said you should positively identify both: venue and hotel.'

This was an opportunity, I told myself, to learn a hard lesson: namely, that you couldn't have everything you wanted all the time. All you could do was force strangers to buy you your favourite kind of crisps and pretend that was all your dreams come true at once.

'You're not keen to revisit the hotel?' Charlie asked me. 'How come?'

'It was hardly the Savoy.'

'We can just walk in, you say, "Yes, this is where I stayed," then we walk out.'

We could walk in? Was she going to insist on coming into the room with me? God, that would be embarrassing. Unless . . .

'Let me tell you now and get it over with,' I said. 'Any hotel room I go into, whether I'm spending the night there or just popping in, I have to take a book into the room with me and put it in a drawer. If there's a Bible in the room, I have to put my book in the same drawer as the Bible. If there's no Bible, any drawer will do.' My face radiated heat as I spoke. I'd have found it less embarrassing if I'd had to admit that I travelled with a bag of sex toys.

'Really?' Charlie wasn't smiling. She didn't look as if she was preparing to mock me. 'Which book? The same one every time?'

'Yes. It's called *Delirium of the Brave*. By Terence Nithercott. I guarantee you won't have heard of it. Please don't ask me why I have to take it to every hotel with me. There's literally no reason. The book has . . . *had* . . . sentimental value. Soon after I got it, as a present, I took it with me to a hotel because I wanted to try and read it – turns out it's unreadable – and then it kind of became a thing. A mascot, or . . . I don't know.'

Why was Charlie Zailer suddenly paying such close attention to my every word?

'What would happen if I said, "I want you to go into hotel rooms without that book from now on"?' she asked.

I shrugged. 'I'd probably take the opportunity to persuade myself it's turned into an irrational obsession, and now's a great moment to break the habit.'

She nodded. 'And if I say, "Do what you like with regard to the book"? Then are you going to bring it or leave it at home?'

'Bring it. Don't you have any irrational superstitions?'

'Have you read *Beloved* by Toni Morrison?'

'No, I don't think so. I've read one of her books – *The Bluest Eye*. Why?'

'Billy Dead Mates sent a copy of *Beloved* to Sondra Halliday, a journalist who's been—'

'I know who Halliday is. I've been reading her commentary on the murders. With mounting incredulity. I wish someone'd get her the help she needs.'

'What do you mean?'

'From the few autobiographical columns of hers I've read in the past, I know she should be crying on a shrink's couch and drinking hot milk with honey in it till she feels better, not trauma-laundering to create unrest.'

'I've seen her mention PTSD but never anything specific.' The hardness of Charlie's voice suggested she wasn't convinced. I was. You don't end up like Sondra Halliday if nothing terrible's happened to you; you don't harm others unless you've been harmed yourself first.

You think I'm wrong? You have counter-examples? That's so sweet and naïve – which is tactful-speak for 'fucking stupid'.

Whenever people say about someone who's committed an evil act, 'But he had a happy, loving childhood,' feel free to say to them confidently, 'No, he didn't.' Not all wounds or causes of hurt are visible to those on the outside.

'Halliday had an abusive stepfather from a really young age – seven or eight, I think – and a mother who colluded,' I said.

'Simon calls her the Hate Preacher,' said Charlie.

'I feel sorry for her. She so desperately wants to believe women aren't as venal and vicious as men. Maybe she never went to school with other girls between the ages of twelve and eighteen. Why did Billy Dead Mates send her a Toni Morrison novel?'

'We don't know. He also sent her *Jude the Obscure* by Thomas Hardy. Books are everywhere in this investigation. Billy's little white ones with lines from poems in them . . .' Charlie gave me a pointed look.

'And now my copy of *Delirium of the Brave*.'

'Yes.'

'Books don't commit murders,' I said. 'Even the very worst of them. That's why books are so much better than people.'

Sophie Hannah

Lifeworld online, 14 January 2015
BILLY DEAD WOMEN STRIKES AGAIN
by Sondra Halliday

Yesterday, Culver Valley Police revealed that the killer they're failing to catch, while affectionately dubbing him Billy Dead Mates, has struck for a fifth time. Guess what? Once again, the victim was a woman: 82-year-old Marion Hopwood from Silsford. Unlike Billy's other victims, Marion wasn't shot. That would have attracted too much attention, given she was in hospital at the time of her death. Instead, she was injected with something very similar to battery acid.

How do the police know Marion was killed by Billy and not by one of the many other lethal male death machines freely roaming our streets? Well, a little white book containing one line of poetry was found in her hospital bed shortly before she died, and, as we all know by now, Billy serves a little white book to each of his targets before killing her, like a sinister murder-subpoena.

By murdering Marion Hopwood, Billy Dead Women proved the validity of my adapted nickname for him. For those of you who aren't following each new permutation of the story, Billy has now murdered four women. In chronological order: Linzi Birrell from Combingham, Rhian Douglas from Poole, Angela McCabe from Chiswick, and now Mrs Hopwood. And just as Billy's latest foray into brutality shows us, as if we were in any doubt, that ending the lives of women is his top priority, it shows us something else about him too. It's not enough for him that women's lives should be snuffed out; he personally wants to be the one to make it happen. He's even willing to put himself out to achieve that goal, being no slouch when it comes to practical misogyny.

How do I know this about him? Because Marion Hopwood was in the process of dying of cancer when he killed her. She had somewhere between twenty and seventy hours left to live when he injected her with poison. All Billy had to do, if he wanted Marion dead, was wait. Like so many violent misogynists, however, he craved more than that. He needed to feel his own power surge through him as he played God with a helpless, terminally ill grandmother's life. After all, belonging to the superior sex class is more fun if you get to exterminate the subordinates once in a while – right, guys?

This latest murder enables us to draw a further conclusion: if you want to be a killer who gets away with it apparently forever, kill women. It's that simple.

For the ambitious career murderer, targeting women is a sensible move. Does anyone honestly imagine the police wouldn't have caught Billy by now if it were men he was shooting dead? Of course they would; like the rest of us, all the investigating officers were born and socialised into a world that believes men's lives matter and women's don't. I'm the first to admit that it's hard to train yourself out of thinking that way. Evidently the police have failed to do so.

Marion Hopwood's life mattered. She was a devoted wife until her husband died in 2008, a loving mother, a beloved grandmother. She never worked outside the home, but spent her whole life doing the unpaid work expected of women: caring for her family, bringing up her grandson Drew when his teenage mother couldn't cope with the responsibility.

Drew Hopwood was kind enough to speak to me yesterday and it was from him that I learned a fascinating fact about Marion, something about which the news coverage of her murder has so far been silent: she had no best friend. She was on nodding terms with her immediate neighbours, but her grandson described her as 'always so immersed in family that she never had time for friends'. The only people she saw regularly were Drew and his half-sister, comedian Kim Tribbeck, who was adopted by another family at birth.

No. Best. Friend. Are you going to break into the police briefing to tell them the bad news, or shall I? Their theory that Billy is killing pairs of best friends has just died on its arse. Now all those brilliant detectives are going to have to look for another pattern and I'm willing to bet my vital organs that they'll *still* fail to notice the glaringly obvious: that Billy is a dedicated practitioner of the misogynistic murder of women.

Think I'm wrong? Then ask yourself this: if a serial killer murdered four chiropodists and one tightrope walker, would or wouldn't the papers and the blogs be full of speculation about what grudge he might have against chiropodists? How often do you think you'd hear the word 'chiropodist'? I think we all know that aspect of the story would be central in our communal narrative. But substitute 'women' for 'chiropodists' and it's not thought by mainstream reporting to be a detail worth dwelling on.

And why should we dwell on it, especially if we're women? What does it matter what we think, when we're so insignificant? Most of us aren't chiropodists, and we certainly aren't human beings with innate value. We can't be, or else how do you explain the way we're treated in the world and the way the phenomenon of our mass slaughter for centuries at the hands of men is ignored and erased by the very police officers whose job it ought to be to keep us safe?

---

3 Comments:

From: Colin, Culver Valley

You're properly off your trolley, aren't you?
1) The police are trying to keep people safe and prevent further deaths. All right, they haven't got there yet. Think you can do a better job? Feel free to catch Billy and bring him down the nick at your earliest convenience – maybe having all the right thoughts about violent men and misogyny will make you a better detective than trained and experienced officers.
2) The police haven't ignored or erased any murders. All their official communications mention all of Billy's victims –

including Joshua Norbury, the man Billy murdered whose name you don't even mention in passing. So if anyone's erasing anyone's murder, it sure as shit ain't us.

3) 'After all, belonging to the superior sex class is more fun if you get to exterminate the subordinates once in a while – right, guys?' Unless I'm mistaken, you're implying that all or most men would find it enjoyable to murder women. This is an out-and-out lie. The vast majority of men don't want to kill anyone, just like the vast majority of women.

4) Your chiropodist point, and what you think it proves, is a load of crap. If a killer kills only men, or only women, then it's noteworthy. If he kills a mixture of both, it's seen as not relevant, for obvious reasons. Men + women = people. People = everybody. What use is it to say a killer's targeting people? It doesn't narrow down his victim field at all. All Billy's female victims were straight. His male victim was gay. According to your logic, does that make it the ritual slaughter of heterosexuals? Or would you say that, no, that makes no sense because there's one gay victim? If so, I'd agree with you.

5) Best friends pattern. It was there in four out of the five cases. In the fifth case – Marion Hopwood – you're right, it seems not to be there. Let's hope that means there'll be no sixth victim. Or, to put it in terms you'll be able to relate to, let's hope that if there is a sixth victim, it's only one of those potentially lethal male murder machines you talk about (otherwise known as 'men') and not a fellow human being that you dane to consider worth caring about and writing about because she happens to share certain body parts with you.

From: David Howard, Oxford

Well said, Sondra! Your analysis is, as ever, superb. Unfortunately, your brain is too large and brilliant for most people to be able to cope with. I wish everyone would listen to you! I have been spreading the feminist word as best I can!

From: Herr Jennda, Wolverhampton

So only men and women are people, Colin? Wow. Just . . . wow.
What about those of us who don't slot neatly into your bigoted
gender binary? Please, educate yourself. Also, there is no point
trying to reason with Sondra Halliday – she too is a bigot, though
of a different stripe from you.

1 Reply:

From: Sondra Halliday, London

Fuck all the way off, Herr Jennda. David Howard – you seem to be
suffering from White Knight Syndrome, AKA Entitled Tosser
Syndrome. I don't need the endorsement of any man, so stop
trying to insert yourself into feminism, which belongs to women and
has nothing to do with you. You're not wanted or needed. As for
you, DC Conker Deep (you gave yourself away with 'it sure as shit
ain't us' when you should have said 'them' if you were pretending
not to be a detective) . . . sorry once again if I hurt your delicate
manfeelz, and, yes, please do educate yourself. 'Deign' is the word
you're looking for. 'Dane' is Hamlet.

13

14/1/2015

The red-brick semi-detached house on Thress Street in Rawndesley had nothing to distinguish it apart from the colour of its door – an unusual shade that Sellers, if forced, would have described as sea green – and a small metal fountain in the mainly paved-over front garden, with water spouting from it. Around the fountain's base were flat smooth stones of different sizes that hadn't got there by accident; someone had arranged them in a kind of three-hump circle shape. Sellers wasn't surprised, given whose house this was and what he'd learned about her in advance from her website. Still – it was nice that there were people who cared enough to make a shape out of matching stones around a fountain in their garden.

The door opened and a woman appeared.

'Ms Baillie?'

'DC Colin Sellers? Welcome!' She beamed at him. 'Please, call me Lane. All my friends and family do.'

Well, that was easy. Sellers told himself not to leap to conclusions.

Lane Baillie was in her late fifties or early sixties and dressed in a red tunic with a wide black belt, black leggings and slip-on pumps. Her outfit was too young for her, but it looked okay. Her smile made her seem much younger too, though her neat, short hair was silvery-grey, like tinsel, and her skin was lined. Sellers checked with himself: was she definitely middle-aged to old? Yes, her hands were covered in liver spots. She might even have been getting on for seventy, in fact.

It must have been the radiant smile that had confused him,

creating a momentary illusion of youth. It was unusual for someone her age to beam like that – like a kid who'd just found some buried treasure and realised it was better than she'd hoped it would be. Sellers was as taken aback by the smile as by Lane's enthusiastic cry of 'Welcome!' She was doing a convincing impression of someone whose day had been greatly enhanced as a result of his sudden arrival in it; no one had ever looked at him that way before – not his mother, not Stacey, not either of his kids, none of the women he'd shagged. Literally no one.

Sellers decided it meant Marjolein Baillie was probably hoping to try and con him out of something, like all his money, or into something, like a freaky religious cult. He'd done his homework. As well as being a counsellor and psychotherapist, she was – and she admitted it; she advertised it – an Ishaya of the Bright Path. There were articles on her website explaining what this meant, or purporting to, though Sellers had read all of them and was none the wiser. The Bright Path was described in several places as being a kind of meditation, though there were no instructions for how to do it, and in other paragraphs it was referred to more as if it were a religion.

'Please come in,' Lane Baillie stood aside and gestured with her left arm to indicate that he should enter. Using a series of arm movements that made Sellers think of ballet dancing, she directed him, wordlessly, into the second room they came to.

It was a lounge with hardly anything in it. French doors at one end led onto a small, tidy, fenced-in garden. The focal point of the room was a white marble-effect fireplace. There was a matching armchair and sofa – pale green with a white leaf pattern – a beige carpet and a rug that was made out of tiny wooden beads strung together. Sellers hadn't met a wooden rug before. He wondered if Bright Path meditation might involve lying on it naked, with the wooden beads digging into your back. He stopped thinking about this in time to save himself from embarrassment.

'Please have a seat.' Still beaming at him as if he was the best visitor she'd ever had, Lane indicated the sofa.

Sellers sat, wondering what would have happened if he'd ignored the arm signal and gone for the chair.

'I'll be with you very soon.' She turned and left the room, closing the door behind her.

Sellers stared at the fireplace. Along the edge of the bottom bit were five small white pebbles and two royal blue ceramic bowls full of what looked like water. Water, fire, stone. Perhaps Bright Path meditation involved thinking about the different elements. Was stone an element?

The door opened again and Lane appeared with two pint glasses full of water. 'Here you are,' she handed one to Sellers with a new smile. 'You can put it down anywhere: on the arm of the sofa, on the floor. And please feel free to put your feet up on the sofa if you'd like to. You can remove your shoes if you want – if it would make you more comfortable. It's up to you!'

'Thank you.' Sellers wanted to hold his glass of water in his hands, sit upright and leave his shoes on, but he appreciated the general message: whatever he wanted to do was okay with Lane Baillie.

Whatever Colin Sellers wanted to do had never been okay with anybody before.

'So, then.' Lane sat down in the armchair, curling her legs under her body. 'What brings you here?'

'I'm one of the Culver Valley detectives working on the Billy Dead Mates investigation. I'm sure you're sick to death of hearing about it.'

Lane shook her head. 'Billy . . . Dead Mates?'

'It's all over the news. I assume you've been following it, along with the rest of the country.'

'I'm sorry, I haven't heard anything about it.'

Sellers laughed. 'You're kidding?'

'No. I don't read newspapers or watch the news.'

'Oh. That's . . . pretty unusual!'

'Yes, it is.' She smiled. 'Do *you* keep up to date with the news?'

He was supposed to be interviewing her, not the other way round, but since she sounded genuinely interested . . . 'Yeah, pretty much. Depressing as it usually is these days.'

'But you don't stop watching? Or reading, or listening?'

'No. It's tempting, sometimes. It can get you down.'

'Yes, that's what so many people say. I think – I mean, this might not be of interest to you, and I know it's not what you came here to talk about, so forgive me – but I think a lot of people with social consciences imagine they have a duty to immerse themselves, via the media, in the misery of others less fortunate than themselves. Having a social conscience and caring about others is of course a *great* thing. But there's a danger that the misery that can seem to be everywhere will affect people negatively, and – quite understandably – they'll internalise that negative energy and spread it around, causing more pain and suffering. I believe positive change can only come from *positive* energy. Meeting new people, seeing that *everyone* has good in them – which is incredibly obvious when you sit face to face with even the most troubled person and try to help them. I prefer to devote my attention to that instead of the news.'

'Well, I read the news, but . . . I couldn't in all honesty describe myself as someone with a social conscience,' Sellers said. 'If I had my way I'd win the lottery and live out my days as a tax exile with my own private island. My wife says I'm a selfish . . . er, a selfish git.'

Lane laughed. 'We're all selfish much of the time. That's only human. But of course you have a social conscience! You're a policeman. Every day you do your best to make the world a safer place for everyone in the Culver Valley. Don't you?'

'I s'pose.'

'Well, then. Anyway, I'm not saying for a moment you should

stop watching the news. In fact, I think it's great that you can and do, and still remain the person you are!'

Sellers didn't know what she meant. He was about to ask when she said, 'I want to help you in any way I can, but insofar as it's possible, I'd rather not hear any details of murders or cruelty – if that's all right?'

'Oh.' Normally people wanted to hear all the repulsive details and weren't nearly as keen on the helping part. 'Yes, that's no problem at all. I mean . . . if you want, I can tell you nothing about Billy and stick to asking questions. If you don't mind not knowing any context?'

'That's fine.' Lane smiled.

'Although because you're involved – only at several removes, so it's nothing to worry about . . . But because your name's been . . . mentioned in connection with Billy – this case, I mean – I'm going to need to ask you where you were on several dates, if that's possible. It's really nothing to worry about.'

'Absolutely fine. Shall I get my diary?'

'That'd be great, thanks. For this year and last year, if you have them.'

'Yes, I do.'

Lane rose gracefully and left the room, closing the door carefully. Sellers heard footsteps on the stairs, then nothing for about ten seconds, then more footsteps.

The door opened silently and she reappeared with two black leather A4-sized books. One by one, Sellers told her the dates of the five murders. It soon became apparent she wasn't a suspect. Two of the five days Lane had spent at a private hospital in London doing group therapy with breast cancer patients from 9 a.m. until 4 p.m. Another two had been spent here at her home, seeing private clients. She couldn't share their details now, she explained, because of confidentiality, but she could certainly contact them and ask if any of them were willing to speak to Sellers and vouch for her. On the most recent Billy-kill day, Tuesday, 6 January, Lane and her husband Duncan had been in Paraty, Brazil, on holiday.

'Don't worry about asking your patients – clients, whatever – about the November and December dates,' Sellers told her. If Lane Baillie was anything other than the kind, gentle person she appeared to be, he would walk through Spilling town centre naked. Though that particular gesture would mean less coming from him than it would from someone who hadn't already once done that while very drunk, in the early hours of a particularly disappointing-on-the-picking-up-girls-front morning in 1999. Sellers shuddered. What a state he'd been in that night: his absolute low point, and, let's face it, there was stiff competition.

'Are you all right?' Lane Baillie was leaning forward to inspect him, with a concerned expression on her face.

'Fine, thanks.' He grinned. 'Sorry! All right, so we've dealt with the dates. Moving on . . .' He produced the printout of the 'Two Sisters' story and passed it to Lane. 'Is this familiar to you?'

'Yes!' It was as if Sellers had reintroduced her to an old friend. 'This is a wonderful story. I give it to most of my clients. I have a few others like it – stories that contain unusual and, I hope, enlightening insights about life. I like to share them with as many people as I can.'

'Let's talk numbers: how many clients have you had in the last year, say, and what percentage of that number have you shared the stories with?'

'I have no more than ten private clients at any given time. That's my upper limit, if I want to give each of them the very best of myself, which I do. I also have the people I see at the hospital. There are about sixteen in that group.'

Cancer patients, thought Sellers. Marion Hopwood had been murdered on a cancer ward.

'I think the percentage must be a hundred,' said Lane. 'There's a wonderful website, Boundlessconsciousness.com. It has many stories on it. Sometimes I print a particular one for a particular client, but I try to make sure I tell *all* the people I work with about the site, so that they can discover the wonderful stories for themselves. And I've put some of them on my website – with permission, of course. Have you read this one, "The Two Sisters"?'

Sellers nodded. 'We all have. It's funny, actually – when I first read it, I thought, this is daft. It's trying to make out that people who fight for good causes are doing more harm than selfish, greedy people.' *And then I met Sondra Halliday.*

Lane laughed. 'It does seem upside-down at first glance, doesn't it? But in fact, if you read it closely, the story says nothing critical about those who *work hard* for good causes. The world urgently needs those people – you're one of them! Saving us from harm, keeping us safe.'

Sellers felt positively heroic.

'What the story *is* saying, though, is that people who devote their energies to *fighting* are helping neither themselves nor others. Whereas someone who enjoys life and spends their days having fun and feeling happy – remember, in the story the words "greedy" and "selfish" are negative value judgements unilaterally imposed by the sister whose every moment is spent fighting. The other sister would probably describe herself as fun-loving and jolly – someone who makes sure to enjoy all life has to offer! Someone like you.'

Lane smiled. 'I hope you don't mind my saying so, but you have a strong positive energy about you. I think you're someone with a real zest for life, aren't you?'

'Undoubtedly. But . . . well, some would say not in a good way. I don't always . . . behave all that well. Anyway, I think you're right about the moral of the story. This case has brought me into contact with a journalist who shares a personality type with the fighting, negative sister. She claims to be fighting for justice and equality, but all she does is spew venom all day long.'

'How sad.' Lane looked shocked, and pressed the palm of her hand flat against her collarbone. Sellers wondered if the words 'spew venom' had been too much for her.

'To take your two points one by one . . .' she said. 'Nobody always behaves well. It isn't only you. If you'll pardon my outspokenness, I do sense that you have many clouds close to the surface, but I sense more strongly that if you could clear those clouds away, your positive energy would burn even brighter than it does at present. You're someone who is capable of doing endless good in our world. I hope you know that. I felt it as soon as I opened the door.'

Sellers didn't know it, and wasn't sure he wanted to. He concentrated on sipping his water, to avoid eye contact.

'With regard to your other point – the journalist – like so many people, she's completely unaware of the harm she's doing. So when she produces anger in you, or hurt feelings, try to remember that, while those feelings are valid and understandable and you certainly mustn't judge yourself for them, what this person needs is not blame but kindness and empathy. She's probably as she is because she was deprived of both in her earliest years. Or perhaps she suffered a trauma and could only make herself strong enough to survive it by building a shell of hate and blame. What I would say about a person like that is: there's *always* hope. One day, with luck, and if she's treated with kindness and understanding, she'll see a better way forward and, as she stops causing pain to others, her own pain will fall away.'

To anyone else, Sellers would have said, 'Yeah, dream on – you haven't met Sondra Halliday.' To Lane Baillie, he said, 'I hope you're right.'

Did he hope that? Did he give a toss about Sondra Halliday's welfare? He decided to stick to the questions he came here to ask.

'So everyone you've helped, all your clients, they probably know about these stories. Let's try a different tack, then. I know you're bound by confidentiality, and I'm not asking for a name or names at this point, but has any of your more recent clients asked you to help him or her resist the urge to kill somebody?'

Lane straightened up in her chair. 'I'm just thinking about whether I can responsibly answer your question. Yes, if I don't give you a name, I think I can. So . . . yes, that is the case. Not a current client. Someone who came regularly towards the end of last year.'

'I assume people come to you with all sorts of problems – was this an unusual one, or do you hear it all the time?' *Don't ask to know the name too soon.*

'Very unusual. No one has ever said anything like that to me before. I will say this, though: from the first session, I never for a moment feared there was a real danger my client *would* kill the person in question. I was absolutely sure sh . . . he or she wouldn't. There was a real determination not to. The head was saying no as loudly as the heart was saying yes.' Lane sighed. 'I was sad and disappointed when the client stopped coming. A lot of help was still needed, and I . . . well, I was worried. I tried the number she'd given me a few times but it seemed not to be in use any more.'

'Was the person this client was trying not to kill a journalist called Sondra Halliday, by any chance?'

Lane looked scared. 'Oh, no,' she said. 'I hope . . . I don't know what I hope, really. I was going to say, "I hope she hasn't hurt anyone or been hurt", but then if she hasn't, someone has – or else you wouldn't be here.'

This was the problem, thought Sellers. Bad things existed and always would, no matter how many smooth stones and bowls of still water you sat next to.

'Can you answer the question? Was it Sondra Halliday?'

'Yes, it was.'

Bingo. 'And this former client of yours was a woman, I take it? You said "she".'

Lane nodded. 'Has . . . has something happened to the journalist?'

'No.'

'Thank goodness.' Lane closed her eyes, clearly relieved.

'Something's happened to other people, though, and your former client is a suspect.'

'I very much doubt . . . I mean, you wouldn't try so hard not to kill the person you hate most in the world if you're willing to kill other people, would you? It wouldn't make sense.'

'Did she say that she hated Sondra Halliday more than anyone in the world?'

Lane nodded.

'Did she say why?'

'Yes. It was because she – the journalist – was telling lies about my client. In the press: misrepresenting her character and her motivation. She didn't say in relation to what, so that's all I know. The client chose not to share any more details.'

I bet she did.

'I . . . I must admit, I did think it might be a delusion of some sort.'

'Sondra Halliday's the person I was talking about before,' said Sellers. 'The spewer of venom.'

'Oh!' Lane's eyes widened. 'I see. Well, I told my client the same thing I told you. What Sondra Halliday needs is what we all need: love, kindness, compassion. I expect she's not been given nearly enough of it in her life. Most of us aren't. I'm sure that was true of my client also, though unfortunately I didn't know her long enough to find out, really. She was reluctant to discuss feelings and preferred to talk about ideas. For example, she was fascinated to hear the . . . philosophical underpinnings of my spiritual practice, but absolutely unwilling to talk about how she felt.'

By 'spiritual practice', Sellers assumed Lane meant being an Ishaya, whatever that was. He'd have liked to ask, but was afraid it might lead to more embarrassing talk of his surface clouds or his brightly burning positive energy. He wondered if Lane had been contacted yet for a DNA sample; her name was on the list. She probably had special, glittery, spiritual DNA.

'My client showed me no more of herself than her desire to

kill this particular journalist. I learned nothing else about her life or her feelings. I was hoping I'd be able to persuade her to lower her defences, gradually, but she stopped coming, so I couldn't.'

'Ms Baillie, I—'

'Do call me Lane, please.'

'I really need to know the name of this former client. Is it any of the following: Kim Tribbeck, Isobel Sturridge, Lisa Norbury, Gisela Bloor, Muriel Pearson, Faith Kendell, Samantha Granger?'

'I would *love* to be able to help you.' Lane frowned.

'If you recognised one of those names . . . I have reason to believe its owner might have committed five murders.'

'Well, yes, quite,' said Lane apologetically. 'But I can't betray client confidentiality. I'm so sorry. This is a terrible situation. I *really* can't break confidentiality, but . . . oh, goodness, this is difficult.'

Sellers waited, confident that she'd talk herself into helping him eventually.

'It sounds as if you don't know for certain that this person committed these crimes?' she said hopefully.

'Not yet. It's highly likely, though. And even more likely that she'll try it again and probably succeed.'

'Oh, dear.' Lane looked stricken. She closed her eyes and took a deep breath. When she opened them a few seconds later, she smiled. All signs of distress had vanished. 'I know what we'll do,' she said. 'In situations where two opposing needs clash, there is always a solution that will satisfy both sides.'

Sellers was certain that couldn't be true.

'You don't believe me? Sometimes it requires one side, or both, to realise that their prior definitions of "need" and "satisfaction" must be deconstructed and rebuilt, but . . . there's always a way of getting there.' She stood up. 'I have to do something that will take about ten minutes. Please wait here.'

Sellers was confused. Was the something that would take

ten minutes connected to their conversation or not? Did she need to use the bathroom, or ring a friend?

He resolved to stand firm. His definition of 'need' was, and would remain, 'I'm not leaving this house without the name of the person in question'.

After a while, Lane returned with a grey felt bowler hat in her hand. She was holding it the wrong way round. As she walked towards him, Sellers saw that it was full of torn up bits of paper.

'I've separated the first names and the surnames of several of my clients,' she said. 'Therefore, if you find a "Philip" or a "Jane" or a "Thompson" or a "Townsend", it will mean nothing to you. You won't know who it is with only one half of the name to go on, will you? Even if you have an old friend named Philip Townsend, it's unlikely to be him that's my client. Do you see how it works?'

'Yes.' Sellers was impressed. 'Because I'm not looking for a specific Jane, she could be Jane Fonda the actress or my ex-girlfriend Jane Gregson. I don't know it's the one I know because Gregson could just as easily be the surname of a different client of yours. But if there's a first name *and* a surname in this hat from our Billy case notes . . .'

'Precisely.'

'That's clever.'

Lane looked delighted. '*Thank* you,' she said, handing the hat to Sellers.

He shook out the pieces of paper and laid them out flat one by one: Judy, Sally, Annabelle, Peter, Crompton, Liz, Scott, Richman . . . When he saw a first name that made his heart beat louder in his ears, Sellers continued to lay out the rest in neat rows. There might not be a match. He didn't want to get excited prematurely. He smiled to himself, imagining the joke Gibbs would have made if he'd heard that last thought.

Sellers gasped when he saw the surname he'd been hoping against hope to see. *A match*. And – oh, fuck – a massive oversight on the part of him and his team. Waterhouse would break all previous records on the foul mood front when he heard the news.

Slowly, Sellers bent to pick up the only two pieces of paper on the floor that mattered.

The name on the first was Faith.

The second: Kendell.

~

An hour later, having apologetically postponed his meeting with Joshua Norbury's sister Lisa, Sellers was in the cancer ward at the RGI talking to the hospital's head of oncology, Radimir Nowak. He was a tall, thin Polish man with the neatest haircut Sellers had ever seen – almost like a graph in haircut form.

'You're absolutely positive?' Sellers asked him.

'I am positive, yes. We know our patients and we know their families – we pride ourselves on keeping a record of all such information. Otherwise, we would not be able to monitor—'

'Thank you, yes, I understand,' Sellers cut him off. The list of things on which Radimir Nowak prided himself was long, and the doctor seemed determined to talk Sellers through it item by item. For example, there had been his insistence that everybody – especially a policeman who must have touched many guns and criminals – disinfect their hands at the mobile handwash station in the ward corridor. Then there were Nowak's exemplary colleagues, the well-run ward. *Not quite exemplary and well run enough to prevent a patient from being murdered*, Sellers had thought but not said.

'So no one by the name of Faith Kendell had a mother in this ward, being treated for cancer, on Tuesday, 6 January?'

'Definitely not.'

'And no one called Faith Kendell was a patient here herself on that day?'

'No, there was not. I mean *she* was not. I apologise for my flawed English.'

'It's all right – my Polish's nonexistent.'

'I would not have expected it to be otherwise,' said the doctor. Sellers thanked him and left.

There were no two ways about it: this was a cock-up of heinous proportions. Everybody had forgotten all about Faith Kendell as soon as it had emerged that the 'Death devours all lovely things' book had been found in Marion Hopwood's bed.

At that point, Faith had become, in all their minds, just someone who happened to be at the RGI because her relative was sick. No one had checked.

Faith Kendell, who also happened to start a conversation with Kim Tribbeck outside the hospital, one that made Kim decide she liked this stranger rather a lot . . .

Alone in the lift on the way down to the ground floor, Sellers kicked the mirror and swore.

They'd all been so busy trying to cast Faith Kendell as Billy's fifth victim, then rejecting her when someone else came along and claimed the part, that they'd failed to audition her for the role of murderer.

Not that she needed them to do that. She'd given herself the part; her schedule of lethal performances had begun long before any of them knew her name.

There was no point regretting the past – Sellers imagined Lane Baillie would impress this upon him if she were here. The important thing now was to move fast and get some answers. Who was Faith Kendell, and why was she killing people?

When the lift doors opened on the ground floor, Sellers pulled out his phone, took a deep breath and rang Simon.

14 January 2015

Dear Sondra

You haven't read the books I sent, have you? You've
had no time. I know this because I've been watching
your activity on Twitter, and it's clear that you
spend the majority of your time exchanging insults
with those you perceive as your enemies. Or if you're
not scrapping on Twitter, you're writing your articles
for *Lifeworld*, in which you say the same thing over
and over again.

Your confusion about the nature of reality is severe.
There's no shame in that. I used to be as deep in the
dark as you are. Now I can see the light even if I
can't reach it myself, and, surprisingly, that's good
enough for me. It's a huge step forward. Perhaps you
could make similar progress?

Since you're probably never going to stop tweeting
'Fuck you, misogo-splainer' for long enough to read
Beloved or *Jude the Obscure*, I thought I'd try
something quicker and more fun: a quiz. Lane showed me
something similar the first time I went to see her. I
kept it because it made such an impression on me, and
I've adapted it below for you, to reflect your
interests. Don't worry if you get all the answers
wrong. Read the correct answers I've provided
underneath each question.

HOW ENLIGHTENED ARE YOU?

1. Which statement is most accurate?

    a) Men and women are not two separate groups.

b) Men and women are socially conditioned to behave
   differently.
c) Men and women are biologically and
   psychologically different.
d) I refuse to pick any option that puts 'Men'
   before 'women' in the word order. That's a
   syntactical reinforcement of oppressive gender
   structures.

Answer: a. 'Men' and 'women' are irrelevant
categories the human mind has created. Every man,
woman and child on the planet is Awareness,
irrespective of his or her bodily configuration or
set of opinions. The people you attack on Twitter
are you, and you are them, because at the level of
the true self, we are all that same Awareness or
Consciousness with no limit, beginning or end.

2. You, Sondra Halliday, insult and Twitter-block
dozens of people every day because:

a) They are abusive misogynists who deserve it.
b) Women shouldn't have to repress their feelings to
   placate the patriarchy.
c) You are fighting for a fairer world, which means
   you can't always be nice.
d) You have a pool of unhappiness inside you that
   has nothing to do with what anybody tweets to
   you, and that is easily triggered.

Answer: d. The objects of your anger tap into a
discontent - or rage, or pain - that you carry
around with you as a result of your misunderstanding
of the nature of reality. The source of negative
emotion is *always* the belief that one is small,

separate, inadequate and incomplete. It is never what the other person has done that has made you angry or upset. Once you understand that your essential self is limitless Awareness that cannot be harmed, you will cease to be angry or miserable.

3. A truly enlightened person is:

a) Someone who agrees with you, Sondra Halliday, about everything.
b) Someone who understands that there is no such thing as 'brain sex', and that we are all individuals who happen to be biologically male or biologically female - therefore gender must be abolished.
c) Someone who knows that both biological sex and gender are irrelevant.
d) Someone who wears a T-shirt with 'This is what a feminist looks like' printed on it.

Answer: c. Boundless Awareness, which is neither the mind nor the body, is the innate nature of every human being. Awareness has no biological sex, no gender, and remains unaffected by social conditioning. Therefore, focusing on these issues as a source of division will always take us further away from our true selves and create more inner pain and external conflict and suffering. Instead, for greater fulfilment and peace all round, we should focus on our oneness and on the insignificance of the apparent differences between us.

4. 'Not All Men are sexist pigs' is a bad thing to say because:

a) Male supremacists say it all the time, so it must be part of the apparatus of oppression.
b) No man is a sexist pig. Not a single one.
c) Everyone knows it's true that not all men are sexist, but one shouldn't say it because men as a class have created this violent world, and we need to talk about that, and so to pop up and say 'Not all men . . .' diverts attention away from that vital discussion.
d) It's unfair to pigs.

Answer: b. People behave in a range of unhealthy ways as a result of the private pools of pain and rage their egos carry around. However, no man's true self is sexist. The ego is not the self. At the level of self, all men and all women are the same, and all are boundless Consciousness. The mind is not the self, therefore all our opinions and behaviours, if we are unenlightened, have nothing to do with who we are.

5. The vast majority of murders are committed by men. Therefore anyone who disputes that male violence is the biggest problem in our society:

a) Is a misogynist or an idiot.
b) Is a victim of patriarchal brainwashing, and therefore should not be blamed. Patriarchy is to blame, not individuals.
c) Should be blocked and reported.
d) Is correct.

Answer: d. The biggest problem is not male violence but our collective misunderstanding of reality. Once we recognise reality for what it is, we understand

that things like murder and death are not real. They
are merely concepts - the dream-like projections of
our minds. Our true self, the one we all are and
which is neverending Awareness, cannot be killed.
(With regard to the murders of physical bodies,
which do occur, these will happen less and less
often as we gradually come to learn that the hatred
and anger that drives a killer to kill is not, in
fact, a hatred of his chosen victim, but, instead,
either the dangerous chasm that has opened between
his ego and his true self - which we call
'unconsciousness' - or the mistaken belief that his
self can be harmed by the actions of another.)

6. If one day women are liberated by feminism from the
male oppression that they have always endured:

a) I will be proud of the part I played in making
   that happen.
b) I will DM Deepak Chopra and demand that he
   endorses sneering and sniping online all day long
   as a healthy spiritual practice.
c) I will say, 'This has nothing at all to do with
   me.'
d) I will need to find something else to start
   attacking people about, because I'm full of rage
   and I misunderstand its cause.

This is a trick question, since the true self of
every woman is already free, so there is no need for
liberation. But if we interpret the question in the
way most people would, there are two correct
answers, c and d. C because once you are
enlightened, you no longer think of the self as an
agent of action. Enlightened people know that they

```
are actionless Consciousness. D is also correct:
your pain and rage will not dissipate until you stop
mistaking yourself for your ego. Your desire for
liberation is a thirst that can only be quenched by
getting in touch with your true self.

Regards,

Your Secret Detractor

PS. I've enclosed another story, 'The Dress'. Read it
and think.
```

~

The Dress
from *Stories of Enlightenment*

One day, a fashion designer named Perdita went out to buy a birthday present for her personal assistant, Dolores. Perdita was passionate about clothes, so she decided to buy Dolores a beautiful new trouser suit, knowing they were Dolores' favourite thing to wear. She went to the exclusive department store near her home and pressed the button to summon the lift, since all the clothes were on the third floor.

When the lift doors opened, five or six women tumbled out, all clutching carrier bags to their bosoms and all enthusiastically talking about 'the most wonderful dress'. As they walked away, Perdita heard them laughing about how they'd have to make sure they didn't all wear the fabulous dress at the same time, or to the same parties, otherwise that would be embarrassing.

As she took the lift up to the third floor, Perdita felt confused. Surely those women couldn't *all* have bought the very same dress! That never happened, unless it was a group of bridesmaids whose outfits had to match – but from what she'd overheard, Perdita didn't think that applied in this instance.

When Perdita arrived at the women's clothes department, a shop assistant pounced on her. 'How lucky that you're here!' she exclaimed. Perdita was a regular customer and everybody knew her. 'We have the most amazing dress in stock,' the assistant gushed. 'It's made from a new fabric I've never seen before – honestly, it's like magic! Just touch it and you'll see! I've never seen a dress sell so fast – but luckily for you, we have one left!' When Perdita told her that she was looking for a present for her PA, the shop assistant said, 'Oh, well, then – it's her lucky day! This dress will change her life!'

A few seconds later, Perdita was examining the item of clothing in question. She was rather embarrassed to admit it, but she wasn't impressed at all. She could sort of see why everyone else was so keen, because the dress was very different from any other that she'd seen or worn, but she thought it looked cheap and ugly. In fact, it struck her, in its design, as deliberately trying to make a mockery of fashion and of dresses – so much so that Perdita wondered if this was what the designer had intended.

'Isn't it spectacular?' said the shop assistant. '*Everyone* adores it.'

Perdita wondered if perhaps Dolores might agree with everyone else rather than with her. She ignored her misgivings, bought the dress, and left the shop with it a few minutes later.

When Dolores unwrapped the present, her first thought was, 'Oh, please, God, no – this thing is hideous. What is it? I mean, is it even a dress? Perdita says it is, but . . . ugh!'

Not wanting to be rude, however, Dolores smiled, said thank you, and hung the dress up at the back of her wardrobe, planning never to wear it.

The next morning, in their separate houses, Perdita and Dolores woke up and knew instantly that something was badly wrong. Their hands were raw and blistered, seeping and oozing. But the most terrifying thing was that on both women's hands, the skin (where it was still intact) had turned the exact colour of the dress.

Horrified, and dosed up to the eyeballs on painkillers, the two women together hurried back to the department store to complain. 'It must be the dress! Look at the colour of our hands!' they screamed, in terrible agony from their weeping flesh. The shop assistant said, 'I'm so sorry to have to contradict you, ladies, but it simply *cannot* be the dress, or else all my other customers would have been back to complain too, and none of them has. So, no, I'm afraid you can't have a refund.'

On their way out of the department store, Perdita and Dolores tripped over the log-thick legs of a street-sleeper. It was hard to tell if this person was a man or a woman. 'Your poor hands,' he or she intoned in a deep voice. 'Your poor hands. Ah, but you can't pretend you didn't have a hand in it! Four hands, I should say.'

'Are you a man or a woman?' asked Dolores.

'I'm a sage,' said the Sage.

'What did you mean about us having a hand in it?' Perdita demanded to know.

The Sage startled her by pointing straight at her. '*You* gave something that you knew to be a vile thing to someone you care about. You would never have bought one for yourself, yet you bought one for Dolores here. And *you* . . .' – she turned on Dolores – '. . . *you* accepted this gift, though you didn't want it and would never have bought one for yourself. You spotted its ugliness straight away, yet you accepted it. Both of you recognised instantly the horror of the dress, yet you said and did nothing against it – quite the opposite. You colluded with it. You acted against your own judgement and your own hearts. When we do that, we allow evil to prosper. That is why you have sore hands today.'

'Oh, come on!' snapped Perdita. 'That's superstitious twaddle and demonstrably untrue. *Hundreds*, maybe thousands of people have bought that same dress in shops all over the world. It's a global fashion craze!' Perdita had only just realised this, but she was quite right. She'd noticed that every woman walking past her, as she and Dolores stood on the pavement talking to the Sage, was wearing the horrible dress that barely resembled a dress.

'Look at all these people in the dress!' she cried. 'Their hands look fine!'

'Ah, yes – because they are fools who genuinely love the dress, so they are protected,' explained the Sage. 'You see, we are all human, frail and flawed. We all find it impossible, sometimes, to resist our own strong desires. When we do harm to ourselves or to others, it is often because our better judgement has been paralysed by what feels like an urgent need. But the important thing is this: when our hearts are fully engaged in our actions, even the harmful ones, we are not beyond redemption. All hope is lost, however, when we are not infatuated, not helpless with desire, and yet still, from a position of clear-eyed objectivity, choose to behave in ways that promote evil. Neither of you would ever have bought the dress for yourself – you both instantly recognised its loathsomeness – and yet one of you bought it, and one accepted it into her home *without a word of protest*. Hence: your hands. But know this: whatever happens to the body, the true Self – who we really are – cannot be destroyed. We are Awareness, not flesh.'

Perdita and Dolores didn't believe the Sage for a minute. Still, their hands were causing them such torment that they were willing to try anything. They hurried to Dolores' flat and, together, they tore the dress apart and burned the shreds of it in the barbecue on Dolores' patio. Within seconds, the skin on their hands was once again skin-coloured and all their wounds had healed.

14

How typical of me that the one and only friendship fantasy I've ever entertained turned out to involve someone who wasn't real. Ten minutes ago, Charlie Zailer's phone rang and guess what? It looks as if there is no such woman as Faith Kendell. No bone cancer sufferer with a daughter by that name was on Ward 10 of the RGI on Tuesday, 6 January. There's apparently more evidence that Faith was a fabrication, but I'm not allowed to know what it is.

You've got to hand it to her, whoever she is. Inventing a fake identity? Why not choose the name Faith, to make anyone who falls for it feel extra stupid when they find out they've been duped?

Instead of viewing this incident as embarrassing, I'm going to interpret it in the most flattering way possible, as confirmation that I've been right all along about friends. In short: they're hopeless. My ideal friend doesn't exist in this world.

Maybe I sensed that Faith wasn't carrying masses of tedious actual-person baggage; maybe that was why I liked her. Thinking about it now, all she did was reflect me back to myself. The person I liked more than I'm accustomed to liking my fellow human beings was me. If only an attractive man could endeavour to do the same, that would be ideal: work out exactly what I'd like to hear and then say only that, in between bouts of amazing sex. That's a relationship that might work, unlike all my others.

I don't get it, though. Faith's come to the RGI to murder my grandmother – why strike up a conversation with me outside the hospital, try to ingratiate herself? Does it matter to her that the grandchildren of her victims should warm to her? Absurd.

Or perhaps it was a test: if she says things I'm bound to like and I fail to smile and agree, that proves there's an impediment to my liking her – that might mean I noticed her sneaking into Marion's room with a syringe in her hand.

It's thinking about the timing of it that disturbs me most. How long before she stood outside the hospital, talking to me and smoking, did she inject poison into my grandmother? Ten minutes? Twenty? Did she wait until Drew and I had both left the ward, or did she sneak into Marion's room while we were in the corridor arguing about catheters and bladder infections? Would we have noticed?

The conversation I willingly had with her about friends and dead houseplants would have reassured her that I suspected her of nothing.

Charlie says I shouldn't assume she's killed anyone. She asked the obvious question: if Faith Kendell is Billy Dead Mates, who was the man who gave me the little white book? 'Maybe Billy is two people,' Charlie said. I didn't tell her I'd made the same suggestion to Simon Waterhouse and Chris Gibbs.

One, two, three, seven . . . I don't care how many people Billy turns out to be. More than one murderer doesn't interest me unless there's more than one motive, and I don't believe there is. It has to be something to do with pairs. At first it seemed to be pairs of best friends, but then Marion and I ruined it.

I have a theory I've not yet shared with Charlie. The labels we put on relationships often conceal the emotional truth. Marion and I were grandmother and granddaughter: a bond that ought to be close but wasn't in our case. Could something similar have been true of Linzi Birrell and Rhian Douglas, and of Angela McCabe and Joshua Norbury? Did one of each pair grievously wrong the other, and did the other secretly never forgive them?

~

Thursday, 15 January 2015

I shout, 'Not now!' at whoever's knocking on my hotel room door. It must be someone from housekeeping. They come earlier and earlier. At one time – when I first started touring – you could count on no one bothering you before 11 a.m. Now, unless you put up the 'Do Not Disturb' sign, you're at risk of hearing the rat-a-tat-tat of the virtuous early riser any time from nine o'clock. The White Hart Hotel in St Albans, where Charlie and I spent last night, doesn't even provide any kind of 'Sod off and let me sleep' sign for its guests; I should have known that didn't bode well.

There's more knocking, slower and quieter, as if the person responsible has decided I can't handle the strong stuff.

'Fuck's sake.' I pull on my jeans in order to be dressed enough to open the door.

It's Charlie. 'What the fuck? I thought we were meeting for breakfast at nine thirty.'

'We are. I thought you'd want to see this straight away.' She holds up today's *Times*. I take a step back from the face of the man who gave me the white book.

'Thanks, but I've already seen it.'

'Oh. You ordered a paper too?'

'No. I saw it when the artist did it – at the police station.'

'I thought you might like to see it in the actual newspaper.'

'I'm famous, remember? Getting something into the paper no longer holds any element of thrill for me.'

Charlie's looking over my shoulder into my room. 'Is the book in the drawer?'

'What? Oh. Yes, I told you, I always do it.'

'Same drawer as the Bible?'

'Yup.'

'Can I have a look at it?'

'The Bible?'

I know that's not what she means.

'No. *Delirium of the Brave* by Terence Nithercott.'

The normal, rational thing to do would be to get the book out of the drawer and hand it to her. Standing between a police officer and a hotel room drawer in order to protect an inanimate object that isn't under attack: abnormal, irrational.

'So you still think my dusty old copy of a long-forgotten novel is implicated in five murders, then.'

'Did I say that?'

'I don't understand why you want to look at it.'

'Curiosity. Why don't you want me to see it?'

'I don't *not* want you to . . .' Already this argument's too boring. I pull open the drawer, take out the book and hand it to Charlie. 'It's not hiding anything, I promise. There's nothing remarkable about it apart from that it's dedicated to the same person as that copy's signed to.'

'Really?' Charlie checks. 'So it is. That's a coincidence. Is that why you bought it?'

'I didn't buy it.'

'Oh, that's right – it was a present, wasn't it?'

And that was an attempt to trap me, wasn't it? See if my story about the book's changed?

'Yes, it was.'

'From?'

'Liam Sturridge.'

'Your ex-bit on the side. So it has sentimental value. Is that why you take it with you everywhere?'

'It had no sentimental value to him.' Charlie isn't Liam. It's not her fault. I should have snapped at him while I had him there to snap at. 'He said so when he gave it to me. He thought it was an unusual object, but he didn't care about the relationship implied by the dedication or the handwritten message, or both together – didn't give a shit about it.'

Charlie's leafing through it, and I can't help seeing it through her eyes: just some dull old tome. She's in Liam's camp, not mine. It means nothing to her. Why should it?

I lunge forward and pull it out of her hands. Feeling as if someone's taken a serrated blade to my heart, I start to tear out pages. 'It's a fucking pile of shit and I'm sick of carrying it to every fucking . . . every . . .'

What have I done? What have I done?

I sink to the floor, sobbing, clutching what's left of the book against my chest, trying at the same time to scoop up the scattered pages.

I thought I was ready to live realistically – without a pointless symbol of my fleeting belief in love. I'm not. Too late, though: I've ruined it, like I ruin everything I care about.

'Kim? It's okay. Those pages can be glued back in, I think.'

Charlie's voice seems to come from miles away.

'Even if they can't, you haven't ripped out any of the bits that matter. The dedication's still in there, and the signature.'

I can't get myself together to check if she's right. What if she's wrong? She can't know. I've got the book pressed against my stomach. She can't see what I have or haven't torn out. I lie on my side, howling as if I've lost everything, though I know I haven't. I've never lost anything because I've never had anything, not the way most people do.

'Kim, take deep breaths.'

'I . . . I can't . . .'

Charlie kneels down beside me. I clutch at her sleeve.

'You can. Shall I get you some water?'

'No.' If she moves away, I don't know what I'll do.

I didn't expect this to happen at a random hotel that has nothing to do with anything. I was afraid I'd have a bad reaction to the room at the Narrow Bed Hotel, but not this bad.

This can't be me. I don't cry. I'm scared I won't survive this, and even more scared I will and I'll die of shame. At the moment, I feel nothing but a need to cling on.

'I think water would be a good idea,' says Charlie quietly. 'Why don't you try to get up and come with me to the bathroom?'

'No. I can't move.' My heart's beating too fast but the beats are wrong: each one hurts, like a big ball being forced through a hole that's too small. 'Tell me . . . something.'

'What?'

'Anything. A story. An old case. Anything.' *Something I can concentrate on that isn't sad*. The tears have stopped and I've started to shake. It makes it difficult to speak.

'How about a mystery?'

'Yes,' I whisper.

'Okay,' says Charlie. 'I'm going to tell you a story about my sister Olivia.'

~

'You've got to find out,' I say once we're back on track after a wrong turn on the way out of St Albans. Next stop is Watford Colosseum. 'If it was my brother, or even an acquaintance, I'd have to know.'

'Simon thinks I should stop obsessing,' she says. 'Advice I've never heard him give before. I think I've finally made him realise how boring someone else's obsession can be.'

'I wouldn't call it obsession, I'd call it due process.'

'How so?'

'If someone significantly deceives you and they're not clever enough to conceal their lie, you're entitled to go after them with the full force of your snooping capacity.'

'Yes! Exactly. That's how I feel.'

'Snoop and be proud.' As I say this, the driver of a car we're overtaking turns and stares long and hard at me, as if encouraged by my words, though he couldn't possibly have heard them. He grins and waves. I turn away pointedly. 'I think I just saw Kim

Tribbeck,' he'll be saying to his passengers now, and they'll be asking him if he's sure, or saying, 'So what?' or 'Who's she?'

'The one thing I can't see a way to do is get into Liv's Gmail account,' says Charlie. 'That's really all I'd need. Whatever's going on, she'll be corresponding with someone about it – Nikhil and Natalie, probably. I can't risk it, though. It's unambiguously illegal. I'd need to enlist someone at work to help me, and then we're talking criminal conspiracy.'

'You can't guess her password?'

'I've tried more than a hundred guesses.'

'So you only mind the illegal part if there's a witness? It's okay, I get it. I'd be the same.'

'Shit. I shouldn't have told you that.' Charlie looks at me out of the corner of her eye. 'If Simon knew I'd even *tried* . . . He's not Liv's greatest fan, but Gibbs is the closest thing he has to a best friend.'

'I need to tell you something I haven't told Gibbs or Simon,' I say. 'About the night the man gave me the white book.'

I don't need to, though, do I? It'll make no difference to anything. That means I must want to. I hadn't planned to confess this part but now that I've started, I'd better see it through. 'I told Gibbs that my husband Gabe was with me on the night that I was given the white book – that he came to my gig, then drove back home afterwards because he had an early start at work the next day.'

'And it's not true?'

'True about work but not about the specially early start. If I'd wanted Gabe to stay over, he'd have stayed. I lied to him: told him I wasn't staying overnight in that town, wherever it was. Sometimes I have a driver when I'm on tour: Dmitri. He often picks me up after a gig and drives me on to the next town. That's what I told Gabe was happening that night. It's why he drove home. Otherwise he'd have stayed with me at the Narrow Bed Hotel, got up at 5 or 6 a.m. and driven back to Rawndesley then.'

'You didn't want him with you overnight?' says Charlie.

'No.' I take a deep breath. 'Also in the audience that night was Liam Sturridge, the man I was seeing behind Gabe's back.'

'I see – and Liam was the one you wanted to take to the hotel?'

I nod. 'By pure chance, Liam was in the area for a work away-day. He wanted to come along. I warned him Gabe would be there. Any normal man would have said, "No problem, I'll stay away," but Liam had already decided he and I would be having sex in my hotel that night.'

'You remember Liam saying he was going to be in the area but not which area?'

'I remember everything visually – the feel and the look of the hotel, our room, what we did that night, how I *felt* . . . but the town? No. Names of towns are pretty much interchangeable at this point in my touring career. There are some places on the list that I'm almost certain it wasn't – though even there I'm not positive. And I had a policy of instant deletion when it came to emails and texts from Liam, so I've got no record of where it was.'

'Hang on – surely Liam would remember where the two of you stayed in a hotel? He doesn't spend every night in a different city, does he?'

'No, he doesn't. And yes, I'm absolutely convinced he remembers and even more convinced he'll never part with the information. Soon as I made the connection between the book I was given at a gig and the murder investigation on the news, I rang Liam – from my car, on my way to get the other white book, the one I'd seen on the hospital noticeboard. I asked him where we spent our one and only night in a hotel together. He said, "Don't you remember?" I told him I wouldn't have needed to ask him if I remembered, would I? He said, "I see. In that case, I don't remember either." Bastard went out of his way to be unhelpful. I told him why I needed to know, but he said Billy and the murders had nothing to do with him.'

I was supposed to provide Liam with hassle-free sex, not involve him in a murder investigation. Having screwed up in this respect, I was stupid to give him the chance to punish me for it. When I told DC Gibbs my secret – a lover who visited at night, while my husband was asleep upstairs – I made it sound daring, maybe even glamorous. I was too ashamed to add, 'Oh, by the way: my ex-lover's now refusing to tell me where it was that we spent that night together – he'd rather make me search the entire country for the hotel room we shared.' Even thinking about saying it makes me shudder. I don't mind people thinking of me as immoral but I'd rather no one knew I'd been made a fool of.

So why tell Charlie all this? You didn't have to.

'You didn't suggest to your husband that he miss that gig and come to the next one instead?' asks Charlie. 'It must have been stressful having them both in the same room.'

'It wasn't great. I hoped Gabe'd change his mind about coming with me that night, but . . . we were trying to save our marriage at the time. Well, Gabe was trying. I'm not sure what I was doing. Gabe's got a drug . . . issue. I call it a problem, he doesn't. He's a committed weed-head. I'd been telling him for years that I'd leave if he didn't give it up, and he'd tried to wriggle out of it a million different ways. His latest line was, "Well, you're away all the time on tour – what am I supposed to do when I'm bored and lonely?" So I said, "Okay then, come on the road with me." I didn't really want him there, moaning about having to watch the same set over and over, but if the only way to stop him smoking that crap was not letting him out of my sight . . .' I sigh. 'It didn't work. Nothing worked apart from leaving him. Now I don't give a shit how much he smokes. It's his problem. *Non*-problem, I should say, since it's now his alone to define.'

Charlie's signalling to come off the motorway.

'Where are we going?'

'I'm stopping to ring Simon. He needs to know this. Liam didn't mind coming along to an event where you were with your husband?'

'God, no. Liam knew he was getting laid that night, knew Gabe was going home after the gig. That was all he cared about.'

'I bet he was pleased to be the chosen one,' Charlie says.

'I wouldn't count on it. I'm not sure Liam's ever happy, sad, angry, guilty. He doesn't show any emotion at all. I called him the sex robot.'

Charlie smiles as we pull into the car park of a disused Little Chef with boarded-up windows and part of its sign missing.

She says a quick hello to Simon when he picks up, then passes her phone to me. 'Tell him exactly what you've just told me.'

I assume she doesn't want me to include the sex robot part, so I stick to the facts.

'You're saying Liam Sturridge was with you the night you were given a white book by a man you didn't recognise?' Simon asks.

'Yes.'

'The night you told Gibbs about – the room you described, but didn't remember where it was. You're saying that as well as your husband, Liam Sturridge, your . . . boyfriend at the time, was in that room?'

Haven't I just answered that question? 'That's right.'

'Your husband went home after the gig, correct?'

'Yes. I've already told you that.'

'I'm asking again. Your story's changed, so I need to start from scratch.'

'No, you don't. Everything I told you before still stands. Just make one addition: Liam Sturridge, there that night.'

'Who left the venue first, Liam or your husband?'

'Gabe, obviously. Liam stayed there because he knew he and I would be going on to the hotel.'

'Which hotel?'

'I don't know its name. Or where it was. You *know* this! That's why I told Charlie about Liam, so that you could ask him. He remembers, and he wouldn't tell me, but he might tell you.'

'Can you tell me anything about the hotel at all?'

'Are you serious? I've already—'

'What can you tell me about that hotel?'

'The bed in my room was too narrow! Not a proper double. As you already know.'

'Did Liam Sturridge share that narrow bed with you?'

'Yes.'

'All night?'

'Yes.'

'Until what time in the morning?'

'I don't know. Maybe . . . eight, eight thirty?'

'Didn't he have work the next morning?'

'I don't remember. He'd been at a work team-building thing that day . . . I'm not sure about the day after. Why don't you ask him?'

'I will.'

Beside me, Charlie lights a cigarette.

'The white book you'd been given – where was it at this point?' Waterhouse continues with his grilling. 'In your bag at the hotel?'

'No. I've told you, and I've told Gibbs: I either left it at the venue on the table or I chucked it in a bin there.'

'So it wasn't among your possessions at the hotel?'

'I've just answered that question.'

'Could it have been among Liam's possessions? What if he picked it up at the gig after you discarded it? Is that possible?'

'I don't know!'

Charlie takes the phone from my hand. 'Enough, Simon,' she says. 'Calm down. We'll ring you from the hotel in a bit.'

I watch her press the end-call button. *Thank God for that.*

'Sorry,' she says. 'It's the buzz of an influx of new information. There's been a lot today. He gets like that, I'm afraid.'

'Please don't say I have to speak to him again today. Please.'

She laughs.

~

Let me say upfront that I approve of Simon Waterhouse. He's a frighteningly intelligent force for good, and I'm glad he exists. I've also never had such a powerful feeling of escape successfully achieved as I did when he declared our second telephone conversation of the day – much longer and more laborious than the first – to be over. There was a catch, however: what had struggled free from his sustained interrogation was not the richly complex person I'd been beforehand but a squinting husk whose brain matter had largely been sucked out through an invisible straw.

I lay down on the bed in my room at the Bradley Park Hotel in Milton Keynes – a place with nice big beds and therefore not The One but simply the one for tonight – and stared at the ceiling, allowing myself to drift into a welcome trance state. I couldn't speak, couldn't close my eyes. I needed an urgent transfusion of everything it was possible to transfuse.

Charlie laughed as if it were the funniest thing ever, and told me that conversations with Simon were often like that and I shouldn't take it personally. Other times, she said, he clammed up and could hardly be persuaded to say a word. It depended on how close he was to an answer: very close and he'd go quiet, too busy thinking. Endlessly browbeating people with questions was what he did when he was angry about getting closer but still not being close enough.

As I lay there listening to this, I thought to myself, 'This is the man who called his wife obsessive for wanting to know what her sister's lying about, who says it's none of their business and they should be content to remain blissfully ignorant.'

If that's what he thinks, then why wasn't it his attitude from the start? Why had he agreed to follow Liv and Gibbs to Cambridge? Charlie said he seemed to want to solve the mystery as much as she did at that stage. And then he changed his mind, for no apparent reason?

I didn't believe it. The man I'd just been grilled by on the phone would never decide he didn't want to know the answer. Never. Whether it was a professional matter or a personal one.

The most likely explanation for his change of heart seemed so obvious to me, I couldn't believe it hadn't occurred to Charlie: whatever was going on with Liv and Gibbs and this other couple, Simon already knew.

He knew, and he'd decided it was best if Charlie never found out.

Loyalty

from *Stories of Enlightenment*

There were three friends who lived on the same street: Amelia, Pearl and Jasmine. They met for coffee every morning, jogged around the local park together every weekend and went out for cocktails together on Friday nights.

One morning, Amelia arrived at Pearl's house for coffee (they took turns to host and it was Pearl's turn) and was shocked to find both Pearl and Jasmine in tears. 'What on earth is wrong?' Amelia asked.

Pearl and Jasmine told Amelia that a new neighbor, Tara, had sent them each a poison pen letter full of horrible insults.

'Why did she do that?' asked Amelia. 'And how do you know the letters were from her?'

Apparently another neighbor had seen Tara putting the notes in Pearl and Jasmine's mail boxes.

'She thought no one was looking,' said Pearl.

'She did it because she's jealous,' said Jasmine. 'She's got a thing about you, Amelia. She knows we're your best friends, which is what she wants to be. She hasn't got any friends at all.'

'Oh dear! How awful,' said Amelia. Then she said, 'Wait! I've got a fantastic idea.' She ran back to her house and made a few secret phone calls.

The next morning, when Jasmine and Pearl arrived at Amelia's house for coffee, Amelia presented each of them with a gorgeous puppy. Pearl's was a miniature English bull terrier: white with a black circle around one eye, and one black ear. Jasmine's was a lilac horse-coat shar pei. Both women squealed with delight and rushed over to give Amelia a hug. They forgot all about the poison pen letters Tara had sent them and cheered up immediately.

Later that day, Amelia took a bassett hound puppy round to Tara's house. 'You're obviously feeling miserable if you're sending poison pen letters,' she said. 'Here's a gift for you: a lovely dog. He will give you lots of love and cheer you up!'

Tara was incredibly touched. 'Thank you,' she said, cuddling the puppy against her body. Amelia left feeling happy. She was sure that Tara would never again send a poison pen letter. The basset hound would be her new best friend, and he'd enable her to make other friends too while she was out walking him.

The next day, over coffee, Amelia told Pearl and Jasmine about Tara and the bassett hound. Their reactions could not have been more different. 'That's such a neat idea,' said Pearl. 'I know how much I already love my puppy after only one day. No one with this much love inside them could sit down and write a vicious letter. Let's hope you've solved all Tara's problems, and all of ours too.'

Jasmine, meanwhile, had a face like a thundercloud. 'How *could* you?' she raged at Amelia. 'You bought a *present* for the bitch who wrote me a nasty anonymous letter? You're supposed to be my friend! Give me one good reason why I shouldn't throw you out of my house right now, you disloyal bitch!'

'But I bought a puppy for you too,' Amelia pointed out. 'I demonstrated my loyalty to you by trying to make you happy when I saw that you were sad.'

'But . . . then you also bought one for that bitch Tara! If you were my loyal friend, you'd spit at her in the street, snub her, shun her.'

'No, I wouldn't,' Amelia explained. 'I would never spit at, snub or shun anyone. To behave that way would make me feel terrible.'

'Get out!' screamed Jasmine. 'Betrayer! Judas!'

'I'll leave if you really want me to,' said Amelia, 'but I think you've misunderstood my actions.'

Jasmine turned to Pearl. 'What do you think?' she demanded.

'I . . . I. . . .' Pearl stammered, sensing that anything but complete agreement would be treated by Jasmine as treachery. Still, she wanted to speak up for Amelia. 'I think Amelia's a loyal friend to both of us,' she plucked up the courage to say finally. 'After all, she's been kind to us for as long as we've known her. That's how we should judge her loyalty.'

'But her kindness is worth nothing if she's also kind to that bitch Tara,' Jasmine wailed.

'Why?' asked Pearl. 'I don't think that's true. Her kindness to Tara means that hopefully Tara won't attack us now.'

'She's refused to denounce someone who hurt us, therefore she's disloyal,' Jasmine insisted. 'And now *you're* refusing to condemn her for her betrayal of us – which makes you disloyal too! Get out, both of you!'

That night, in the back gardens of the street on which the four women lived, the three new puppies whispered over garden fences to one another in dog language that humans couldn't understand. One of the puppies declared herself happy because her owner was truly enlightened. Another said he was cautiously optimistic: his owner was a bit screwed up, but had very recently resolved to be less of a disaster area in future (thanks to him, he couldn't help thinking, rather immodestly). The third puppy sighed and confessed to a feeling of deep despair. His owner had a shockingly unhealthy belief system and he saw no hope of her ever changing or learning. She had completely misunderstood what loyalty truly meant.

15/1/2015

'Anyone heard from Dunning? Or the eye-rolling DC Wing?' Proust looked around the table. He, Simon, Sellers, Gibbs and Sam were at the Brown Cow. It was shallow breathing room only again today. Every table had been taken when they'd arrived. They'd only got the one they were sitting at because the Snowman had glared its occupants out of the building. His talent for making strangers feel they'd rather be a thousand miles away, even if that meant abandoning a perfectly decent pudding, was useful at times.

'Wing, Dunning, they've all gone quiet,' said Gibbs. 'It's Marion Hopwood – third Culver Valley murder and the others are all breathing a sigh of relief. Hopwood's death makes it squarely our problem, far as they can see. That and what they know about Waterhouse's reputation as a legend . . . They're all sitting tight, hoping we'll have a solve in hours or days. Then they'll be front and centre, sharing the credit.'

'Waterhouse, you must have heard from Wing,' said Proust. 'Doesn't he stay up all night texting you love-hearts?'

Simon had known something like that was coming. The Snowman had taken to calling the Dorset detective 'the Wing beneath your wind'. 'I've heard nothing,' he said. 'Gibbs is right: everyone's waiting on us.'

'I just can't see a way forward.' Sam sounded despondent.

'Don't say that.' Simon looked up from his pint of Diet Coke. 'We're making solid progress. We'll get the DNA results from our recent batch of samples soon – we might strike lucky.'

'How soon?' asked Gibbs.

'They can't tell me. Not today, that's for sure.'

'Knowing Backlog Towers, all our potential Billies will be dead before we get those results,' said Proust. 'I'm surprised they're still answering their phones.'

'I told them it was top priority,' said Simon. 'I think they'll do their best to get to it. They said they might send the samples on to another lab if they couldn't get to them in the next day or so.'

'Pathetic,' the Snowman snapped.

'Anyway, Liam Sturridge is the latest piece of the jigsaw to slot into place,' said Simon.

Sellers and Sam exchanged a baffled look.

'I thought Sturridge told you nothing,' said Gibbs.

Simon nodded. 'That's right. He must remember the town where he and Kim Tribbeck stayed in a hotel last year. He pretended not to – why? Both of them say it was the only time they ever spent a night anywhere but Kim's cellar. I asked him if he often stays in hotels. Never, he said. So it's not plausible that he doesn't remember where it was. He was lying, and he knew I knew it.'

'And you call that a piece of the jigsaw slotting into place?' Sellers asked.

'It's not an answer – the opposite – but it's part of the whole picture. The things that don't make sense are as vital as the things that do. Liam Sturridge lied. Why? Could mean something, could mean nothing. He wouldn't answer at all until I'd answered his question: didn't Kim remember where it was? When I told him no, she didn't, he said, "Neither do I". I sensed he didn't want to give us any information we hadn't already had from her – either because he cares about her and thinks he needs to protect her, or . . .' Simon broke off and shrugged. 'For what it's worth, I don't think he gives a crap about Kim, or about helping us stop a killer or anything. I've never spoken to a more disengaged-sounding person.'

'Simon's right,' Sellers confirmed. 'I interviewed Sturridge face to face. The radiator on the wall next to him had more personality.'

'Main message I got?' said Simon. 'He wants out of all things Billy. Doesn't want to talk to me on the phone, doesn't want to give me any new information. That'd be too much involvement for him. If I'd said, "Kim's told us the hotel was in Leicester," he'd probably have said, "Yeah, that's right," but he doesn't want be a source. That'd be playing a bigger role than he's comfortable with.'

'Have you checked his alibis?' Proust asked. 'Are they solid?'

'Yes, and yes,' said Gibbs. 'We're also waiting on a list of away-days from last year that his company organised and that Liam attended. Once we've got them, we can see if any are a match with Kim Tribbeck's gig dates from the first half of last year.'

'What about Vincent Van Cop's sketch of the man at the comedy gig? Has no one called in to say it's Liam Sturridge?'

'No.' As always, Simon was pleased to be able to disappoint the Snowman.

'Looks nothing like him, sir,' said Sellers. 'If he was Sturridge, Kim wouldn't have needed to describe him to a sketch artist, would she? She'd have said, "I was given a white book by Liam, the bloke I was shagging at the time."'

'Assuming we can trust her,' said Proust. 'Assuming she's not a fabricator. Has that possibility been thought of? Because – and I wasn't going to say this but I will – I detect no signs of recent brain activity from any of you. You've been flatlining since Marion Hopwood came along and disrupted the neat best friends pattern. Her brain activity's probably outpacing yours at the moment, and she's dead.'

'I think we're all constructing hypotheses all the time, sir,' Sam leapt into auto-mollify mode. 'It's just that at this point anything seems possible.'

'Anything isn't possible,' Simon told him. 'It's not possible that Faith Kendell had a relative on Ward 10 of the RGI the day Marion Hopwood died, as she claimed. And the address and phone number she gave Lane Baillie? Nonexistent. Everything we know of her behaviour suggests guilt, I'd say.'

'I don't see your point,' Proust told him. 'You surely aren't saying that because Faith Kendell is a liar, that must mean Kim Tribbeck isn't one?'

'We know Tribbeck's a liar – to her husband, with another man,' said Simon. 'But we've no reason to think she's lied to us, whereas we know Faith Kendell did, so let's work with what we've got and concentrate on her instead of making things up. We're almost certain it's Billy who's been sending New Age stories to Sondra Halliday, and we know Faith Kendell was a client of Lane Baillie's. Lane Baillie is in the habit of introducing her clients to New Age stories. Liam Sturridge, Drew Hopwood, Gabriel Kearns – they've no connection to Lane that we know of. Faith Kendell's more likely to be Billy than any of—' Simon broke off. 'Than anyone,' he concluded after a second or two, frowning.

'Nobody here has argued that Kendell isn't our most likely suspect, Waterhouse,' said the Snowman. 'You're defensive for no reason, as usual.'

'You accused me of having less brain activity than a dead woman,' Simon reminded him.

Proust turned to Sam. 'That fake phone number Kendell gave to Lane Baillie – contact service providers. Find out if it ever belonged to anyone.'

'Already underway,' said Sellers.

'You were going to say "than any of the men", weren't you?' Gibbs grinned at Simon. 'Faith Kendell's more likely to be Billy than any of the men?'

'What if I was?'

'Nothing. Pointing it out, that's all.'

'I didn't say it, did I?'

'All right, keep your pin in.'

If Simon was more of a sexist than he'd been previously, it was Sondra Halliday's fault. Never before on a murder case had he so ardently hoped the killer would turn out to be a woman.

~

Sergeant Robbie Meakin of Spilling Police knew his obsession with PC Iain Chanter wasn't doing him any good. These days he seemed to spend more time watching Chanter on the sly than doing his own work. He wondered if his antipathy was anything to do with his recent promotion from constable to sergeant. Maybe he felt unworthy of his new rank, and found it easier to focus on the shortcomings of a junior colleague than on his own.

It worried him, too, that he was starting to enjoy disliking Chanter. It was becoming the closest thing he had to a hobby – something he looked forward to. He felt disappointed on the rare days when Chanter said and did nothing to annoy him, and had to resort to taking offence at the young PC's clothes and physical appearance. The knot of his tie was always too knobbly and tight, like a fabric-wrapped walnut, and his arms were too short.

Today wasn't one of the rare days, so Chanter's arms didn't enter Meakin's mind. Chanter was doing a stint fielding responses to the Billy Dead Mates police artist sketch, which had been widely circulated yesterday. That's what he was supposed to be doing, anyway. Instead, he was ignoring the phone ringing on the desk in front of him and staring at his iPad as if nothing existed beyond it. Passing behind him, Meakin spotted the words 'Senior Business Analysts Ref 30' on the screen. He reached over Chanter's shoulder and picked up the phone. Chanter looked up, smiled, and slid his chair out of the way – in the helpful spirit, Meakin imagined, of 'Anything I can do to help you do my job for me, just say the word!'

The caller had nothing useful to offer. She'd thought at first, she said, that the sketch might be of Eric, the pushy Amnesty International volunteer who'd come to her house three nights in a row – always interrupting her supper – to try and persuade her to donate money, even though she'd made it clear from the start that she didn't have much to spare. And he'd had the cheek to say that a one-off tenner wouldn't be ideal and that he'd prefer a regular monthly amount by direct debit! Eric had tried to make her feel guilty, but the thing was that it *couldn't* be Eric in the police sketch, did Meakin see? Because the man in the picture was at least twenty years younger. Still, in all other respects he did look like Eric – the same eyes.

Meakin thought the man in the sketch looked all right – like the sort of person he might want to watch the rugby or have a pint with. This was unusual. Most faces brought into being by police artists looked capable of far more ruthless acts than interrupting three consecutive suppers. Still, if Billy Dead Mates didn't look harmless and amiable, how had he talked his way into four people's kitchens and persuaded them to make him cups of tea? His benign face was part of his M.O., presumably.

Meakin told the caller that if she wanted something to be done about Eric, Amnesty were the people she needed to talk to, not the police. Putting the phone down, he said in his clearest, most deliberate voice, 'That was yours to get.'

'Mm?' Chanter looked up from his iPad, surprised – like a Lord of the Manor disturbed by a presumptuous butler. 'Oh, right. Ha!' As if Meakin had said it to entertain him. 'As you just discovered, these calls are a waste of our time and will continue to be. No one knows who the guy in the picture is. If they did, we'd have had the same name from a few different people by now. That sketch is hopeless. I'd do a better job and I failed my Art GCSE.'

'Talking of jobs, I see you're applying for another one?' Meakin nodded at the iPad.

'Yep. Think I'm in with a strong shot this time.'

No shame at all. For months, Meakin had been asking himself why Chanter made no effort to hide what he was up to. Now he thought he knew the answer: Chanter believed he had every right to apply for other jobs, and saw no need to be sneaky about it. He probably had no idea everyone at the nick called him 'Yosser'. Jack Zlosnik had started it. Apparently Yosser was a character from an old TV show who'd been fired, was skint, and went round saying, 'Gizza job?' to anyone who'd listen.

Chanter hadn't been fired, much to Meakin's consternation, and wasn't skint, but nevertheless was seen at least four times a day circling a job advert in a newspaper, or photocopying one, or filling in an online application form; or else he was heard ringing up to make enquiries about posts that were advertised here, there, everywhere. He didn't seem to be committed to a particular field; anything that wasn't his present position was eligible for consideration.

Meakin had had enough. He was going to say something, right now. Was he? Yes, he damn well was.

'Not happy where you are?'

'What?'

'Your job, here. Don't you like it? I can only assume not, since whenever I see you you're applying to be an airline pilot, a fireman, a farmer—'

'I've not gone in for any of those. A *farmer*?'

'I was exaggerating for comic effect.'

'Oh. Ha, ha!' Chanter was always ready with a smile. Forgetting he hadn't answered Meakin's question, or else deciding not to, he turned back to his iPad.

'It's not going to make you popular,' Meakin tried again.

'What, if I leave? Well, arguably, one doesn't need to be well liked in a place where one no longer is. Eh?'

Meakin was taken aback. There was no question about it: Chanter had put on an aristocratic English accent to make his last statement. His usual was standard Culver Valley, the middle-class version.

'I mean constantly applying for jobs,' said Meakin. 'And being seen to apply for them by all your colleagues. Yes, it's your right to apply for whatever the hell you want, and leave the police when you want, but . . . isn't it a bit tactless to do it so openly?'

Chanter looked confused. 'Er . . . no? No one would mind if I left. There's no one here whose career depends on me staying. If I thought anyone'd be hurt or offended, I wouldn't do it in public, but—'

'You don't think it's rude? A bit like saying, "This job you lot have given me is so not my priority that I can't even spend a single day concentrating on it"? "Instead, I'll take my salary, thanks very much, and spend the hours the police have paid for applying for jobs that'll get me out of here" – you think that's okay?'

'I'm getting the sense that you don't,' said Chanter. 'Look . . .' He put his iPad down on the desk and leaned towards Meakin, as if about to confide something. 'There's not that much for me to do around here that's worthwhile, is there? Sometimes it feels as if this job's a bit . . . well, made up. You know?'

Meakin laughed at this. He couldn't help it.

'I mean, today, these pointless calls about the Billy sketch . . .'

Chanter's explanation of why he was a misused resource was cut short when the phone started to ring. Meakin moved to answer it but Chanter got there first. 'Spilling Police,' he said. 'Yes. Yes, we do. Thank you – we do. That'll be me.' Charming laugh. 'What's the name?'

Meakin was immune to Chanter's charms. He liked to think that if he'd ever interviewed Chanter for a job, he'd have seen through him straight away and sent him packing.

'I've made a note of that, and in fact, it's the first I've heard twice so I'm going to take it seriously,' Chanter was saying.

Made a note? No, he hadn't. Meakin had watched as the younger man had made a note of precisely nothing.

'What? Oh. That was you who rang before? Oh, right, I'm with you. Well, you're the second caller who's given me the name Niall Greeves. What? Well, so you're the first *and* the second caller. I get it. Where's the . . . note . . . I made?'

Chanter's distracted tone while asking this question, suggestive of minor physical exertion as it was, would have left the caller in no doubt that the officer he was speaking to was straining to reach the relevant pile of papers. In fact Chanter was sitting quite still. *Brazen as all hell*.

'Yes, here it is: Niall Greeves. Excellent! I probably shouldn't tell you this, but you've been the most helpful caller so far. You win the award! Ha, ha. Thanks again. Thanks. Bye.'

To Meakin he said, 'It's true, though God knows where I put the list of names – but I'm positive: Niall Greeves. Someone else rang up and said the exact same thing, so maybe we're in luck.'

'Not someone else, by the sound of it,' said Meakin. 'The same person.'

'Huh? Oh – yeah, I guess so!' Chanter grinned, unperturbed.

'You've lost the list of names that've been called in so far? You need to find it.'

'No, it's not lost. I haven't looked for it yet, that's all. I will do, but first I need to nip to the little boys' room.' Chanter picked up his iPad and sauntered off in the direction of the gents.

Meakin was wondering how many more jobs he might manage to apply for while emptying his bowels when the phone rang again. He picked it up. A man's voice said, 'Is that you – the man I was speaking to a minute ago?'

'No, that was PC Iain Chanter. I'm Sergeant Robbie Meakin.'

'He didn't listen to anything I said! I don't want an award for helpfulness, but it'd be helpful to *me* if he listened, if I've made the effort to ring up. Sorry to take it out on you, but I've been trying for an hour and no one's picked up. You're running more of a stone-cold-line than a hotline, are you?'

'I'm so sorry, sir. PC Chanter—' Meakin broke off. Slagging off your colleagues to random callers was as unprofessional as leaving job application forms scattered all over your desk at work.

'You don't need to say it.' The caller sounded as if he was smiling now. 'I can well imagine.'

'Sir, please tell me what you tried to tell PC Chanter. I'll listen carefully. I was listening to Chanter's end of the conversation and from that I've got the name Niall Greeves – is that right?'

'Exactly right.'

'Great. And how certain are you—'

'That the man in the sketch is Niall Greeves? Oh, very certain. It's a brilliant sketch. And now I feel like the old duffer in that ancient *Yellow Pages* advert: J. R. Hartley. Do you remember it? Where he wants to track down a copy of his own book that's been out of print for ages, and he's ringing round second-hand bookshops? "Do you have a copy of *Fly Fishing* by J. R. Hartley? My name? Oh, yes, it's J. R. Hartley." I loved that advert.'

'Sir, are you saying—?'

'Sorry, yes.' He sounded embarrassed. 'You don't want to hear me bang on about old TV adverts, do you? Sorry, I'm a bit nervous – hoping you won't arrest me, to be quite honest. *I'm* Niall Greeves – that's what I rang to tell you. I saw the sketch in the paper yesterday and my first thought was, "Well, I won't ring up because it's me and I know I haven't murdered anyone." But I read the small print and it clearly said to ring *if you knew who the person in the sketch was*. And since I did, I did – ring, I mean. To do my duty as a citizen and say it's me: Niall Greeves. And I'm not a killer.'

~

Proust's head appeared in the CID room. The rest of him was still in his glass-walled cubicle in the far corner. He craned his neck to the left, then turned slowly back, like a moving security camera that pans round to take in a wider area. 'Where is everybody?' he asked Sam Kombothekra, who had walked into the room not three seconds earlier. 'I've noticed a discrepancy and no one's here. I'm supposed to have a team working under me. Where are they?'

'I'm here, sir.'

'Not *you*,' the Snowman said.

Sam knew what he meant. He wanted to talk to Simon. In moments of crisis, the rest of the team didn't count.

'I've got some good news, sir. A development.'

'So have I,' said Proust defensively, as if Sam's report of progress might nullify his own. He slid the rest of his body out of his glass compartment. 'Let's hear it, then.'

Sam told him about Niall Greeves identifying himself from the police artist's sketch. 'Robbie Meakin directed him my way and I've just got off the phone with him. He remembers giving the white book to Kim Tribbeck, and where it happened: the Kennett Auditorium in Canterbury. Kim did a gig there on 11 March last year. Greeves was in the audience. He kept his ticket, so he was able to be exact about the date, and it squares with the list of tour dates Kim's agent's given us. Greeves is a fan of hers.'

'I don't care. Is he Billy Dead Mates? I don't care what else he is or isn't.'

'I think it's very unlikely he is,' said Sam. 'We'll check with his work, but that's where he is every weekday afternoon apart from when he's on holiday. He works for the British Cartographic Society in London, lives in Tunbridge Wells. I told him the Billy dates and he wasn't on leave for any of them, so with any luck his colleagues will be able to vouch for him.'

'In which case, Mr Greeves would need a plausible explanation of why he gave the signature small white book of a serial killer to Kim Tribbeck that night in Canterbury. Did you ask him that?'

'I did, sir. And the good news is, his answer gives us a solid lead.'

The round face reddened. 'Please stop proclaiming good news. It's like talking to a TV evangelist.'

Sam wished he didn't have to waste his progress report on an unappreciative audience. 'After Kim did her show, Greeves said, she came down from the stage at one end into the main part of the room. The audience was sitting at tables below the stage. There was a man sitting at one right near the front and Kim seemed to be with him. From Greeves' description it sounds like Gabriel Kearns, whom we know was there that night. Greeves was there alone—'

'Why? Does he not have a wife?'

'No wife or girlfriend, no. He did have a wife but she died in 2010 from complications relating to an ectopic pregnancy. Greeves was on his way out after the gig – just finishing his pint and about to head home – when he saw a petite woman with very short, mid-brown hair approach Kim and her husband's table. They were having a conversation and standing with their backs to the table. Kim had hung her bag over the back of a chair behind her, and the short-haired woman crept up and seemed to be rummaging in Kim's bag. Greeves didn't want to cause a scene, so instead of shouting "Hey!" or anything, he approached the table, stood right next to the woman and gave her a pointed look. At the same time, another bloke from the audience apparently did the same, so there were two people homing in on her, about to yell, "Stop, thief!" for all she knew. She panicked, as a thief would, as a killer would, stopped what she was doing and made a swift exit – unobserved, still, by Kim Tribbeck and Gabriel Kearns. On her way to the door, she dropped something. Guess what it was?'

'No.' The Snowman was a tough crowd.

'A small white book. Niall Greeves picked it up, had a look. It contained no words apart from "Every bed is narrow", which meant nothing to Greeves. He assumed the woman had *taken* it from Kim's bag, then dropped it during her escape after she was caught in the act. Naturally, being a fan of Kim's and an honest guy, Greeves wanted to return her property to her. But he didn't want to interrupt her conversation, so he waited. He considered putting the little book back in her bag, but he didn't want to look like a rummager himself. When Gabriel Kearns left and Kim was alone, Greeves approached her. He said he sort of froze because he's such a huge fan, and he couldn't think what to say. He was afraid he'd sound weird, and the other guy who'd spotted the woman fiddling with Kim's bag was still hanging around too. In the end, Greeves said, he just passed the book to Kim with an incoherent mumble. She looked at him as if he were a complete freak, apparently.'

'All right, so his account of the giving of the book matches Kim Tribbeck's,' said Proust. 'Do we assume this short-haired woman is Billy, then?'

'I believe it's a strong possibility, sir.' Sam tried not to show his excitement. 'Greeves describes the woman as having very short brown hair. Faith Kendell, the woman Kim Tribbeck chatted to outside the hospital while Marion Hopwood was dying, also had very short brown hair. Now that we know Marion was murdered and a white book left in her bed . . .'

'You don't need to spell it out, Sergeant.' Proust perched on the edge of the nearest desk. His trouser legs rode up to reveal black socks with a pattern of purple fish. 'I have an alternative hypothesis: Faith Kendell doesn't exist.'

'Pardon, sir?'

'A woman with a different name was planning to kill Kim Tribbeck, but disaster struck: she was caught trying to put a white book in Kim's handbag and realised that she could be identified if Kim were to turn up dead. So she didn't kill Kim, but she *did* shoot four other people and she poisoned Marion Hopwood. She used a false name – Faith Kendell – to protect herself because she was at the RGI on 6 January, not to visit a relative with bone cancer but to murder Granny Marion.'

'We agree, sir. I was calling her Faith Kendell because we don't know her real name.'

'I do,' said the Snowman. 'At the start of this conversation, I told you I had a development to report. You waved that aside to make way for your own progess bulletin—'

'Sir, that's not quite—'

'This morning I decided to review all the paperwork – the archive of our ongoing shameful failure to catch Mr Dead Mates. I spotted something that didn't tally: the alibis of Isobel Sturridge, sister of Liam Sturridge.'

Isobel Sturridge. Sam let the name sink in. Once he had, he could think of no possible motive for her to commit Billy's five murders. For the desire to murder Kim Tribbeck, maybe; Isobel could have been a jealous, overly possessive sister. But Kim was still alive. What could Isobel have had against Linzi Birrell, Rhian Douglas and the others?

'Isobel Sturridge can't have been where she says she was when the first four murders were committed,' said Proust. 'She told Sellers she was at work – at Rudolphy's, Silsford's famous bookshop.'

So famous that Sam had never heard of it. He felt immediately guilty. He and his wife Kate bought all their books from Amazon. They kept agreeing that they shouldn't, but it was so much easier than making time to go to a physical shop.

'Do you know why she can't have been there on those dates?' Sam shook his head.

'I used to go to Rudolphy's as a boy,' Proust said. 'In those days, it occupied three different buildings on Guggle Lane, Silsford's only remaining cobbled street. Two were side by side, with a door connecting them that was sometimes locked and sometimes not. The third was across the street. Two of the three buildings were unmanned – no till, no staff presence at all. Just rooms full of books, new and second-hand, piles of them everywhere. There was a noisy till in the corner of one room that looked and sounded like an old typewriter. Someone would always be behind it to sell books, but if you wanted something from Rudolphy's mark two or three, you had to take it next door or over the road to buy it. Imagine that these days!'

Sam waited. This was the most personal thing Proust had ever said to him and it made him feel uneasy.

'The third shop, the one across the road, didn't last. It closed, then reopened as a record shop. Later still, the two adjacent buildings were joined properly and became one big Rudolphy's, though the ceilings were as low as they'd always been and the thick beams didn't help. My brother Edward nearly knocked himself out more than once. There was a girl we'd see in there sometimes, the owners' daughter. Elise, her name was. Elise Rudolphy. About my age, maybe a couple of years older. Once I was in there on my own flicking through a second-hand book and she came up behind me and said, "You want that, don't you?" It was Gibbon's *The History of the Decline and Fall of the Roman Empire*. There were three volumes – faded red hard-backs – and I was holding the first in my hands. "If you want it, take it," Elise told me. She had a terrible voice: a drawly half-English, half-American hybrid. The family was from America originally. Both parents had American accents. I said I couldn't take the book, that it would be stealing, and Elise said, "I dare you. I won't tell my parents." Do you know what I did, Sergeant? I took it.'

'Wow.' Sam laughed appreciatively.

'It wasn't funny, it was a crime. I'd expect you of all people to know the difference, or else what are you doing here?'

'Well, I . . . I just thought—'

'I was sickened by what I'd done, as soon as I got home. Couldn't look at myself in the mirror. The next day I took the book back to the shop and gave it to Mr Rudolphy. I confessed all, and told him that his daughter had encouraged me to defraud him.'

'Right.' Sam was struggling. What was the point of this story? What was he, the audience, supposed to be thinking, and what was he actually thinking? He ought to know the answer at least to the last question, but he didn't.

'Mr Rudolphy thanked me for returning the book. My apology seemed to be enough for him, but it wasn't for me. That day, I made up my mind to become a policeman. And I did.' Proust nodded vigorously. 'You don't see what any of this has to do with Billy and his victims. Only that Rudolphy's is where Isobel Sturridge claims to work, and she doesn't work there. She lied. Incidentally, I read the transcript of Sellers' interview with her and he describes her as having very short brown hair.'

'So you think she's Faith Kendell?'

'You will too when I tell you this: Elise Rudolphy's mother, who often sat behind the till, whose creation the bookshop was . . . *Her* Christian name was Faith. I'd often hear her husband's disembodied voice calling her. If she was busy when he called, she'd smile at the customer and ignore him until she was good and ready.'

'But . . . for Isobel Sturridge to give us an alibi involving a job in a shop *where she doesn't work at all*? Would she be so reckless?'

'She *has* been. So, yes, she would. My foray into the case files also told me that Kim Tribbeck believes Liam Sturridge's sister works nights.'

'I think you're right,' Sam murmured. Had he known that? It rang a bell. Trouble was, when you had five murders, the paperwork mounted up; it was impossible to keep all the details in mind at once.

'Bookshops aren't open overnight, therefore Isobel Sturridge can't possibly work in a bookshop,' Proust underlined his point.

'Sir, how did you find out she'd lied? Did you ask at Rudolphy's?' Sam assumed he was still a regular customer.

'Sadly, that would have been impossible. Rudolphy's closed down in September 2013. There are no other branches. It was a Silsford institution that travelled no further. Rudolphy's is no more.' Proust launched himself off the desk in the direction of his private cubicle. 'Therefore Isobel Sturridge couldn't have been working there in September 2014 when Linzi Birrell was murdered, or on any of Billy's other kill dates. She gave as her alibi a shop that no longer exists.'

~

Sellers hadn't wanted to risk following Sondra Halliday on Twitter under his own name in case she blocked him, so he'd called himself @howmanywomen. It sounded feminist enough to fool Halliday and it was the first three words of the driving question of Sellers' life: how many women could he bed before he died?

He'd stopped short of using a double-bladed axe as his avatar, as Halliday and many of her Twitter associates did; there was a limit to how deranged he was prepared to pretend to be. Instead, he'd picked a cartoon of a woman who looked a bit like Miss Scarlett from the board game Cluedo, but wasn't.

Halliday's latest tweet was a response to someone called @SterlingDervish. It read, 'So you'd tar me with the brush of my oppressors? Fuck you.' Sterling Dervish, whoever they were, had replied, 'Brush? Have you been oppressed by landscape painters, then? Why didn't you say?' Sellers chuckled to himself and pressed the 'favourite' button. On a whim, he clicked on the tweet to see who else had favourited it, seeing that one other person had.

His heart jolted when he saw the name. Isobel Sturridge: sister of Kim Tribbeck's ex-lover Liam.

Isobel Sturridge had favourited a tweet that mocked Sondra Halliday. It had to mean something.

Didn't it?

Sellers put Isobel's Twitter ID and Halliday's into the search box together. They'd never communicated directly on Twitter. Though perhaps Halliday would target Isobel now and lay into her. It was something she'd done before: attacking those who'd favourited tweets she disapproved of.

Sellers had spent a couple of hours today studying her Twitter timeline, and he'd found it genuinely terrifying. One poor person was accused of being 'rape apologist scum' for politely putting forward the view that transgender women ought to be able to use women's changing rooms. Hard as he tried, Sellers couldn't see the connection between that and condoning rape. Transgender women could hardly use the men's changing facilities; they'd be liable to get beaten up. Plus, they weren't men any more, were they? Wasn't that the whole point? In fact, many of Halliday's detractors on Twitter pointed out – every day, it seemed; did none of these people have jobs? Did they never feel in need of a day off from savaging one another? – that women born with male bodies had been women from the start. The problem was that their bodies hadn't matched the people they knew themselves to be.

All this might be interesting, thought Sellers, if it weren't so vicious. Here was Sondra Halliday calling someone a 'malevolent shitbag' further down her timeline. Her unfortunate victim had favourited a tweet addressed to Halliday from one of her opponents, exactly as Isobel Sturridge had. The tweet in question said, 'So genitals shouldn't be life-limiting at all until white m/c Aga feminists decide they're all that matters, amirite?'

Sellers puzzled over that last word for a few seconds before realising it was Twitter language for 'Am I right?'

Many of Sondra Halliday's Twitter friends had names that included 'womon' – probably because some radical feminists objected to 'man' being part of the word 'woman' when spelled conventionally.

Sellers shook his head, mystified.

'Everything all right?' Gibbs had appeared beside him. 'You look worried.'

'I am, about humanity.' Sellers closed Twitter with a sigh.

'I've got something.' Gibbs was trying not to smile and failing. 'Two pretty fucking big somethings.'

'Go on.'

'Have you seen the sarge in the last hour?'

Sellers shook his head.

'So you don't know the Snowman's bookshop story?'

'No. What story?'

'Never mind. It can wait. Rudolphy's, the bookshop where Isobel Sturridge told you she worked—'

'Funny you should mention her . . .'

'—but that in fact closed down in 2013—'

'*What?*'

'Yeah. Before it closed, its owner was an Elise Rudolphy. When I Googled her, pages and pages of results came up. She ran the family bookshop, but she was better known for being a widely published poet. Her stuff looks like dross to me, but what do I know? She was American, too. An American woman poet—'

'With a name that starts with E,' Sellers finished Gibbs' sentence. 'Like Edna St. Vincent Millay and the other two.'

'Right. She died in December 2013 – heart failure, according to Wikipedia.'

'Then she's not Billy,' Sellers stated the obvious. 'His murders didn't start till September 2014.'

'Oh, did I forget to say?' Gibbs grinned. 'Before she died – long before – Elise got married and had a family. Guess who she married?'

'I can't. Tell me.'

'A man called Norman Sturridge.'

'Sturridge? Then . . . ?'

'Yep. Liam and Isobel Sturridge are Elise Rudolphy's children.

And that's not all I've got. The fake mobile number Faith Kendell gave Lane Baillie? I've just heard back from O2. That very same number, until 2013, belonged to guess who?'

'Isobel Sturridge?' Too easy, surely.

'Got it in one,' said Gibbs.

16

from Origami *by Kim Tribbeck*

Should I tell Charlie what I suspected: that Simon knew the truth about Liv and Gibbs? I kept asking myself the question and coming to the same conclusion: no, I shouldn't. Unless you're wise, don't interfere – that's my motto, and wisdom isn't a quality I've ever possessed. I've met sticks of chalk that are capable of forming better judgements than I can. Instead, I told Charlie my theory about bad liars.

The worst liars imagine a lie must be the literal opposite of the truth. Like (forgive the comedy reference – I am a comedian, after all) in *Blackadder Goes Forth*, when Blackadder is on trial for his life, accused of shooting Speckled Jim, a carrier pigeon, and the thick soldier played by Hugh Laurie says in an attempt to defend him, 'We didn't receive any messages and Captain Blackadder definitely didn't shoot that delicious, plump-breasted pigeon,' in a way that makes it apparent to anyone with a brain that he did precisely that.

What if Liv and Gibbs had told a childlike, literal-opposite lie?

I'd done it myself, I realised: told Liam that I couldn't see him any more because Gabe and I were renewing our vows, when in fact I'd dumped Gabe that same day and ordered him to move out.

What was the opposite of breaking up? Surely it was *not* breaking up. But that was the situation before Liv and Gibbs' lie. That was the boring old status quo; everyone apart from the two deceived spouses had known about the affair for years, so why suddenly announce a change?

Leaving their respective marriages and moving in together: that could be another opposite to splitting up – but then everyone would find out in due course, so why bother with an elaborate hoax to put people off the scent?

And what did Nikhil Gulati and his girlfriend Natalie have to do with anything? Why bring another couple into the mix? There were three already where there should only have been two: Liv and her husband, Gibbs and his wife, Liv and Gibbs – and now these complete strangers.

Of course, to me they were all complete strangers. That's why I was happy to spend time thinking about them.

~

Friday, 16 January 2015

'No way.' Charlie sounds disappointed. She was hoping to like my theory better. 'The opposites thing's a great idea in principle, but there's zero chance of Liv and Gibbs ever moving in together. He would, she wouldn't. She doesn't believe they could be happy after destroying two marriages.'

'Most marriages exist in a state of semi-permanent destruction anyway,' I say. 'Put them out of their misery: it's the kindest way. I did it to mine. Sorry – I don't normally say that to married people.'

Charlie smiles. 'If only you'd stuck to your policy. Now I've heard your opinion, I'm going to have to get divorced. You're *that* influential.'

I laugh. We've had a can of Fruit Rush and a packet of pickled onion Monster Munch each, so we're in a good mood. Today so far we've ruled out Bristol and Bath, and we're about to arrive in Yeovil. All I remember about my gig here was that when I stepped outside afterwards, there was nobody in the town centre: no human beings in evidence, no cars, no sounds to be heard. I'd had nearly a thousand people at my show – where had they all gone while I was checking my messages and getting showered and changed? I couldn't believe any town could be so still and silent at half past ten at night.

Was Liam with me when I had those thoughts? Had I, a few minutes earlier, been handed a little white book with a line of poetry in it, and was I on my way to spend the night in a too-narrow bed? I don't remember. I'm about to revisit the venue where I did my gig, after which I'll be able to declare that it's the one or cross it off the list.

My clothes are going to reek of smoke tonight. Like all nicotine addicts, Charlie imagines exhaling in the direction of an open window actually works. Sometimes she holds the cigarette out of the window, and chooses not to notice the wind blowing the smoke back in.

She says, 'So if they're not taking things to the next level, which they're not, because Liv won't, then the most opposite it could be to the break-up lie is same old, same old: they're still having an affair. In which case, what changed to make them want to pretend to split up? I'm not expecting you to know, by the way. I keep thinking if I ask myself the same question for the millionth time, I might come up with the right answer. My starting point has *always* been that there's only so many things a person might conceivably want to hide: infidelity, a drug habit, alcoholism, a secret life as an escort or a porn star, a second identity, an embarrassing illness . . .'

She mutters something I can't make out. Then she says: 'Nikhil and Natalie have got to be the key, right? They and Liv and Gibbs aren't just normal friends. They're . . . involved in something together, some business or arrangement.'

'If your sister won't leave her husband to move in with Gibbs, what about a baby? Could she be pregnant with his kid? Maybe . . . okay, this is far-fetched, but maybe Nikhil and Natalie are going to adopt it?' I want to argue with myself already. 'No, because how's Liv going to hide a pregnancy from her husband? She'd be more likely to pass the kid off as his, wouldn't she?'

'Liv can't get pregnant. She's had ovarian cancer. The treatment left her infertile.' Charlie sounds excited. She reaches for the Marlboro packet again. 'Hang on – let's not rule this out too quickly.' The more interested she is in the conversation we're having, the more she smokes. She ought to go on a road trip with Liam; she'd have clean lungs by the end of it.

'Liv and Dom aren't short of money . . .' she murmurs.

'So?'

'I'm thinking surrogacy.'

'*What?*' Have I missed a stage?

'Liv can't conceive. She and Gibbs are in love, they want to make a baby together. That's something most people in love want, right?'

'Apparently. I don't get it myself.'

'Me neither, but we're not typical, I don't think.'

I file away that 'we' to mull over later. 'Wouldn't Liv want a baby with her husband if she wanted one at all?'

'No. Liv loves Dom like a . . . big old sheepdog. A sheepdog who gets a million-quid bonus every year. She's *in love* with Gibbs: he's the one whose kid she'd want – but she can't because she can't get pregnant, so . . .' Charlie shrugs. 'It's too ridiculous.'

'So she takes some of her husband's money, hires Natalie to be artificially impregnated by Gibbs?'

'Something like that, yes. Don't you think it's possible?'

'But what does Liv do with the baby she's bought? Take it home to Dom and say, "Here's my lover's child and we're going to raise it – hope that's okay"?'

'Don't be daft.'

'Then what?'

'She gets Dom to give her some sperm. Tells him all about the surrogacy but pretends the kid'll be his. Secretly, she, Gibbs, Nikhil and Natalie all know the truth – it'll be Gibbs' kid. Liv gets to raise the child of the man she loves, and Natalie probably gets paid extra for keeping quiet about the deception aspect.'

'That's beyond gross if it's true,' I say. 'It's too gross to be plausible, unless your sister's a monster with no conscience. For God's sake, whip out your badge in front of Natalie one day and make her tell you what's going on. I would.'

'Can't.' Charlie pulls into the car park of the Yeovil Playhouse. I look at the outside of the building, hoping for a hint, but it's no use. This might be the venue I'm looking for or it might not. No way of knowing until I get inside.

'Why not?' I ask.

'I work in Spilling, not for NYPD, so I don't have a badge.' Charlie grins. 'And I want to find out secretly, so that I retain the advantage of surprise. Does that sound stupid?'

'It sounds more disciplined than I'd be. I'd just want to know, any way I could. The quickest way.'

'Maybe you're right. But I've held out this long.' Charlie sighs. 'Come on, let's go and stick our heads in.'

The Yeovil Playhouse is the wrong place. The inside of the building matches nothing in my memory. If I didn't have documentary evidence proving I'd performed here, I'd be convinced I'd walked into this auditorium for the first time today.

'No,' I say to Charlie.

'Definite no?'

I stare at the curved rows of black seats. The walls and even the ceiling are black too. 'Definite.'

'Okay, good. One more ruled out. We're narrowing it down. Do you need the loo or shall we hit the road? Wait, that's my phone.' She pulls it out of her pocket. 'Hi. Yes, we're making good progress,' she says, then mouths 'Simon' at me. 'No, not yet . . . Good progress in the sense of ruling places out. What? We're going as fast as we can, Simon. It's not my fault the UK's roads are the length they are. Really? Go on. You're *joking*? Fuck.' Charlie looks at me, then quickly looks away. 'No, I won't. That won't be a problem. Tell me.'

If I'm not mistaken, he's ordered her not to share it with me, whatever it is. It's kind of appropriate; an enormous black room is the perfect place to be when you find out you're about to be kept in the dark.

'What else?' Charlie asks Simon. 'You said two things.' There's a long silence while she listens. Eventually she says, 'Okay. It was him, ringing up about himself? I suppose that must happen from time to time. I will, now. So when did this happen? *What? Well, fuck you too!* That's just perfect, isn't it? For fuck's sake!'

I try not to look surprised. What's happened? Seconds later, I realise it's obvious. Marriage is what's happened: unnatural proximity to another human being over a prolonged period. It's bound to be the world's leading cause of Sudden Violent Swearing Syndrome.

'Do you think I'm having fun driving up and down bloody motorways all day?' Charlie rants. 'Do you think my lungs enjoy collecting diesel fumes? What? Oh. Right.' She sounds a different kind of annoyed now. I recognise this mode too: fuming at the prospect of having to apologise to someone you know to be guilty in general, if not on this particular occasion. 'Whatever.' She sighs. 'I'd still have appreciated being told.'

She stuffs her phone back in her pocket. 'We've got a name. The man who gave you the book: Niall Greeves. He rang up *yesterday*. Thanks to an administrative cock-up at *his* work-place, it's taken Simon until today to verify that he's legit.' Charlie shakes her head. 'I only want to know as much as everyone else knows or doesn't know – is that too much to ask?'

'They're The Detectives, capital T capital D,' I say. 'You're not. They're going to take every chance they get to pull rank – even, especially, the one you're married to.'

'I used to be a detective. I used to lead that team! I was Simon's boss.'

'So now it's payback time, right? Look no further for an explanation!' I definitely shouldn't ever go into marriage guidance counselling.

Charlie curls her lip. I imagine there are plenty more

swearwords tucked inside it, waiting to be fired later, when she and her beloved are reunited. 'Come on, let's make a move,' she says. 'I'll fill you in on the way.'

'To where?' I ask. As far as I'm aware, we haven't decided where we're going next.

'Canterbury. That's where it was.' Charlie grins at me. 'Niall Greeves has saved us days of driving.'

I ought to be pleased, given how much I didn't want to come on this trip, but all I can think is *Please let Niall Greeves be wrong. I don't want to have to go home.*

～

Welcome to the Narrow Bed Hotel. There ought to be a sign with those words on it. This is definitely the right place: the Whitworth Hotel in Canterbury.

Everything is the same apart from Liam not being with me: the leaflet rack, the navy fleur-de-lis carpet, the battered skirting boards in the reception area that look as if a gang of thugs in steel-toecapped boots have kicked them hard every day for the last twenty years.

Charlie's busy asking the receptionist to look at her records and try to find out which room Liam and I stayed in last year. All I can remember is that it was on the first floor. It might have been room 10, 11, 12, 13, 14, 15 or 16.

I don't understand why Simon needs to know, or why Charlie accepts all his orders without question, as if they're commands sent from God. Is this what's required for a successful marriage?

I don't want to go back into the room Liam and I shared. Even though it has no sentimental value, I tell myself firmly. How could it, when there was nothing special about me and Liam and what we had together? He once bought me a book that was signed by hand and dedicated in print to the same person: so what? Only a fool would make a big deal of that the way I did.

I wanted it to mean that Liam loved me. It didn't. I wanted his outwardly blank manner to mean that his affection for me was so powerful, he didn't dare express it for fear it would overwhelm us both. It didn't.

When I was five years old and still an optimist, my adoptive parents bought me a book called *The Stone Doll of Sister Brute*. It was about a girl who had nothing to love, so she gave a stone a name, pretended it was a person, and determinedly loved it. That's what I did with Liam. I was so desperate to believe I could extract love from him. Easy to fool myself that all I wanted was sex; it was all Liam had to offer, so how could I possibly have been hoping for more? I'd have had to be stupid, and I knew I wasn't. I could prove to myself any time I wanted that Liam meant nothing to me. Evidence of insignificance poured out of all our interactions. I kidded myself that was coming from me as much as from Liam.

Fuck him. Fuck Gabe too, who told me endlessly how much he loved me, when what he really loved was himself and skunkweed, in that order. It's the opposites thing again; I assumed, because of Gabe, that Liam must love me; he was the one not saying it every time he opened his mouth.

Which makes me an idiot. It's possible for one, two, four, eight, a thousand men not to love you, each in his own special way.

I wish I hadn't already torn up *Delirium of the Brave* and thrown it away. I should have waited till I got here, to the Whitworth Hotel. This would have been the perfect place for its desecration.

'You okay?' Charlie appears at my side. 'Have you thought of something else? You look weird.'

There's a feeling of emptiness inside me that's so powerful, it's obliterating all the words I might use to describe it. I do what any self-respecting comedian would do and try to make light of it. 'It's just dawning on me: I'm far more fucked up than I thought I was. And I thought I was pretty bad.'

'I often feel that way,' Charlie says airily. 'Then a few minutes later, I'm convinced I'm the only sane person in a world full of nutters. You and Liam were in room 15, by the way.'

'You're going to ask me to go up and look at it, aren't you?'

'Just a quick peek inside, to confirm it's the room you remember staying in with Liam. Please?'

'Why? Because Simon says so?'

'Look, I don't get it either, but . . . his infuriating pedantry seems to work.'

'Okay, fine. Let's get it over with.' Halfway up the stairs, I stop. Agreeing to this doesn't mean I agree to everything. 'Do I have to meet Niall Greeves? Confirm he's the man who gave me the little book?'

'No, I don't think so. Greeves has confirmed that himself.'

'Good. I don't want to meet him.'

We arrive at the door to room 15. Charlie unlocks it. I walk in first. Soonest in, soonest out – that's the idea.

How can someone as gobby and obnoxious as I am be so scared of everything? I don't understand it.

'It looks like the same room,' I say in a monotone. 'Narrow bed, horrid pink curtains with a silly pelmet. What if all the rooms here look the same?'

'I think you saying it looks the same and the receptionist saying this was the one will be good enough even for Simon.' Charlie smiles. 'Come on, I'm starving. Let's go and find something to eat.'

I stay where I am, staring out of the pelmeted window at the row of buildings opposite and, beyond them, a big Tesco in the distance. There was no reason to avoid room 15, it turns out. I don't feel worse than I did downstairs. I feel better, if anything.

'I've been avoiding thinking about him out of fear, but it's not fear he'll kill me.' The words rush out before I can stop them.

'Who?'

'Niall Greeves. He's not Billy, is he?'

'Simon doesn't think so, no.'

'I knew it. Knew he wasn't dangerous – not in that way.'

'You think he's dangerous in a different way?'

'It was a relief when it seemed he was probably Billy. I could pretend that was why I was scared of him, but I knew deep down that wasn't it. When he gave me the white book, he looked at me as if . . . as if he was really *noticing* me. I mean, *me*. As if I was someone who mattered. Liam and Gabe never did that. Both of them initially approached me in a . . . well, in a way that most people'd find offensive. That was what made me feel secure: I knew I'd never have to feel morally inferior to either of them.'

I walk over to the window. Standing several inches away, I can smell the dust on the pink curtains. 'I felt more comfortable with Liam's way, Gabe's way. They both saw me as an object to be manipulated. That was how I felt happiest relating to them too: manipulating. It's how I am with everyone. I'm a piece designed to be pushed around a board and so is everyone else. It makes life easier.'

'And Niall Greeves?'

'He looked at me as if I was a real person. As if he . . . thought highly of me. It was only for a few seconds, but it freaked me out. What scared me even more was . . .' I stop.

Charlie gives me a 'Don't even think about it' look.

'I thought he was gorgeous,' I admit. 'He was. Is – objectively. Not sexy in a louche way like Gabe, not a strapping specimen like Liam, but stand-out gorgeous, like a film star or a model. And *nice*. He looked kind. I saw him coming towards me with something in his hand and I thought, "Great – he's going to give me a note with his number on and some lovely message, and I won't be able to resist ringing him."' I can see from Charlie's face that she doesn't get it.

'He was too good for me by a long way,' I explain. 'I didn't want to try to start something with him and fail, and I knew I was unlikely to be able to resist trying.'

'So . . . you get involved with badly behaved less attractive men, while fearing really hot ones who seem like decent blokes?'

'Yup. Exactly.' I never want to see Niall Greeves again. Maybe it's me I'm scared of, not him. The physical pull I felt when I looked at him; how little power I'd have in any exchange with him as a result of that.

I was so sure that the object he was determined to put in my hand was a note declaring his interest. The disappointment I felt when it wasn't . . . Fuck you, Billy Dead Mates, for putting me through that humiliation. Thank God it was one I was able to suffer privately.

Later that night, in this room I've returned to with Charlie, I closed my eyes and pretended Liam was the man who'd given me the white book. I had sex with Niall Greeves all night long in my mind, without knowing his name or seeking his permission.

What kind of person does that? What kind of woman ignores both her husband and her lover as if they don't exist, in order to build a sexual obsession around a stranger she's seen for no more than a few seconds?

'Who does Simon think is Billy?' I ask Charlie. 'I know he told you something and asked you not to tell me. He knows, doesn't he?'

'I'm not . . . I mean, *he's* not sure, so . . .' She stumbles over the words.

'Who?'

'Faith Kendell. Or rather, the woman who introduced herself to you as Faith Kendell.'

'Who is she really?'

'Did she – hospital woman – have funny kind of grooves on her teeth?'

'I don't know. I didn't notice if she did. We were standing side by side, not facing one another.'

'Simon wants you to look at a photograph, see if it's of the woman you met. It should be a match, and then we'll hopefully be able to give you a name. Is that okay?'

'I'm happy to look at a picture, but I want a provisional name now. I want to know what you and Simon think you know.'

19) *If Kim has been helpful to you in your hunt for a serial killer, you may not withhold from her any relevant information.* One to add to my terms and conditions.

I should have tried a more subtle approach. I've only strengthened Charlie's resolve to keep it from me. 'Let's just see if the woman in the photo is the one you know as Faith Kendell,' she says. 'Make sure it's the right person.'

~

When she said those words – 'the right person' – Charlie was thinking of Isobel Sturridge, though I didn't know it at the time. She, Simon Waterhouse, Chris Gibbs, the whole lot of them – they'd decided that Isobel, Liam's sister, was the infamous news-monopolising serial killer known to the world as Billy Dead Mates.

It's lucky Charlie wouldn't give me a name; I'd have laughed till I ruptured every internal organ.

I'd never met Liam's sister Isobel, but I knew a few things about her. Sometimes I'd withheld sex until Liam agreed to talk to me for a while first, like in a normal relationship. 'What do you want me to say?' Liam would ask, and a few times I suggested he tell me things about his sister. So I knew that in the top year of primary school, Isobel had once copied another pupil's answers in a Maths test, then burst into tears and confessed all to her parents as soon as she got home that afternoon. She'd cheated successfully and got an excellent mark, but couldn't enjoy it because of the guilt she felt. Her parents and Liam had advised her that she'd be fine as long as she never cheated again, but Isobel insisted on handing herself in to her Maths teacher, who was far less horrified by the transgression than Isobel herself was.

Liam once told me, trying to prove that women create unnecessary work for themselves and for men, 'My sister's revision *plans* for her GCSEs – not her essays or her coursework, just the plans for the work she intended to do – took up more sheets of paper than every essay I wrote in all my exams put together.'

At the age of fifteen, Isobel announced on New Year's Eve that she'd given up making New Year's resolutions and would never make another one as long as she lived. She felt too guilty when she didn't stick to them, Liam said.

Does this sound like a serial killer to you? Is that someone who's going to imagine she can get away with killing four innocent people? (I'm afraid I can't bring myself to think of Marion as innocent.) Is it someone who would want to?

Murderous sociopaths are supposed to spend their childhoods torturing animals and setting fire to buildings, aren't they? Not learning the flute as Isobel Sturridge did; carrying their instruments around in shiny black cases, diligently practising every night and then sticking their grade certificates up on their bedroom walls with Blu Tack.

The overlap between conscientious flautists and serial killers must be minimal to nonexistent. That's what I'd have said if Charlie had put me in the picture at that point. There's simply no way that Isobel Sturridge could be Billy, I'd have told her.

17

16/1/2015

Simon couldn't help it: he was excited to be in a room with Isobel Sturridge. He was making a special effort to appear subdued so that Sam, also present, wouldn't guess how big a deal this was for him. He'd always found it excruciating, the idea that others might observe him caring passionately about something.

For Simon, Isobel Sturridge was a first; noticeably different from all the others.

All the other killers? Are you sure that's not because she's no more a murderer than you are?

Yes, Simon was sure. Especially now he was in an interview room with her at the nick where he'd worked for most of his adult life, a backdrop against which he'd seen many guilty people and many innocent ones. Isobel Sturridge moved, spoke and dressed like a good girl who wouldn't dream of causing any trouble: neat, short hair like a fitted cap around her head; a flowery blouse with a shiny pink trim around the collar and cuffs; apricot-coloured flat shoes that fastened with a strap and a buckle, like the shoes girls in Simon's class at primary school used to wear. Even her perfume smelled innocent: light and flowery. But the reek of her guilt was stronger.

Simon couldn't work it out. All the aspects of Isobel Sturridge that ought to have made him fear he'd erroneously cast her in the role of killer only convinced him more: it was her. The more benign she seemed, the stronger grew his certainty that she'd committed five murders.

The clothes. He'd start with the clothes.

'When you spoke to Kim Tribbeck outside the RGI on Tuesday, 6 January, you were dressed very differently to how you're dressed today: jeans, black hoody, trainers. Quite masculine. Yet here you are in a floral blouse, a skirt, schoolgirl shoes. Is that because you were in disguise when you went to the cancer ward on 6 January?'

Isobel said nothing. A tear trailed down her cheek. Sam was fidgeting, no doubt worried they were bullying her. She'd refused a lawyer. Simon wondered if part of her plan was to look bullied: the helpless victim of insensitive interrogation. He rejected the idea straight away; her unhappiness had nothing to do with their words or behaviour. She gave the impression of being a distraught person trapped in a sealed bubble. Simon felt that he couldn't get to her, though there were fewer than ten inches between them.

'You were in disguise as Faith Kendell, I believe. Where did you get that name from?'

She shook her head.

'Isobel,' said Sam gently. 'If you don't know what we're talking about—'

'She does, though,' Simon cut in. 'Faith Kendell was the maiden name of her maternal grandmother, Faith Rudolphy. She knows that. And now she knows we know it too. This late in the day, denial's not your best option, Isobel. We know you were at the RGI the day Marion Hopwood was murdered. We know you lied when we asked you where you were on the days of the other four murders: you said you were at work at Rudolphy's, the bookshop. You weren't. There is no Rudolphy's any more. You used to work there, but then the shop closed down – more than a year ago, in September 2013. At the time of the first four Billy Dead Mates murders, you worked nights at Rawndesley Services on the A1. You still do. Which means you have afternoons free – to sleep, usually. Except I don't think you slept on those four days. Did you?'

Isobel made no attempt to speak, though her mouth was

working. With her bottom teeth, she kept trapping her top lip as if trying to bite the tears as they fell.

Simon wondered how and why someone who'd worked for her family's bookshop had ended up working nights at a motorway service station. Why not look for another job in the bookselling trade, or train to be a librarian?

Perhaps it wasn't so jarring a lifestyle change; it was simply that Simon could sort of imagine himself working in a book-shop – Word on the Street in Spilling, for example, where he bought all his books – whereas he'd regard serving sausages to refugees from the M1 in the middle of the night as a form of torture.

'I'm wondering if we made a mistake referring to our unknown killer as Billy for so long,' he said to Sam. 'Must have made it easier for the real killer – Isobel here – to imagine her crimes were being committed by someone else. Her name's not Billy, so it can't be her. And she's certainly not a man, so it really can't be her. We must be looking for someone alto-gether different.'

'Are we, Isobel? Look, if we've got something badly wrong here, tell us. Please. If you're scared of somebody, if you've been threatened . . .' Sam ran out of imaginary afflictions. 'We can help you.'

'And if you're Billy, we can also help you,' said Simon. 'We've got enough to charge you already. Any jury'd convict. The way you're treated from here on in, the experience you have as a convicted criminal, that can go one of two ways. If you want it to go the better way, start helping us. Then we'll help you.'

A noise from her at last.

Simon's heart did a jump-start. 'Pardon?'

'I've tried to help you.'

'How?'

Silence.

'What do you mean?' Simon pushed. 'Do you mean the letters

you've written to Sondra Halliday? The weird stories you've sent her? You must have known she'd pass them on to us.'

'You can trust us, Isobel. Really.'

Christ, could Sam not rein himself in? Handling suspects sensitively was one thing, but there was only so much of his soft-consonant smarming that Simon could take. Gibbs was right; he'd been letting off steam about it in the Brown Cow recently, after he and Sam had interviewed two armed robbers who'd shot and killed three women at the Combingham branch of Santander. 'His voice was one step away from being a fucking spa treatment,' he'd said about Sam.

Isobel Sturridge had stopped talking and was tear-biting again.

'Has your brother helped you to commit these murders?' Simon asked. Liam Sturridge's alibis had been proved solid, but that didn't mean he hadn't arranged it all and delegated the dirty work to his sister.

Isobel looked disorientated for a second or two, then shocked, as if something outrageous had been suggested. 'Liam has nothing to do with any of this,' she said in a clear, matter-of-fact voice.

'Whereas you do – correct?' *Fuck*. Simon had pounced on that too quickly. Isobel drew her head back, as if afraid he might spit at her.

'We know you're Elise Rudolphy's daughter,' he told her. 'An American poet, name beginning with E. Like the three poets whose words you've used in the little white books you give to your victims. Why do you do that, Isobel?'

No answer.

'Why did you give Kim Tribbeck a book first and then not kill her? All your other victims, you've planted the white book, unseen, and then killed them very soon after. Why's Kim different? Is it because you didn't manage to slip the book into her bag – you were interrupted? Or because she was your brother's girlfriend for a while?' Simon's adrenaline morphed into anger without warning. 'Crying's not an answer! Tell me!'

'Simon,' Sam murmured.

'All right then, don't tell me. Tell him. Look at him! Look at that face: ready to lap up any bullshit you cough up. Why not take advantage? Did you know Linzi Birrell and Rhian Douglas personally? You worked at Rudolphy's until it closed. Was Linzi a customer? She lived locally, so she easily could have been. Was Josh Norbury a customer? Rhian Douglas and Angela McCabe didn't live in the Culver Valley – how did you persuade them to let you into their homes?'

'Browbeating her's not going to achieve anything,' said Sam quietly.

'Yeah, well, not everything has to be an achievement.'

Simon stood up and moved his chair further away from Isobel's. Sitting down again, he said, 'I don't get it. Help me. You kill five people – I reckon you were planning on Kim too, so let's say six. One's been involved with your brother so there's a connection there, but why the others? What links all six? Something must.'

'I can't tell you anything!' Isobel screamed. Coming from her silence, it was more shocking, like a small earthquake in the room. Simon saw Sam flinch. He'd done the same himself.

'I haven't murdered anybody, but I can't tell you . . . I just can't *tell* you.'

'Why not?' Simon asked.

'Because then everything would be ruined,' she said.

~

'This is the first time I've been here in a few days,' Lisa Norbury told Sellers. They were in Josh's flat in Spilling, in the large L-shaped kitchen. Sellers was sitting at the breakfast bar and Lisa stood at the kitchen sink, looking out over the large shared garden. Sellers had met her only once before, immediately after her brother's murder. She looked much thinner today, and the skin of her face seemed somehow to have the wrong texture, as if she'd exchanged it for its synthetic equivalent.

She wasn't holding up well, that much was clear. She was supposed to be making Sellers a coffee but had got no further than the window. It looked as if she'd forgotten. She reached out to pick up a cocktail shaker from the windowsill, then put it down again.

Josh had been something of an amateur mixologist, and this room had accommodated many a cocktail party. Before Billy and this investigation, Sellers hadn't known the word 'mixologist'. His two teenage children had laughed at him when he'd asked them if they knew it. 'Of course, Dad. Everyone knows that!' They'd then proceeded to test Sellers on other modern terms they suspected he'd be unaware of: bae, beasted, pwned.

'I keep thinking, if I can stay away one day longer each time . . .' Lisa laughed self-consciously. 'I feel awful when I don't come, though. It's like the flat's become a substitute for Josh. If I don't come, it's like I'm not visiting *him*. Crazy.'

'Not at all,' said Sellers. 'For what it's worth, I don't think you should try to stop yourself if your instinct is to be here more often. Whatever makes you feel better.'

Lisa nodded. 'Josh was killed a month ago. I keep worrying that I ought to be getting over it faster.'

'You know that's daft. It'd be normal to feel that way after two years. Look, I'm no grief expert, but I don't think you ought to be wondering if you're doing anything wrong. Do whatever makes you feel better. But I mean . . . at the same time, don't put pressure on yourself to feel better. A lot of misery comes from telling yourself you're feeling the wrong way. If that makes sense.'

'Yes, it does.' Lisa smiled. 'Thanks.'

'You're welcome. And thanks for letting me take another look at Josh's flat. I might not see anything that I and my team didn't see all the other times we were here, but it's still helpful for me to be here.'

'But you *might* find something new.' Lisa's voice rose in pitch.

Sellers decided to be honest. 'It's possible. I don't think there's much of a chance, but I'm still hoping I will, and feeling as if I might. A lot of my friends think I'm a deluded optimist. It's stupid, but – for reasons I won't bore you with – I care more about catching Josh's killer than I've ever cared about catching any scrote before.'

'Well, I'm all for deluded optimism,' said Lisa. 'For as long as I live, I'm going to believe you lot are just about to catch him.'

Sellers felt winded. What she'd just told him, without realising it, was that she expected them never to catch Billy. Corresponding with Sellers' own fears as it did, that wasn't an easy thing to hear.

'It's the only way I can live. If this were a movie, I'd say, "When you catch him, don't arrest him – bring him to me. Let me deal with him." God, the fantasies I have about what I'd do to him. And then I wonder if I've allowed a monster to turn me into a monster,' Lisa added tearfully.

'You're no monster. Every single relative of a murder victim has those same revenge fantasies. The police have them too.'

She sniffed, then giggled. 'Hey, do you fancy a cocktail? I'm no mixologist, but how hard can it be? It's just shaking up some booze and sticking it all in a glass at the end of the day, isn't it?'

Sellers, who'd had too much to drink the night before, couldn't think of anything he wanted less. 'Tell you what,' he said. 'You make us cocktails – though not too much of the hard stuff in mine, if that's okay. While you're doing that, I'll do my walkaround of the flat.'

'Deal,' said Lisa. 'Josh had a silly song he used to sing whenever he made a cocktail. He called it his magic ingredient. If he didn't sing the song, the cocktail wouldn't taste right.'

Please don't sing.

She waited, at least, until he was out of the kitchen and the door was closed. Sellers listened from the hall. It sounded like a skipping song schoolkids might sing: 'Happy llama, sad llama, mentally disturbed llama, super llama, drama llama, big fat mama llama. Llama llama llama! Who is this big llama causing all the drama? It's me, bitch!'

Sellers raised his eyebrows at the abrupt ending. Lisa started to sing the same words again. Josh's cocktails must have been amazing, thought Sellers, if his guests were willing to put up with the llama song on an endless loop. Or perhaps the aim was to instill in them a desire to get drunk as quickly as they could.

Josh's bedroom and lounge looked exactly the same: nothing had changed, moved or been added. There was only so much looking at two small rooms one could do. Standing around hoping for something to magically appear was pointless.

Doesn't make this a pointless exercise. You've already learned something new: Josh's llama song. It might be ridiculous, but you didn't know it before. No one working on Billy did. Which means something else, something useful, might also be here for the taking.

Sellers opened the drawer in the TV stand, looked under the chair and the two sofas. Nothing.

He decided to try the bathroom. That looked the same too, though there was a blue carrier bag leaning against one wall that he hadn't seen there before. Probably Lisa's, he thought. He peered inside the bag and saw a name he wasn't expecting to see – not here, at any rate. Having a word with his racing pulse, telling it not to get ahead of itself, he slowly and carefully removed all the other items from the bag – a Kindle with a green cover, a cream butter dish, a hideous man's tie with a purple background and little characters from *Star Wars* all over it – so that he could concentrate on the item that interested him.

Slowly, he took it out of the bag and examined it.

Jesus Christ.

Sellers wasn't prepared to believe it was a coincidence. And, come to think of it, this couldn't be Lisa's bag. Why would she have brought these four items to her dead brother's home?

Sellers found her in the kitchen and asked her, taking care not to let his excitement show.

'Oh, those things?' Lisa's face coloured. 'I decided to take them home with me. Is that okay? Sergeant Kombothekra said you'd finished—'

'It's fine, don't worry. But do you mind me asking why those four particular items?'

'All presents from Angela. They had sentimental value for Josh. "And *only* sentimental value," as he regularly used to say. But he kept them all in the drawer under his bed, because they were from her.' Lisa's eyes filled with tears again. 'Josh didn't make friends easily. He could be quite intense. Angela really meant a lot to him.'

'What did you mean about only sentimental value?'

Lisa made a face. 'Angela was a bit rubbish when it came to presents – not for want of trying! Did you see the *Star Wars* characters tie?'

'Yeah.'

'I mean, Josh adored *Star Wars* but he didn't want to wear it round his neck! He had no use for a Kindle – screens were for work and porn, he said – and the butter dish and recipe book . . . Angela kept trying to inspire him to cook and host dinner parties in his nice big kitchen, but Josh was a takeaway and leftovers man through and through. Cocktails were all he was interested in making himself.'

'I need to step out into the garden and make a phone call,' Sellers told her. 'I'll be back shortly.'

Aware that people sometimes didn't answer their phones when you urgently needed them to, Sellers willed Simon to pick up.

He was in luck.

'I'm at Josh Norbury's flat with Josh's sister,' he said, realising how breathless he was when he tried to speak.

'I don't want to know,' Simon said. 'Why are you telling me? Fucking hell, man, what's wrong with you? Her brother's just died!'

'What?' Sellers was momentarily confused. 'No, not like *that*. I haven't thought about her from that angle, not once.'

'Then I don't get it. What are you doing there?'

'I asked her to meet me. I wanted to have another go at—' Sellers broke off. 'Look, that's not important. Here's what is: Angela McCabe bought Josh various presents he didn't want, but that he kept anyway. Lisa's about to take them home with her, knowing they mattered to Josh on a sentimental level. I happened to see them in a bag, waiting in the bathroom to go to her house. One of them struck me as being possibly significant.'

'In the bathroom?' said Simon. 'Do you think she was trying to hide them from you?'

Sellers frowned. 'No. At least . . . that hadn't occurred to me. I mean, I was bound to go into the bathroom at some point, so she didn't hide them very well.'

'Go on. What were they?'

'A butter dish, a Kindle, a grotesque tie with *Star Wars* characters on it and a recipe book – written by guess which celebrity chef?'

When no answer came, Sellers examined his phone to check he hadn't lost reception. 'Simon? Are you there?'

Still silence.

'Simon!'

'Yeah, I'm here.'

'Oliver Halliday – that's whose recipe book Angela McCabe bought Josh Norbury. Other half of Sondra.'

'Obviously. Who else was it going to be but the Hate Preacher's husband, if you're this excited about it?'

'You don't sound excited.'

'I'm not.'

Sellers felt winded for the second time in one day. He'd made a fool of himself yet again.

'The reason I'm not excited is that we're there now. We have our answer, thanks to you. We've got Billy.'

'What?'

'You ought to understand the thrill-of-the-chase factor better than anyone. It's being close to getting there that's exciting. Once you know all the answers . . .' Simon sighed. 'Obviously we still need to get the confession, but that's a different kind of challenge.'

'*All* the answers? I don't know any of the answers.'

'Really? Think about what you've just told me.'

'But . . . So you reckon it's definitely significant? I mean, people all over the country have got Oliver Halliday's book. It was everywhere when it first came out. There's probably a copy in my kitchen. Stacey buys more food books than she makes meals these days.' Sellers' new healthy eating regime had apparently put his wife off cooking.

'So? Two, two hundred or twenty thousand people might own copies of Oliver Halliday's book. It's irrelevant.'

'Okay.' Sellers ran his free hand through his hair. 'Okay, so . . . who's Billy, then?' Everything had been pointing towards Isobel Sturridge, but Sellers couldn't see how Isobel could have anything to do with this recipe book.

So who could Billy possibly be?

'Lisa Norbury?' said Sellers tentatively. 'The only other two people associated with this copy of Oliver Halliday's book are dead: Angela McCabe and Josh, but . . . I *know* Lisa's not a killer.'

'So do I.'

'Then who?' said Sellers. 'Sondra Halliday? Oliver Halliday himself?'

The silence in his ear sounded more dead than alive.
'Simon?'
Had he cut him off?
The bastard. He'd gone.

18

from Origami *by Kim Tribbeck*

Saturday, 17 January 2015

I stare at the screen of my laptop, unable to believe what I'm seeing and what it means.

Jolly voices chirp from my TV in the corner of the room: a woman in a red blazer and brown corduroy trousers and a small, bespectacled man in a yellow shirt. They seem happy about something I'm fairly sure I wouldn't give a toss about if I'd paid attention. I reach for the TV remote control and mute them. Normally I like the company of two-dimensional screen people and the loneliness-alleviating background noise, but now I need to think without distraction, because if this means what I think it means . . .

No way. It can't be that I tried something and it worked. Can it?

But here's her face on my screen: more than one photo. And when I typed her name into Google images, I must have done it because I thought it might be her: Isobel Sturridge. I knew she'd been interviewed by the police, along with Liam, so I typed her name into the search box.

The first pictures to come up were three of Faith Kendell. My stomach started to hurt when I saw her – a sharp jabbing pain at first that faded and spread until it felt more like a dull ache radiating through me.

I clicked on them one by one: 'Isobel Sturridge of Rudolphy's receives the Independent Bookshop of the Year Award', 'Author Naomi Alderman with Isobel Sturridge from Rudolphy's bookshop', 'Isobel Sturridge asks: Do Bookshops Have a Future?'

It's her. Isobel Sturridge is Faith Kendell.

Does that mean she killed my grandmother? Could it mean something else: a possibility I don't want to put into words?

Whether I want them or not, the words are there: *is Liam a killer? What if Isobel gives out the books and then Liam does the killings?*

I push sofa cushions out of the way in search of my phone. I deleted Liam from my contacts, but I still know his number by heart.

I don't want to ring him. I want to ring Charlie. I want us to be still driving around, still working together . . .

Will you listen to how pathetic you sound? She spends her days attending suicide and domestic violence yawn-fests, and you're a comedian. You're not fucking Cagney and Lacey.

If I can get something useful out of Liam, I'll have a reason to ring her.

'Liam Sturridge.'

'Why didn't you tell me your sister was in Canterbury that night?' I wouldn't have been able to ring him if I'd allowed myself to think about what I'd say, or how. This was the only way it could happen: a current of need-to-talk-to-him coursing through me.

'Excuse me? Who is this?'

'Who d'you think it is, Liam?'

'Kim?'

'Oh, well done.'

'I'm surprised to hear from you, that's all. How are you?'

'Caught up in a murder investigation, in a possible-next-victim kind of way. You?'

'I'm fine.'

How did I ever imagine a relationship of any sort with this man might be possible? I wait a few seconds, then say, 'Well, okay, if you have no follow-up questions, I'll press on with mine.'

'Okay.'

How do most people resist the urge to flatten you with a meat hammer?

'Isobel, your sister, was in Canterbury the night I gigged there. You were there too. We stayed in a hotel together, remember?'

'Yes.'

'There was a man there that night who gave me a small white book with some words from a poem in it. I didn't mention it to you at the time. Then, the day my grandmother died, I found out that Billy Dead Mates is in the habit of giving books like that to his victims shortly before killing them. Liam? Are you still there?'

'Is there a reason why you're telling me all this?'

'The police have found the man who gave me the book. He's told them he saw a woman trying to take something from my handbag, and he saw the white book drop to the floor – and so he picked it up and handed it to me, assuming she'd pulled it out of my bag. In fact, she was trying to put it in there. This man also told the police about another man who was there that night, lurking nearby, who witnessed the same thing.'

Silence.

'The man he described was you, Liam. And the woman trying to plant the white book in my bag was your sister, Isobel.'

I wait. And wait. 'Well?'

'Well what? You didn't ask me a question.'

'Was your sister there that night? Did you see her?'

'Yes.'

'Did you see her trying to do something to my handbag? Because that's what this man's account suggests.'

'Yes.'

'Then why the fuck didn't you say anything to me?'

'You didn't ask.'

'I didn't . . . Jesus Christ, Liam! You see your sister with her hand in my bag and you say *nothing*?'

I can't see him, but I hear the shrug in his voice when he

says, 'If she'd taken anything, I'd have stopped her. The other guy was watching her, she saw him and left immediately, empty-handed. There was no harm done. Why would I say anything?'

'Because . . . any normal human being would!'

'I find it stranger that you didn't tell me a man had given you a book with nonsensical words in it.'

I squeeze my eyes shut and listen to my heartbeat in my ears until the urge to scream 'Fuck off!' has subsided.

'When you came to meet me that night, did you know your sister would be there?'

'No.'

'So you were surprised to see her?'

'Very.'

'And surprised to see her rifling through my bag?'

'That surprised me less.'

'Really? Is she in the habit of doing that?'

'No. I often catch her doing things I don't understand, though.'

'Such as?'

'The toilet roll.'

'Pardon?' I snap.

'When a new roll needs putting on the thing attached to the wall, I just put it on. I don't care how. Isobel usually takes it off and puts it on a different way, saying I've done it wrong. She insists it has to be . . . I don't know how to describe it. Rolling down from over, not pulling from under.'

I rest my forehead against the wall. 'What did Isobel say the next time you saw her, when you asked what the hell she'd been playing at?'

'I didn't ask.'

'You . . .' All my words have evaporated. What's the point?

'I didn't want to embarrass her. She knew I'd seen her, therefore she knew I knew she was obsessed with my sex life, enough to follow me to your gig. It would have been as distasteful a conversation for me as for her, so I didn't bother. I assumed she wouldn't try it again, since she'd been caught.'

'And you didn't think I had any right to know? You didn't fancy telling me so that we could discuss it just because it was interesting?'

'I didn't find it interesting. I didn't realise you'd think there was anything to discuss.'

'Liam, are you Billy Dead Mates? Have you murdered anybody, or helped to?'

'No,' he says in a monotone.

I turn cold. This man has been inside me, inside my body.

'That's the best you can do? An offhand "no"?'

'It's not any particular kind of "no", it's just "no".'

'It didn't reassure me.'

'I didn't realise I was supposed to reassure you. I thought you wanted a simple answer to a simple question.'

'I asked if you were a serial killer,' I remind him. 'Weren't you offended? Upset that I might think you could kill people? Five of them?'

'Not really. You might believe, as I do, that anyone's capable of killing in certain circumstances. I didn't take your question personally.'

Ignoring the warning voice in my mind, I say quickly, 'Why the pairs? What do they mean? And why change from pairs of friends to a grandparent and grandchild? Why Linzi Birrell and Rhian Douglas, Angela McCabe and Joshua Norbury? What could you and Isobel possibly have against these people?'

'If I were you, I'd stop tormenting yourself with questions,' Liam says. 'Other people's reasons are always a mystery.'

No. Not good enough. I have to understand. I have to know.

'Goodbye, Kim. We probably shouldn't speak again.'

I hear a click, then nothing.

~

Monday, 19 January 2015

Nothing ever goes the way you want it to. I came here to find Charlie Zailer but the first person I see when I get out of my car is White Book Man: Niall Greeves.

He's probably the kind of attractive that starts to look dull after a while, I try to persuade myself. Or sickly; too much, like eating a box of chocolates all at once.

What's he doing here? He saw the police artist's sketch in the paper, helpfully identified himself and has been eliminated from the investigation. *Alibis for all five murders, all solid,* I recite to myself. His role in the proceedings is well and truly over. He shouldn't be striding purposefully up the steps of the police station like a man with something urgent to say to a detective.

I run across the car park, mount the steps two at a time, and burst in through the doors after him. If he turned, he'd see me, but he's busy at the reception desk. I hear the end of his request: '. . . talk to someone involved in the, er . . . the investigation. Is that possible?'

Why? Don't give him what he wants: make him explain himself.

'I mean, it's not at all urgent. It's something that . . . well, it's awkward. I probably shouldn't be here at all.'

Oh, God, his voice.

For Christ's sake, Tribbeck, it's just a voice. Imagine it coming from the mouth of someone with yellow toenails and dandruffy shoulders.

'Come with me.' A uniformed officer wearing a badge with a strange name on it – Zlosnik, I think it said – leads Niall Greeves away from reception into the same corridor I walked along with DC Gibbs nearly two weeks ago. It feels more like a hundred years. As he and Zlosnik shrink with distance, I notice that Greeves is protesting. The closer he gets to the detectives he came here to see, the more he's changing his mind.

I fight the urge to scream. Anything he knows, I deserve to know before anyone else. No one would be aware of his existence if it weren't for me.

Could he be Billy? The police are certain he isn't.

Please let him not be Billy. Not that it's any business of mine. Just . . . for his sake, it's better if he's not a serial killer. The same would apply to anyone.

A uniformed policeman walks in from outside, holding a sheet of paper in front of his face. Unaware of my presence, he rams into me. 'Watch it!' I say.

'Sorry! So sorry – are you all right? How clumsy of me!'

'I need to see Sergeant Charlie Zailer. Can you find her for me?'

'I can't, I'm so sorry. Got to run. I'm in the middle of something urgent.' He holds up the piece of paper. It's an advertisement for a job. I read the words 'permanent position' and 'remuneration' before he snatches it away and moves on.

He's almost out of the reception area by the time I manage to say, 'Hold on a minute.'

He stops with a sigh that I'm not supposed to be able to hear.

'You're in a hurry to apply for a job?'

'Yup. The deadline's today, so . . .' His charming smile probably works on most people and only makes a tiny minority want to pluck out his eyes and spit into the sockets.

'But for the moment, as things stand, you work here, right? You're a policeman?'

'Well . . .' He laughs. 'Yes, obviously. The uniform's the clue.' Is he for real?

'I'm a member of the public who's come in needing help. Instead of prioritising a job you might not get, why not do your current one properly? Help the woman who's come in needing help. That's me. Just a thought.'

His eyes widen: a mixture of shock and recognition. The message, or at least the one I'm getting, is along the lines of 'I've heard about scary people like you, but I never for a moment dreamed I'd meet one in real life.'

'Look, I've got to run,' he pleads. 'Someone else will help you. I'd like to, but I can't. Sorry. I've done my best to explain. Forgive me.'

He darts off down the corridor, leaving me open-mouthed, hysteria rising inside me. He doesn't know I've come to see Charlie about her sister; I might have vital information that he's refusing to help me pass on: someone on a high ledge threatening to throw themselves off, or a class of primary school kids held hostage by a maniac.

'Kim! No one told me you were coming in.'

I turn. It's Charlie.

'What kind of shit-show are you guys running here?'

'You seem angry. Did the servants forget your pickled onion Monster Munch this morning?'

This makes me laugh, though I don't want to. I describe my brush with her unhelpful colleague and she groans. 'That's Iain Chanter. He doesn't do a stroke of work – just obsessively applies for other jobs all day long. I think he's got an actual problem. As well as *being* an actual problem. They're trying to give him the boot, I think, but it's hard. Anyway: you wanted me and here I am!' She smiles. 'What's up?'

'You've driven me around. I thought I could drive you around for a change.'

'Kim, why are you here – really?'

You can hardly blame liars; so often the truth is mocked or rejected as unacceptable.

'You said you'd ring me with any news,' I say.

'I will. There's none yet, I'm afraid.'

'Who's Faith Kendell? Whoever she is, is she Billy?'

Charlie frowns. 'I don't have a definite answer to that question yet. Sorry. They're still waiting for DNA test results, and

Simon's at the refusing-to-tell-me-what-he's-thinking stage of the case. I have a special hitting pillow that he knows nothing about. At the moment I'm beating the mouldy feathers out of it several times a day.'

'Isobel Sturridge is Faith,' I say. 'Even if she isn't Billy, she's Faith Kendell.'

Charlie nods. 'That's . . . yes.'

Of course she was never going to tell me. Why should she?

'I did a bit of digging around online,' I say. 'I think I've got something on the Liv and Gibbs front.'

Charlie grabs my wrist. 'You'd better not be joking.'

'I'm not. I've found Natalie – Nikhil's girlfriend. Her surname's Burge. She has a long job title: Director of Science and Plants for Schools at Cambridge University's Botanic Garden. She's on Twitter – not as herself; as Science and Plants or some such – and she's going for a wedding dress fitting tomorrow afternoon in Cambridge city centre at a place called The Tailor's Cat. It's a bridal boutique. Guess who's also going?'

'I've no idea.'

'Charlie. You used to be a detective.'

'Liv's going too? How do you know?'

'From Natalie's tweet last night: "So excited about wedding dress fitting on Tuesday at The Tailor's Cat" followed by Liv's Twitter handle. They hadn't been tweeting each other, there was no conversation – just that one tweet with Liv included. And – I think this is strange, I don't know if you will – they don't follow each other on Twitter. They've never communicated there before. Natalie's tweets, all apart from that one, are "Picture of rare monkey puzzle tree" and stuff like that.'

'Wow.'

'Yeah, that's what I thought. Liv didn't reply to the tweet about the wedding dress, but she did favourite it. Then, next time I looked, the tweet was gone. Vanished.'

Charlie nods. 'Typical of Liv. She favourites to suck up, then

DMs to say, "Actually, would you mind deleting that?" How did you find Natalie on Twitter with no surname to go on?'

'I searched for "Natalie" and "McElwee" together – Nikhil's wine company. There was something from a years-old McElwee Christmas party . . . Look, it doesn't matter. What's more interesting is: why did Liv want that tweet deleted?'

Charlie looks at me oddly. 'She didn't want anything online linking her and Natalie. I agree, it's interesting – to me. I just can't see why it matters to you.'

'It's my mystery too,' I say. 'You gave it to me in that godawful hotel in . . . wherever it was, and I'm keeping it until I've solved it.'

I can't tell if Charlie's impressed or annoyed.

'So Natalie and Nikhil are getting married,' she says, eyes darting back and forth as she processes the new information. 'Liv and Gibbs must be their . . . best man and woman, witnesses, whatever. But so what? Why does that have to stay secret? Why has my sister never mentioned the name Natalie Burge in my presence?'

'Maybe the wedding's tied up with the surrogacy plan. Something like "We pay for your wedding and honeymoon – you then have a baby for us and allow us to buy it from you." It sounds far-fetched, but why else would Nikhil and Natalie choose witnesses they've known such a short time? Let's face it, if they'd been part of your sister's social circle for ages, or Chris Gibbs', you and Simon would have heard their names.'

'True. But there's no surrogacy plan that we know of. We made that up, remember?'

'There might or might not be a surrogacy plan. If there isn't, there's something else. I want to find out what it is, tomorrow. Do you?'

Lifeworld online, 19 January 2015
OPEN LETTER TO BILLY DEAD WOMEN
by Sondra Halliday

Dear Billy Dead Women

I've decided to use this week's column to write to you directly. You've been writing to me and sending me presents, and I don't believe you'd have done that if you didn't want a reply. The trouble is, I don't know who you are or where you live. I don't know your email address. If I'm going to communicate with you at all, it has to be in public.

I am proud to say that, although I am no kind of detective, I know more about you than those whose job it is to investigate your crimes. They're still clinging to the overwhelmingly unlikely possibility that you might be a woman. It's victim blaming at its most flagrant, masquerading as open-mindedness. All but one of the murder victims are women, so the killer must be a woman too, or else how can it turn out that all female suffering has a female cause that conveniently absolves the lethal bulldozer that is patriarchy, the one we're not allowed to notice even as it crushes the life out of us?

If you're wondering what you've just read, Billy, let me explain: it's called a radical feminist rant. Don't pretend you didn't know that's what I am. Every journalist in the country is writing about you, yet I'm the only one you've chosen to bombard with books and stories and letters. Why me, Billy? It's because I'm not keeping my head down like a good girl, isn't it? I've looked up and seen the hostile pattern all around me – a pattern of woman-hating – and I've correctly identified how you fit into it.

You target me, Billy, for the same reason I target you: you would annihilate my kind as irreversibly as I would annihilate yours if I had the chance. What I'm trying to say is: I understand why you feel as if you know me. It works both ways.

The detectives pursuing your bloody trail don't know who you are, but I do. Your name starts to seem more and more irrelevant when I know the rotten core of you so well. Unlike the police, I know you're one of the millions of men on this planet who don't believe the lives of women and girls are worth anything. Unlike them, I know it's going to be almost impossible to find you or stop you because you are not an aberration; rather, you're the logical extension of male socialisation in our repugnant society.

The truth is, Billy, you could be any or all of the men I've encountered throughout my life, with the exception of my husband Oliver. You share your attitude to women with the majority of males. To you, and to them, we females are not people in our own right, with hopes and dreams and inherent value; we're whatever you need us to be at any given time – receptacles, muses, caterers, heir-producers – or else we're obstacles, impediments, witches, lunatics. That's when you decide it might be simplest to murder us.

And when you do, once you have, the next step is to control the story: 'I did it because I was drunk', 'I only smashed her head against the fireplace because I loved her and she broke my heart.' You tried to tell a story about pairs of best friends, didn't you, Billy? Except you couldn't stick to it. Your fifth victim didn't have a best friend. Never mind, eh? At least she was a woman – you got the important part right, and you and I know that, in the true version of the story, not much else matters.

You like stories, don't you, Billy? This Lane person you're so fond of: she teaches through stories – you wrote that in the first letter you sent me. She's your mentor and your inspiration, so you're mimicking her methods. In an attempt to teach me how wrong I am to call you a misogynist even though you've murdered five women, you've sent me two novels – *Jude the Obscure* by Thomas Hardy and *Beloved* by Toni Morrison. I've been too busy to read either, but you'll be pleased to hear that I've read the shorter pieces you sent me: 'The Two Sisters', 'Loyalty' and 'The Dress'. All three are sanctimonious New-Age drivel and I felt physically ill when I read them.

Credit where credit's due, though. 'The Dress' deserves full marks for ingenuity. It contains the following line: 'Know this: whatever happens to the body, the true Self – who we really are – cannot be destroyed. We are Awareness, not flesh.' When I read that, I laughed out loud. I *had* thought that men, collaborator-women and all the enemies of feminism in between might have run out of ways to invalidate and erase the lived experience of female-bodied humans by now. It seems I was wrong. You've broken new ground, Billy, in approaching it from a spiritual angle. If all that matters about women is our spirituality in the form of cosmic Awareness (which you coyly capitalise), if our bodies are neither here nor there, then of course it's no big deal if we're shot, stabbed, raped or mutilated – and who better to tell us so than self-proclaimed enlightened men whose souls still comfortably inhabit their highly privileged but allegedly irrelevant physical shells long after they've destroyed ours?

Don't bother sending me any more stories, Billy. I won't read them. I didn't sign up to attend your Spirituality for Misogynists class, and I won't let you inflict it on me. And let's face it, you're no deity. You're not even the guru you seem to think you are. You're just another run-of-the-mill man whose idea of metaphysics is woman as disposable body, man as essential soul. And there was you, thinking you were special. Bless.

19

19/1/2015

'He-ey, Simon.'

Simon hated speaking to Dr Kerensa Moore on the phone. Her greeting never varied, which told him that at some point she must have decided always to answer the phone in that way. Simon wished she'd amend her 'He-ey' to a more palatable 'Hello'.

'What can I do for you?' she said. 'I'm just rushing out to a dinner.'

'Can they manage without you for ten minutes?' Simon couldn't help feeling superior because he was having his evening meal cooked for him at home by someone who thought cooking was a waste of time. Like many of his feelings, it made no sense. 'This is important,' he told Moore.

'All right. I'm all ears.'

In the kitchen, Charlie was singing along to her current favourite song on her iPod: 'No water in the water fountain, no phone in the phone booth . . .' What a stupid racket. Simon imagined she was dancing around with her headphones on. That's why she took so long to cook when it was her turn. All she ever did was open a jar of something and pour it over pasta; she made sure it took an hour and a half so that she could stage a kitchen disco.

Simon kicked the lounge door shut so that he could concentrate, then sat down on the sofa. 'I've been thinking about what you said about serial killers whose targets aren't individuals,' he told Moore. 'Billy's unusual not so much because he chose pairs as his victims but because he didn't kill them together. Do you stand by that?'

'Absolutely. Any serial killer that's ever gone for groups or pairs as opposed to lone victims has attacked the victim unit together, whether that's two people, three, five . . .'

'And Billy's not doing that.' Simon confirmed what he already knew. It helped to say it out loud. 'He's eliminating them individually.'

'And I'm afraid to say that Marion Hopwood's murder really throws a spanner in the works,' said Moore. 'She had no best friend; she wasn't shot. Billy's now atypical of a serial killer in more ways than he was when I last spoke to you.'

'I'm not worried about the not-shot part,' said Simon. 'Shoot someone on a crowded hospital ward and you're going to get caught. Billy doesn't want to get caught, so it makes sense for him to vary his method.'

'And the no-best-friend thing?'

Simon chewed the inside of his lip. 'Yeah. That would be a problem if killing pairs of best friends was what Billy thought he was about. We all assumed it was at first, understandably. Marion Hopwood's changed that – now we know it's not about friends.'

'And we have no clue what it *is* about.' Moore sighed.

Simon pitied her. He knew what it was about. It was becoming rather obvious. No one else seemed to see it, though.

'Let me ask you something,' he said. 'Linzi and Rhian were best friends and so were Angela and Josh. But let's imagine that's not why Billy wants them dead. He wants them dead because of something they've *done*. In his mind, they all need to be punished.'

'Okay. Carry on.'

'I'm going to narrow it down to one pair, though I could use the other just as easily: Linzi and Rhian. Billy wants to kill them both because of something they've done. If that thing was, for example, that they got drunk one night and made prank phone calls to Billy's sister, teasing her and driving her to suicide – if the thing they'd done wrong, in other words, was something they'd done *together*, then maybe Billy would have murdered them *together*.'

Simon didn't generally allow himself to think about the time two of his classmates had spent a whole evening telephonically harassing his mother, and the trauma his family suffered as a result. Kathleen Waterhouse had taken months to recover from the upset, and it was nearly a year before she was prepared to answer her telephone again.

Kerensa Moore laughed. 'I love the idea of prank phone calls. It sounds so lovely and innocent.'

Simon scowled. Innocent? When, seconds ago, he'd described a scenario, albeit fictional, in which prank calls led to suicide? He added Moore's tone-deaf response to his ever-growing list of evidence that so-called psychology experts knew fuck all. 'Let's now look at a different hypothetical situation,' he went on. 'Linzi and Rhian *each* did something wrong that Billy deems worthy of punishment by death, but they didn't do the *same* thing.'

'So Linzi drives Billy's sister to suicide with prank phone calls, and Rhian . . . runs over his pet dog on her Vespa?'

'In the case of two separate crimes, might Billy decide separate executions were appropriate – to do full justice to both? Might he kill the two halves of the pair separately because, in his mind, they'd committed two distinct offences rather than jointly colluding in a shared one?'

Why bother asking? Simon knew it was not only possible but likely. He knew Kerensa Moore wasn't as clever as he was. This was a pointless conversation, a box-ticking exercise.

There was a long silence from Moore. Then: 'You know what? I want to say yes. Yes! It makes absolute, perfect sense that he'd do that *if* everything you've outlined were to turn out to be the case. But then that wouldn't work for the second pair, would it? Angela and Josh. Or for Marion Hopwood.'

The lounge door opened. Charlie mouthed 'Food' from the doorway.

'Yes, it would,' Simon told Moore. 'It'd work for Kim Tribbeck, too, though she's still alive. This is about pairs, just not pairs of best friends. And all three pairs work in exactly the same way. Thanks for the chat. It's been useful. Got to go.' Simon put down the phone.

'That was *better*,' Charlie said uncertainly. 'You thanked her and explained you had to end the call.'

Simon was about to roll his eyes, then stopped himself as he remembered that was James Wing's tick. He was Wing's favourite person at the moment, even more than usual. Strangely, he found he didn't mind so much now that real progress was being made. Simon had decided there was no point him driving to Poole when Wing was already there and would welcome the chance to be a long-distance conspirator. It had worked like a dream, and Simon had agreed to go for some beers with Wing next time they were in the same place, even though he wasn't overly keen on beer.

'One small suggestion,' said Charlie. 'Stay on the phone for three seconds longer so that whoever you're talking to has the chance to say, "Okay, bye, see you soon" – so they don't feel they've had the phone slammed down on them. But overall? Definitely a move in the right direction.'

'It's almost mathematical,' Simon muttered. 'Three twos. But also . . . two threes.'

'Any chance you could relocate your cryptic pondering to the kitchen? For once, a meal I've produced looks quite tempting. I must have taken the lid off the pesto jar differently.'

Simon stayed where he was.

'Okay, well, I'm going to the kitchen to eat. See you when I see you.' Halfway there, Charlie stopped and turned back. 'What threes?' she asked.

'Linzi Birrell, Josh Norbury and Kim Tribbeck. Billy's punished them all – or wants to punish, in the case of Kim – for the same crime.'

'And his other three victims: Rhian, Angela, Marion?'

'Same. Rhian Douglas, Angela McCabe and Marion Hopwood – those three also committed the same crime as each other, different from the one committed by Linzi, Josh and Kim.' Simon looked at Charlie properly for the first time since she'd entered the room.

'Okay, so . . . hang on. Group 1 – Linzi, Josh and Kim – all committed the same crime as one another, but not together, right?'

'No. Separately and at different times.'

'And the other three also? They committed the same crime on different occasions?'

Simon nodded. 'Want to know the worst thing? None of these people did anything wrong at all. Billy's idea of a capital offence . . .' He finished his sentence non-verbally, with a small shake of his head. He looked utterly defeated, Charlie thought. For a second, she felt afraid.

Pasta was the solution. She fetched Simon's heaped plate and a fork from the kitchen table and brought it to him in the lounge. 'Here. You must be starving. I'm assuming you've not eaten all day, since you've been AWOL on one of your secret missions.'

Charlie had woken this morning at six to find Simon's half of the bed empty. Normally, his getting up would wake her, so he must have set off at some ridiculous hour when she was still deeply asleep. On the kitchen table, he'd left some stories. Charlie recognised the titles: 'The Two Sisters', 'The Dress', 'Loyalty' . . . These were stories from the website of Bright Path Ascension Ishaya Lane Baillie (Charlie liked to include Lane's full title every time she thought of her, in order to enjoy its ridiculousness) that Billy Dead Mates had sent to Sondra Halliday. New Age moral fables: not Charlie's favourite genre. Simon had summarised each one briefly and dismissively when he'd first mentioned them to her. Since then he'd evidently decided they mattered. On the back of an unpaid gas bill beside the pile of stories on the kitchen table, he'd written,

'Read these CAREFULLY'. Charlie hadn't – she'd had to go to work – and was annoyed with herself for having felt guilty all day.

'So did you go to Poole to see the Asda van biddy?' she asked Simon.

'Muriel Pearson? No. I sent Wing to do it for me. Gave him a script, told him to stick to it word for word.'

'And?'

'A good result. Muriel Pearson confirmed what I've known for a while.'

'I hope you praised Wing to the skies. From what you've said about him, that would make his year.'

'I went one better and told him what I know: why Billy's doing what he's doing. Not for general consumption – yet.'

'You didn't!' No way had he told James Wing before her; no way.

'I did.'

'You bastard. You want me to be angry, don't you?'

'No.'

'Well, I'm not.' Charlie consoled herself with the knowledge that she too was keeping something secret: the plan she'd made with Kim Tribbeck for tomorrow. Perhaps she'd ring James Wing and tell him, make him swear not to tell Simon.

She went to fetch her own dinner. By the time she returned to the lounge, she thought she'd worked something out.

'The different crimes committed by the two groups of three – they must be connected,' she said. 'If they weren't . . . I mean, imagine Group 1 have all driven after necking a bottle of gin and then run over and killed a small child. Meanwhile Group 2 are all embezzlers who've defrauded the companies they work for. If each member of Group 1 is paired with a member of Group 2, as best friends or family, that's too unlikely.' Charlie was frustrated. She knew what she meant but couldn't express it. 'It's too much of a coincidence if Group 1's crime has nothing to do with Group 2's. Billy wouldn't just happen to know three pairs of people in which one has embezzled and the other's a drink-drive killer. So the only other possibility . . .'

'Go on.' Simon sounded interested.

'Group 1's crime must be linked to Group 2's. Like, imagine the pairs were married couples instead of best friends or grandmother and granddaughter. Married couples with children. Let's say all three husbands beat up the children, and all three wives turned a blind eye and let it happen because they were scared of their husbands. In that scenario, you'd have three pairs of two but also two groups of three: one from each pair who did the beating, and one who condoned and looked the other way.'

Simon smiled. His mouth was full of pasta, but that was a definite smile. 'Bang on,' he said once he'd swallowed the mouthful. 'And now that you've got that far, it ought to take you three seconds to work out the rest.'

One. Two. Three.

'Um . . .'

'All right, three's a bit ambitious. Five seconds.'

Charlie sighed. 'Can't we spend even one second concentrating on the bit I've cleverly worked out, instead of berating me for not knowing everything there is to know?'

'Did you read the three stories?'

'Not yet.'

'Read them. See if you can spot the odd one out. That's the last piece of the puzzle – it was for me and it will be for you. No, on second thoughts, this isn't charades at Christmas.' Simon put his pasta bowl down on the floor and stood up. 'Where are they? Still on the kitchen table?'

He returned with a handful of papers a few minutes later. 'Here. This is the one you need to read.'

'You're *telling* me which is the odd one out?' Charlie squinted up at him suspiciously. 'You're helping me to get the answer?' There was no precedent for this.

'The other two stories are Lane Baillie standard issue – naïve moral message, be kind, give off positive energy, think the best of everyone. Lane Baillie knows the other two stories. She gives them out to her clients. This one, the odd one out – she's never heard of it. Billy sent it to Sondra Halliday, but Lane had never laid eyes on it till I put it in front of her. I don't think she was impressed by the general principles it promotes. She described it as "concerning".'

'Can we stop saying "Billy"?' Charlie asked. 'Isn't it Faith Kendell AKA Isobel Sturridge we're talking about here?'

Simon's face froze – as if he were trying to imitate a wax model of himself. 'Is it?' he said. 'Why do you say that?'

'Because the evidence suggests that Billy Dead Mates is Isobel Sturridge – doesn't it?'

'A lot of it does, yes.'

'But not all of it?'

'Why would Isobel Sturridge want to kill Linzi Birrell? Why would she want to kill Josh Norbury?'

'All right, fine,' Charlie snapped. 'Billy it is.' She tried to expel all the air from her lungs, hoping to breathe out her frustration along with it. After inhaling new supplies to see her through the next stage of the conversational ordeal, she said, 'So if one of the stories Billy sent Sondra Halliday didn't come from Lane, maybe he wrote it himself.'

'Correct,' said Simon.

'Twice in one day! I intend to let this go to my head.'

'Not only is the moral of the story very different from the others, it also sticks out like a sore thumb linguistically. Billy's a Brit, so "favourite", "neighbour" – those words contain a "u" when Billy writes them. And words like "realise" are spelled "i-s-e" not "i-z-e". The stories on Lane's website were written by an American – hardly surprising – so we have "neighb*or*", "fav*or*ite", "reali*z*e" with a zed. Or a zee, as a Yank would say.'

'Billy snuck in a story of his own, camouflaged within Lane's collection,' said Charlie.

'Yes, and do you know why? Because psychologically, symbolically, Billy needs these killings to be good deeds – saving all of us, not doing irreparable harm, *not committing murder*. That's the most dangerous kind of killer there is. By clutching on to Lane – her obvious kind nature, her benign, naïve stories – Billy's making a statement: "I too am good. All I want is what Lane wants: for the world to be a better place."'

Charlie took the pages from Simon's hand. 'I'd better read this odd story out,' she said.

'Yeah. Don't be surprised if you feel sick when you work out what it means. I did.'

Charlie was about to say that maybe she ought to finish her pasta first, but Simon had already taken the bowl from her hand and left the room.

'Wait,' she called after him. 'If you weren't in Poole today, where were you?'

'At an Indian restaurant called the Khaybar in the morning.'

'But you don't like spicy food.'

'I wasn't eating. Then in the afternoon I went to Hot-n-Tasty in Combingham – the caff opposite Linzi Birrell's flat.'

'Why? Oh, God – not that bloody row about the lasagne?'

'No, actually – nothing to do with lasagne.'

'Then why?' Charlie asked.

Simon shook his head and said nothing.

20

from Origami *by Kim Tribbeck*

Tuesday, 20 January 2015

'Will you trust me? Us being parked here is the worst idea. It's a *pedestrianised street*. Cambridge traffic police are fanatics. Bad combination.'

'Exactly – pedestrianised,' I say calmly, trying to lead by example. 'So unless the traffic police appear on foot . . .'

'They will! Any second now – maybe at the exact moment Liv and Natalie arrive, and then we're fucked. We need a better plan.'

We're in my car, parked opposite The Tailor's Cat in Cambridge. Charlie is proving to be a twitchy and irritating stakeout partner. As big a pain in the arse as I was when she was the calm, sensible one driving me around. Why are human beings all so determined to cock up the things that matter most to them?

I'm not sure that, deep down, Charlie wants to find out the truth about her sister.

I'm sure I do and that we will. Today.

'Cambridge traffic police are like a weird religious cult. When Simon and I followed Liv and Gibbs here last year, they swooped down on us *every time* we stopped the car for even a few seconds. They're inflexible, they don't smile—'

'Can you be quiet?' There's nothing for us to see at the moment, but I want to watch in silence in case something happens.

Charlie lights another cigarette. She's got through about fifteen since we set off. 'It's not surrogacy,' she mutters. 'Does the Director of Science and Blah-blah at Cambridge University's

Botanic Garden sound to you like the kind of woman who'd sell her own baby?'

'Possibly. A certain kind of eco-posh person might think it was biological fascism to believe that flesh-and-blood relationships count for anything.'

Charlie ducks down in her seat, startling me. Then, just as suddenly, she springs back up. 'Here she comes – Natalie on her own. No Liv. I thought they'd arrive together.'

So did I. I rang and checked, claiming to be the sister of the bride and using my Don't-even-think-about-saying-no-to-me voice: Liv was the one who booked Natalie's appointment. They ought to be arriving together in a stupid, arm-linked, girly way.

Natalie Burge is tall and slim with centre-parted glossy dark hair. She's wearing black boots with brown square heels and a long fawn-coloured coat with a belt. She's the kind of woman who'll look brilliant in any wedding dress. I married Gabe wearing black trousers and a cream linen shirt. I knew that if I attempted traditional attire I'd only end up looking like a psychopath who'd murdered The Good Fairy and stolen her outfit; I have the wrong range of facial expressions, and hair that's too unruly for frilly white dresses.

Natalie passes my car without taking an interest in its inhabitants. She's hurrying towards The Tailor's Cat. In she goes.

'She's going to be pissed off with Liv for being late.' Charlie sounds like a jaded sports commentator describing a match that's a let-down from the start. 'Hopefully she'll realise she's asked a selfish twat to be her best woman.'

I'm about to reply when Natalie reappears on the street, phone pressed against her ear, talking in an animated way.

I open my window. At first the wind blows her words away, but then I manage to catch a few.

'I can ring you in an hour, hour and a half maybe? That okay? I'm busy with a friend in town at the moment – long-standing commitment. Okay, cool. Thanks, I appreciate . . .'

Four young men dressed in black gowns and mortarboard hats walk past, complaining about how early they have to get up the next day for rowing practice.

Once they've passed, I can hear Natalie again. 'That'll be perfect. Looking forward muchly. Okay, I'll quickly let Debjani know and then I'd better get back to my friend – I've abandoned her in the shop!' She turns and glances over her shoulder at The Tailor's Cat. 'Okay, ciao ciao!'

Anyone capable of two 'ciao's and one 'muchly' could sell a baby for cold, hard cash without flinching, I decide.

Charlie elbows me hard. 'Did you hear that? Liv's in there.'

'Sounds like it.'

'She must have been earlier than us and more than half an hour early for the appointment. That's not like her. What the fuck's going on?'

The person who knows the answer to that question is pressing buttons on her phone, still standing outside the shop.

If I don't do this now . . .

I'm out of the car and heading for my target before Charlie can protest. Natalie might know me from the TV but she doesn't know *me*. With any luck, she'll think I'm someone who looks a bit like the comedian Kim Tribbeck.

'Natalie! How *are* you? God, how long has it been? How's Nikhil?'

'Um . . . hi.' She looks surprised. Understandably.

'How's life at the Botanic Gardens? Still keeping you busy? You were a bit stressed about it all last time we spoke.'

'Oh . . . ha! Yes, the stress is pretty much a constant, but I love it really.' She finds a smile for me at last. As I hoped: her only ambition is to come out of the conversation without me twigging that she hasn't a clue who I am.

'So, you and Nikhil are finally tying the knot, then!' I point over her shoulder at The Tailor's Cat.

She frowns. 'Um . . . well, no. I mean . . .'

'You're *not*?' I make sure to sound suitably incredulous.

'We tied the knot ten years ago.'

Did you indeed?

She's worried. If I know her and Nikhil so well, how come I don't know they're married?

There's no ring on her wedding finger.

Brazen it out, Tribbeck. Brazen is your number one characteristic.

'Oh, that's right – I remember Nikhil explaining about the no wedding ring thing!' I say brightly.

'Yes, well . . . there's no point having one when your fingers are buried in soil most of the time. Nik doesn't wear one either – we bought each other a much-needed new car instead of wedding rings.'

I nod as if I've known this for some time. '*Such* a great idea. But . . . you're about to have a wedding dress fitted, right? Nikhil definitely said that – or I thought he did.'

'Oh, I see!' Natalie laughs. Whatever suspicions she had are gone. People are such trusting fools. 'No, I'm here with my friend Liv. *She's* getting married. Next week.'

Oh Jesus Christ. Is Charlie hearing this?

'Look, um . . . it's been nice chatting but I'd better go – I've left my friend stranded on her pre-big-day big day and it's not fair.'

'Liv . . . Zailer, isn't it?' I say as if I'm not sure. 'Yes, that's right – Nikhil did tell me it was her dress being fitted, now that I think about it. I remember saying, "That's an unusual surname".'

'Listen.' Natalie moves closer. When our faces are only a few inches apart, she says, 'Nikhil *shouldn't* have told you. Please don't mention Liv's name to anybody else, or anything about her wedding or . . .' She breaks off, blushing. 'It sounds stupidly melodramatic, but Liv and her boyfriend are getting married in secret. They're not from the Cambridge area. Apparently all their friends and families have been just *awful* about them getting together – not supportive at all – so they decided to do it without telling anyone. I don't know whether you know, but . . .' She stops, looking hesitant.

I say nothing. I can afford to wait. She's the one who needs something from me now: a promise that I'll be discreet.

'Ah, sod it, I might as well tell you. It doesn't matter if you didn't know already. Nikhil and I have a small business – I mean, like, *tiny*. We both have full-time jobs, and this is really just an occasional thing we do, but it's important to us. When we met and fell in love, both our families cut up rough – mine because Nik's brown and his because I'm white and not Hindu.' Natalie shakes her head at the stupidity. 'We got married in Vegas – yes, I know! – with strangers for witnesses. It was kind of horrible, you know?'

'I can imagine.' I assume that's what someone who thinks like Natalie would say. Personally, I think a Vegas wedding with only strangers present sounds ideal. You don't yet know and resent strangers, so they're less likely to ruin things for you in a range of overt and subtle ways.

'We could have invited some friends, but I didn't want to try and patch together a wedding with *some* of the people close to us but not all,' Natalie goes on. 'The absence of our families would have been a huge embarrassment. Everyone would have been aware of it and trying not to mention it. Anyway, this is nothing to do with anything really, except to explain why Nik and I set up our business: Your Secret Wedding, it's called. We help couples who've got no one else. We don't just turn up and do the impersonal witness thing – we get to know them properly beforehand, join in with all the preparations. The idea is that by the time the wedding comes round, we're proper friends.'

Natalie likes talking about her business. Her voice is full of energy. 'It *really* works,' she gushes. 'Never fails. Nik and I are still good friends with all the couples we've helped. Liv and Chris aren't just customers to us any more – they're our good mates.'

'They're paying you, though?'

'Yes, there's a fee, but . . . well, just because something's a paid-for service doesn't make it an emotionless transaction. That's the whole point of our venture. We feel we're doing a really valuable thing.'

I should have guessed, or at least wondered. Liv Zailer booked the appointment at The Tailor's Cat. It was in her name. I assumed, based on nothing, that it was an appointment for Natalie that she'd booked. As best woman, I thought, Liv was the one in charge of all things administrative.

But Liv Zailer is already married. Chris Gibbs is already married.

Bigamy. That's what they're planning. Nothing to do with surrogacy. Nikhil and Natalie have no idea a crime's about to be committed. They'll be complicit in something illegal, without their consent. Gibbs is a police officer, for Christ's sake. What's wrong with people?

Obvious answer: just about everything.

I'm wondering what to say to Natalie when Charlie calls my name. 'We need to go,' she says. Her patchy, contorted face tells me she's heard every word. Left to my own devices, I'd probably tell Natalie the truth and let her save her business from involvement in a scandal, but it's not my decision to make. It's up to Charlie. If Drew were the one at risk of going to prison, I'd want to be in charge.

Do bigamists go to prison? Is bigamy still a common crime? Was it once? I think it must be rare. I've hardly ever heard of it happening, unlike every other illegal act I can name: murder, rape, burglary, fraud and the gang.

'I'd better dash. I've also got a friend waiting.' I smile at Natalie. 'Good luck with everything – and let's get together very soon!'

'Yes, let's!' she agrees.

I go back to the car, inside which the mood has changed into something almost frightening.

'Drive,' Charlie orders in a voice I don't recognise. 'Drive, and say nothing.'

After she's been silent for an hour and smoked eight cigarettes, I ask her what she's planning to do. 'No idea,' she says.

'I think Simon knows.' I'm not sure if I'm helping or making things worse. All I know is, I needed to tell her. Gabe deserves to be lied to; Charlie doesn't.

At least I'm not a bigamist. At least I'm not a murderer. There are worse people than me out there.

Whose birth families didn't give them away.

'Of course Simon knows,' says Charlie.

From: billydeadmates@hushmail.com
To: Sondra.Halliday@Lifeworldmag.co.uk
Sent: 20 January 2015 04:16:12

Dear Mrs Halliday

I read your latest column in *Lifeworld*. So, you've been 'too busy' to read the novels I sent you, have you?

That says it all. Now I understand something about you that I missed before, and it explains why you're trying at every turn to sabotage my project and to misrepresent me.

At first I thought you genuinely believed me to be a misogynist. I thought you were so blinkered by your own dogmatism that you were incapable of seeing past it, but now I wonder if you and you alone have known from the start why I'm doing what I'm doing. I've no idea how you could know – I have confided in nobody, and if the police are still clueless in spite of having put all their investigative muscle into it then I can't see how you could have beaten them to the correct conclusion – but perhaps I'm being naïve. Journalists sometimes set out to investigate, don't they? Especially when they're obsessed.

You can't deny you're obsessed with me, Sondra (if I may?). Nor can you deny that, in all the thousands of words you've written and published about me, you've been silent on one much-publicised aspect of Billy's *modus operandi*: the white books containing fragments of poetry that he leaves for his victims to find before he kills them. I know you know about the books; it's inconceivable that you would not know.

Finally I put together two of your omissions and worked out what they jointly mean: your failure to mention the Billy books and your failure to read the two novels I've sent you.

Because you've read the three Stories of Enlightenment, haven't you? Even though they had no authors' names attached to them – certainly not famous names like Toni Morrison and Thomas Hardy. You will no doubt claim this is because the stories were much shorter, but we both know that's an excuse, a glossing-over of what's really going on here.

Which is quite simply this: you, Sondra Halliday, are a bibliophobe.

Yes you are.

I've seen you (on Twitter, countless times) accused of transphobia and whorephobia, and I've seen you protest bitterly as I imagine you are now, reading this, but I am in no doubt: you suffer from bibliophobia. You hate and fear books. It's a rare condition, but it's real. Look it up online if you don't believe me.

Books – the actual physical objects with paper pages and covers and printed words – disgust you. I bet you don't have a single one in your house, do you? The smell, even at a distance, wafted from another room or floor, is enough to make you gag.

Not all bibliophobes are frightened of precisely the same thing. In most recorded cases, reading is what they fear: the ideas contained within books. Whereas you love ideas as long as they're exactly the same as yours. You love reading as long as it's a tract by Andrea Dworkin and as long as you don't have to read from or touch an object with covers and pages. That's a prospect that makes you shudder.

I won't bother sending you any more brilliant novels. Why waste my time? You're a book-hater. You despise books. If you do happen to have any in your home, it's as a smokescreen, to hide the truth. Your husband the celebrity chef will of course have his collection of recipe books prominently displayed in the family kitchen, and you wouldn't dream of asking him to move them to an outbuilding, though secretly you'd love to. I'm certain Oliver Halliday has no idea he's married to a book-hating low-life. You're ashamed of your phobia, as you should be, so you hide it from those who matter.

Why don't you quit the charade and admit it? Why don't you start your next *Lifeworld* column with the words 'I, Sondra Halliday, am a hateful bibliophobe'?

Yours sincerely,
Billy

21

20/1/2015

'There's no truth in it,' Sondra Halliday said, red-faced and buzzing with indignation. 'None whatsoever. It couldn't be less true if it tried. Ask anyone who knows me – they'll all tell you I only read on a screen when I have to. On holiday I *always* read paper books. I love them, especially second-hand ones. That smell of old books is one of my favourite things. I'm always going on about it. I mean, it's one of the things I'm *known* for.'

'That and spreading hatred of men?' Simon asked. 'We believe you about the books. Not pleasant when someone lies about you, is it?'

Sellers wasn't so sure he believed Halliday. Why was Billy convinced that she was a bibliophobe if she wasn't? It was such an odd accusation to pull out of nowhere. Perhaps he'd been pointlessly baiting her, but Sellers wanted to hear more before he dismissed the claim altogether.

To his astonishment, he and Simon had been invited to Halliday's home for this interview – though 'required to attend' would be a more accurate way to put it. He'd assumed Halliday meant her home in London when she'd first issued him with a visiting order; she and her husband Oliver had a flat in Farringdon, which, as far as Sellers had been aware, was their only home. No, there was another house in the country where Halliday was holed up working on an important project for a few days. That was where Sellers and Simon were talking to her now: in the kitchen of her white-painted, timber-framed farmhouse in the village of Brettenham in Suffolk.

Sellers hadn't visited the kitchens of any other celebrity chefs, and he wondered if they were all so large. The canteen at the nick was bigger, but only just.

'Yes, it's distressing to be slandered, as you'd know if it had ever happened to you,' Halliday snapped in response to Simon's question. She was sitting across from the two detectives at the long table that took up a substantial part of the room and looked home-made – as if she and her husband had one day decided to chop down a tree in their garden, carve an uneven slice from it and stick it on legs. At one end of the table there was a pile of old copies of *Lifeworld*; at the other, nine bulging Sainsbury's carrier bags that needed unpacking. The point of a cucumber protruded from one, a packet of bacon from another, the neck of a bottle of red wine from a third. A delivery man had turned up with the shopping five minutes after Simon and Sellers had arrived.

Halliday was wearing jeans and a black long-sleeved sweatshirt that was mercifully slogan-free. 'You believe me about the books but not in general?' she said to Simon. 'Are you accusing me of lying about something? What?'

'Billy. You've claimed he's motivated by hatred of women. He isn't.'

'How do you know? Do you know who he is? No. You haven't got a fucking clue! Of course, it's much more fun to demonise me than to focus on your own shortcomings as detectives.'

'I've got more than a clue,' Simon told her.

'That's news to your friend DC Conkers. Look at him, poor startled goldfish. He wasn't expecting you to say that.'

'Why do you call him DC Conkers?'

'Private joke.' Halliday smiled. 'Isn't that right, Conkers?'

Sellers confirmed with a nod.

'So you know who Billy is – well done! That's great! And you're not arresting him why?'

'We're on our way to making an arrest. There are other things that need to happen first.'

'Like disturbing me when I've got work to do, to demand proof that I'm not a bibliophobe? Billy said I am, so it must be true! Naturally, you believe the man and not the woman, even when the man's a multiple murderer. I'm wrong and mean and a bitch to say he's a misogynist, but *he* has authority – he's male! – so he must be speaking the truth!'

'No, I don't think he is,' said Simon.

'He damn well isn't! I love books. I love their yellowed pages and their old musty smell. I'd bottle it and wear it as perfume if I could. I used to have fantasies of opening an antiquarian bookshop.'

'I think the bibliophobia thing is Billy's idea of a joke,' said Simon. 'He might think anyone who has a double-bladed axe as their Twitter avatar is tough enough to take a bit of teasing.'

Sellers' throat was dry. There had been no offer of a drink. He'd have to make an effort not to keep looking at the carton of apple and raspberry juice he could see through the plastic of one of the Sainsbury's bags.

'Billy's being disingenuous,' Simon told Halliday. 'He knows you're not a book-hater. He's giving you a taste of your own medicine, saying, "How do you like it when I make up obviously untrue things about you and spread them around, the way you've been doing to me?" He's saying – subtly – that for you to call him a woman-hater is as far off the mark as him accusing you of bibliophobia. Two can play at that game, that's his message.'

Halliday considered this for a few moments, head down. 'You know, you're probably right. He can't admit to himself that I'm right about him, so, yes, consciously, he might well be doing what you say. In one sense, you'll inevitably understand him better than I ever can, since he's one of your own.'

'One of our own?' Sellers laughed. 'That's a bit rich, even from you.'

'He's a man, Conkers. You and DC Waterhouse are both men. It matters, however much you're all pretending to be enemies and enjoying your game of cops and robbers. Your true enemy – that's "you" plural, all three of you – is, was and always has been women who challenge the oppressive hierarchy that ranks men above women.'

Sellers would have loved to be able to say, 'Actually, we know Billy Dead Mates is a woman.' Or to hear Simon say it. If it weren't for Sondra's husband's recipe book muddying the waters . . .

Everything had seemed nice and clear for a short while, all pointing in the direction of Isobel Sturridge being guilty – or at least Sellers had thought so, though her possible motive had remained elusive. Everyone else had appeared to think so too, until Sellers had gone to Josh Norbury's flat and found Oliver Halliday's book – since when Simon had been insisting he knew everything, while refusing to say a word about what this 'everything' might be.

Sellers had fielded a phone call from a furious Neil Dunning earlier in the day. 'What's wrong with your chain of command up there?' Dunning had raged. 'Kombothekra needs to get Waterhouse in line, or, if he's not up to it, let Proust do it. Is this Isobel Sturridge person Billy or not? If not, who is? You lot are a fucking anachronism! You're a joke. Nowhere but the Culver Valley would a detective – a DC, for Christ's sake, not even a DI – get away with swanning around claiming to know all the answers and refusing to pool his knowledge.'

Sellers, thinking of Lane Baillie and what she might advise, had told Dunning he understood his frustration and sympathised; being Neil Dunning, in the present circumstances, couldn't be easy. That had mollified him a bit.

'My true enemy – or one of them – is anyone who can write about a serial killer three times a week and not once mention Josh Norbury, who's just as dead as the four female victims,' Simon was saying to Sondra Halliday.

She scowled. 'It's not my job to care about Joshua Norbury. I'm a feminist. Violence against women and girls is my concern.

It's my *work*. That's why I don't centre everything around Norbury, or feel obliged to refer to him every time I write or speak about Billy having murdered four women. Tell me this: while he was alive, did Norbury care about the liberation of women? Did he ever challenge the status quo, or own his part in the subjugation of the subordinate sex class? Prove to me that he did and I might care about him.'

'We need you to do something for us,' Simon told her. 'It's important.'

'Wash and iron your undies? Make you scrambled eggs on toast?'

Simon pulled a folded sheet of paper out of his jacket pocket and put it on the table, print-side down. 'I need you to send this to *Lifeworld*, word for word, not changing so much as a comma, and tell them it's your next column. Let them publish it. It has to be published in two days' time, not before – not even online. No sooner than forty-eight hours from now.'

Sellers wondered why this time lag was necessary. There was a lot Simon was keeping to himself, apparently: not only the identity of Billy Dead Mates.

'Don't tell anyone you didn't write the column, not even your husband,' he ordered Halliday. 'Everyone has to believe you've written it.'

Her eyebrows shot up. 'Come again?'

'I need you to—'

'What is it? Who wrote it?'

'I did.'

'*You*? Ha! Fuck that! You expect me to publish *your* words as my own? Of course!' Halliday rolled her eyes. Sellers noted that she was better at the gesture than DC James Wing. 'I'm only a woman, so naturally I'm going to leap at the chance of replacing my trivial pink lady-words with your superior alpha-male ones. If I'm lucky, people might fall for it and imagine I'm capable of saying something that matters! Though, actually – silly me! – that *won't* happen, because the column would still have my name on it right? In which case, it could be the wisest thing ever written and no one would recognise it as such. Whereas a man—'

'Could publish any old shite and have it taken seriously,' Simon supplied the end of the sentence. 'That's what you were going to say, isn't it? If I were a programming genius, I could write software that'd churn out Sondra Halliday columns and no one would be able to tell the difference.'

'Wow. You really are the misogynist *king*, aren't you?'

'No. I just don't like fantasists, that's all. You whine on about the subjugated class, meaning women . . . Every single man who lives on the Winstanley estate in the Culver Valley – *every single skint jobless one of them* – is more oppressed and subjugated than you are.'

'DC Waterhouse.' Halliday took a deep breath. 'Be sensible. A man tells a female journalist that he could write software to replicate her words, and you're honestly claiming that's *not misogyny*?'

'Yes, I am. I wouldn't say it to Emily Brontë or George Eliot. I don't think I could replicate *Wuthering Heights* or *Middlemarch*, or anything truly interesting or original. I don't care what sex the author is.'

Simon stood up and walked over to the Sainsbury's bags. He pulled a six-pack of Diet Coke out of one, tore away the plastic wrapping, freed a can and opened it. After taking a sip he passed it to Sellers, who was too parched to worry about etiquette. No doubt Halliday would care even less about the deaths of men henceforth and Sellers' thirst would be partly to blame.

'You think your thoughts and writing style are so unique? Let's put it to the test,' said Simon. 'Publish this column I've written as your own.'

'Get the fuck out of my house.'

'I'll put money on nobody being any the wiser. If anyone suggests it's not all your own work – if there's even a hint of suspicion from any quarter – I'll give you a thousand quid. There won't be – I can promise you that. I made sure to use all your buzzwords: manfeelz, erasure of lived experience, it's all in there. Read it. You might like it.'

'You're trying to use me as bait, is that it? Of course it is. Why *wouldn't* you? What's one more dead woman between misogynist friends?'

'Make sure it's not published until Thursday, 22 January – 9 a.m., not before – and I guarantee you'll be safe,' said Simon. 'Billy will be with me by then – and won't have any more opportunities to kill anyone. I wouldn't put anyone's life at risk, not even yours.'

Sellers was looking forward to leaving this room and its atmosphere of hostility behind. He didn't know where people found the energy for so much anger. In some ways, Simon and Sondra Halliday were perfectly matched. Why couldn't they both abandon their grudges and concentrate on having a laugh instead?

Halliday stood up and held out her right arm in the direction of the kitchen door. 'Goodbye, tossers. Request to commandeer my *Lifeworld* column denied. This conversation's over.'

Simon picked up his piece of paper and put it back in his jacket pocket. 'Any more Billy murders happen, you're responsible.' He walked out of the room, slamming the door behind him. A minute later there was another bang from further away: the front door.

Sellers stood up to follow him. He didn't want to leave with the mood as grim as this. If he'd interviewed Halliday alone today, he'd probably have taken offence at her silly distortions and her wilful blindness as he had twice before, but Simon's palpable disgust had made him feel oddly protective of her.

He didn't know why he kept thinking of Lane Baillie. Then, suddenly, he did. He'd spoken to Lane about Sondra Halliday. *What this person needs is not blame but kindness and empathy . . . Perhaps she suffered a trauma and could only make herself strong enough to survive it by building a shell of hate and blame around herself.*

Was Lane right? Would positive energy work? Sellers did massively fancy Sondra Halliday, which he knew would help him in what he was about to attempt.

'I'm sorry about Waterhouse,' he said.

'Thank you. I still want you to leave as soon as possible.' Halliday didn't look at him. She was slamming shopping items into her fridge in the manner of someone launching weapons at an enemy.

'I don't blame you,' said Sellers. It was funny, he thought, how often people said those words without really thinking about their meaning. Normally it was a way of saying, 'I agree' or 'I'd do the same'.

'I'll leave within the next minute, but can I say one thing before I go? I'm asking permission – if you don't give me permission, I'll leave straight away.'

'Make it quick, then.'

'I understand that you care passionately about saving and improving women's lives. I agree with you that Billy, if we don't catch him, will kill again. Statistics suggest his next victim will be a woman. As you've correctly said many times: most of his victims are. Whoever that unfortunate woman is – and we have reason to believe it might be the comedian Kim Tribbeck – I *know* you want to save her life. Don't let Waterhouse's arrogance and the anger it's provoked in you stop you from doing something that could really help a woman.'

Halliday glared at him. 'What are you asking? Spit it out.'

'This idea of Waterhouse's, about your column. He's confident it'll work. He thinks once Billy sees the column, he'll confess. Based on Waterhouse's past record, I'd say that means the odds are good. Better than good: excellent. Look, when this is all over and Billy's no longer a danger, you can write a column about how it all came about. You can print all the misogynistic things Waterhouse said, make the police look *terrible.* Wouldn't that make a great column?' Shit; he was in danger of veering away from the positive here, tempting her with revenge opportunities. Plus, Simon was his mate. The last thing Sellers wanted was to be responsible for him getting a slating in *Lifeworld.*

What might Lane Baillie say to Sondra Halliday next? he wondered.

As it turned out, nothing more was needed.

'All right,' said Halliday. 'If you really think it might help to catch Billy. I mean, we *all* want that, right?'

'We certainly do.'

'If you can keep me safe until you get him, and as long as I can see a draft of whatever that shit Waterhouse has written before it's published under my name . . . Fine. I'll do it.'

'Thanks a million.' Sellers wanted to hug her, but he didn't think it would go down very well. 'You know, I might disagree with a lot of what you say, but you've made me think about these things – men, women, all that – in a way that no one else ever has. You've . . . had an effect. I'm going to carry on reading your column once all this is over.'

'I find that kind of hard to believe.' She eyed him suspiciously. 'Are you still going to say things like, "Wouldn't mind getting conker-deep in *that*?"'

Sellers laughed. 'Probably.'

'I find that very easy to believe,' said Halliday.

~

Simon was standing in the yard with a can of 7UP in one hand and his battered old copy of *Moby-Dick* in the other when Charlie arrived home just before midnight. She could have got back earlier, but had opted to spend the evening alone in a wine bar in Spilling.

She let her bag slide off her shoulder and fall to the ground. 'You knew,' she said.

'Yeah. Are you angry?'

'No. If I'd been the one to find out first, I'm not sure I'd have told you.'

'I'd have been furious. S'pose I'm unreasonable.'

Charlie reached out her hand for the can. Simon gave it to her and she took a sip. 'I enjoyed getting there on my own,' she said. 'Gave me a sense of achievement. And now I'm in the predicament you were trying to make sure I didn't get into: do I let this stupid bigamous wedding happen and then shop my own sister to the law? Or interfere and threaten that, make them call it off?'

'Depends how much you want to see them punished. Or want to save them.'

'What do you think I should do?' Simon always knew the answer. Not necessarily the right answer by anyone else's standards, but his answer. 'Simon?'

'Do you want to hear a story?'

'Not if it's about a guy looking for a whale, no.' Charlie pointed to his book. 'What are you doing reading outside, anyway – in the dark and standing up?'

'Look at this.' Simon held up the book between his index finger and his thumb. 'It's old – almost falling apart. Stained with coffee, bath water, ketchup; so heavy it's hurting me to hold it like this.'

'Boring, overrated, full of some guy's obsession about a whale,' Charlie joined in. 'What's this, a turning point? Do we finally get to chuck it in the bin?'

'Maybe.'

'Have you had a personality transplant?' Charlie peered at him. 'If it hurts to hold it like that, use your other fingers too. That's why you have them.'

Simon looked as if he'd suddenly snapped awake. 'The story I want to tell you's nothing to with *Moby-Dick*. It's about a teacher and a delinquent pupil.'

Charlie made a face.

'I'll make it short,' Simon said. 'One day, the delinquent chucks a desk through the classroom window, smashing the glass. Teacher doesn't see it, but he knows full well who did it. The boy won't confess, though, so the teacher offers a reward to any pupil who'll speak up and say they saw him do it. A girl – best-behaved kid in the class – stays behind after the lesson, and the teacher thinks she's going to inform on the delinquent. She doesn't, though. Instead, she says to the teacher, "He won't confess for as long as you're judging and blaming him for what he did. If you tell him that you *don't* blame him, that you understand his anger and sadness and want to help him, then he'll confess." "Great," thinks the teacher. "I'll try that." He can't wait to see the delinquent again, so sure is he that his plan's going to work.'

'Hang on,' said Charlie. 'This is one of Lane Baillie's Stories of Enlightenment, isn't it?'

Simon nodded. 'From her website, but not one that was sent to Sondra Halliday. If I were Billy, I'd have included it in my selection. Next time the teacher sees the delinquent he says exactly what the girl told him to say. He can't wait for the boy to confess so that he can suspend him, maybe even expel him. But still the boy denies throwing the desk through the window. The teacher complains to the girl—'

'Unreasonable git! She did her best to help him,' said Charlie.

'He tells her he followed her advice to the letter, but it didn't work. "Of course it didn't," she says. "Because when you told the boy that you didn't blame him and weren't going to judge him, you were lying, weren't you? I told you what would be the right thing to say, and it *was* the right thing. It was your mistake to assume you could say it without meaning it and still get a good result."

'"Hang on," says the confused teacher. "You seriously expect me to say – and *mean* – that it's fine by me if a pupil throws a desk through a window?"

'"Think about why he might be sad," says the girl. "Think about why he might be angry. Think about his life, and then ask yourself: how might you behave if his pain were your pain?"

'The teacher goes away and thinks about it. He realises that the delinquent has much to be sad and angry about: a very sick mother, a bad-tempered father who hits him, no money, not much hope for the future. The next time he speaks to the delinquent, the teacher says, "I don't blame you for what you did," and he really means it. "You don't have to admit it was you, and you won't be punished," he tells the boy. "But please come to me if there's ever anything I can do to help you." At once, the boy feels so grateful to the teacher that he confesses to throwing the desk through the window. He isn't punished, and, with the teacher's help, the boy learns to behave better. From then on, he doesn't get into any more trouble at school.'

Charlie groaned. 'Imagine how that story would make you feel if you'd just had your window smashed.'

'We do it all the time, don't we?'

'Do what?'

'Tell scrotes we understand how they feel, how hard it must be for them. Anything to get them to admit what they've done, so we can lock them up.'

'There's nothing wrong with that. We're the police, not their therapists.'

'What about preventing future crimes? All the windows that boy's not going to smash from now on because one person demonstrated that they cared about him, one teacher said, "I understand your pain."'

'I see you've become fluent in claptrap while I've been away,' said Charlie.

Simon flinched. 'I don't think the usual fake sympathy's going to work with Billy, that's all,' he said. 'To get the confession I need, I might have to mean it.'

22

from Origami *by Kim Tribbeck*

Wednesday, 21 January 2015

My phone is ringing in my head. That can't be right. I don't have a phone in my head.

I lurch into a sitting position, eyes still closed, and pat the duvet in search of the source of the noise. By the time I find it (under the covers, along with an empty beer bottle, because I'm so house-proud and wholesome), it's stopped ringing.

I don't recognise the number.

7.45 a.m. Jesus Christ.

The ringing starts again. Same number.

'Hello?'

'Is that Kim?' It's a woman.

'Yes. And if you know who you're ringing, you'll know I'm a stand-up comedian. Stand-up comedians typically aren't awake at quarter to eight in the morning. Who are you? A vindictive postman? A milkman with a grudge?'

'I'm sorry if I woke you.'

'You did.'

'It's Isobel Sturridge. Liam's sister.'

I want to laugh and accuse her of lying but I can't. I know that voice. It's her. 'Oh, hello Isobel, AKA Faith Kendell. Or would you prefer me to use your street name, Billy Dead Mates? Not a milkman or a postman but a murderer, right?' Would I be talking to her like this if there were anything to be afraid of?

She can't be anywhere near my house. Definitely not standing right outside, or else she'd knock on the door instead of phoning.

Did I remember to double lock the front door before going to bed last night? Probably not.

'Liam gave me your number – I hope you don't mind.'

Now I laugh. 'That's right: because of everything you've done, the thing I'm likely to object to most is you getting hold of my phone number without my consent. Injecting battery acid into my grandmother's nothing compared to that.'

'Liam told me there was no love lost between you and Marion.' I freeze.

She's Billy. No one else would have reacted like that.

It's a few seconds before I manage to say, 'That's correct. It's also true that she had cancer that was about to kill her. I still wish she hadn't been murdered, though. Ironic, huh?'

'No. It's understandable. I'm sorry I lied to you about my name.'

'Why have you rung me? I don't want to speak to you – I'd rather be ringing the police and telling them this happened – so unless you have something urgent you want to say—'

'I'm going to be speaking to the police tomorrow morning. I'd like you to be there, and your brother. This concerns you as much as it does me. I asked the police to make sure you and your brother were present, and they flatly refused. So . . . although it's an unorthodox request, and although I'm well aware that no member of your family owes me anything . . . I'm begging you to agree to come.'

'Jesus fucking Christ!' I swear at my phone. 'What the fuck is this shit?'

'Again, I apologise sincerely, but . . . believe me, Kim, you'll want to be there. You shouldn't let the police leave you out of this.'

Damn right. Fuckers. Or is that what Isobel wants me to think? Am I falling into a murderer's trap?

Are you a murderer, Isobel? Are you Billy Dead Mates? I'm not afraid to ask. It's more that to do so would make me feel disgusting.

'If they refused to tell me about it, they won't let me in even if I do turn up, will they?'

'I hope they will. If you make the effort to come, and bring your brother, I'll do my bit to ensure it all runs smoothly.'

'Does "your bit" involve shooting me in the head?'

'No. You have my word that you'll come to no harm.'

Unbelievable.

'I'm sorry I've been . . . so much more trouble than a dead houseplant.' I hear what sounds like a stifled sob.

'Isobel, we're not friends,' I say loudly and clearly. 'Please tell me you know that.'

'Will you come tomorrow?'

'I don't know. I'm going to ring the police and ask their advice.'

'Remind them that I won't tell them what I know without you there. I mean it, Kim. There's no balance without you.'

'Balance?'

'Apart from me and Liam, everyone else at the meeting is going to be police. That's not right. With you and your brother there, it'll be closer.'

'Closer to what, Isobel?' I'm guessing she means a fifty-fifty split between detectives and civilians. Why does she care? I'd ask, but it would mean speaking to her for longer, and I can't bear to.

'Goodbye, Isobel. Don't ring me again.'

'Tomorrow morning, nine o'clock. Please, Kim. Can I at least give you the details of the venue so that you can think about it?'

Venue? The word makes it sound as if she's planning a wedding. Surely she'll be interviewed at the police station in Spilling or at her house.

Before I can answer, she tells me the name and address.

'What?' I can't believe what I've just heard. At the same time, given that she knows I'm going to be ringing the police in the very near future, I don't think she's lying.

What the hell's going on here?

23

21/1/2015

'This is not how police business is conducted,' said Proust. 'It's not how serious murder investigations are conducted. This isn't a parlour game!'

'Sir, we all know that,' said Sam. 'But sometimes, to get results, isn't it wiser to be flexible?'

'You call it flexible, Sergeant; I call it dancing to the tune of a murderer.' The glare dial inside the Snowman's cubicle had been fixed at its maximum setting.

'We've already got the Wing beneath Waterhouse's wind and Kerensa Moore on their way to us – and you're proposing to add Kim Tribbeck and Drew Hopwood to the party?'

'Neil Dunning as well,' said Sellers. 'Sorry, sir. If Wing's coming, Dunning's got a right to be there too.'

'They can and should all be there,' said Gibbs. 'Billy's a big deal. I don't see why we're so keen to take sole responsibility for it.'

'We don't yet know that Isobel Sturridge is Billy, sir,' said Sam almost inaudibly.

Simon only realised they were all waiting for him to speak once the silence had lasted for nearly ten seconds. He was fuming. How could Charlie have done what she did and not realise the effect it'd have on him? Here he was, supposed to be concentrating on an important negotiation and all he could think about was how she'd let him down. Did she not know him or understand him at all?

Concentrate, idiot. On Billy. You're on thin ice here.

Simon had rung up the lab first thing to chase the verdict

on the many DNA samples taken. He'd been given an answer – one he hadn't yet shared with the team, because it wasn't an answer that ought to satisfy anyone. Without understanding why, what was the point of knowing who? No one but him and Billy Dead Mates understood why, even though it was staring them all in the face.

Idiots.

Simon knew he was wrong to think this way, wrong to keep quiet about the DNA results, wrong to be angry with Charlie. His desire to punish, indiscriminately, probably wouldn't have swelled to such a dangerous level today if she'd only kept her overly hospitable mouth shut when James Wing had rung this morning. 'You don't need to stay in a hotel if you don't want to,' she'd said to Wing, having answered Simon's phone while he was in the shower. 'Why don't you crash on our sofa? We'd love to have you to stay. Yes, really – as long as you don't mind the house looking like a squat.'

The prospect of trying to sleep – the night before one of the most important mornings of his working life, in case Charlie had forgotten – with a virtual stranger 'crashing' on his sofa, as she'd put it, made Simon want to punch something or someone: ideally a punchbag with a drawing of Proust's face on it, priggish, whiny fucker that he was. Simon came from a family in which such a thing was unheard of. His parents had never had guests overnight, not even family, and the idea of someone in your living room while you were asleep, perhaps staying awake later than you, watching your TV while you slept . . .

The reasonable part of Simon's brain knew Charlie had meant well. 'You and Wing are getting friendly – I thought this would help!' she'd said. 'You can have a drink and a bit of a laugh. It's a nice gesture, inviting him here. It won't kill you to behave like a normal human being *for one evening and night*, Simon!'

She didn't get it. It wasn't dying he was worried about, it

was his night's sleep and his peace of mind and his sofa. Were sofas the same after they'd been slept on? His and Charlie's was scruffy but that didn't mean he was willing to see it wrecked. What if he felt differently about their house after Wing had stayed? What if it didn't feel like home any more? As for his budding whatever-you-wanted-to-call-it with Wing – it would probably amount to nothing, but why jinx it before giving it a chance? That Wing was to spend a night under Simon's roof had already made him feel differently about the man, which was as ridiculous, Simon knew, as it was impossible to do anything about. By accepting Charlie's invitation, Wing had willingly agreed to play the role of trespasser.

What if he decides he wants to stay longer than a night? What if he never leaves?

'You'll know everything tomorrow morning,' Simon told Sam. 'You all will. I agree, we ought to be flexible. If Isobel Sturridge wants Tribbeck and her brother there, and if they're willing to come—'

'That's settled then.' Proust stood up. 'Let's spend the afternoon sliding cubes of cheddar and chunks of pineapple onto little wooden sticks for all these guests we're expecting, shall we?'

'Don't pretend you wouldn't eat them if we did,' Simon muttered.

'We're not hosting, sir,' Gibbs reminded Proust with a smirk. 'We've, um, subcontracted out the hosting on this occasion.'

Guests, hosting . . . were they talking like this deliberately? Simon tried not to imagine the deep indent James Wing's body would make on his sofa cushions. He headed for the door as fast as he could, desperate to escape the confined space.

Lifeworld online, 22 January 2015
BILLY DOESN'T KNOW WHAT A BOOK IS
by Sondra Halliday

On Tuesday I received an email from misogynist murderer Billy Dead Women, in which he accused me of bibliophobia. That means hatred of books. His evidence? He's sent me two novels that I haven't read.

This can't, of course, be because I'm busy and/or unwilling to drop all my other commitments in order to please a murderer I've never met. If I'm not obeying Billy's instructions to the letter, that must mean there's something wrong with me. I'm a woman and he's a man, so he expects me to do his bidding.

And when I don't, what's his next move? Instead of writing to ask me why I'm passing up this once-in-a-lifetime chance to be the inaugural member of Billy's Book Club, he decides, all on his own, that he knows the reason: bibliophobia! No need to take guidance from me before defining my inner reality; I'm only a woman, after all, and every male person must feel free to invent my thoughts and emotions in accordance with what suits them best.

If anybody more reasonable and less appropriative (in other words, female) wants to know how I'm really feeling, I'll tell you: I'm disinclined to read the novels Billy sent me, and not only because they came from him.

Beloved by Toni Morrison? A woman responds to the barbarism of slavery by murdering her daughter. Why not kill her male master or the male slave traders instead – the men responsible for all the misery? (Naturally, the murdered baby is a girl, as are nearly all murder victims in fiction.)

Jude the Obscure by Thomas Hardy, an author famous for treating women atrociously? Thanks, but I'd rather not read about children who believe they must sacrifice their own lives so that the all-important father figure can live unimpeded, devoting all his precious resources to himself alone. If that storyline isn't the epitome of patriarchy apologism, I don't know what is.

I don't hate and fear books, Billy. I just want to make my own reading choices. Is that okay with you?

By the way, your definition of a book is pure, undiluted horseshit. A book – whether it's a novel, a volume of poetry, a memoir or a macramé manual – is the *words*, not the paper object. Therefore, even if I did hate the paper objects, as you claim, I could still read all the books I wanted to read, on my iPad, and I would not be a bibliophobe at all. I'm surprised I need to tell you this, Billy. You seem to understand it in relation to people: eternal Awareness that can never die and all that? The only part that perishes is the physical body, remember?

Why should books be any different? The soul of a novel is its story, which is made up of words. As long as you've got the words, you don't need anything else – certainly not a brick-shaped paper thing that will start to smell and turn yellow as the years go by.

Unless I'm only saying all this because of my phobia. Yellow, smelly pages? Sounds like bibliophobic language to me – until we remind ourselves of what a book is and what it isn't.

Having trouble keeping up, Billy? Don't worry about it. You might be a murderer five times over, but your denseness in this area isn't your fault. Our education system fails so many. What are you – a car mechanic? A security guard? We can't all be expected to understand such sophisticated concepts. Those of us who know what a book is shouldn't crow about it – especially not within earshot of someone who thinks the word means white pages, folded and stapled in the middle, with a few random words tossed in.

24

from Origami *by Kim Tribbeck*

Thursday, 22 January 2015

Remember that time you met a serial killer, a collection of police detectives, a psychological profiler and your ex-lover in a genteel market town's best Indian restaurant at nine o'clock in the morning?

Of course you don't remember it. It's never happened to you. It doesn't happen to most people.

The restaurant is the Khaybar. It's on a cobbled street in Silsford called Guggle Lane. There are white linen tablecloths on the tables, covered by pink paper ones, and laminated menus standing upright between unlit candles and small white vases of fake red flowers. The interior says traditional Indian restaurant, but the building looks as if it would be better suited to an antique shop.

Along one wall there are booths, like in the Hourglass in Rawndesley. *Ideal for privacy, which, as we all know, means the ability to stick your hand into another person's body without attracting the attention of the wider community.*

I wonder if Liam's also remembering that evening, prompted by the booths. Next to him is the woman who introduced herself to me as Faith Kendell – his sister, Isobel. She's been trying to catch my eye since I arrived, to inflict her grateful smile on me. Liam, by contrast, is studiously avoiding looking in my direction.

Drew's sitting at a table on his own. When I walked in, he looked at me then quickly looked away. The message was clear: 'Don't sit with me.' *Happy to oblige, bro. We're not going to be seeing one another again after today, are we?* It's funny how you can know some things for certain, without a word being spoken.

Despite the number of police present, I don't feel safe. It's not being murdered that I'm scared of; it never has been.

I'm afraid of Isobel Sturridge's peculiar smile. No one's moving to defend me against it as they would if she pulled out a gun, and although I'm not looking at it, I know it's there.

Not understanding precisely what needs to be feared: that's what frightens me.

I count and name police people to keep myself calm and steady: Simon, Charlie, Gibbs, Sam Kombothekra, profiler Kerensa something-or-other, the hilariously named, bare-bulb-headed DI Proust with his horrible jellyfish-like skin, a grinning fat guy with excessive sideburns whose name I've forgotten . . . Then there's the one from London, with a face that suggests someone's rammed a pencil up his arse and he's determined to keep it there. Dunning – that's it. Or is that the one from Bournemouth who rolls his eyes unprovoked, like it's a nervous tic? He has the look of a serial killer more than anyone else in the room, come to think of it.

'Thanks to everyone for turning up,' Simon Waterhouse mumbles like a tongue-tied schoolboy pushed forward by a well-meaning teacher on speech day.

'We all know why we're here, so . . . I'm going to kick off by reading you Sondra Halliday's latest column.'

He's wrong. I don't know why I'm here, apart from curiosity, and because Isobel Sturridge told me I had to be. But Simon allowed me to come – encouraged it, even, without explaining why. Could his reason for wanting me here be the same as Isobel's?

Does Liam know why he's here? I try to look at him without letting him see me. He looks like a stranger disguised as somebody I used to have sex with.

'As Billy Dead Mates knows, Halliday has already devoted one column to writing him an open letter,' Simon goes on.

'Her column in *Lifeworld* this morning, which should have gone live in the last half hour, is also about Billy. It'll be published in the new print edition of *Lifeworld* tomorrow. I have it with me, so . . .' He looks up and surveys the room, apparently uncertain for a second. 'As I said: I'll read it to you.'

I swallow a laugh. Simon's standing poker straight. He pulls his phone out of his pocket, gets ready to read from the screen. It's like being on an aeroplane and being told you have to pay special attention to the safety announcements.

Sondra Halliday's column about bibliophobia isn't quite as dull as instructions about where to find the oxygen masks in the event of a crash, but it's weirdly hard to follow: like an extract from an intense fight that you've missed the beginning of.

Those of us who aren't police all seem equally bemused, apart from Isobel Sturridge. Her eerie smile is gone. She's shaking and looks as if she's about to cry.

When Simon's finished reading the column, he walks slowly towards her. Stopping by her side, he says, 'You didn't like the bit about books being the words and not the physical objects, did you, Isobel? If books are no more than words, who needs bookshops? Like Rudolphy's. Thanks to the opinion you've just heard from Sondra Halliday – thanks to people coming to believe *en masse* that books are only the words – Rudolphy's, your family's shop, is now this Indian restaurant.'

Okay, try to keep up, Tribbeck. The Khaybar Curry House used to be a bookshop called Rudolphy's. And . . . Isobel's family owned it? Which means Liam's family did too.

Simon's eyes are fixed on Isobel. His voice continues hypnotically. 'When I interviewed you before, you wouldn't tell me the truth. If you did, everything would be ruined, you said. I now understand what you meant by that. You know why you killed five people. In your mind, you had a powerful reason for doing what you did. You can conjure up a fantasy in which you explain in good faith, and it all comes out as

Sophie Hannah

you want it to, and the world understands. But in reality – certainly in our first interview when you were scared, facing police suspicion for the first time – you lacked confidence. You feared that if you told me why you'd committed the murders, I'd dismiss you as out-and-out crazy, and then the true purpose and meaning of your actions would be lost. Wasted. Isn't that right?'

Isobel. Isobel Sturridge. She's Billy Dead Mates. Simon Waterhouse has just said so, unequivocally. *Faith Kendell*.

Which means there's something I need to ask her, and it can't wait.

'Isobel, were you planning to kill me?' I say. 'Would you still if you could?'

'No.' Her eyes widen. 'I swear on my life, Kim. I mean, yes, I was, but—'

'Did you murder my grandmother?' Drew asks, cutting her off.

Of course. Because Marion's life is so much more important to him than mine.

Isobel flinches. 'Yes,' she whispers.

Liam expels a heavy sigh, as if having his sister admit to murder is an inconvenience he hadn't bargained for.

'Please.' Simon holds up a hand. 'I know it's hard, but if you could all remain silent unless prompted by me, this'll go quicker.'

Drew makes a whistling noise like an angry kettle. 'She's just admitted to murdering Marion and you're trying to shut me up? What is this "All gather round, speak when you're spoken to" pantomime anyway? This isn't the denouement of a TV drama – it's real life. Real death! My beloved grandmother's, to be specific.' He wants everyone to understand he's the main victim here.

'If it were a TV drama, your lines would be better,' I tell him.

'Denouement's an interesting word, isn't it, Isobel?' Simon

370

takes a step back and looks around the room. 'Do you want to explain why? To everybody?'

'No.'

'No,' Simon echoes. 'That's my job, isn't it? I'm the detective. You're the guilty party. It's my role to explain everything, isn't it?'

She sniffs and nods.

His voice and his demeanour have changed to a weird theatre-in-the-round style that's nothing like the real him, when only a few minutes ago he seemed nervous about speaking in front of a large group.

To Isobel he says, 'Don't you see that the opposite of what you fear is true? If you *don't* tell us the truth, everything will be ruined. You know you can give a good account of your actions; you know you did it all for the best of motives. If you stay silent now, Sondra Halliday's narrative wins; she's the one who gets heard, the only one. She's wrong about everything, isn't she? Wrong about you and, more importantly to you, wrong about books. I know you think that, so why don't you tell us? Your words will express it so much better than mine ever could.'

I'm lost. I catch Charlie's eye as I remember her saying 'Books are everywhere in this investigation', the first time I met her.

Who kills people because of books, for Christ's sake?

'I've spoken to the *Telegraph*,' says Simon. 'It's the UK's bestselling broadsheet newspaper. They want to publish your story – in your words. That'll knock Sondra Halliday's column into a cocked hat. Hardly anyone reads *Lifeworld*, and their numbers are dropping issue by issue.'

The newspaper offer doesn't ring true. I frown at Charlie. Almost imperceptibly, she shakes her head. *Thank God for that*.

Isobel has started to cry. Did she believe Simon's phoney *Telegraph* story? Did she even hear him?

'We know you were at the scene of the crime for three of the five murders,' he goes on, standing awkwardly in the middle of the room. 'Marion Hopwood: Kim saw you at the hospital. And one of the students on his way to a kung fu class at the school in Angela McCabe's garden remembers you being there. He assumed you were from a previous class.

'Rhian Douglas – you were there. You left Rhian's house after shooting her dead, and saw Muriel Pearson, the deaf, elderly neighbour, come to her front door and look around. She didn't spot you, but you saw her. She looked left and right and said something out loud about a blonde lady. "Hello? Where's the blonde lady gone?" or something like that, was it? You'd seen the Asda van too, delivering Samantha Granger's shopping. You put two and two together – worked out that Muriel, when interviewed by police, would mention this blonde woman, and that someone else – a drawing of a woman, not even a real person – would briefly get the credit for your crusade. You couldn't bear that idea, could you?'

Simon turns his back on Isobel and looks at his colleagues. 'None of you saw what was missing when we heard the story of Muriel Pearson realising her mistake. Even you, Wing – you told us the story, but you didn't understand what it meant. Muriel's son rang the police to say that she was terribly sorry but, as it turned out, she *hadn't* seen a woman, only a poster on the side of a van. None of you asked yourselves the obvious question: *what made Muriel Pearson realise her error?* She spends all day sitting in a chair, hardly stirring from in front of the telly. The only reason she didn't instantly know Van Woman wasn't real when she saw her was because she'd never seen the Asda van before – though it delivered to her neighbour regularly and had for years. Everyone was so busy thinking her mistake was hilarious, no one thought to question how she worked out that she'd got it wrong. So I asked DC Wing to ask her.'

'And?' says Charlie.

The eye-roller takes a step forward, then quickly steps back when he sees he's not going to get a turn. So he's DC Wing, then. Pencil-up-the-arse must be Dunning.

'Muriel told Wing that one day, nearly three months after Rhian was murdered, a nice lady from a bookshop popped round with some lovely free books for her,' said Simon. 'Danielle Steel was the author, I believe. That lady was you, Isobel. Muriel IDd you from a photo Wing showed her, printed off the internet. According to Muriel, this bookshop woman had said she was stopping at every house, giving away books. She'd just been next door, she said, talking to them in their lounge, and she'd seen a blonde woman at the window who'd looked so real, but at the same time looked kind of weird – and she'd turned out to be not a woman at all but a picture on the side of an Asda van.'

'Wow,' Charlie murmurs.

'Yeah. That's how Muriel Pearson realised she'd got it wrong – Isobel here made sure she knew.' Simon looks at Sam Kombothekra. 'Remember when Wing was telling us about Muriel's cock-up? After she'd admitted to having made a mistake, he said, he'd wanted to check she was right second time round, so he took a picture of Asda Van Woman round to her house. Muriel was upset by the picture. It was clear from Wing's account: that was the moment she knew *for certain* that she'd made a serious error. That didn't make sense to me, and it shouldn't have to anyone else. Surely in order to contact Wing and his team and tell them she'd been wrong, Muriel must *already* have seen the Asda van again, or seen a picture of Asda Van Woman, or else how had she been made aware of her mistake? Answer: Isobel Sturridge had said things in her presence that had convinced her she'd messed up and given the police false information.'

Liam clears his throat to speak, and I jump. I've got used to the sight of him; now it seems I'm going to have to acclimatise myself to the sound. 'Even if you're right about that part, what you've just said doesn't put my sister at the scene of Rhian Douglas's murder.'

'True,' Simon concedes. 'But she must have been there, otherwise she wouldn't have known Muriel Pearson was bound to tell the police that a blonde woman had been hanging around outside her window that day.'

'"She must have been there" is different from "She was there". You're guessing.'

'So were you in on these five murders too, Liam? Were you helping her?'

'No, he wasn't,' Isobel says quietly. 'Though I think . . .' She turns to face her brother. 'I think you suspected, didn't you, Liam?' Her voice is full of a need for affirmation. She wants him to say yes.

'I don't bother *suspecting* things,' he puts a scathing emphasis on the word. 'I know things, or else I don't know them. There's no in between.'

So he knew. I call it knowing, whatever he wants to call it.

Drew is crying. I catch myself wondering whose brother is more disappointing: mine or Isobel's.

Faith Kendell. My dead houseplant friend.

Isobel looks up at Simon. 'I killed them all – all five,' she says. 'Liam had nothing to do with any of it.'

'Kim.' Liam briefly makes eye contact. 'I didn't know or have any reason to think that Isobel intended to kill you.'

Why did she want to? I want to scream. *Why did she then stop wanting to?*

'I believe you, Isobel,' says Simon. 'I think you acted alone, with a motive that would have crumbled if you'd had to discuss it with anyone else. It obsessed you, but, at the same time, you knew the logic of it was too fragile to prove itself outside of your head. That's why telling the truth would have ruined it for you. Even telling your own brother.'

Isobel's staring at me. 'You were going to be the first,' she says. 'But on the night I was supposed to give you your book, you were there with my brother. I wasn't expecting that. Liam saw me trying to put the book in your bag. My own silly fault! I chose to come and see you in Canterbury of all places because Liam sometimes worked there. It seemed almost meant to be. When I saw that Liam had spotted me, I ran away. Hid outside.' She turns to him. 'I saw the two of you kissing on the street, and you put your hand up her skirt.'

I get a grimace from Pencil-up-the-arse Dunning and a half-smile from DC Sideburns that looks like a secret message of approval.

That's right: I have skirts. I let men put their hands up them sometimes.

'I love my brother – he's the only person I have left – so I knew I had to change my plan,' Isobel goes on. 'I couldn't kill the woman he loved.'

'"Loved" is putting it a bit strongly,' says Liam.

'So, I adapted,' the killer called Billy Dead Mates says in the voice of an educated woman in her early forties. 'I decided I'd leave Kim till last. There were always going to be six deaths. It had to be six.'

'Why?' Simon asks.

'I knew of six cases, and only six, who qualified,' Isobel says with an earnest expression.

'Victims,' says Dunning from the sidelines. 'Victims, not cases. You killed real people, with families who loved them.'

'Do you know anything about numerology?' she asks him. 'I didn't used to either. Lane has a book about it. The number 6 is the most harmonious of the single-digit numbers. It's also about sacrifice, and . . . that's what it was, for me, what I did. Too much harm had been done that couldn't be allowed to stand. A symbolic protest was necessary, or else how would the world ever know that it mattered to anybody – enough to take extreme action?'

Simon nods, encouraging her to go on.

'I decided to wait, see if Kim and Liam broke up. I could kill her then, I thought – later.'

Sure thing, Freakoid. Happy to fit into your schedule wherever's convenient. Let's diarise.

'I expected Liam to talk to me about what he'd seen me do in Canterbury, but he never did,' Isobel says sadly. 'I was too scared – well, more embarrassed, really – to bring it up, so I had no way of knowing what Kim meant to him, or if they were still together. I waited and waited, putting Kim and Marion off till last instead of having them as the first pair as I'd originally planned. I did the others, and didn't mind waiting to finish. I wasn't in a particular hurry. The opposite, really. It was motivating for me to think that there were still some outstanding. It buoyed me up. Without that . . .' Isobel shakes her head as if it doesn't bear thinking about.

Outstanding. The word makes my stomach turn over. Outstanding not as in excellent; as in still to be killed.

Funny peculiar, not funny ha-ha.

'Then one day Liam told me his ex-girlfriend's grandmother was dying. Well, he didn't say exactly that. He asked me what I'd do if I knew someone whose grandmother was about to die of cancer. Would I send a card, and what would I write in it? I asked him who he meant, and he told me: Kim. He didn't need to say her surname. There was only one: Famous Kim, Superstar Kim.'

'For fuck's sake,' I mutter.

'Liam called her his "ex". I didn't realise they'd split up. I managed to get the story out of him: Kim had rung him in a complete state, even though they were no longer seeing each other. Her grandmother was about to die and she . . .' Isobel glances at me, then looks quickly away. 'She didn't think there was any way to make peace or resolve anything before Marion went. Liam didn't want to get involved, but he was thinking about sending a card so that he could do the right thing, at least.'

Cheers for that, Liam. What a big-hearted sex robot you are.

'I offered to buy the card and tell him what to write, but he decided in the end that he was better off not interfering. I think, having lost our mother so recently, he couldn't bear to think about death long enough to do the whole card thing.'

That's one thing Liam and I have in common, then: both allergic to the idea of death.

'With regard to my . . . project, I knew that Kim was once again available to me since she was no longer my brother's girlfriend,' Isobel goes on. 'I had to act fast. Marion Hopwood was dying, but she couldn't just die. I had to kill her. I was upset that I couldn't use my gun that I used for the others, but she was in hospital. People would have heard the shot.'

'Your gun,' says Simon. 'Let's talk about that.' He walks over to the bar area of the restaurant and leans his elbow on it. God, I could do with a drink, though it's not yet ten in the morning.

'You used it to shoot your first four victims, and when you weren't using it, it was here at the Khaybar, safely stowed away.'

'*Here?*' says Kerensa the profiler. 'In an Indian restaurant? But—'

'On a hunch, I asked the manager how often you were here,' Simon tells Isobel. 'This place used to be Rudolphy's, I thought – surely you'd still be obsessed with the physical space that your family's bookshop used to inhabit. Turns out they know Faith Kendell very well at the Khaybar. After every killing, within two or three days, you'd book a table for one and come here for a meal, alone. You did the same *before* each killing, apart from Marion Hopwood. I got the exact dates from the manager, who keeps records of bookings going back about a year, luckily for us.'

Isobel smiles as one might at someone else's good news. As if she's pleased for him.

'You can all see the seats in the booths.' Simon looks around the room. 'Long rectangular cushions set into wood. Each one acts as a kind of lid for the bench it covers, and there's a hollow space underneath. Isobel, you came here and replaced your gun after each shooting. And you'd retrieve it before the next one. You're probably assuming it's where you left it, directly beneath where you're sitting now, but it's not. I had it removed two days ago.'

Her face crumples. 'You shouldn't have touched it. It wasn't yours to take.'

'Where did someone like you – educated middle-class woman who's interested in books – get a gun?' Dunning asks her.

'Derby,' says Isobel briskly. 'Being educated and bookish isn't a barrier to accomplishing practical tasks, you know. It infuriates me when people imply that it is. Without books and the knowledge they contain, we'd none of us know how to exist in the world at all.'

'Tell us about Derby,' says Simon.

'There was a documentary on Channel 4 about a council estate there where little children had guns. That's where I went. It looked perfect. I paid a lot. It was hard to find a child to buy one from, but I did. I was determined not to compromise and buy one from an adult or even a teenager.' She smiles suddenly. 'I had a first edition of a Secret Seven book, you see, and I wanted to give it to whoever I bought the gun from. You have to catch them early.'

'Who?' Simon asks.

'Children. If you want to instill a love of reading.'

'Something I don't get,' says Gibbs. 'Isobel, you're saying you were planning to kill Kim *before* you knew your brother was involved with her?'

'Yes. She was going to be the first. I knew she was famous, which seemed somehow . . . I don't know. Auspicious, I suppose.' Isobel smiles. 'People talk about going out with a bang . . . I wanted to go *in* with a bang, start with someone who was a public figure. That way I knew I'd get people talking straight away, before there were more victims or a pattern or anything.

I set about doing some research and I became a bit obsessed, I suppose. That never happened with any of the others – only Kim. I bought all her "Live at the Blah-Blah" DVDs, and a box set of *The Village Parallel*. I watched them all endlessly, telling myself it was useful preparation, but that was an excuse. You don't need to know someone's work by heart in order to shoot them dead. I . . . I guess I grew to like Kim. I liked her voice and her way of looking at the world. That's why I was relieved when I realised I'd have to put off killing her till last.'

You and me both, Billy.

'Liam watched Kim's DVDs with me because he was there in the room. We ate in front of them. I talked about Kim all the time – he could hardly avoid her. He . . . I suppose he came to share my interest in her and . . . well, I had no idea he'd done anything about it until, as I say, I found them together in Canterbury. And Kim, please believe me – I *did* change my mind about you. I changed the number to five – that would be fine too, I decided. Just as good as six, though it'd be two pairs and an odd one, but I didn't care about that. When we spoke outside the hospital, I knew I'd never be able to kill you. I *liked* you too much – already, from the DVDs, and then we got on so well . . . and I'd read up on you, too, so I knew you'd never really had a proper mother—'

'Yes, I did. I had a mother, a brilliant mother. I just never got to meet her.'

Drew pointedly looks away.

'I lost my mother in 2013,' says Isobel. 'I know your pain inside out.'

'No,' I say. My pain is mine.

'Knowing you'd been through that, I couldn't inflict any more pain on you. I just couldn't.'

To the room, Simon says, 'You must all be wondering why Isobel chose the six victims she did. To understand her choices, we need to look at the story she wrote and sent to Sondra Halliday: "The Dress". You all assumed, and so did I at first, that all three stories Billy sent to Halliday were from the *Stories of Enlightenment* section of Lane Baillie's website. When I looked, though, I only found two of the three. Whoever wrote the stories – and that's not Lane; she only uses them – they're obviously American. They write "realize" with a zed, and "color" and "favorite" without the "u"s.

'I couldn't find "The Dress" anywhere on the internet, and it contains only English words and spellings: "lift" instead of "elevator", "pavement" instead of "sidewalk", "colour" with a "u". That's because it's the original work of Isobel Sturridge. It's her murder manifesto. In it, she describes why she needed to kill, and how she chose her victims. It's not a literal explanation – it's all done metaphorically, but it makes it very clear why Isobel chose to kill the six people she did.'

Simon puts his phone, which he's been clutching all this time, back in his jacket pocket. From the pocket of his trousers, he produces some papers, unfolds them and waves them in the air. 'Anyone who hasn't yet read it and wants to can read it. It's about a dress that's ugly and evil, but most people don't realise. Most people think it's beautiful, and all women start to buy it. They get away with buying the evil dress because they've fallen for it – they genuinely love it – but one woman, Perdita, buys it as a gift for her PA, though she personally hates it. The PA, Dolores, accepts the dress, though she loathes it too. And both of their hands start to ooze and seep with terrible sores. They're mystified about why touching the dress has affected them both so badly when no one else has had that reaction.

'Luckily, a sage is on hand to explain.' Simon reads aloud. '"*You* gave something that you knew to be a vile thing to someone you care about," the Sage tells Perdita. "You would never have bought one for yourself, yet you bought one for Dolores here. And *you* . . ." – here the Sage is talking to Dolores – ". . . *you* accepted this gift, though you didn't want it and would never have bought one for yourself. You spotted its ugliness straight away, yet you accepted it. Both of you recognised instantly the horror of the dress, yet you said and did nothing against it . . . You acted against your own judgement and your own hearts. When we do that, we allow evil to prosper. That is why you have sore hands today."'

Seriously? This sounds like a ludicrous story.

'"We are all human, frail and flawed," the Sage expands on her wisdom. "We all find it impossible, sometimes, to resist our own strong desires. When we do harm to ourselves or to others, it is often because our better judgement has been paralysed by what feels like an urgent need. But the important thing is this: when our hearts are fully engaged in our actions, even the harmful ones, we are not beyond redemption. All hope is lost, however, when we are not infatuated, not helpless with desire, and yet still, from a position of clear-eyed objectivity, choose to behave in ways that promote evil."'

'A dress can't be evil,' I blurt out, unable to sit in silence and listen to this rubbish any longer. How can crap like this be the explanation for anything, let alone five murders? 'What was so wrong with the dress – did it have Nazi propaganda all over it or something?'

Simon shakes his head. 'Remember, all the other women in the story apart from Perdita and Dolores *love* the dress. To most people, it looks like a beautiful dress – highly desirable. But the most important thing to remember about the dress is that it *isn't* a dress, not really. It's a metaphor for something else – something Isobel believes to be evil. It's a metaphor for this.' Simon approaches Charlie from the side, pulls her bag off her shoulder, sticks his hand in and pulls out what looks like an e-reader. Yes, it's a Kobo – I see the name as Simon brings it closer. It's the same as the one Marion gave me on my fortieth birthday, the one I didn't want but accepted anyway. Like Dolores, who accepted the dress she didn't want.

Hang on. That can't be the answer, or anything to do with the answer. Can it?

Simon walks over to Isobel and lays the Kobo down on the table in front of her. 'You blame this machine – this and all the others like it – for Rudolphy's closing down: your family's bookshop. Many, many bookshops have closed since people stopped buying as many paper books and started to read electronically.'

'Proper books, not paper books,' Isobel corrects him. 'Proper books are made of paper.'

Jesus Christ. Jesus fucking Christ. I can't think anything else apart from those words, over and over. The e-reader I never wanted . . .

'Your mother died three months after Rudolphy's closed, didn't she?' Simon asks Isobel. 'Of a heart attack – but I think you believe the closure of the shop was what killed her.'

'This.' Isobel wraps her hand around Charlie's Kobo. 'This killed my mother – this and all the others of its kind. They killed Linzi Birrell, and Rhian Douglas, and all of them.' In a sudden violent movement, she swings her arm up and back, then hurls the machine at the wall.

'No!' Charlie shouts, and Isobel screams something indecipherable, and there's a crash as the Kobo hits the wall.

25

22/1/2015

'It was DC Sellers here who said the magic words that allowed me to put the whole picture together,' said Simon. He was sitting across from Isobel in the booth now. The atmosphere had changed since the smashing of Charlie's Kobo. Something dark and heavy hung in the air, but it wasn't prickly and unpredictable like before.

'Sellers went to Josh Norbury's house. He spoke to Josh's sister, Lisa. She mentioned some presents Angela McCabe had given Josh that he'd never really wanted, but had kept because they were from her. One was an Oliver Halliday cookery book. Another was an e-reader – a Kindle. Sellers assumed it was the recipe book that was significant, but it wasn't, despite its author being the husband of Sondra Halliday. No, it was the Kindle that mattered. When Sellers told me that was in the bag along with the cookbook, I could see it all. Everything came together.'

'Great,' said Charlie. 'We're all thrilled for you, Simon. Any chance you might tell the rest of us what "everything" is? Because I'm still completely in the dark here.'

'It's pretty simple,' he said. 'Josh had been given a Kindle he didn't want by Angela. Soon as Sellers told me that, I had a vague memory of Kim *also* being given an e-reader she didn't want – by Marion. I'd seen that in some of our interview notes for Kim – and when I checked, I found I was right. So . . . it seemed a huge coincidence. I'd probably have discounted it, except for the fact that books are everywhere in this case: Billy deposited them near his victims before killing them, and he sent two novels to Sondra Halliday. So I wondered . . . was it possible, crazy though it undoubtedly seemed, that what our six victims had in common – I'm including you, Kim, though Isobel changed her mind about killing you . . . Was it possible that what the six had in common was the giving and receiving of unwanted e-readers?'

'Oh my fucking God.' Charlie turned away from him.

'Then, hot on the heels of that coincidence, I remembered something else, something that had been bothering me for months. It had always jarred: Linzi Birrell's row with Miff Sheeran, owner of the Hot-n-Tasty café. Ahmed, Linzi's fiancé, had been absolutely adamant that Miff wouldn't hurt a fly and couldn't possibly have killed Linzi. Yet it seemed she'd lied through her teeth to the police even in the face of three witnesses saying otherwise: Miff flat-out denied she and Linzi had ever exchanged sharp words about a dodgy lasagne. She was too lovely and harmless for Ahmed to suspect her of murder, but at the same time she was a barefaced liar, intent on deceiving the police when there was a murder under investigation? That didn't gel for me at all – ever.'

'You also questioned why Linzi had never mentioned the row to Ahmed,' Wing reminded Simon.

'Right. She'd have mentioned it, wouldn't she? According to our three witnesses, Miff was giving Linzi a bollocking for ordering the same dish more than once – that was asking for trouble, apparently. Except any sane person knows that it's perfectly reasonable to order whatever the hell you want in a café. It was totally *un*reasonable of Miff to suggest otherwise – and hilarious that she thought she was right. Would Linzi really fail to tell Ahmed such an outrageous story? I don't think so. I never thought so.'

'We get it, Waterhouse,' said Dunning. 'You're right not just now, but also since records began. Get to the point.'

'Suspecting that the murders had something to do with e-readers – unwanted ones – I remembered another detail from the Hot-n-Tasty witnesses' accounts,' Simon said. 'They all mentioned Linzi walking out without eating her lunch, but only one of them said she picked up her *phone* and her book and walked out. I started to wonder . . . I formulated a little theory, and when I put it to the test, I found it was bang on.

'I went to Hot-n-Tasty and I asked Miff Sheeran again: did she and Linzi have a row or discussion about lasagne? Again, Miff said no, no way, didn't happen. That's when I asked her if she and Linzi had ever exchanged views about e-readers.' Simon looked around at the puzzled faces. Did no one get it, still? What was wrong with them?

'Miff told me that yes, for sure, she and Linzi had disagreed about e-readers. Linzi had come in one day with a Harry Potter book and an e-reader that was a present from her best friend—'

'Rhian Douglas,' supplied Sellers.

'Right. Rhian had given Linzi a Kobo, like Charlie's—'

'Like mine used to be, before it got smashed,' Charlie chipped in.

'It wasn't a phone and a book Linzi had with her on the lasagne day, it was her Kobo and a book. Miff confirmed it. The witness got that detail wrong. Linzi had gone to the café for lunch that day with Harry Potter the paper book and also with Harry Potter the e-book downloaded onto her Kobo. *That* was why Miff questioned her having the same thing twice – why bring two copies of the same book to read at lunch? That was Miff's point. Why not only bring one, when they're both the same? And Linzi had replied that no, actually, they *weren't* both the same – the e-book was *worse*. She couldn't say how, but it wasn't like reading a proper book. She hated the Kobo that she'd kept and tried to use to please Rhian, and she'd ended up taking the paper book with her everywhere she went because, no matter how hard she tried to read on the Kobo, she still hated it, and she always ended up ditching it in favour of the paper version.'

'Unbelievable,' Kim Tribbeck muttered.

'Miff said, "If you don't want it, I'll have it!" but Linzi was determined to keep it. How could she give it away? What would she say to Rhian? Miff admitted she might have tried to persuade Linzi a little too forcefully, and Linzi ended up leaving the café – no doubt annoyed to be pressured in that way – and leaving her lasagne uneaten. At which point, Miff – a very fat woman, as those of you who know her will confirm – sat down, ate the lasagne and pronounced it delicious, *not* as a smokescreen to cover up the café's shameful lasagne problem, but simply because she was enjoying the lasagne.

'So, there we are,' said Simon, after a quick pause for breath. 'We've got three pairs of victims, all connected to an unwanted e-reader given as a gift, an e-reader that's kept by the recipient even though they don't like or want it. And then we have our story, "The Dress", and I quote again: "You would never have bought one for yourself, yet you bought one for Dolores here. And *you* accepted this gift, though you didn't want it and would never have bought one for yourself . . . You acted against your own judgement and your own hearts . . . When our hearts are fully engaged in our actions, even the harmful ones, we are not beyond redemption. All hope is lost, however, when we are not infatuated, not helpless with desire, and yet still, from a position of clear-eyed objectivity, choose to behave in ways that promote evil."

'You believe e-readers are evil, don't you, Isobel? Why are bookshops closing all over the country? Because of e-books – people don't need the paper versions any more. And so Rudolphy's had to close, and your mother died. And you happened to know, probably because Linzi, Josh and Marion were all regular customers of yours, and Rudolphy's would have prided itself on chatting to its regulars and knowing them really well, I'm sure – you knew the full stories behind those three unwanted e-readers, didn't you? You knew the three givers – Rhian, Marion and Angela – weren't keen themselves, and you knew the three recipients – Linzi, Kim, Josh – had no time for e-books and preferred to read their paper equivalents. None of the six was seduced or impressed, yet they helped to promote what you saw as an evil thing.'

'The evil machine,' Isobel corrected him.

'You decided to punish them, didn't you?'

'No. Not punishment. Just . . . something had to be done. To prove someone *cared*, that this *mattered* to somebody. When historians look back in hundreds of years' time, I want them to be able to say: "One woman cared. One woman, Isobel Sturridge, really cared. And she did something about it." The people who . . . who died . . . they had no excuse. There were no mitigating circumstances, so . . .' She stopped and pressed her lips together.

'So you murdered them,' said Simon. 'And now I'm the brilliant detective delivering the ingenious solution in front of a crowd. That pleases you, doesn't it? Because you love books – *proper* books. This is a crime story, isn't it, that we're all in? And you want and need it to be a *proper* one. That's why it mattered so much to you to have a denouement – here, with us all gathered together, like in a detective story, and me explaining everything.'

'Yes,' Isobel said fiercely.

'That's why you wanted Kim and Drew here.'

'Yes, because otherwise it would have been unbalanced. It's still unbalanced, even with them here. There are supposed to be more people who aren't the police than who are – you need plenty of suspects.' Isobel stared at Simon, her mouth twitching. 'There were lots of others you could have invited too: the families of Linzi, Rhian, Angela and Josh would have been a good start. Josh!' she spat, suddenly. 'What was wrong with him? He *hated* his evil machine, but would he throw it away? No, he wouldn't – because it was a present from Angela, who told me herself when she was in the shop once, when she was visiting Josh: she loathed the whole idea of e-books herself – *much* preferred real books. Then why buy a Kindle as a present for your best friend? Angela said, "I'd run out of ideas of things to get him. He had everything else." I mean . . . surely you can see that sort of attitude is unconscionable?'

'And murder isn't?' said Simon. 'We all think it is.'

'Rhian and Marion were the same – bought e-readers as presents, while not thinking much of them. I had it from their own mouths – all the evidence I needed. Rhian used to come into Rudolphy's with Linzi whenever she stayed with her. She didn't like e-readers and didn't want one herself, but an acquaintance from work had told her that Linzi might like one if she was a book-lover – so Rhian listened to this acquaintance instead of to her own instincts. And Marion didn't seem to care that she'd bought Kim something *she herself* thought was a waste of space – nor did she give two hoots that Kim had stuffed it in a drawer, unimpressed, and never once used it.' Isobel turned on Kim. 'So why not throw the damn thing in the bin? Why not destroy it, instead of letting it stay and destroy everything else?'

'You need help,' Kim told her.

Isobel turned her attention back to Simon. 'It has many names: Nook, Kobo, Kindle. It tries to fool us with all its aliases, and it succeeds. I couldn't do *nothing* and live with myself.'

'But you also couldn't allow yourself to kill Sondra Halliday,' said Simon. 'She didn't qualify as one of your targets, did she?'

'No – if I'd killed her it would have been murder. That's the part you don't foresee: that once you've killed four, then five, it's not so hard to keep on and on if you allow yourself to. But I didn't let myself touch Sondra Halliday, and I'm proud of that.'

'Why did you accuse her of bibliophobia?' asked Sellers.

Isobel looked confused for a few seconds. Then her face changed and she said, 'She kept accusing me of things that had nothing to do with me, things she'd made up. I thought I'd show her how it feels to have that done to you.'

Exactly as Simon had suspected.

'Sondra Halliday didn't write the column I read to you this morning,' he said. 'I did.'

Isobel shrugged. 'I don't care. She could easily have written it.'

'What I wrote as Sondra is true, you know. Books are the words, the stories, the facts, the knowledge, the imagination. They're not the paper they're printed on.'

Isobel shook her head. 'You don't know what you're talking about. Yes, of course the words matter, but without the book's embodiment as a distinct physical object, where is it? What space does it have to call its own? Where's its soul? Where's *our* soul? When books are ruined, everything is ruined. It will get worse, too. Much, much worse. When it does, everyone will be sorry but at least they'll know I tried to do something. Me and perhaps a handful of others. Though no one has gone as far as I have.' Isobel looked embarrassed. 'It sounds grandiose to call it a cause, but that's what it is: it's my cause.'

'My favourite novel of all time is *Moby-Dick*,' Simon told her. 'Yesterday I chucked my old copy away. It was knackered. I've ordered an e-reader. A Kindle. I'm going to read *Moby-Dick* on that from now on.'

'No, you're going to give it to me as soon as it arrives, to replace my broken Kobo,' Charlie's voice came from behind him.

'Your electronic *Moby-Dick* will be soulless and lifeless,' Isobel said sadly. 'You'll see it one day. You'll all see it – but it'll be too late by then. Still, at least I'll know I did my best. What more can I do?'

'Why did you send Sondra Halliday two novels?' Simon asked.

'I was trying to teach her. She can't have read much fiction if she has so little imagination. If you reduce everyone to a member of a sex class, as she calls it, and drone on about it endlessly – this group being like this, and that group being like that – well, you miss all the *exceptions*. And, when you think about it, isn't nearly everybody an exception? A special case of some sort?'

'I'd say so, yes,' Simon agreed. It was strange, agreeing with a murderer.

'In *Beloved*, a mother kills her baby daughter to *save* her – from life as a slave. In *Jude the Obscure*, one of the children kills himself and his siblings in a wrongheaded act of altruism – he believes he's helping his parents. Sondra Halliday's blinkered, vindictive sex war has absolutely nothing to do with the killings in either of those stories, yet that's the lens through which she insists on seeing every single thing. I wanted to teach her that there are other possible motives, not just misogyny.'

'How did you persuade them to let you in – Linzi, Rhian, Josh and Angela?' Simon asked.

'Oh, it wasn't hard. They were all so nice to me: making me drinks, inviting me into their homes. I'd met them all at one time or another, at Rudolphy's, so I just did the old, "Remember me? Here I am with free books!" routine. I pretended I'd opened a new shop. I didn't want to kill them, any of them. I wish I hadn't had to. They're not suffering any more from what I did, at least. I am. That's my punishment.'

'How did you know all their addresses, and when they'd be at home?'

'The addresses? Linzi, Marion and Josh had all had books delivered from Rudolphy's over the years, both to themselves and to their friends: Linzi to Rhian, Josh to Angela – so I had all the addresses apart from Kim's – which, as it turned out, I never needed. And I didn't know when they'd all be at home. I tried several times with a couple of them, waited till I found them in. There were a few failed visits, but we got there eventually!' Isobel smiles brightly, as if delivering a happy ending.

'Why did you give Rudolphy's as your alibi?' Simon asked her. 'You must have known we'd find out soon enough that it had been closed for over a year.'

'I don't know.' Isobel looked down at her lap. 'I suppose I wanted to be able to say that I worked there – wanted to hear myself saying it. I was proud to work there . . . here.' She looked around at the Indian restaurant. 'It was a wonderful place. The best. Now I work in a service station. There's no point working with books any more – I don't want to stick around to watch them become extinct. Better to work somewhere shitty now that everything's ruined. Sorry for swearing. I need to ask . . .'

'What?'

'I'll be able to read books in prison, won't I? And write? I can write a memoir, maybe.'

'Yes. Books are allowed,' Simon told her. There was a heavy feeling in his gut. He didn't want to feel sorry for Isobel Sturridge. Why did he? Throwing away his copy of *Moby Dick* had been the hardest thing he'd ever done – his attempt to prove to himself that he was nothing like her.

'Lane will visit me in prison if you ask her to. Will you ask her? I really need her now.'

Simon nodded.

'Lane's got a book, you know – about the effect different words have on water – did I tell you? No. Ha!' Isobel laughs. 'When would I have told you? But it's fascinating. One cup of water had horrible words hissed at it day after day, and the other had only loving words spoken to it, and guess what? The water that kept hearing the hateful words turned murky and foul, while the water in the other glass stayed clear and clean.'

'Water can't hear,' Gibbs contributed from the far corner of the room.

'You're wrong. Lane's got a book that proves it can. Maybe it can't *hear* in the conventional sense, but . . . it can understand.'

'Why the little white books to your victims, with the poetry?' Charlie asked. Simon heard a pronounced lack of sympathy in her voice.

'They were clues,' Isobel directed her answer to Simon. 'Mysteries need clues. Each little white book contained a line of poetry by an American poet whose given name began with

E. My mother was an American poet whose given name began with E. Clue! Right? And . . . books! The clues were books, and my motive was a love of books. Pages that had lost most of their words – to evil machines. I feel like that sometimes, don't you? Like a page that's lost nearly all of its words.' She sighed.

'Do you ever feel evil?' Simon asked her.

'No! Me, evil?' Isobel laughed to cover her shock. 'I played fair with you in every possible way. You can't accuse me of not playing fair.'

'There's nothing fair about killing five innocent people,' said Simon.

She nodded as if she were about to agree, then said, 'Liam says I'm tired more than anything else. I think I'll sleep in prison. I've hardly slept since my mother was murdered by the horrible machines.'

'I'm sorry. About your mother, about Rudolphy's . . . I'll make sure Lane knows you'd like her to keep in touch.'

Isobel didn't seem to be listening any more. 'Little white books,' she murmured to her clasped hands. 'My little white books.'

From: colin.sellers@spilling.police.org
To: zoemcguinness@endfemicide.co.uk
Cc: Sondra.Halliday@Lifeworldmag.co.uk, Sondra@sondrahalliday.com
Sent: 26 January 2015 14:28:03

Dear Ms McGuinness

It was good to talk on the phone just now, and hopefully we at Culver Valley Police and your organisation will, in the near future, find ways to work together to bring down rates of domestic violence and male violence against women and girls. I've passed your contact details on to Sergeant Charlie Zailer, who will be in touch with you shortly to move things along.

Thank you so much for removing as speedily as you did the names and photographs of Linzi Birrell, Rhian Douglas and Angela McCabe from your website's list of victims of femicide. Your site defines the term as 'the killing of females by males because they are females'. As I said on the phone, we have now established beyond doubt that the killer of Linzi, Rhian and Angela was not a male; nor were these three women murdered because of anything to do with their sex or gender.

Warmest best wishes,

DC Colin Sellers
Culver Valley Police

26

Tuesday, 27 January 2015

There's a new email from Liam in my inbox. I've just had a boiling hot, lavender-scented bubble bath and I wish I hadn't pulled the plug. After reading Liam's words, I know I'll wish I could climb back in and get clean all over again.

He won't be able to resist sticking up for his sister. He'll say she did terrible things, yes, but she's not a bad person. If he defends her, knowing how close she came to killing me, what's left of my faith in humanity might break for good.

I should delete his message unread, but I open it – for Simon Waterhouse's sake, I tell myself. There's a chance Liam has something important to add, as the person who lived with Isobel. I might learn something useful from the email that I can pass on to the police.

There's no 'Dear Kim'. There never was, from Liam. The message reads, 'Want to meet? Feeling horny. Jerking off twice a day at the moment.'

No reference to his sister having been charged with five murders.

I click the bin symbol at the bottom of the screen to delete it. Keep my finger pressed down hard.

Disappear, disappear, disappear.

There's nothing he could have said to change my mind. But if there had been, that wasn't it.

I'm about to close my inbox when another new message pops up. The sender is Niall Greeves. What the hell does he want? I make a mental note to get my website changed so that there's no way for strangers to contact me directly.

This is a good opportunity to prove to myself that I've learned something. There's nothing Niall Greeves could want to say to me that I'm interested in hearing. If it's anything important to do with Billy – with Isobel Sturridge, as I must now learn to say – then he can contact the police and leave me alone.

I click on the envelope icon to open the message. Might as well know what I'm punitively deleting.

No 'Dear Kim' at the top of this one either. Where are men's manners these days?

The subject heading of the email is 'Do you know the woman in this sketch?'

I'm looking for a woman whom I think I might like a lot if I could only get to know her. (Yes, I'm afraid I'm the kind of person who says 'whom'.) I did once ham-fistedly try to approach her, and ended up, briefly, as a suspect in a serial murder case. As a result, and most inconveniently for me, I now feel unable to consider dating anyone who hasn't at one time or another become entangled in a nationwide hunt for a serial killer. I'm told I'm too fussy, but I disagree. I don't think a basic level of shared experience is too much to ask for.

Enclosed is a drawing of the woman I'm looking for, penned by a talented police artist from the Culver Valley, though not an official police sketch artist of the kind that drew me.

Let me explain: I went to Spilling police station in the hope of persuading someone there to pass on my phone number and a message to this woman, since I knew they'd have her contact details. Sadly for me, they weren't inclined to help me (well, they said they weren't allowed to, to be fair) but then the strangest thing happened. It would have been enough to make me start believing in fate if I weren't far too sensible.

As I walked out of the police station, there was a man – a PC in uniform – walking ahead of me, talking on his mobile phone very loudly and confidently. He seemed to be in the middle of a long-distance job interview with a graphic design company. As I listened to him going into great detail about what a design whizz he was, and how brilliant he was at drawing, I had an idea which I could see at once was either totally brilliant or a hideous embarrassment that I'd regret for the rest of my life.

I waited for the policeman to finish his phone call, then approached him and asked him if he'd be willing to do a one-off piece of freelance work for me. It involved drawing, I told him. I should stress that I wouldn't usually approach an officer of the law in this way – normally I'd assume they were too busy catching criminals – but this man did not (I mean, really did not *at all*) seem too busy with policing. And as it turned out, he was happy to help me – and I was delighted to discover that he's every bit as good an artist as he'd boasted he was to the graphic design firm, as you can see from the attached sketch. I felt a bit sorry for him when we said our goodbyes and he asked me rather desperately if I thought I might have some more freelance assignments for him in the future.

But back to the main point of this communication: do you know the woman in the attached sketch, by any chance? If you do, please get in touch. If you could bring her to a restaurant of her choice so that I can buy her dinner, that would be even better. Just don't forget to tell me which restaurant, when, etc.

Thanks in advance,

Niall Greeves

So that's what he was doing at the police station the other day. It was nothing to do with Billy Dead Mates. He was there because he wanted to get in touch with me.

In the sketch that he's scanned into the email, I look wary, unapproachable, lonely. It's a better likeness than all my official publicity photographs.

Damn Niall Greeves. Damn him to damnation for making me want to put him in his place by proving I'm funnier than he is.

I click on 'Reply'.

From: inessa.hughes@goochandhughes.com
Sent: 17 July 2016 10.52:13
To: Susan.Nordlein@nordleinvinter.co.uk
Subject: *The Billy Dead Books* by Kim Tribbeck

Dear Susan

I'm so sorry we've ended up where we are. I don't know what to say. I love the book as much as you do, and am bitterly disappointed. It seems almost a tragedy that no one apart from us will ever get to read the inside story of the Billy Dead Mates investigation, but Kim is adamant. I think it would be unfair to blame Niall. Yes, it's because of him, but he certainly hasn't applied any pressure. And there's the Charlie factor, too: as she and Kim have become closer friends, Kim has wanted to protect her, understandably (if not her appalling sister). Anyway, rest assured: no one has leaned on Kim at all. This is one hundred per cent her decision.

I can sort of understand it. She was willing to put her life and feelings out there for public consumption while she was unhappy and lonely (I almost wonder if the book wasn't a cry for help, in some ways) but now that she is neither, now that she feels she has something worth preserving, she doesn't want to be the butt of everyone's disapproval and derision.

As you might imagine, Charlie Zailer is simultaneously relieved and disappointed. She seems to think Kim will write a different book in the not too distant future – perhaps crime fiction – so we can always keep our fingers crossed for that!

Once again, I'm so very sorry. I wish I could have come back to you with better news. I suppose the only silver lining is that I don't now have to convey your anxieties about *The*

Billy Dead Books as a title. That would not have gone down well!

Very best wishes,

Inessa

Acknowledgements

Huge thanks as always to the stupendous team at Hodder, especially Carolyn Mays, Ruth Tross and Abby Parsons, who helped knock this book into shape; to Peter Straus and Matthew Turner at Rogers, Coleridge & White; to Dan, Phoebe, Guy and Brewster, to Morgan White, for being the exact person Jermain Defoe and I needed at the exact right time; to Emily Winslow, who provided brilliantly incisive editorial comments; to Adele Geras, who read an early draft and said nice things about it as always; to Dan Mallory for his boundless enthusiasm and faith in my writing; to the lovely and brilliant Al Murray, on whose tour dates Kim's were based; to Mathew and James Prichard and family, and everyone at Agatha Christie Ltd; to Anne Grey, my source of infinite wisdom; and to Jim Swarz, whose website www.shiningworld.com and whose book *The Essence of Enlightenment* formed the basis of Lane Baillie's spiritual outlook! And enormous thanks to my right-hand man Jamie Bernthal, who spotted many plot continuity errors that I missed.

Also, a massive thank you to everyone who supports my books – readers, international publishers, Twitter friends who cheer me up in between bouts of hard writing!

The Teacher, The Thug and The Helper

An original short story by
Sophie Hannah exclusive to Sainsbury's

I've often thought that books ought to have a section at the end called 'The Gossip Behind the Book'. It's easy to look at the blurb and see roughly what the story's about, but what I always wonder is: 'What made this author want to write this particular story?'

One of the many inspirations for *The Narrow Bed* was my growing awareness that there was a whole area of psychology that, to my knowledge, had not yet formed the basis of a psychological thriller. When we talk about 'psychological crime fiction', we rarely go into detail about what that 'psychological' label means. As a result, one glaringly obvious truth is never mentioned: ninety-nine per cent of the time, it's *Freudian* psychology that we find in this sort of thriller – a serial killer strangling tall, slim blonde women because his neglectful mother was tall, slim and blonde, for instance. This is fine, of course . . . but then an experience I had in my own life made me wonder if there might not be another equally fascinating kind of psychology that would also work well in crime fiction.

In 2001, I went to see a woman most people would describe as a New-Age therapist. I did so because I thought of myself as a bitchy, hardened cynic (rather like Kim in *The Narrow Bed*, in fact!) and I decided it would be good for me to do something so completely out of character. My therapist, Anne, turned out to be so wonderful that I saw her for many years, and I still do from time to time. She completely changed the way I looked at the world, and although I was still bitchy and cynical, I could at least see and understand the virtues of being the opposite (rather like Billy Dead Mates, who is fully clued up about how to be an enlightened person in theory, while being a murderer in practice!). Anne introduced me to a new and exciting way of looking at psychology, from what some might call a 'spiritually enlightened' perspective (yes, I know that sounds rather mung-bean-and-hessian, but there we are!) and I realised that this way of thinking would lead someone trying to solve a mystery or puzzle to form radically different conclusions from those they might form using Freudian psychology. I was soon very excited about how this different kind of psychology could be used in crime fiction, and *The Narrow Bed* was the result.

Lane Baillie, the New-Age therapist in the book, is based on Anne and is the main force for good in the novel. Lane is a minor character, but a crucial one nonetheless. Her role in the story is to demonstrate that the anger and resentment personified by characters like Billy Dead Mates and Sondra Halliday, the radical feminist extremist, are not an inevitable result of suffering, but an active choice. Lane Baillie, by contrast, chooses always to be kind, compassionate and non-judgemental even in the face of cruel and destructive behaviour, and this approach demonstrably succeeds far more than the berating and grudge-holding preferred by Billy and Sondra. This is not a coincidence; I firmly believe that compassion and kindness are always the way forward (though I must admit I am regularly unable to achieve both, especially when someone says something daft on Twitter that makes me really cross!).

There are several self-contained 'enlightened' stories in *The Narrow Bed* that play a role in the plot – inspired by what I've learned from Anne and also from Jim Swarz, one of the world's leading experts on Vedanta philosophy. There was originally one more story, but it didn't make the final cut because too many would have felt self-indulgent and over the top. So, in the final draft of the novel, Simon summarises the key points of the fourth story for Charlie's benefit – but here is the story in full, just for those of you who have bought or stumbled across this limited edition of *The Narrow Bed*.

Sophie Hannah

The Teacher, The Thug and The Helper

A teacher was writing on the blackboard, with his back turned to his class, when he heard something smash. Startled, he turned around and saw that one of the windows was broken. All the glass had shattered, and wind and rain were blowing into the classroom. Assuming somebody must have thrown something in from outside, the teacher walked over to see what had been hurled in, guessing that it was bound to be lying on the floor.

When he reached the smashed window, however, he found nothing on the classroom floor, so he looked outside. There on the grass he saw a wooden desk on its side. It was exactly like the ones in his classroom.

He turned back to face the room and saw immediately what, in the shock of the smash, he had not noticed until that point: the spare desk was missing, the only one at which no pupil sat. As far as the teacher could see, there was only one possible explanation for all of this.

'One of you must have picked up the spare desk while I wasn't looking and deliberately thrown it out of the window,' he said to the class. 'Who did it? Please own up.'

Nobody spoke. Most of the students looked nervous and lowered their eyes. Only one boy stared the teacher in the face and smirked. Unsurprisingly, it was the boy the teacher secretly thought of as 'The Thug'. He was a disruptive, rebellious child who never put any effort into his work and was often rude, sullen and aggressive.

'Did you throw the desk through the window?' the teacher asked him.

'Nah, mate,' said The Thug.

'I think you did,' said the teacher. 'I know for a fact that no other child in this class would do such a thing.'

The Thug shrugged.

'Go outside *right now*, pick up that desk, and bring it back into this classroom!' the teacher yelled.

'The fuck I will!' The Thug sneered. 'Wasn't me that did it.'

What was the teacher to do? He knew there was no point asking any of the other pupils what had happened; they were all terrified of The Thug. No one would dare say a word. He considered doing that thing teachers do of punishing the entire class until someone comes clean and reveals the individual culprit, but he couldn't bring himself to do that to the twenty-eight lovely students in his form.

The bell rang: end of lesson. Dejectedly, the teacher mumbled, 'Class dismissed.'

One girl stayed sitting at her desk after all the others had left the room. She was a small girl with very long white hair – the colour of hair that an albino would have, except she wasn't one. She had dark blue eyes, almost navy blue. In his mind, the teacher had always thought of her as 'The Helper'. She regularly volunteered to tidy the classroom, and put her hand up first in response to a question every time. She was kind, obedient and almost suspiciously mature, the teacher sometimes thought.

'I have an idea, sir,' she said.

'An idea?'

'Yes. Do you think you might know who threw the desk through the window?'

'I know perfectly well who it was,' said the teacher angrily.

'But you don't know for sure,' said The Helper. 'And there's only one way you'll ever find out: if the culprit confesses.'

'Well . . . you could always tell me?' the teacher suggested.

The white-haired girl shook her head. 'Even if I did, it would be one person's word against another's. Whereas if whoever did it were to confess . . .'

The teacher grimaced. 'That will never happen – not with this boy. He has no conscience. He's incapable of remorse or cooperation.'

'I'm not sure that's true,' said The Helper.

'Oh, really? Then what do you suggest? How on earth can I persuade him to confess when he knows full well that a confession would lead to a serious punishment for him?'

'Tell him you understand why he did it. That you haven't judged him, because, after all, who are you to do so?'

'Well . . .' the teacher began to protest. 'I'm someone who's never thrown a desk that didn't belong to me through a window that didn't belong to me.'

'Well, then, maybe you should,' said The Helper. 'When we forget that we're as flawed as everyone else and delude ourselves that we're fit to sit in judgement, that's when the real problems arise.'

'Now look here, young lady—'

But The Helper ignored him and went on. 'Once you've hurled a desk of your choice through a window of your choice, find the boy again and tell him that you know he's had a tough life: both parents dead before he was five, growing up in care, separated from his siblings. They both found adoptive families but he didn't. The same family, actually.'

'How the hell does she know all this?' the teacher wondered. He'd never seen her and The Thug chatting. They belonged to completely different social circles. His was all cigarette breath and slouch and stubble, while hers was hairband, satchel and choir practice.

'It must have been very traumatic for him to be left behind when his brother and sister were given a second chance with a new family,' she went on, 'so explain to him that you understand that. Tell him that if you were struggling with the pain he must struggle with day in day out – if you'd lived most of your life with the fear that the world was a hostile place, full of threats, and no one cared about you – you too would have picked up that desk and hurled it through the classroom window, propelled by a violent rage you didn't understand that felt like lava burning inside you. And then, finally, let him know that you aren't going to punish him. Instead, ask how you can help him to feel happier.'

'Wow – that was some speech,' thought the teacher to himself. The Helper, though always helpful, was not normally so talkative or sure of herself. The teacher also wondered how she knew so much about The Thug.

Suddenly, light dawned. Or, at any rate, it felt like light to the teacher at that moment. He laughed and said, 'You know what? I think that might be an excellent idea. You're very clever, young lady. You'll go far.'

The white-haired girl sighed, as if the teacher's words had not made her happy, but the teacher hardly noticed. He was thinking ahead, looking forward to his next encounter with The Thug.

He didn't have to wait very long. The following day presented an opportunity, and the teacher took the sullen, angry-eyed boy to one side.

'Going to start on at me again, are you, sir?' asked The Thug.

'No,' said the teacher. He then said, almost word for word, everything that The Helper had told him to say, from, 'I understand why you did it. I know you've had a rough life . . .' all the way to ' . . . and so I'm not going to punish you if you confess. Instead, tell me what this school and I can do to make you happier.'

For a few seconds, The Thug was silent. Then he smirked unpleasantly and said, 'That's a very touching little lecture, sir. I'm sure if you find whoever threw the desk through the window, they'll appreciate your concern. But you're talking to the wrong person. I'm an innocent man.' He held up his hands in a 'don't shoot' gesture.

The teacher was bitterly disappointed. While he felt certain that The Thug was the only possible culprit, his doubts grew a tiny bit bigger with each denial he heard. He started to go through all the other potential suspects in his mind. Yes, there was that girl who'd had a metal brace fitted on her teeth the day before. Might having a brace fitted make you suddenly volatile and aggressive? It seemed unlikely.

Later that day, the teacher ran into The Helper. She was walking along a corridor with her satchel over her shoulder, carrying a pile of books. 'It didn't work!' the teacher couldn't help blurting out, though he had no wish to blame the girl who, after all, had done her best.

'No,' she said. 'I knew it wouldn't.'

'What?' The teacher was taken aback. 'But then . . . why did you tell me to do it?'

'Oh, there was nothing wrong with the advice I gave you. If you'd done it in the right way, the result would have been quite different.'

'But . . .' The teacher frowned, bewildered. 'I repeated what you told me, word for word.'

'I'm sure you did,' said The Helper, 'but did you *mean* it?'

At this, the teacher looked more confused. 'Mean it?' he asked.

'Yes. While you were telling the boy that you understood how tough his life must have been and that you'd probably have thrown a desk through a window yourself if you'd had similarly painful experiences, what were you thinking in your head?'

'I . . . I don't remember, exactly,' the teacher muttered.

'Try,' said The Helper, fixing her navy blue eyes on him.

'Well . . . um . . . I guess I was thinking some version of, "This is totally going to work. There's no way he won't fall for it."'

'Aha!' said The Helper. '"Fall for it". So, in other words, everything you said to the boy was a lie, wasn't it?'

'Well, a trick more than a *lie*, I'd say. A ruse – suggested by you – to induce him to confess. So that I could land him with a big, fat punishment: Saturday detention every weekend for a month.' Gleefully, the teacher rubbed his hands together.

'I never suggested you trick him,' said the girl. 'You chose to interpret what I said in that way. When I suggested you say those words, I hoped you might mean them.'

'But . . . but . . .' the teacher spluttered. 'That's impossible, I'm afraid. It's unthinkable that I wouldn't punish him for what he did if he admitted it. Cloud cuckoo land! And I would never vandalise school property, no matter how many painful experiences I'd had.'

'Oh, dear.' The girl closed her eyes. 'You still haven't thrown a desk through a window, have you? I can tell.'

'Of course I haven't,' said the teacher. 'We all suffer, young lady, but we *do not* all turn to delinquency and antisocial behaviour.'

'And so you'll punish this boy, and he'll remain full of pain and rage. And soon after his punishment, he'll probably throw another desk through another window. Whereas if you show him some compassion and give him a reprieve on this occasion, who knows how he might respond? I mean, clearly, as a member of school staff, you must do what you can to prevent further violent acts. I can quite see that. But what if the best way to do that is by *not* punishing him?'

'Hmph.' The teacher was not convinced.

'As to your other point,' said The Helper, 'you can't know who you'd have grown up to be if you'd had the childhood he's had. Don't you think it's rather arrogant to claim that you can know such a thing? Were you orphaned as a young child, and then separated from your only remaining family when they were adopted by people who made it clear they wanted your siblings but not you?'

'No, that didn't happen to me,' the teacher conceded. 'But I mean . . . I can *imagine* it.'

'Standing at the window, watching them getting into the car,' said The Helper. 'Crying – screaming in panic at being left alone – only they can't hear you. You're six years old, only just tall enough to see through the glass above the window sill.'

'Yes, yes,' the teacher snapped. 'I do have an imagination, you know!' But even as he was saying it, he felt something draining away inside him: his certainty. He could imagine a broken leg, but he'd never personally felt the snap of a shin bone or the subsequent fear of walking on slippery surfaces. He could imagine being lost in the snow with no clothes on, and conjure up a bit of a shivery feeling, but even if he did that all day long, he'd still have all of his nice pink fingers and toes; he wouldn't lose a single one to frostbite.

Crying – screaming in panic at being left alone – only they can't hear you. You're six years old, only just tall enough to see through the glass above the window sill.

The Helper was quite right. Until one has experienced something, one cannot fully know its effects.

Something else the girl had said wouldn't leave his mind: 'people who made it clear they wanted your siblings but not you'. For the first time, the teacher thought about the boy as a person with an inner life of his own and not simply as a nuisance to be managed.

He realised he'd been wrong. He had no idea what sort of person he might have become if he'd had as painful and unstable a childhood as The Thug.

Perhaps it was time to stop thinking of him as The Thug and start thinking of him as The Unhappy Boy. The next time he saw him, the teacher said, 'I have a confession to make: I lied to you.'

This got the boy's interest.

'When I spoke to you before and said all that about how I'd probably have done the same if I were you – thrown the desk through the window – I wasn't being sincere. I just wanted you to admit you'd done it.'

'No fucking shit,' said The Unhappy Boy.

'Yes. Look, the truth is, I've no idea what I would or wouldn't have done if I'd had the childhood you had – there's no way of knowing. But . . .' The teacher stopped. He found himself wanting to say something that was very different from what The Helper had told him to say. It felt right to him, but how did he know if she'd approve? And why did he care? She was just a random pupil at the school.

I'll just say it, the teacher decided to himself. It was the truth after all. 'I *do* know that whereas before I was furious with you, I'm not any more. Whereas before I wanted to punish you, I no longer do.'

'I didn't. Fucking. Do it,' spat The Unhappy Boy in the teacher's face.

'No, I know,' the teacher agreed.

'Huh? You what?' Now the boy looked confused.

'I no longer think it was you who threw the desk through the window.'

'Why the fuck not?'

'It was the anger in you that did it. Not you. Your anger is not you. You are not your anger.'

The boy didn't like the sound of this at all. 'Well, guess what? It *was* me. I chucked that desk at the window and smashed it. I was bored.'

'Your boredom is not you,' said the teacher. 'Your pain is not you. That means you can hope to be free of it one day.'

'Are you going to punish me or what? Am I, like, suspended and shit?'

'No, I don't want to punish you. But if you ever need someone to listen, I'm here. I'll help you in whatever way I can.'

'Listen to what?' the boy asked. He looked scared. 'Help me with what? Sir, is there something wrong with you? I mean, like, mentally?'

'I wouldn't have thought so,' the teacher replied with a self-deprecating smile. He suspected that maybe there was, hoped there wasn't, and thought this answer would cover him either way.

'Well, I don't need you to listen because I haven't got anything to say,' said The Unhappy Boy defiantly. 'Look, I'm sorry I fucked up your window, but . . . I don't need any touchy-feely therapy or anything.' He stuck two fingers into his mouth and mimed being sick.

'Well, you know where I am if you change your mind and ever want a chat.' The teacher smiled as he walked away. The boy had taken responsibility for his misdemeanour and apologised for it. Instead of a punishment given, there had been a reward received. The teacher no longer cared even slightly that his classroom window had been broken.

As he made his way along the quiet, dark corridor, he saw the white-haired girl, The Helper, walking in his direction. He felt no urge to hurry towards her and tell her what had happened. The impulse to tell her how he'd adapted the speech she'd prepared for him, and how his approach had worked brilliantly with The Unhappy Boy, was simply not there. Talking to the girl about it wasn't an unpleasant prospect; it was simply a conversation he didn't feel the need to have. 'Well, whether or not I feel the need to tell her, I'll have to, because she's bound to ask me,' thought the teacher to himself.

He slowed his pace, expecting The Helper to do the same, but she hurried on, with only the most casual of smiles for him as she passed.

The teacher, alone in the corridor, heard the bell ring as if to say 'Lesson over!' but when he looked at his watch, there were still ten minutes of that particular period left – just enough time to throw a desk through a window – perfect! The Helper had encouraged him to do that, and he didn't doubt for a second that her advice was sound, or that he'd interpreted it correctly.

The teacher left the school building and made his way to the patch of grass outside his classroom where the desk thrown by The Unhappy

Boy had landed. After a few failed attempts, he finally managed to lift the thing. With all his might, he threw it in the direction of the already-broken window. It landed in the exact spot where it belonged in the room – not on its side and not upside down, but in precisely the right position.

LITTLE FACE

It's every mother's nightmare...

'Ingenious' *Sunday Times*

HURTING DISTANCE

**Sometimes love must
kill before it can die**...

'Superbly creepy' *Guardian*

THE POINT OF RESCUE

**It began with an affair.
And ended in murder.**

'Addictive' *Marie Claire*

THE OTHER HALF LIVES

'Utterly gripping' *The Times*

'Thrilling' *Sunday Telegraph*

A ROOM SWEPT WHITE

Murder begins at home...

'Beautifully written' *Daily Express*

LASTING DAMAGE

Don't go into the other woman's house...

'Jaw-droppingly assured'
Daily Express

KIND OF CRUEL

Some secrets are so dark, you keep them even from yourself...

'Truly hair-raising'
Independent on Sunday

THE CARRIER

He swore he was a killer. The truth was worse.

'Another gripping triumph' *Heat*

THE TELLING ERROR

Knowing the secret will kill you.

'Fiendishly clever' *Sunday Express*

A chilling standalone novel from the queen of psychological crime...

SOPHIE HANNAH

a game for all the family

Justine thought she knew who she was, until someone seemed to know better . . .

After escaping London and a career that nearly destroyed her, Justine plans to spend her days doing as little as possible in her beautiful new home.

But soon after the move, her daughter starts to withdraw when her new best friend, George, is unfairly expelled from school. Justine begs the head teacher to reconsider, only to be told that nobody's been expelled – there is, and was, no George.

Then the anonymous calls start: a stranger, making threats that suggest she and Justine share a guilty secret. And then the caller starts talking about three graves – two big and one small, to fit a child . . .

Stay up to date with Sophie Hannah.

@sophiehannahCB1

/SophieHannahAuthor

www.sophiehannah.com

Do you wish this wasn't the end?

Join us at www.hodder.co.uk, or follow us on Twitter @hodderbooks to be a part of our community of people who love the very best in books and reading.

Whether you want to discover more about a book or an author, watch trailers and interviews, have the chance to win early limited editions, or simply browse our expert readers' selection of the very best books, we think you'll find what you're looking for.

And if you don't, that's the place to tell us what's missing.

We love what we do, and we'd love you to be part of it.

www.hodder.co.uk

@hodderbooks

HodderBooks

HodderBooks